James Warburton Begbie, Dyce (1840-1928 : Sir) Duckworth

Selections from the works of the late J. Wharburton Begbie

James Warburton Begbie, Dyce (1840-1928 : Sir) Duckworth

Selections from the works of the late J. Wharburton Begbie

ISBN/EAN: 9783744741446

Printed in Europe, USA, Canada, Australia, Japan

Cover: Foto ©Andreas Hilbeck / pixelio.de

More available books at **www.hansebooks.com**

SELECTIONS FROM

THE WORKS OF

THE LATE

J. WARBURTON BEGBIE, M.D., LL.D.,

FELLOW OF THE ROYAL COLLEGE OF PHYSICIANS OF EDINBURGH;
PHYSICIAN TO, AND LECTURER ON CLINICAL MEDICINE IN, THE EDINBURGH
ROYAL INFIRMARY, AND LECTURER ON PRACTICE OF PHYSIC
IN THE EXTRA-ACADEMICAL SCHOOL.

EDITED BY

DYCE DUCKWORTH, M.D. Edin.,

FELLOW OF THE ROYAL COLLEGE OF PHYSICIANS; ASSISTANT-PHYSICIAN TO ST. BARTHOLOMEW'S
HOSPITAL; SOMETIME EXAMINER IN PRACTICE OF PHYSIC IN
THE UNIVERSITY OF EDINBURGH.

THE NEW SYDENHAM SOCIETY,
LONDON.

———

MDCCCLXXXII.

EDITOR'S PREFACE.

THIS volume is the result of a proposal which I made last year to my colleagues on the Council of the New Sydenham Society, and which they were so good as to accept. It seemed desirable that the writings by which Dr. Warburton Begbie was so well known in his day should be collected and placed within easy reach of the Profession. I accordingly offered to select from his numerous contributions to medical literature such of his essays as seemed to me best to represent his clinical powers and to illustrate the influence he exerted upon his contemporaries. It may be that this intention was in our author's own mind, to be carried out at some future time. He may have contemplated producing, in place of an *opus magnum*, such a collection of his fragmentary writings as was formed, in his later years, by his eminent father.[1]

Acting, then, as far as possible in accordance with this idea, I have made the attempt to carry out what could only have been properly achieved by the author himself.

To accomplish this purpose has been for me most truly a labour of love. The lines on which Warburton Begbie worked so successfully were just those which were traversed in my own impressionable student days by the best minds in Medicine, and the level of excellence reached in the essays in this volume may fairly be taken to represent that which had been attained in the Edinburgh School some twenty years since. This book,

[1] 'Contributions to Practical Medicine,' by James Begbie, M.D., F.R.S.E., Physician-in-Ordinary to the Queen in Scotland. A. & C. Black, Edin., 1862.

then, may prove of interest, if for nothing more than that it illustrates the standard of medical teaching and the modes of thought prevailing at that time in Edinburgh, in the days when Hughes Bennett, Laycock, Syme, Simpson, Goodsir, Gairdner, Sanders, and others were all engaged in the work of that great School.

Amongst all these remarkable men, Begbie held no unimportant place. His teaching was very different from that maintained in the University Clinical Wards and the Systematic Chair, and was attractive from causes peculiar to itself. Unlike Bennett, he had neither the inflexible will nor the dogmatic temper which brought a discipline, almost military in its character, to bear upon clinical teaching, nor did his genius, like that of the gifted Laycock, lie in the direction of speculative philosophy. He secured the devotion of his pupils by his enthusiasm and his charming manner, no less than by his qualities as a great clinical teacher.

I have endeavoured to arrange Begbie's writings as far as possible in the order in which they appeared. I think no inconvenience will arise from this, because I have formed so copious an index as will enable every point of importance in these papers to be seized at once.

I have discarded all of his essays which seemed deficient in interest at the present standpoint of our Art. I have not thought it necessary to ask for the reproduction of his several articles from Dr. Russell Reynolds' 'System of Medicine,' because they are readily accessible.

Dr. Lauder Brunton bade me search for public expression of Warburton Begbie's recommendation of arsenic as a drug of much value in some forms of albuminuria. Dr. Brunton believes that Begbie advised this remedy, and Professor Arthur Gamgee tells me he was under the same impression. I can, however, find no written recommendation to that effect in any paper I have met with.

Perhaps I may be allowed to indicate that the subjects with

which Warburton Begbie's name may be best associated are treated in Papers I, III, IX, XII, XVI, XIX, XXIV, XXV, and XXVII. His work in connection with the whole subject of vascular bronchocele is, perhaps, his best, and together with that achieved by his father on the same subject,[1] almost completes the clinical conception of the malady which is held at the present moment.

My thanks are due to Messrs. Oliver and Boyd, of Edinburgh, for permission to republish many of the articles in this volume, also to Mr. Joseph Bell, the present editor of the 'Edinburgh Medical Journal,' and so, too, must I acknowledge similar obligations to Mr. Maclehose, the publisher of the 'Glasgow Medical Journal,' to Dr. Lionel Beale, Dr. Lauder Brunton, Messrs. Macmillan, and to the British Medical Association. Dr. James Carmichael, of Edinburgh, has been so good as to furnish me with some copies of these articles, which I could not otherwise procure.

For further kindness and assistance I have been much indebted to the Rev. Sir William H. Gibson-Carmichael, Bart., of Castle Craig, Dolphinton (a connection by marriage of Dr. Warburton Begbie), to Dr. Claude Muirhead and Mr. John Dalziel, W.S., of Edinburgh, his trustees, also to Professor Gairdner, of Glasgow. To Mr. Thomas Rodger, the eminent photographer at St. Andrews, I am under obligation for permission to have Dr. Begbie's likeness engraved for the frontispiece of this volume.

In the biographical memoir which precedes the text, I have tried to record such traits as will vividly recall his presence and character to the minds of all who were familiar with "young Begbie," as he was often called in his father's lifetime.

I cannot doubt that this book will prove acceptable to many of Warburton Begbie's former pupils, who must now be scattered in all parts of the world. They can have none but bright

---

[1] Op. cit., p. 116.

memories of their old teacher. To those who never knew him, and never came within the sphere of his influence, these chapters may be commended as pieces of clinical portraiture executed by a master's hand.

LONDON;
July, 1882.

CONTENTS.

MEMOIR OF JAMES WARBURTON BEGBIE.

BY THE EDITOR.[1]

JAMES WARBURTON BEGBIE was born on the 19th of November, 1826. He was the second son of Dr. James Begbie, the pupil, friend, and successor of Abercrombie. He was educated at the Edinburgh Academy, where he made some firm and lasting friendships. For some time he was also at a private school in England. In 1843 he matriculated at the University of Edinburgh, and began the study of Medicine.

In 1847 he proceeded to the degree of M.D. and wrote his ' *Dissertatio Medica Inauguralis* ' on " Some of the Pathological Conditions of the Urine," receiving special commendation for this thesis.

He twice was honoured by election to the chair of the Royal Medical Society, one of the " blue ribbons " of Edinburgh medical undergraduates, first as senior President in 1847, and secondly as junior President in 1848. He was known as a " quiet and industrious

---

[1] In preparing this memoir I have been indebted to various friends and pupils of Dr. Warburton Begbie, and have largely availed myself of an admirable biographical notice which was published in the ' Edinburgh Medical Journal ' for April, 1876, and issued from the pen of its editor, my accomplished friend, Mr. Joseph Bell.

student, and impressed his fellow-students with his ability and earnestness."

Dr. Warburton Begbie next proceeded to Paris, where he appears to have continued his studies and added largely to his experience. His writings often bore witness to the influence of the teachings of the French school upon him. He seems to have specially studied skin-diseases at the St. Louis Hospital under Cazenave and Devergie.

In the summer of 1849 he was selected to reside for some months with the family of the Earl of Aberdeen at Haddo House, Aberdeenshire, and late in the autumn of that year he travelled on the Continent with the only son of the late Right Hon. John Hope, Lord Justice Clerk of Scotland. He visited Italy, and subsequently wrote a paper upon the surgical instruments exhibited in the Museum at Naples, which had been discovered in the ruins of Pompeii.[1]

About 1852 he settled in Edinburgh and engaged —as has not unfrequently been the custom for the younger physicians in that city—in family practice. In that year he became a Fellow of the Royal College of Physicians of Edinburgh, and was appointed one of the medical officers of the New Town Dispensary.

Dr. Warburton Begbie married, in December, 1852, Miss Anna Maria Reid, and had seven children, three sons, the eldest of whom is deceased, and four daughters.

He was a member of the Free Church of Scotland and of Dr. Candlish's congregation. By nature a deeply religious man, he was entirely void of the bigotry and narrow-mindedness that, in his day, were wont to be attributed to that important body. Warburton

---

[1] This was a review, written in 1853, of Vulpes on 'Ancient Surgical Instruments discovered in Herculaneum and Pompeii.' 1847.

Begbie was in warm sympathy with all Christendom, his mind was too broad, and his soul too big, either to find concern in petty questions of ecclesiastical polity, or to be vexed about disputed points in Biblical exegesis.

In 1854 he was elected to fill a very onerous and responsible office, that of Physician to the Cholera Hospital in Surgeon Square. How admirably he utilised his opportunities there, the very excellent record of his experience, incorporated in this volume, amply testifies.

In 1855 he secured the most coveted post of young Edinburgh physicians, and was appointed Physician to the Royal Infirmary. Here he was in his proper sphere. At the same time he joined the Extra-Academical School, and delivered a summer course of lectures upon the History of Medicine, a subject which had always had a great attraction for him, and one which his extensive reading, knowledge of languages, and correct scholarship, allowed him to do full justice to. These lectures were highly appreciated. They were never published, and were delivered for about eight years, long indeed after the labours of systematic and clinical teaching had begun to make large inroads upon their author's time. For ten winter sessions Dr. Warburton Begbie lectured on the Practice of Physic to large classes, and shared the clinical lectures in the Royal Infirmary with his colleagues Dr. Gairdner, Dr. Haldane, and Dr. Sanders, throwing all his energy into hospital work and teaching, and spending four hours of each day in his wards and lecture room. The Infirmary appointment, lasting but for ten years, had to be resigned in 1865, much to his own and the regret of his numerous pupils, and his systematic course of lectures was also suspended at that time. Thus,

Warburton Begbie's career as a teacher came to an end, and, with the exception of a course of lectures on Practice of Physic which he delivered in the University in the winter of 1866-67, by appointment of the Senate, during the illness of Professor Laycock, he never taught more in public.

Before this period, Dr. Begbie's practice was increasing steadily. His pupils were very loyal to him and preferred his opinion to that of most of the Edinburgh consultants, many, if not all, of whom were much his senior.

Thus, when about forty years of age, Dr. Begbie was in large practice, and after the death of his father, in 1869, he altogether gave up family practice and took none but consulting work. At this time, too, he was appointed Physician to the Scottish Widows' Fund Life Assurance Society in succession to his father, and after five years of office he wrote a Report on the Deaths, which was published in the ' Edinburgh Medical Journal' for December, 1874, and which piece of work constitutes a very valuable contribution to the statistics of life assurance.

From the time of his father's death, Warburton Begbie continued in the full tide of practice till overborne by his fatal illness some seven years later. He had acquired a splendid reputation, and had the largest consulting physician's practice north of the Tweed. He was richly endowed for the work which poured in upon him from all sides, and he never spared his labour or his skill. Prosperity wrought no change in him, he remained the same simple-minded, unselfish man he always was. No Scottish physician was ever more justly popular in the best sense of the word.

We shall best study his life by contemplating, first, his personal, and secondly, his professional character.

Having had myself the privilege to know Dr. Warburton Begbie from my earliest student days, to watch his practice, and to have been closely associated with his pupils, I may seem to have some qualification for the task, but I am sensible that many others whom I could name, could better convey to posterity all that should be told of such a man. My recollections are still vivid, and the veneration in which I held Begbie upwards of twenty years ago grows not less, but more, as time rolls on. All who knew him in any degree loved him. He was one of those guileless men who could never have an enemy. As I look back upon the strife and distracting elements which raged in the Edinburgh School of Medicine some twenty years since, and which are now all subdued and known only as matters of history, I reflect with some wonder, and much admiration, that amidst all the turmoil the gentle figure of Begbie went to and fro, and was never embroiled, or even ruffled, in the varied conflicts of that time. For all this, his influence was very great, and he was conspicuous as a teacher, in full power of work, and with a large following.

Personally, he was of commanding stature, with large frame and well-cut features. His expression was calm and sweet almost to effeminacy. I think I never saw him frown, or roused to exhibit a trace of ill-temper or vexation. Equable and uniformly bland and courteous, never, apparently, worried or pressed, he had a simple, friendly, modest manner, and a marvellous power of attraction for everybody. Any one could readily approach him, and secure his aid or counsel. None who worked under him can ever forget his manner either as a physician or a teacher.

Without any affectation, he was truly in charity with all mankind. " Homo sum, humani nihil a me alienum puto " was his life's motto. His manner at the bedside was gentler, if possible, than that of any woman, and almost gave rise at times to ridicule, as, for instance, when he addressed the roughest of his sex, or the most forlorn of the other, with genuine tenderness and sympathy in such terms as—" Tell me, dear man, or dear woman, have you any pain." But none misdoubted the real humanity and heart-felt overflow of the wise clinician. It was unmistakable and true, exhibiting the humility and unselfishness of the man. He was neither hypocrite nor mannerist, and everybody knew it. There was nothing small or mean about Warburton Begbie. His magnanimity and charity were indeed boundless.

He much venerated his great teacher Professor Alison, and expressed his obligations to him, and to his father, perhaps more than to any who had shared in moulding his character. He was jealous of his father's reputation and sagacity, and frequently referred to these in his various writings with much loyalty. " Few knew what an admirable mimic he could be when he chose, and he had a strong sense of humour, but always under the control of a peculiar tenderness for the feelings of others."

Viewed from its professional side, Dr. Warburton Begbie's character was one possessing great charms and many noteworthy features.

As a systematic lecturer, his style was somewhat dry, and he followed his manuscript too closely. That he might have well trusted to extempore utterance all who knew him could testify. His clinical expositions in the wards and in the side-room could not be surpassed for perspicuity. It is believed that he was always exercised by the fear that he should give anything less than his best, and that he so far distrusted his powers. He was, however, greatest at his clinical visits. "He taught not only how to win the patient's confidence, to get his whole history, to examine him carefully yet rapidly, with consideration for his feelings, but he was great in diagnosis and prognosis, and, with a rarer power still, had the faith and patience to use and profit by the use of remedies—not drugs merely, but diet, regimen. With him the student learned manners as well as physic, nursing along with diagnosis. His faith in therapeutics was very great, not greater than was his success in using medicine, a success due partly to his training, partly to his extensive reading and experience."

His confidence in treatment was indeed remarkable, and he never had misgivings as to the value of drugs at a time when expectant methods and nihilism were somewhat rampantly vaunted in the Edinburgh School. The secret of this confidence, which I, for one, believe to have been well-placed, was that he made a rigid study of the action of remedies, and that he had acquired the art of employing drugs, an art which was then, as indeed it is now, too little cultivated. If to say this is to place faith in mere empiricism, I maintain that a large part of our best practice is of this nature, and I am no more ashamed of such a confession than was the gifted subject of this memoir, who vigorously defended the position.[1] Begbie was, however, no mere drug-administrator. He was a student of pathological processes, he was a keen observer, possessed of a logical mind, and, above all, he had that rare and invaluable faculty, one begotten and hardly to be acquired, of clinical intuition, which penetrates deeply, and with almost unerring certainty, into the intricacies

[1] See his address on 'Ancient and Modern Practice of Medicine,' pp. 411, 413.

of disease, and thereupon determines a definite line for action. He had confidence in his own powers, he inspired his patient with the vigour of his will, and marshalled all the forces of recovery to his aid.

His industry was remarkable. Like many truly great men he found time to do much outside the bare lines of his regular duties. He wrote much. In his earlier professional life he contributed many reviews and critical notices to the 'Edinburgh Medical Journal,' and the 'British and Foreign Medico-Chirurgical Review.' His readers will find that all his writings bear the stamp of thoroughness and honesty, and he never failed to give full credit to the labours of others who had worked in the same field with himself.

It has been said that even his best writings did scant justice to the merits and qualities of their author, and some have expressed disappointment with the results of his literary efforts.

An attached pupil, and one of his former resident-physicians, writes to me as follows :—" How much greater and better was *Begbie himself*—man and physician—than anything he ever wrote ? "[1] It would be strange if his numerous writings were of equal merit. I imagine that few men maintain an equal standard of excellence in the literary productions of a busy professional life. Yet in Begbie's writings one may always feel that his primary motive is to publish what he believed to be true, and worthy to claim the attention of the profession. He was most unlikely to write for the sake of writing or of keeping his name before his brethren. He must have felt that his large opportunities for observation constituted a responsibility of his life to further the advance of practical medicine.

[1] Dr. William Jeffrey, of Jedburgh.

Certainly, I think it may be affirmed that his best work was that which came spontaneously from him, and not that which may be supposed to have been written by request, and it is probable that little, if any, of the latter has been suffered to appear in this volume.

He wrote several of the articles for Dr. Russell Reynolds' 'System of Medicine,'[1] and was under promise to contribute one on "Life Assurance" for Dr. Quain's forthcoming 'Dictionary of Medicine.' The only book he ever published was written in his early days, and was entitled 'A Handy Book of Medical Information and Advice, by a Physician.'

"In his relations to his friends in the profession, whether in town or country, Begbie was inimitable, unapproached. To his town brethren, who used to rush in upon him with their troubles and difficulties at any hour of the day, he was uniformly gentle and obliging. An example of punctuality, never hurried or bustling, uniformly tender in manner, and patiently attentive, he had the faculty of, even when differing in prognosis or treatment, never shaking the confidence of the patient in his own doctor. An utter absence of pomposity, self-consciousness, and self-assertion, a 'moral loftiness, which kept his marvellous sweetness of manner from ever becoming less than reality,' as one of his most distinguished pupils has described it,[2] contributed in no small degree to his unexampled popularity and success as a consultant.

---

[1] "Neuritis and Neuroma" vol. ii; "Local Paralysis from Nerve-disease," vol. ii; "Local Spasms," vol. ii; "Local Anæsthesia," vol. ii; "Colic," vol. iii; "Colitis," vol. iii; "Dysentery," vol. iii; "Fatty Liver," vol. iii; "Cancer of the Liver," vol. iii; "Hydatid Disease of the Liver," vol. iii; "Waxy Disease of the Liver," vol. iii; "Pneumo-Pericardium," vol. iv; and "Hydro-Pericardium," vol. iv.

[2] Dr. Jeffrey, of Jedburgh.

"His country brethren knew well with what readiness and unselfishness he would alter his plans, or give up his rest, to suit their wishes. One who knew him well, and with whom his relations were those of mutual respect and esteem, writes :—'His kindness to the families of country doctors was beyond all expression, and his consideration for the doctors themselves absolutely faultless. Conceive his coming to me, in the circumstances I mentioned (circumstances involving a long railway journey, and a night spent chiefly in a post-chaise), just because he knew, from the nature of the case, that I must be very anxious.'[1] Another says 'the only excuse Begbie ever made for postponing a consultation was, that he must go and see poor Dr. —— who was so ill.'

"Of his abounding beneficence, his charity shown with infinite tenderness and delicacy of feeling, combined with judicious selection of objects, we hardly like to speak, knowing how he himself shrank from publicity. He considered himself only the steward of the wealth he had to work so hard to win; and very few but the recipients knew the numberless ways in which he helped the widow and the orphan, the student, or the clergyman; and all was done as if the recipient was conferring, he only receiving, the favour."

His reputation and excellence were not left unrecognised by his University, and at the graduation ceremonial in August, 1875, just before the meeting of the British Medical Association in Edinburgh, the Senate conferred upon him the degree of Doctor of Laws *honoris causâ*. He was presented for this distinction at the same time with Hughes Bennett, Sir William Fergusson, Matthews Duncan, and Burdon Sanderson.

Doubtless, had he lived, many other honours would

[1] Dr. Turnbull, of Coldstream.

have come to him, and in no quarter would they have been grudged, for no man of his time had a more unblemished personal reputation, nor, in Edinburgh, had any physician higher professional merit.

His valuable life declined somewhat rapidly. His sturdy frame and temperate habits encouraged his friends to expect a long and brilliant career for him.

During the last seven years of his life, his engagements came pressingly upon him, entailing long and exhausting journeys. He neglected his health, became irregular in his meal hours, and often worked without taking any midday repast. The first indication of failing power which was brought home to him was a swoon, which occurred while he was dressing on the day on which he delivered the address on Medicine before the British Medical Association at Edinburgh.[1]

Following this, other symptoms indicating weakened action of the heart appeared, and were cause of grave anxiety to himself.

He resisted these warnings, however, for some months, hoping to get rest, which he believed was all he needed.

When he left home to journey south it was too late. He did not get beyond Carlisle where Mr. Page saw him. Recognising the gravity of the case he returned with him to Edinburgh, and left him in the hands of his most devoted friends and colleagues, Drs. Haldane, Sanders, and Muirhead.

" Others of his old friends kept watch by his bedside, and witnessed his patience, gentleness, courtesy, and manliness which were maintained to the last.

" There was little change on the grave, sad firmness of the face, that had so often by its human sympathy helped others to bear ; there was much of the old

---

[1] *Vide* p. 381.

humour and marvellous power of observation, which those who knew him best saw under his calm, almost grim visage. There was the most perfect simplicity of faith, and patience of hope.

" He died on 25th February, the immediate cause of death being general dilatation of the heart, which was increased to about twice its natural size and weight. This condition had probably existed to a small extent for years, but at last it made rapid progress, dyspnœa and dropsical swelling of the limbs coming on only about ten days before he died.

" Dr. John Wyllie made an inspection of the body, and found the heart greatly enlarged, weighing 21½ ounces.[1] Some atheroma existed on the mitral and aortic valves, and in the coronary arteries. The right ventricle was almost covered with a layer of adipose tissue, which in the right auriculo-ventricular groove was three quarters of an inch in thickness. The muscular fibres were found somewhat granular, and almost free from fat, and all the other organs were healthy except as affected by the heart-lesion."

His remains were interred in the Dean Cemetery, Edinburgh.

" Having reviewed[2] the prominent facts of a bright professional career, and indicated the solid claims of Dr. Warburton Begbie upon the esteem, respect, and gratitude of his generation, we may now ask, by way of improvement, what was the secret of his eminence, and of the wide-spread confidence reposed in him as a physician ? That these were quite exceptional, while at the same time he had competitors of at least equal talent and professional aptitude, cannot be denied. Our answer is, that he possessed a combination of

[1] *Vide* Dr. Wyllie's Report, ' Edin. Med. Journ.,' April, 1876.
[2] From the pen of Mr. Benjamin Bell, of Edinburgh (1876).

qualities which very rarely meet in the same individual. Besides availing himself, as others did, of all the opportunities of instruction which the schools afforded, both at home and abroad, he enjoyed, like his predecessors Abercrombie and Begbie senior, the decided advantage of being a family attendant for many years before he came forward as a consultant, and of thus gaining a familiarity with important details of practice, which one who starts as a consulting physician *ab initio* slowly and painfully acquires. Moreover, from the beginning and all along, he was an enthusiast in his profession, *believed* in the efficacy of remedies, and persistently aimed at practical skill in their administration. Add to these recommendations an inherent benevolence of nature, which impelled him both to feel and manifest a genuine interest in his patients—poor and rich alike—and a charming manner, perfectly natural to him, in which decision, firmness, cheerfulness, and tenderness were seen exquisitely combined. Hence it often happened that, even when a case was hopeless, his genial presence and sympathy soothed the sufferer, and conquered the hearts henceforth of sorrowing friends. Let it be noted that, even when oppressed with business and personal anxiety, he never allowed it to be seen, but applied himself to the circumstances of every case as if he had no other to think of. Can it be wondered that, when a man has gained a reputation for such qualities as these, his circle of confiding friends should rapidly widen, his professional experience grow in proportion, and in a few years his pre-eminence be firmly rooted?

In all his intercourse with his brethren he was remarkably considerate and agreeable—respectful, almost deferential, towards those who were his seniors; friendly, sympathetic, and affable towards younger

men. In short, all who met him in consultation found
him most satisfactory and pleasant; and it is our
opinion that no distinguished member of the profession
in recent times has departed with a more unsullied
personal reputation, or with a tenderer feeling of
regret on the part of his brethren, than James
Warburton Begbie. He was a good man, in the
highest sense—righteous, without pretence or self-
consciousness of any kind; benevolent, loving, and
munificently liberal.

The older members of the profession will look back,
not without emotion, on the comparatively brief, but
bright and altogether pleasant, career which has so
unexpectedly terminated; the younger have lost an
example which promised to assist in moulding their
generation into something nobler than that which went
before."

It needs little reflection to be convinced that he, of
whom all that has now been told, was no ordinary man,
and that his death left a blank which it was not easy
to fill. The profession throughout the country was
the poorer for Warburton Begbie's early removal, as it
had justly looked upon him as one of its brightest
ornaments in the Scottish metropolis.

Though little more than six years have elapsed since
he left us, the Horatian sentiment is still, and will long
be, apt respecting him—" exstinctus amabitur idem."

OBSERVATIONS

IN

CLINICAL MEDICINE.

I.

ON TEMPORARY ALBUMINURIA,

MORE PARTICULARLY AS OCCURRING IN THE COURSE OF
CERTAIN FEBRILE OR OTHER ACUTE DISEASES.

(Read to the Medico-Chirurgical Society of Edinburgh, 5th May, 1852.)

" It appears to me most remarkable," writes Dr. Adams, in
his learned translation of the works of the father of medicine,
" that the important observations made by Hippocrates on the
state of the urine in febrile diseases should have been lost sight
of in an age when the chemical characters of the urine have
been so much studied."[1] M. Littré has make a remark to the
same effect, in his edition of ' Hippocrates,' and it will, I think,
be acknowleged by all to be a just one. The observations on the
urinary secretion contained in the aphorisms are such as to fill
the attentive reader with wonder, as well at the amazing
observation as at the vastness of the knowledge possessed by
their immortal author. It has, indeed, been contended by some,
that the fact of the occasional albuminous nature of the urine
was known to Hippocrates,[2] and, if this notion be correct, then,

[1] ' Hippocrates.' Sydenham Society's edition. Vol. i, p. 98.
[2] On this point, see Dr. Adams' Observation on Aphorism 34, Section 7 ;'
also Dr. Adams' translation of ' Paulus Ægineta,' vol. i, p. 552—(this page
is erroneously printed 352).

more wonderful still, he had already associated it with a protracted disease of the kidney.

Whether known to Hippocrates or not, this connection of disease and symptom long lay neglected, and it is indeed only within our own days that Blackhall,[1] by showing the frequent association of coagulable urine with dropsies, and then the well-known researches of Drs. Bright, Christison, Gregory, and many others, allying albuminuria with alteration of the structure of the kidney, have added to our knowledge regarding it. At the present time, though *well-known*, there is perhaps no symptom the value of which is more frequently misunderstood than the existence of albumen in the urine. Unless the occasion of its presence can be referred to some such certain cause, as the admixture of pus or blood, &c., it is apt too generally to be linked with organic change in the kidney. That the difference of opinion which prevails as to the pathological importance to be attributed to the existence of albumen in the urine arises mainly from two sources, most will, I apprehend, be ready to admit. These are—either from an imperfect knowledge as to the causes of, or conditions under which, the coagulability of the urine occurs; or from an incorrect appreciation of the indications that coagulability, even when observed, affords. In illustration of the first of these, I need only here refer to the condition of the urine in a febrile disease, to which I shall afterwards have occasion in this communication more fully to direct attention—I mean scarlatina; and now speak more particularly of the condition of the urine in the dropsy which so frequently follows that disease. In such cases I have found the urine almost *always* to contain a considerable, in some a very large, amount of albumen; Becquerel[2] appears to have had the same experience; and Dr. Anthony Todd Thomson,[3] in whose posthumous work on skin diseases there occurs this passage :—" The urine is *always* found albuminous where dropsical symptoms appear." Opposed to this are the statements of Simon,[4] and Dr. Scott Alison,[5] and the observations

[1] 'Observations on the Nature and Cure of Dropsies.' London, 1813.

[2] 'Semeiotique des Urines,' p. 267.

[3] 'Diseases of the Skin,' edited by Dr. Parkes, p. 8.

[4] Simon's 'Chemistry.' Sydenham Society's edition. Vol. ii, p. 313.

[5] 'London Journal of Medicine,' March, 1849.

of Phillip,[1] in Berlin,—the former speaking of the disease under the two heads of albuminous and non-albuminous. In illustration of the second reason which I have assigned as causing difference of opinion on this subject, I need only here remind the members of the Society of many cases which must have fallen under their own observation, in which they did experience difficulty in referring the occurrence of albumen in the urine to its proper cause, where perhaps they too rashly concluded its dependence on organic change, and only after further reflection and more careful examination, detected a much more simple cause, which had been previously overlooked, and which neglect had led them, in the first instance, unreasonably to magnify the importance of the disease. This is no supposititious case—such a one I have not unfrequently encountered—and the class of which it is the type will appear by examples in the sequel.

In the present communication I propose directing the attention of the Society to the condition of the urine in certain febrile or other acute diseases. Though the inquiry is important, the subject is too vast to permit me to discuss it wholly. I have, therefore, selected for present investigation one of the most striking characteristics of the urine in such diseases—its frequent coagulability. In a word, my object is not so much to deal with the aphorisms of Hippocrates on the state of the urine near and at the crisis of fevers, as it is to illustrate the observation of M. Martin Solon,[2] that at the resolution of diseases the urine is apt to become albuminous.

By *Temporary Albuminuria*, I mean the manifestation and continuance of albumen in the urine during a limited period, and unconnected with any serious organic change in the kidney. This albuminuria, as occurring in the course of certain febrile or other acute diseases, I shall at present consider under the three following heads—*Desquamative Albuminuria, Inflammatory Albuminuria*, and *Critical Albuminuria ;* and these I shall best illustrate by an immediate reference to the diseases in which they occur.

Under Desquamative Albuminuria, then, I shall speak

[1] Casper's 'Wochenschrift,' 1840, No. 35 ; and Simon's 'Chemistry,' Sydenham Society's edition, vol. ii, p. 280.
[2] ' De l'Albuminurie,' &c. Paris, 1838.

shortly of the urine in Scarlatina, Asiatic Cholera, and Erysipelas.

Under Inflammatory Albuminuria, of the urine in the Dropsy following Scarlatina.

And under Critical Albuminuria, of the urine in Pneumonia and certain cases of Typhus.

First, then, of Desquamative Albuminuria, and of the urine in Scarlatina. In speaking on this subject, we have to deal with a mass of conflicting evidence; for, unlike the condition of the urinary secretion in most febrile diseases, the characters presented by the urine in scarlatina have of late excited the attention of many accurate observers. Of continental authorities, I may quote the names of Martin Solon, of Simon, Romberg, and Phillip, with whose statements most of the members of the Society are probably familiar, and to which I need not allude more particularly than to say, that while some afford evidence of the frequent coagulability of the urine during the period of desquamation after this disease, others from very careful observations oppose it : thus Dr. Frerichs,[1] in his very excellent work, says it is not the rule to find the urine albuminous in simple scarlatina. In a short paper, published in the ' Monthly Journal of Medical Science ' for January, 1849, I gave the results at which, after careful examination of the urine in many cases of scarlatina, I had at that time arrived. Particularly referring to twenty-one cases, because the experiments in regard to these were free from all conceivable sources of fallacy, and were possessed of this additional value, that they had been performed by me *coram publico*—in the Infirmary, in the presence of, and frequently aided by, my then fellow-clerks, more especially Drs. Littlejohn and Absolon. These experiments and others led me to entertain the belief, "that if careful examination of the urine were made, albumen in small amount would be found to exist in every case of scarlatina." The prevalence of the disease in this city and in many parts of Scotland, about and since the same period, afforded opportunity for the further investigation of the subject, which was not lost sight of. From Dr. Fleming and Dr. Chalmers, then house-surgeons of the Dundee and Perth Hospitals respectively, I

[1] ' Die Bright'sche Nierenkrankheit und deren Behandlung'—in a note at foot of p. 207.

early received communications corroborative of my own experience. In June, 1849, Dr. Patrick Newbigging communicated to this Society an interesting history of an epidemic of the disease, as observed in John Watson's Hospital, and from his own experience there in regard to the urine, expressed his concurrence in the belief I have just quoted.[1] I conclude this short historical account by referring to a most interesting paper, from which I have derived much instruction, giving an account of an epidemic, observed under very much the same circumstances as that by Dr. Newbigging, and also communicated to this Society by Mr. Benjamin Bell.[2] Mr. Bell's experience antagonises Dr. Newbigging's and my own; the urine, however, was not tested from day to day—a condition I had been led to regard and to express as a *sine quá non*. Mr. Bell, I feel sure, will pardon me if I now state that, to a certain extent, the want of daily examination, in my opinion, invalidates his experiments. I am, however, willing to admit that, even had the diurnal testing been executed, the albumen might not have appeared—an opinion held in deference to Mr. Bell's, and to that entertained by others, as well as formed from my own more recent experience. In speaking a little more in detail in regard to the urine in scarlatina, let me direct attention more particularly to the following points :—

I. The period of the occurrence and duration of the albumen in the urine, and its amount.

II. The microscopic characters of the urine with which the albumen is invariably associated.

III. The pathological import which its existence denotes.

IV. Whether it possesses any diagnostic value.

I. As to the period of its occurrence, &c. It is just after the commencement of desquamation of the cuticle that the albumen first makes its appearance. In most of the cases I have seen, the third and fourth days after desquamation had set in were the most common. I have found it, however, on the first day of desquamation, and as late in its appearance as the eighth and ninth : this was the case in the urine of a patient I had occasion to attend lately. I had been examining the

[1] 'Monthly Journal of Medical Science,' September, 1849.

[2] Since published in 'Monthly Journal of Medical Science,' August, 1851.

urine from day to day, and finding no albumen on the eighth day after the desquamative process had commenced, I had begun to doubt the likelihood of its appearing, when on the morning of the ninth day I detected the albumen; it continued visible on the tenth, and passed entirely away on the following day. Here let me say a word as to the examination of the urine; in this, as indeed in all cases, both tests—*i.e.* the application of heat and the addition of nitric acid, *must* be employed; nor must the examination be made once or twice, and only on those days when the presence of the albumen is deemed most likely—it should be made every day, beginning before desquamation has commenced, and continued till that process is nearly completed. As a general rule, the duration of the albumen in the urine will be short, probably not longer than a few days; differences, however, exist in this respect; I have known it to disappear in thirty-six hours, and have found it to continue for ten days. There is one interesting fact in regard to its continuance—that after its disappearance it will not return, at least so I have always found; in other words, whenever the albumen was not detected after being first seen, its disappearance was a final one. The amount of albumen will generally be small, seldom more being present than to allow the urine to be called slightly coagulable—a feature of great importance in distinguishing the urine of the simple from that of the dropsical scarlatina.

II. The *microscopic character* of the urine, with which the albumen is invariably associated, is the presence of a considerable amount of epithelium, derived from the different parts of the urinary apparatus. Sometimes the entire epithelial lining of the small tubes of the kidney was present, though certainly not frequently. I do not remember to have ever seen in the urine of simple scarlatina the albuminous or fibrinous casts of the small tubes of the kidney, the appearance of which is so common in the urine of the dropsical affection. Besides epithelium, the urine generally contained amorphous urate of ammonia, sometimes crystalline uric acid; and occasionally, though very rarely, the urine, though examined very soon after micturition, contained crystals of the ammoniaco-magnesian phosphate. In all such there existed a greater than usual amount of epithelium and mucous sediment. It is not uncommou to find octohedral crystals of oxalate of lime in the urine at the same stage of the disease.

III. The pathological import which the existence of albumen in the urine denotes. This is a point on which difference of opinion must still be expected to exist, seeing not only how very different are the facts recorded in regard to the occurrence of albumen, but how varying is the estimation of the importance which is awarded to its presence. While many believe its manifestation to be accidental, and of no importance, there are others who conceive it, if at the time unaccompanied with dropsy, to be its certain prelude. Both of these opinions I have attempted to show are erroneous, and, at least as far as my own observations go, founded on incorrect data. What, then, is the cause of albumen in the urine in simple scarlatina, and what its pathological import? I conceive it to be as essential a symptom of the disease as is desquamation of the cuticle,—to be associated to a certain extent with that desquamation,—to be, in fact, the result of a desquamative process, which the mucous membranes in this disease, equally with the skin, are subject to. Granted, then, that this desquamation occurs when such a change is taking place in the epithelial membrane lining the minute tubes of the kidney, the office of the cells composing which is to eliminate from the blood the matters, solid or fluid, which, in the normal exercise of the renal function, compose the urine, it surely is not surprising that the albumen from the former should, to a slight amount, enter into the latter. Such I believe to be the cause of its occurrence; nor can I regard its presence as indicating any pathological condition further than the separation of epithelial cells and their passage in the current of the urine. No symptoms referable to any such condition occur, no febrile reaction, no lumbar pain, no non-elimination of urine, no suppression of its watery parts, not even any diminution in its quantity, and, with the exception alone of the presence of albumen, no marked alteration in any of its sensible qualities. I have said that this albuminous condition of the urine in scarlatina is associated with the cuticular desquamation, it is so in the time of its occurrence, and so it is also as regards its amount; for I have noticed the albumen in the urine to be greatest in amount, and to continue longest, in those cases in which the process of desquamation had taken place to the greatest extent. In those cases in the urine of which no coagulability has taken place—for my more recent experience has shown me a few such—there has been no very marked desquamation, and no direct evidence of any epithelial separation, as shown by examination of the urine. We know that in many cases of scarlatina, especially in those where the eruption, though well-marked, has not been brilliant, extensive, or lasting, it is not uncommon for the desquamative process not to take place at all, or at most to a comparatively very slight extent. Such are the cases in which the coagulability of the urine will perhaps not occur. I say *perhaps*, for in some such I have, notwithstanding, found it. I am still, therefore, disposed to regard the temporary albuminuria of scarlatina as probably as frequent in its occurrence, and of somewhat of the same importance as a symptom, as the desquamation of the cuticle.

IV. Does the existence of albumen in the urine of scarlatina possess any diagnostic value? I shall best illustrate this point, by relating shortly the particulars of a case which came under my own observation at the time I was making these investigations.

A female servant, æt. 28, was admitted, early in December, 1848, into the Royal Infirmary, under the care of Dr. Paterson, with whom I then acted as clerk. Her chief complaint was of sore throat, which, however, was less severe than for some time before her admission, and was then not very characteristic, and of feebleness and incapability for exertion. She mentioned that she had lately undergone much fatigue and anxiety, having acted as nurse to a lady, who died while she was so employed. I need not detain the Society by relating all the particulars of the case, suffice it to say, that a few days after admission the cuticle, which had been dry, but the skin free from eruption, began to desquamate. The idea then occurred to me that, probably, this had been a case of scarlatina. I examined the urine; on the first and second occasions, and these on different days, detecting no albumen, but on the third found it slightly coagulable, and confess that, upon doing so, I felt less difficulty in deciding on the nature of the case. The albumen continued for three days, and no dropsy occurred. The interest of this case was increased by my being informed, on making careful inquiry, that the mistress of the patient, in whose house she resided, and on whom, when ill, she attended, was supposed to have died of scarlatina, before, however, the eruption had been fullly developed, so that the servant had remained in ignorance of the cause of death. I conclude what I have to say in regard to simple scarlatina, by urging the importance, as well as interest, attending the existence of albumen in the urine of that disease. It is during that period when desquamation is taking place, not so much from the cuticle, I believe, as from the kidneys, that dropsy, from exposure to cold or other causes, is apt to be developed. Let regard then be had to the condition of the urinary secretion ; till the stage of temporary albuminuria is gone by, the patient should be strictly confined, and no hygienic rule relaxed; but after that, even though the old cuticle is as yet only slowly separating, I am inclined to think the danger of a dropsical attack is passed ; the renal function, never inactive, but only slightly involved, is again entirely healthy and efficient.

Second.—In regard to the occurrence of albumen in the urine in Cholera. The very frequent occurrence of albumen in the urine of persons suffering from this disease was, I believe, first noticed in the Cholera Hospital of Edinburgh, during the epidemic of 1848–49. At nearly the same time Dr. Parkes and others in London found the first urine passed in cholera to be coagulable. In the end of spring 1849 the disease became epidemic in Paris, and the same character of the urine speedily attracted attention—Messrs. Levy, Martin Solon, Rostan, and others, making observations in regard to it.[1] During the prevalence of cholera in Edinburgh, 1 had, thanks to Dr. William Robertson, the opportunity of examining the urine in nearly 100 cases.[2] On the general morbid characters of urine in cholera I shall not now enter, except in so far as these are connected with, or illustrate, its coagulability. One of the most invariable symptoms of Asiatic cholera is the entire, or almost entire, suppression of the urine ; and one of the most favorable symptoms throughout the whole course of the disease is the return, or the decided increase, in quantity of that secretion. The mode of fatal termination in many cases of cholera had

---

[1] See Valleix, 'Guide du Médecin Praticien,' tome deuxième, p. 707.
[2] See 'Monthly Journal of Medical Science' for November, 1849 [and p. 65 of this volume].—ED.

satisfactorily shown that the cause of death might reasonably be attributed to the existence of a poison in the blood, whose effects were produced in very much the same way as those of opium and other narcotics; death in such cases as those now referred to taking place by way of coma. All who have seen any number of cases of cholera are familiar with the circumstances now alluded to; and the painful experience of the almost certainly fatal issue of the cases which presented such symptoms cannot soon pass from the mind. Hopes of ultimate recovery given rise to by an unexpected rally from a state of prostrate collapse; by a wasting diarrhœa checked, and urgent vomiting controlled, by a returned pulse and genial warmth taking the place of a deadly coldness of the surface, were too often disappointed. Many such promising cases being cut off in the way already adverted to, it soon became manifest that the only certainly favorable symptom was the restoration of the urinary secretion. The urine, then, first passed in cholera is found to present the following characters :—To be dark in colour, muddy in appearance, to be deficient in specific gravity, to be generally acid in reaction—when treated with nitric acid, to manifest the presence of bile or biliary colouring matter— when tested by heat and nitric acid, to yield a precipitate of albumen; to be remarkably deficient in urea; and lastly, when viewed under the microscope, to contain a large amount of epithelium, derived from different parts of the urinary system, and generally one or other of the common crystalline deposits— most frequently uric acid. The morbid character most intimately connected with the mode of death adverted to is the extreme deficiency of urea, the retention of that substance being, as we know, a frequent source of mischief in other diseases; but the two characters which chiefly concern us in this investigation are the presence of albumen and the deposit of the epithelium. In several examples the albumen existed in such amount as to allow the urine to be called highly coagulable; but more generally the expressions coagulable, or slightly or faintly coagulable, more correctly described it. The albumen continued present in general for some days, usually decreasing in amount, but occasionally increasing for a day or two. This coagulability of the urine was associated invariably with the presence of a large amount of epithelium; as in the case of the

urine in simple scarlatina the epitheum was derived from the
bladder, as well as from the kidney; it was, however, more
common in the cholera urine to find the entire epithelial lining
of the minute tubes.   Attentive observation enabled me to note
these further points; the amount of epithelium and the degree
of coagulability of the urine always stood in exact ratio the one
to the other.   They generally appeared together, and again in
company disappeared.   I have found the epithelium present
alone before the albumen appeared, but have never observed
the opposite case.   Again, the period of the disease at which
the albumen and epithelium in the urine appear, is an interesting consideration in regard to their cause and pathological
import. .I have just referred to the favorable nature, as a
symptom, of the return of the urinary secretion.   It is indeed
just as the period of the resolution of the disease is arrived at,
just as convalescence begins, as bile returns to the stools, and
as the general appearance of the patient commences to improve,
that the first urine is passed; and these are the characters it
presents.   Now, I have called the albuminous urine of simple
scarlatina a *desquamative* albuminuria, and for the same reasons
I call the passage of albumen in the urine of this disease a *desquamative* albuminuria.   The examination of both most
emphatically indicates the progress of a desquamative change
in the lining and secreting mucous membrane of the kidneys;
and both diseases afford the evidence of desquamation taking
place in other parts of the system.   The desquamation of the
cuticle in scarlatina is not more constant than that of the
mucous membrane of the intestinal canal is in cholera.   These
peculiar features of the urine in cholera I have always found
best marked in the severest cases of the disease.   There remains
one other point of still higher consideration, because beyond its
mere interest there is a weight of value, namely, that by a just
appreciation of these evidences furnished by the urinary secretion, means may and have been adopted whereby the condition
of the patient may be improved, happily his restoration from
otherwise certain death secured.

    Third.—Albumen in the urine of erysipelas.   I need not
occupy the attention of the Society long with this example.   I
have found that after severe attacks of idiopathic erysipelatous
inflammation, and most frequently when a large surface of the

skin has been affected, that the urine has, during the progress of convalescence, become albuminous. I do not regard temporary albuminuria as so invariable or frequent a symptom of erysipelas as I conceive it to be of scarlatina, at least I have not found it so. But since my attention was directed to this subject, I have found albumen in the urine during the early progress of convalescence from a large number of severe cases of the disease, more especially when these two symptoms had been present—severe gastric or intestinal irritation and derangement, and considerable desquamation of the cuticle. The quantity of the albumen present was never great; the period of its occurrence was at the resolution of the disease, as convalescence commenced, and during the progress of desquamation. It was, as in the other examples of albuminuria I have already referred to, invariably associated with epithelium, affording evidence of desquamation, but more closely resembling the urine of scarlatina in being less charged with this ingredient than that of cholera. The question arises, that seeing this temporary albuminuria is a symptom of certain of the exanthematous diseases, is the fact of the frequent occurrence of albumen in the urine of erysipelas, when its symptoms most nearly resemble those of that class of diseases, to be considered as at all proving that identity?

In the interesting paper[1] read to the Society at its last meeting, by Dr Alexander Wood, the relations of erysipelas with scarlatina were sought to be established by a reference to other but very important facts. The temporary albuminuria which occurs in the course of both adds, I think, another link to the chain of connection and relation.

In now taking leave of the subject of desquamative albuminuria, I have only to add, that the three examples now considered are not the only ones I could have adduced. There are others, of which variola and certain febrile affections of the skin are instances; but the three I have selected differ in no very marked degree from these and others, while they have served sufficiently to illustrate the temporary albuminuria dependent on desquamation. I have, it will further be observed, not claimed for the urine in these three diseases an entire similarity in their characters; it is sufficient for my purpose,

[1] Since published in ' Medical Times and Gazette,' July, 1852.

if you agree with me in thinking that they so nearly correspond in certain particulars, that, setting aside their differing characters, I am entitled to conclude that the *temporary albuminuria* common to the three arises from the same cause in each.

And now. *Secondly*, I have to consider the case of *Inflammatory Albuminuria*, which I propose to do very shortly, by reference to one example—*the dropsical disease following scarlatina*. Every one who has paid attention to the condition of the urine in this most interesting affection, must have noticed the great dissimilarity subsisting between its external and other characters and those of the urine in simple scarlatina; while in the latter the amount of urine passed, except during the continuance of febrile symptoms, is undiminished, one of the most certain forerunners, as it is always the most invariable accompaniment of dropsy, is the excessive reduction of the quantity of urine. This urine, when further examined, is found to contain a large amount of albumen; while, under the microscope, frequently blood, not unfrequently exudation corpuscles or compound granular cells, always much epithelium, and the fibrinous casts of the renal tubes are recognised. The symptoms which accompany these changes in the urine are generally well-marked, the most prominent, save the dropsy, being a very uneasy, often severe, lumbar pain and marked febrile excitement. But, independent of these general symptoms, it will, I think, be admitted, that the characters presented by this urine, while they differ from those of the urine in simple scarlatina, indicate also the existence of a much more serious change in the secreting mucous membrane of the kidney than a merely desquamative one. In order, however, to arrive at a correct opinion in regard to the pathological importance of the change undergone in the kidney during the dropsical disease, it is necessary to bear in mind both the symptoms presented by the patient and the hints afforded by the characters of the altered urine. These taken together give evidence of general febrile excitement, and of renal congestion, inflammation, and exudation. I have examined the urine in many such cases, and have found the albuminous condition much more lasting than in the simple cases—indeed observation and experience show now pretty plainly that the long-continued albuminuria of dropsical scarlatina may, and often does, lead imperceptibly—insidiously it may be—to organic renal disease. In many instances I have found the albumen, though large in amount and associated with all the general and local inflammatory symptoms alluded to, speedily and entirely disappear. I have not seen many cases of the dropsy following scarlatina, which I had watched from the commencement of the primary disease, but I have seen a few, and in all such the dropsical and aggravated symptoms appeared at the time the temporary albuminuria was going on, and were evidently the result of exposure to cold. This variety of albuminuria, then, which I have called inflammatory, may or may not be *temporary :* it is to be feared that not unfrequently neglected, or even unskilfully treated, the affection it accompanies lays the foundation of permanent renal disease. In most cases, however, it is fortunately otherwise, while in nearly all it may be looked upon as, under judicious management, a curable disorder.

Thirdly.—*Critical albuminuria.*—1. *Pneumonia.*—Becquerel,[1] Simon,[2] Andral,[3] Finger,[4] and others, have all noticed the not unfrequent occurrence of albumen in the urine of pneumonia. Several observers in this country, though perhaps on a less scale, have done the same; in particular, Dr. William Aitken[5] has recorded several cases of pneumonia in which albuminuria occurred. The peculiar appearance presented by the urine about the critical period in acute pneumonia is well-known. The urine, perhaps clear and transparent, perhaps even pale in colour, though in general not remarkable for any of these characters, becomes at that time almost suddenly dark and muddy, loaded with amorphous urates, which speedily subside in the form of a dense deposit. This characteristic is known to all attentive observers, but I do not think that it is so generally known that that urine, cleared as it is by the first application of heat from the solution of the urate of ammonia, is, by a continuance of the heat, and by the addition of nitric acid, caused to manifest the presence of albumen. Such, how-

[1] 'Semeiotique des Urines,' p. 327.

[2] 'Chemistry.' Sydenham Society's edition, vol. ii, p. 214.

[3] Quoted by Becquerel, 'Semeiotique des Urines,' p. 332.

[4] 'Präger Vierteljahreschrift,' 1847, No. 4; also 'Monthly Retrospect of Medical Sciences,' edited by Drs. Fleming and Gairdner, volume for 1848, p. 66.

[5] 'Edinburgh Medical and Surgical Journal,' No. 178.

ever, I have found to be the case in a large number of instances. It is undoubtedly, as Schönlein and others have pointed out, by the increased energy of the kidney that the mass, in many cases very large amount, of exudation poured into the substance of the lung is got rid of. That exudation is found in the urine in a very different form. The deposit being for the most part composed of amorphous urate of ammonia, of uric acid, and of a large number of very small molecules or granules, which are unaffected by heat, and unaltered by acetic acid, and which are, I think, to be recognised as the *débris* of the exudation—finally, of albumen, deposited by heat, or on the addition of nitric acid. These are the ingredients of the deposit found in the urine of pneumonia, this the manner in which the inflammatory exudation to a certain extent chemically tranformed, but to some degree having only undergone a breaking down, is as effete matter discharged from the system. In respect to the period of occurrence of the albumen, I have already mentioned that about the crisis of the disease is the time I have detected it.

By critical period in pneumonia is meant the time at which resolution begins, when the exudation, which had rendered a portion of the lung useless—impermeable to air—is being got rid of. The occurrence of the albumen in the urine I have, on a few occasions, noticed a day or two before the more general deposit appeared. This, from observation, I was led to regard as a very favorable symptom—it certainly was a very interesting one, because, just as certainly as the returning crepitation, and the less dull sound on percussion over a condensed lung, indicate the breaking up of the exudation and the return of the air to the previously closed vesicles, did the albumen in the urine advertise the approach of the more dense deposit, consisting of the amorphous urates, &c. The continuance of the albumen is very variable. I have never known it to disappear under five or six days. In chronic pneumonia, more especially when the disease has advanced slowly, and when, as is not unusual, a considerable portion of the lung is affected, and when, as is certain, cure is tedious, resolution slow, I have found the duration of the albumen longer than in acute pneu-. monia. In such instances I have known it to continue for weeks; it did so in one most interesting case, to which I shall presently refer. As the duration of the albumen is variable so is its amount. It was always present unmistakably, allowing no doubt of its existence; often it was present in considerable amount, not unfrequently in very large. Such are the facts I have observed in regard to the existence of albuminuria in pneumonia, or rather in the convalescence from it. In regard to the frequency of its occurrence, I may mention that in almost all the cases of pneumonia[1] admitted into the Royal Infirmary under the care of the senior physician during a period of nine months, and which I carefully examined, the appearances were such as I have detailed; and that the casual examination of many other cases in wards under the care of other physicians served to strengthen my belief in the almost uniform occurrence of the facts now noted.

I shall here give the particulars of one case—that before alluded to.

In August, 1848, a hale man, aged upwards of sixty, was admitted into the infirmary with acute pneumonia affecting the inferior lobes of both lungs. The disease ran its course with marked severity, but at the end of fourteen days from his entrance to hospital the patient was convalescent. As I was in the habit of doing, in the case of every patient at that time, I examined this man's urine,[2] and found it highly coagulable; still it was passed in normal amount and maintained a good specific gravity, while under the microscope it was found to contain a large deposit of amorphous urates, and a considerable amount of the granular matter I have already described. In this case the opinion first formed (after the discovery of the albumen) was that he laboured under Bright's disease, and that the acute affection which caused his entrance into hospital was an example of one of those intercurrent inflammations which, whether affecting the pericardium, pleuræ, or lungs, we know to be common in that disease. The general symptoms of the patient, however, in particular his appearance and marked convalescence, together with his freedom from dropsy, and the

[1] Of at least eleven cases I have preserved notes, and these in connection with some other features of interest in the urine of pneumonia I shall hereafter lay before the Society.

[2] The first examination had not been made till the fourteenth day of the disease.

characters presented by his urine, appeared to me to militate against the idea of his suffering from renal disease. Accordingly, I kept him under careful observation for some time longer, both while he remained in the hospital and after his dismissal from it; and examining his urine from day to day, perceived its characters to undergo those modifications I have described; and, finally, found it to present those of a perfectly healthy secretion. Had this examination not been continued, or this cause of temporary albuminuria been unknown or unregarded, the probability is, that incorrectly appreciating the evidence afforded by examination of the urine, and particularly the detection of albumen, instead of considering the coagulability as evidence of the progress of a healthy action, we should unreasonably have concluded it to be that of the existence of a permanent organic change. To this albuminuria, then, I have given the title of *critical albuminuria*,—because my data being correct, and my conclusions justifiable, it is to be regarded as an evidence of a critical action, and commencement of a change undergone by a diseased part before its return to a healthy state. But I can further illustrate this subject by a reference to changes which occur in some cases of typhus fever. I have have found albuminuria by no means an uncommon attendant on the convalescence of typhus; not, however, nearly so invariable in its occurrence as in scarlatina, or even so common as in pneumonia; so frequent, however, as to lead me to examine all cases in which it occurred, and that with very great care. The result has been, that no one of any such cases has, either at the time or during a considerable period of observation afterwards, afforded the evidence of any organic change in the kidneys to account for the albumen in the urine.

The albuminuria in the case of typhus appears to me of special interest, as occurring much more frequently, if not entirely, in certain cases of typhus. It is in those cases in which we know, or have reason to suspect, that the deposits, generally called typhus deposits, have taken place in internal organs, that we find albumen in the urine. Two or three observations of a somewhat different nature have led me to this conclusion; for example, I have found the urine albuminous in cases of abdominal typhus—that is, in those cases in which we

2

generally find severe diarrhœa as a symptom during life, and
deposit in the intestinal glands as the most prominent lesion
after death. In several cases of this kind, which proved fatal,
I have found albumen in the urine for days before death; and
in others, which happily recovered, I have as frequently noticed
its occurrence. In both these instances the albumen appeared,
for the most part, at an advanced period of the disease, at least
after the particular symptoms had continued for some time;
while in the former the albuminuria continued up to death;
in the latter, in some it disappeared as convalescence was fairly
established; and in others it lasted for a longer period. The
amount of albumen in these cases, and the other characters
with which the coagulability was associated, were exactly as I
have described them in the example of pneumonia; and finding
the albuminuria to bear a relation to the deposits in internal
organs in typhus, I have been led to regard the kidneys as the
emunctories by which the morbid matter so deposited is to a
certain extent at least removed from the system—and so doing,
to regard the temporary albuminuria of typhus as a critical
albuminuria. It is, I think, no objection to this view that
deposits, such as those referred to, remain in organs for a
lengthened period; for, firstly, I do not think we can pretend
to limit the period of their removal or disappearance; and I am
inclined to believe that, when they do so disappear, the urine
will very probably contain the ingredients I have noticed; and,
secondly, the calcareous masses found in the spleen, and other
organs, accepted as the earthy remains of the deposits spoken
of, certainly attest the removal by some channel or other of the
animal matter, of which, in their original condition, these
deposits were partly composed. This is an interesting subject,
and invites further inquiry.

And now, in conclusion, I have thus brought under the attention of the Society some of the various causes, as I have
observed them, of temporary albuminuria, more particularly as
occurring in the course of certain febrile or other acute diseases.
Let me again state that I am far from supposing that in this
consideration I have included all its various causes, or the diseases in which it may occur. There exist several others, as
puerperal fever, phthisis, &c.; these, however, I have not
hitherto been able to observe in numbers sufficient to justify

any deductions, though from what I have seen I feel inclined to attribute the albuminuria in these, and some others, to a blood change. Temporary albuminuria occurring in the course of certain diseases has in this paper been considered under three heads—Desquamative, Inflammatory, and Critical—and to one or other of these three I have referred the coagulable urine of scarlatina, cholera, and erysipelas, of dropsical scarlatina, and of pneumonia and certain cases of typhus fever ; it remains for the Society to consider whether or not these divisions are authorised.[1] The study of the morbid qualities of the urine is one of confessedly great interest and importance, and so also is the pathology of the kidney ; both of these have individually received great attention—not, however, sufficiently in respect of the relation to, and dependence of, the one upon the other. It is in this direction that our labours must now advance ; and doing so, we cannot fail to arrive at facts equally instructive as important.

[1] For an account of an interesting discussion which followed the reading of this paper before the Medico-Chirurgical Society, in which Dr. Christison, Dr. Andrew Wood, and Dr. W. Gairdner took part, see the 'Monthly Journal' for July, 1852, p. 92 ; also the 'Medical Times and Gazette,' June 19th, 1852, p. 623.

II.

CASE

OF

ACUTE RHEUMATISM

SUCCEEDED BY

CHOREA AND AFFECTION OF THE HEART.

(*Read to the Medico-Chirurgical Society of Edinburgh, Nov. 24th, 1852.*)

THE relation subsisting between the two diseases, rheumatism and chorea, has now for some time been recognised by the profession, while from many of its members the subject has received much attention and study. That an amount of obscurity, however, still exists in regard to it is evident from the various explanations which have been advanced to account for the association of the rheumatism with the nervous disorder; and although the subject has engaged, and does still engage, the notice of many fully qualified for its investigation, it will not, I think, be considered that the recording of any accurately observed case is to be looked upon as superfluous or uncalled for. Acting on this belief, I beg to submit to the Society the following case, and the few remarks which succeed it :

J. O—, æt. 10, daughter of a groom, was placed on the roll of the New Town Dispensary on the 7th June last. I saw her that afternoon, in the house of her grandmother, in Jamaica Street. She was a delicate-looking but comely child, of fair complexion. In infancy she had suffered severely from measles and hooping-cough. Her grandmother, with whom she resided, had for many years been a cripple from rheumatism ; and her own father had had two attacks of rheumatic fever. The little patient had been seized two days before my visit with shivering, followed by the occurrence of severe pains in the larger joints of both legs and arms. At the time I saw her, the knees, ankles, and all the smaller joints, were much swollen, red, and very painful. The shoulders, elbows, and joints of hands, were similarly, though to a less extent, affected. There was much fever, quick pulse, and furred tongue. The urine was dense, and the bowels confined. Heart's action violent, but unattended with any morbid sound.

She was ordered a purging dose of calomel with half a grain of opium, and a black draught to be taken the following morning.

June 8th.—The pains and fever much as yesterday. Has slept pretty well. Ordered a pill with one grain of calomel and one fourth of a grain of opium to be taken four times in the twenty-four hours.

It is not my object to dwell on this portion of the case, and I need not, therefore, weary the Society by detailing the daily condition of the patient; let it be sufficient to say, that she passed through a very severe rheumatic fever, being only convalescent on the seventeenth day. She did not, however, so far as I could make out, suffer during that period from any extension of the rheumatic inflammation to the heart or pericardium. There certainly was not on any occasion during these fifteen days any morbid sound to be detected on auscultation, or any increased precordial dulness to be made out on percussion. The mouth had been slightly affected by the mercury, which had immediately thereafter been suspended. Up to the 23rd of June I saw her daily; from that date she was convalescent, and thereafter, up to the end of the first week of July, I saw her frequently; on more than one occasion examining her chest, and always with the same result. On the 20th of July, not having seen her since the 7th, I was requested to visit her, on account of a peculiar shaking and nervousness, to use her mother's words. I found her suffering from confirmed chorea. The mother informed me, that the disease had been creeping on for some days, and that ever since her rheumatic fever she had been nervous, and very easily excited and alarmed, which was different from her previous character. She could not attribute the occurrence of the disease to any particular cause, indeed it had come on gradually; but she was quite sensible that it had been augmented by a fright, sustained the day previous to my visit, when a cat had somewhat incautiously attacked a favourite hawk, which was kept in the room in which my patient slept. She had given a loud scream at the time, and during the following night had awoke from sleep with the same. When I saw her, the choreic affection of the lower limbs was so aggravated as to render progression nearly impossible; the arms, especially the left, were similarly affected. The left side of the body was, on the whole, more markedly affected than the right. Articulation also was greatly impaired, and she made most singular grimaces. She had never suffered from any nervous disorder before. The tongue had become furred.

On examination of the heart, I now, for the first time, noticed a deviation from the natural sounds. A distinct blowing murmur took the place of the first, as heard towards the apex of the heart, and this was accompanied by a greatly increased action of the organ.

Ordered a purge of jalap, to be repeated each day for three days.

The purges improved the tongue, but did not apparently influence the nervous disorder. Accordingly I ordered her to take five drops of Fowler's solution twice daily immediately after meals.

The arsenic was continued regularly, without the intermission of a single dose, from the 24th of July up to the 20th of September, when the physiological action of the mineral being induced, as represented by a very white tongue, swollen eyelids, and a somewhat irritable state of the mucous membrane of the stomach and bowels, I ordered its suspension. During that period the nervous affection had preseveringly continued, at times augmented in severity, at others apparently yielding, at one period so severe as to cause the strict confinement of my little patient to the house, at another, permitting her to walk, assisted by her mother, and even to visit me at home.

On the 23rd of September I made the following note of her

condition :—Chorea almost entirely disappeared; walks well
and steadily, though she still complains of occasional sinking
at the knees; slight twitches of the muscles of the face. The
cardiac murmur continues distinct, clearly heard over the
whole cardiac region; it is most distinct towards the apex, and
is not propagated in the cervical vessels.

November 17th.—Is quite free from all choreic movements;
expresses herself as well, except for the beating at the breast.
The palpitation is at times inordinate. No decided increase of
precordial dulness exists. The murmur continues as before.

Remarks.—This case is similar to many others which have
been placed on record, and is, with one point of difference, the
same as more than one case alluded to by Dr. Kirkes in his
most interesting papers[1] on this subject, the only dissimilarity
being that the evidence of the affection of the heart, though
looked for during the rheumatism, was not detected, but
became established about the time of the recurrence of the
chorea. I had indeed come to the conclusion, that happily the
heart had escaped implication in the disease. The case is
interesting from the speedy manner in which the choreic
affection succeeded the declension of the rheumatic. There is
one question of great interest to which I should wish to draw
the attention of the Society, and that is—The association of
disease of the heart, unattendant on rheumatism, with the
nervous disorder. I think that the evidence of some affection
of the heart will be found in many cases of chorea. In Dr.
Kirkes' analysis of thirty-six cases, three were of this nature.
In some cases the cardiac affection will no doubt be found to
be inorganic—functional derangement merely—attended by a
murmur with the heart's first sound, heard most distinctly over
the upper sternum, propagated in the cervical vessels, and in all
probability asssociated with the so-called venous murmur in
the neck. Further, the general appearance and symptoms of
such patients point to the probable dependence of both nervous
and cardiac affection on a disordered state of the blood, in short,
on anæmia.

But apart from these, there is another class of cases, in which
the evidence of organic disease of the heart, independent alto-

[1] 'Medical Gazette,' 1850.

gether of rheumatism, is quite as marked as its functional derangement is in the former. I remember to have seen one such well-marked case under the care of Dr. Paterson—now of Tiverton—in the Royal Infirmary, an account of which, with Dr. Paterson's concurrence, I afterward published.[1] The patient, a boy of seven years of age, was admitted into the hospital, suffering from a first, but very severe, attack of chorea. Immediately on his admission a loud musical murmur was detected accompanying the first sound of the heart, heard most distinctly towards its apex. Neither in this boy's history, nor in that of any of the members of his immediate family, which were carefully inquired into, was there any account of rheumatism. Under treatment the chorea speedily subsided, and after a residence of nearly a month he left the hospital, the cardiac murmur remaining as before. Scarcely six weeks thereafter the little boy died suddenly, sitting at his tea table —he dropped down dead. Unfortunately I was unable to obtain an examination of the body, but the manner of the death certainly corroborated the opinion formed from the observation of the symptoms and physical signs of disease during life.

I do not propose to allude to the various theories known to all the members of the Society, which have been advanced to account for the association of rheumatism with chorea.[2] That which has been suggested by Dr. Begbie[3] has received the willing assent of Dr. Watson and of Dr. Kirkes, appears to accord with the views entertained by Dr. Todd, and finds no adverse facts in the numerous observations of M. Sée, whose elaborate memoir on this subject, read to the Academy of Medicine, and published in their ' Transactions,' has left nothing to be added to its historical bearings.

The case I have now related certainly goes to establish the correctness of Dr. Begbie's theory, that the morbid condition of the blood which gives rise to rheumatism also gives rise to chorea. The child had inherited from two generations the rheumatic diathesis, and only became a sufferer from chorea on the declension of a rheumatic attack. Assuredly no other theory which has been advanced so simply or correctly explains the now frequently observed facts of one member of a family being

---

[1] ' Medical Times,' 1849. [2] ' Monthly Journal,' 1847.
[3] The father of the writer.—ED.

affected with chorea, another with rheumatism, and perhaps a third being the subject of both affections. But I acknowledge, with Dr. Kirkes, that there still exist several very interesting circumstances, which require more attention and investigation, before the association of these two diseases shall become thoroughly understood.

III.

ON THE USE

OF

BELLADONNA IN SCARLATINA.

(This paper appeared in the 'British and Foreign Medico-Chirurgical Review' for January, 1855, as a review of the following works:—
1. *Cure and Prevention of Scarlet Fever.* By SAMUEL HAHNEMANN. ('Lesser Writings' of the Author, collected and translated by R. E. DUDGEON, M.D.). 2. *Travaux Thérapeutiques sur la Belladone.* Publiée par A. L. J. BAYLE. (Tome Seconde de 'Bibliothèque de Thérapeutique.')— Paris, 1830. 3. *Homœopathy: its Tenets and Tendencies.* By Professor SIMPSON.—Edinburgh, 1853. 4. *Homœopathy fairly Represented.* By Professor HENDERSON.—Edinburgh, 1853.)

SINCE the immortal discovery of Jenner, whereby one of the most frightful and most fatal diseases from which the human race has ever suffered was deprived alike of its terrors and its victims, the cultivators of medicine have been justly animated by the hope that their science might be caused to yield other services of a kindred nature to mankind.[1] Nor has there been any want of real and earnest activity in a work which, since the introduction of vaccination, all must have had more or less at heart. For whether or not we concede to belladonna the prophylactic virtues in scarlatina which not a few have claimed for it, we are at all events called upon to acknowledge, that from very many the subject has, at various times during the

[1] "I believe," says Dr. Simpson, "medicine will yet most probably discover prophylactic measures against scarlet fever, measles, &c."—'Homœopathy,' p. 230, note at foot of page.

five-and-fifty years it has been under discussion, received all
that attention and patient investigation which every right-
thinking man will readily and heartily admit to be its due.[1]
That a disbelief in the alleged power of belladonna should have
taken possession of the mind of the profession generally, and
more particularly in this country, was scarcely to be wondered
at, when we consider the quarter from which the recommendation of its vaunted virtues proceeded, and the manner in
which the test of its efficacy was required to be determined.
But though apologising for the feeling at first entertained by
the bulk of medical men in regard to the announcement of the
prophylactic action of belladonna, we are not to be held as
thereby approving it, far less defending the course of procedure
which it in some cases engendered; for, on the contrary, when
regard is had to the frequency as well as to the extremely fatal
nature of many epidemics of scarlet fever, whose ravages it was
upheld both to mitigate and repress, we do feel that the mere
circumstance of Hahnemann being its originator and strongest
advocate formed no excuse for belladonna being either

---

[1] We may remind our readers that very many other prophylactics have
been recommended and actually employed in scarlatina besides the exhibition of belladonna. In regard to such we find Joseph Frank writing: "Ad
scarlatinam præpediendam commendata fuere : errhina et collutoria ex
ammoniâ cum sufficiente quantitate aquæ; acida mineralia diluta tum
interne, tum externe sub formâ gargarismatis : subfumigia vel ope acidi
muriatici sive simplicis sive oxygenati, vel ope acidi nitrici; minimæ doses
succi inspissati herbæ atropæ belladonnæ; et ipsa scarlatinæ insertio, de
quarum autem rerum effectibus, cum non quivis homo necessario scarlatinæ
subjici debeat, arduum est judicare."—' Praxeos Mediæ Universæ Præcepta,'
vol. ii, par. i, p. 221, Leipzig, 1815.

"Si l'action de la belladone est encore douteuse, malgré le grand nombre
de ses partisans, celle des autres préservatifs est encore bien plus hypothé-
tique. Ainsi on a prôné une combinaison de soufre doré et de calomel. La
dose, pour les enfants de deux à quatre ans, est d'un sixième ou d'un
huitième de grain de calomel uni à autant de soufre doré d'antimoine, et
mêlé à un peu de sucre ou de magnésie; on répète cette dose trois ou quatre
fois par jour. Cette méthode a été conseillée par un médecin Hollandais.
(E. J. Thomassen, à Thuessink), qui affirme que dans toutes les familles où
l'on fit l'usage du préservatif, la scarlatine ne sévit pas. Il cite l'observation d'un enfant qui sous son influence n'eut ni mal de gorge ni éruption,
mais la desquamation consécutive."—' Traité Clinique et Pratique des Maladies des Enfants,' par MM. Barthez et Rilliet, deuxième édition, tom. iii,.
p. 308.

neglected or passed by. Some there were who entered at once upon the examination and investigation; and during the lengthened period that has since elapsed, abundant opportunities have been seized and turned to the best account.

But while we readily allow the same privilege to Hahnemann and his followers as we claim for the disciples of our own School, in so far as the propriety of investigating the peculiar virtue claimed for belladonna by the former was incumbent upon both, we at the same time do conscientiously believe that had it owed its suggestion and enforcement to such a physician as Laennec, or even to Bayle,[1] the question of the prophylactic action of belladonna would have long ere this been settled in the one way or in the other. Once propounded, the claim advanced would have been rigidly examined, and not accepted as correct by some upon what we shall presently show to have been most insufficient grounds, nor rejected in several instances, as we believe, upon grounds certainly not more reliable. For ourselves, we are clearly of opinion that the time and occasion have now arrived when the question of the prophylaxis of belladonna can readily and satisfactorily be answered—and, as we think, in the negative. But, desirous as we are of doing our opponents—we have now declared our own view—every justice, and the subject itself being full of interest, we shall devote this article to a reconsideration of the whole matter.

Although the discovery of the supposed prophylactic action of belladonna in scarlatina has been attributed to Castelliz, of Vienna,[2] there appears little doubt that the idea originally occurred to the mind of Hahnemann, and no doubt that by him the subject was first introduced to the notice of the profession. The former happened when he was resident at Königslutter, in 1799. Two years thereafter he published a pamphlet, entitled ' Heilung und Verhütung des Scharlachfiebers,'[3] from the translation of which, in Dr. Dudgeon's edition of the 'Lesser Works of

---

[1] Bayle manifestly gave it his support, but to a certain extent, and in a certain sense, the theory whose associated facts Bayle has done much service in recording, was tarnished in its propounder.

[2] See " Lectures on Materia Medica and Therapeutics," by G. G. Sigmond, M.D., Lecture xiii ; 'Lancet,' vol. ii, 1836-37.

[3] Originally published at Gotha in 1801.

Hahnemann,' we extract his own account of the manner in which his discovery was made.

"The mother of a large family, at the commencement of July, 1799,[1] when the scarlet fever was most prevalent and fatal, had got a new coun terpane made up by a sempstress, who (without the knowledge of the former) had in her small chamber a boy just recovering of scarlet fever. The first-mentioned woman on receiving it examined it, and smelt it, in order to ascertain whether it might not have a bad smell that would make it necessary to hang it in the open air; but as she could detect nothing of the sort, she laid it beside her on the pillow of the sofa, on which some hours later she lay down for her afternoon's nap. She had unconsciously, in this way only (for the family had no other near or remote connection with scarlatina patients), imbibed this miasm. A week subsequently she suddenly fell ill of a bad quinsy, with the characteristic shooting pains in the throat, which could only be subdued after four days of threatening symptoms. Several days thereafter her daughter, ten years of age, infected most probably by the morbific exhalations of the mother, or by the emanations from the counterpane, was attacked in the evening by severe pressive pain in the abdomen, with biting itching on the body and head, and rigor over the head and arms, and with paralytic stiffness of the joints. She slept very restlessly during the night, with frightful dreams, and perspiration all over the body excepting the head. I found her in the morning with pressive headache, dimness of vision, slimy tongue, some ptyalism, the submaxillary glands hard, swollen, painful to the touch, shooting pains in the throat on swallowing and at other times. She had not the slightest thirst, her pulse was quick and small, breathing hurried and anxious; though she was very pale she felt hot to the touch, yet complained of horripilation over the face and hairy scalp; she sat leaning somewhat forwards, in order to avoid the shooting in the abdomen, which she felt most acutely when stretching or bending back the body; she complained of a paralytic stiffness of the limbs with an air of the most dejected pusillanimity and shunned all conversation. 'She felt,' she said, 'as if she could only speak in a whisper.' Her look was dull and yet staring, the eyelids inordinately wide open, the face pale, features sunk.

"Now I knew only too well that the ordinary favourite remedies, as in many other cases, so also in scarlatina, in the most favorable cases leave everything unchanged; and, therefore, I resolved in this case of scarlet fever just in the act of breaking out, not to act as usual in reference to individual symptoms, but if possible (in accordance with my new

[1] The 14th of May, 1796, was, as Dr. Watson happily terms it, "the birthday of vaccination;" it is not unlikely that during the period from May, 1796, to July, 1799, the mind of Hahnemann had been strongly directed to the subject of the prevention of contagious diseases.

synthetical principle) to obtain a remedy whose peculiar mode of action was calculated to produce in the healthy body most of the morbid symptoms which I observed *combined* in this disease. My memory and my written collection of the peculiar effects of some medicines furnished me with no remedy so capable of producing a counterpart of the symptoms here present as *belladonna*.

"It alone could fulfil most of the indications of this disease, seeing that in its primary action it has, according to my observations, a tendency to excite even in healthy persons great dejected pusillaninity, dull staring (stupid) look, with inordinately opened eyelids, obscuration of vision, coldness and paleness of the face, want of thirst, excessively small rapid pulse, paralytic immobility of the limbs, obstructed swallowing, with shooting pains in the parotid gland, pressive headache, constrictive pains in the abdomen, which become intolerable in any other posture of the body besides bending forwards, rigor and heat of certain parts to the exclusion of others—*c. g.* of the head alone, of the arms alone, &c. If, thought I, this was a case of approaching scarlet fever, as I considered was most probable, the subsequent effects peculiar to this plant—its power to produce synochus, with erysipelatous spots on the skin, sopor, swollen hot face, &c.—could not fail to be extremely appropriate to the symptoms of fully developed scarlatina.

"I, therefore, gave this girl, ten years of age, who was already affected by the first symptoms of scarlet fever, a dose of this medicine ($\frac{1}{432000}$th part of a grain of the extract, which, according to my subsequent experience, is rather too large a dose). She remained quietly seated all day, without lying down; the heat of her body became but little observable; she drank but little; none of her other symptoms increased that day, and no new ones occurred. She slept pretty quietly during the night, and the following morning, twenty hours after taking the medicine, most of the symptoms had disappeared without any crisis; the sore throat alone persisted, but with diminished severity, until evening, when it too went off. The following day she was lively, ate and played again, and complained of nothing. I now gave her another dose, and she remained perfectly well, whilst two other children of the family fell ill of bad scarlet fever without my knowledge, whom I could only treat according to my general plan detailed above. I gave my convalescent a smaller dose of belladonna every three or four days, and she remained in perfect health. I now earnestly desired to be able, if possible, to preserve the other five children of the family perfectly free from infection. Their removal was impossible, and would have been too late. I reasoned thus: a remedy that is capable of quickly checking a disease in its onset must be its best preventive; and the following occurrence strengthened me in the correctness of this conclusion. Some weeks previously, three children of another family lay ill of a very bad scarlet fever; the eldest daughter alone, who, up to that period, had been taking belladonna internally for an external affection on the joints of her fingers, to my great astonishment, did not catch the fever, although during the prevalence of other epidemics she had always been the first to take them.

"This circumstance completely confirmed my idea. I now hesitated not to administer to the other five children of this numerous family this divine remedy as a preservative, in very small doses, and as the peculiar action of this plant does not last above three days, I repeated the dose every seventy-two hours, and they all remained perfectly well, without the slightest symptoms throughout the whole course of the epidemic, and amid the most virulent scarlatina emanations from their sisters who lay ill with the disease. In the meantime I was called to attend another family, where the eldest son was ill of scarlet fever. I found him in the height of the fever, and with the eruption on the chest and arms. He was seriously ill, and the time was consequently past to give him the specific prophylactic treatment. But I wished to keep the other three children free from this malignant disease. One of them was nine months, another two years, and the third four years of age. The parents did what I ordered, gave each of the children the requisite quantity of belladonna every three days, and had the happiness to preserve these three children free from the pestilential disease, free from all its symptoms, although they had unrestricted intercourse with their sick brother. And a number of other opportunities presented themselves to me where this specific remedy never failed." (p. 434.)

Such is Hahnemann's account of the mode in which the efficacy of belladonna was first suggested to his own mind. We shall anon revert to the passage we have quoted at such length; meantime, let it be observed, that over and above the prophylactic virtue in scarlatina which Hahnemann claims for belladonna, he also asserts its potency as a specific remedy in the disease itself, modifying its symptoms, removing its "after sufferings," or consequences, "often worse than the disease itself;" and capable, too, of suppressing the fever "in its first germs," when its invasion has already occurred. Further, that, *so far as the prophylaxis of belladonna* is concerned, Hahnemann makes no restriction of the cases of true scarlatina in which the drug may either be inadmissible, or may, in his own experience, have proved useless.[1] On the contrary, we are led

---

[1] Indeed the *only* restriction made mention of is "in some particular cases, where the original disease has been very violent, and advice has been sought for the *after sufferings* too late . . . . that belladonna is no longer of service;" but in this restriction we recognise a very great amount of speciousness; what is it but to say that whenever and wherever the disease baffles the belladonna, it is not to be laid to its charge, but to the mistake of a too-late advice or consultation?

to suppose that, in his experience, no such cases occurred. And this view of his own opinion is rendered more than probably correct, when we find him speaking in his greater work thus :[1]—" Et qu'en prenant une dose de belladone aussi faible que possible, on se garantit de la fièvre scarlatine."

One of the earliest notices, if not the first mention of the alleged virtues of belladonna, which appeared after the publication of Hahnemann's own pamphlet, and corroborative of his views, was in ' Hufeland's Journal' for May, 1812, from the pen of Dr. Schenck, having reference to an epidemic which occurred in the department of Hilchenbach, in the Grand Duchy of Berg. It and the other testimonies which follow, both in favour of and against belladonna, are detailed, for the most part, with much precision in the learned work of Bayle.[2]

In 1812, when Shenck witnessed the effects of belladonna at Hilchenbach, the epidemic had, before his arrival, lasted for three weeks. Eight persons had already died, two of whom were previously healthy and robust young men, and two young women in like condition. Twenty-two were then affected; almost all were children, or young persons below the age of twenty. Of 525 persons who used the belladonna, 522 were unattacked by the disease. The three persons who suffered were a mother and her two children, who were, it is said, peculiarly exposed to the contagion, and had only taken the drug four times. The manner of making and administering the preparation of belladonna adopted by Schenck, to whom it was

---

[1] 'Organon : Nouvelle Traduction,' par Jourdan, p. 85.

[2] The title of Schenck's paper, as published in ' Hufeland's Journal,' is " Versuche mit dem Hahnemann'schen Präservatif gegen das Scharlachfieber, von Hrn. Hofrath Schenck."—It is from no desire to find fault, but, on the contrary, with great reluctance, that we must, at the outset of our references to Bayle, express our extreme astonishment and disapprobation of the course Dr. Henderson has adopted. He writes at p. 112 of his work :— " Before adverting to the experiments made in Edinburgh *I shall adduce from an article by M. Bayle*," &c., &c. Now, it is quite clear that Dr. Henderson has never had recourse to Bayle, but only to Dr. Black's very inaccurate representation of what Bayle has written; for he even copies Black so literally as to transcribe his errors, one of which, miserable as it is, we must beg Dr. Henderson to correct. He follows Dr. Black in referring to the ' Bibliothèque Thérapeutique,' tom. ii, p. 583, *et seq.*, being unaware that there are only 532 pages in the volume.

suggested by Hahnemann himself, is thus recorded, and as this
is important we shall quote the French of Bayle :

"M. Hahnemann eut la bonté de me faire parvenir trois grains
d'extrait de belladone qu'il avait préparés lui-même, attendu qu'on le
confectionne pas dans toutes les pharmacies avec assez de soin pour
qu'on puisse compter sur son effet. Il m'envoya en même temps
l'instruction suivante : On triture ces trois grains dans un petit mor-
tier, avec une once d'eau distillée qu'on y ajoute peu-à-peu, de manière
à ce qu'ils soient exactement dissous. On ajoute à cette solution une
autre composée d'une once d'eau distillée et d'une once d'alcool purifié ;
on agit le tout, et on laisse déposer. On met une seule goutte de cette
liqueur bien claire, dans une bouteille contenant trois onces d'eau
distillée et une once d'alcool rectifié : on agite bien le tout. C'est cette
liqueur qui sert de préservatif. On en donne aux enfans au-dessous
de neuf ans une seule goutte, et aux personnes au-dessus, deux gouttes
sur du sucre, tous les quatre jours, de manière à ce qu'on reste deux
jours pleins sans en donner. . . . M. Hahnemann me conseilla en
même temps de recommander qu'on préservât les enfans de toute com-
motion vive, ainsi que de lésions externes : mais de ne rien changer
d'ailleurs à leur genre de vie. . . . Le 7 février l'on commença
l'usage des gouttes, et on les continua pendant quatre semaines."
(p. 391.)

In this experience of Schenck, let it be noticed that three
individuals who had taken the belladonna four times were
attacked, and let the possibility of the epidemic having
approached its termination before his observation of it began
not be lost sight of. To M. Schenck, M. Rhodius writes as
follows :

"Altenkirchen, ce 15 Juillet, 1809.

"L'application de la belladone, comme préservatif de la fièvre scarlatine a eu ici un grand succès. Lorsque je reçus ce moyen, cette der-
nière régnait déjà fréquemment dans la ville. Les trois enfans de M.
l'architecte de Trott étaient dangereusement malades dans la maison de
M. le gouverneur de Poelnitz, dont les deux enfans habitaient l'étage
au-dessous. On donna aussitôt le préservatif à ceux-ci, et ils ne furent
pas atteints. L'enfant de M. Furchel, qui demeurait dans le voisinage,
fut préservé par le même moyen. La bonne d'enfant de M. Hertel était
très-dangereusement malade ; on donna le préservatif aux deux enfans,
et ils n'eurent pas la maladie. Une de mes trois domestiques avait
également la fièvre scarlatine : les deux autres, quoique habitant la
même chambre que la malade, furent garanties de la contagion par le
préservatif. Je pourrais ajouter plusieurs autres faits à ceux que je
viens de rapporter : mais je regarde cette énumération comme superflue,

et crois en dire assez, en affirmant que tous ceux qui ont fait usage du préservatif ont échappé à la contagion.

" Signé,   RHODIUS."

MM. Himly[1] and Hufeland each add a note to M. Schenck's communication ; both speak favourably of belladonna as a prophylactic ; the former confirms Schenck's observations, but adds no new ones.

The experience of the observers just named, whether contained in Schenck's original paper in ' Hufeland's Journal,'[2] or as quoted by Bayle, appears to us as scarcely warranting the language which the latter employs in regard to it, and which Dr. Black[3] transcribes. Bayle, let it be observed, gives, in the first place, numerous details of individual experience, and then, as is usual with him, adds a condensed view of the evidence in the form of a report. Now, to say the least, the deductions made by Bayle do, in some instances, scarcely tally with the evidence in detail. We have found it the best way to compare the two, and, when possible, to refer to the original paper from which the French physician quotes. The experience of Hufeland and Rhodius is thus given in the report of Bayle—" gave perfect immunity to all the individuals to whom they had administered this substance in several very violent epidemics."[4] We leave our readers to judge whether or not the statements of Rhodius, in the letter already quoted, authorises the employment of such terms as " gave perfect immunity," and " several very violent epidemics."

M. Masius, professor of medicine at Rostock, furnished a paper to ' Hufeland's Journal ' in 1813. His belief in the efficacy of belladonna is founded on his own immunity from scarlet fever, when occupied during two years at Schwerin, along with M. Sachse, in treating cases of a malignant type. He took half a grain of the extract every day on which he visited scarlet-fever patients, in four doses—" Et je fus préservé." At another time when, during winter, scarlatina was prevalent at Rostock,

---

[1] Himly, who was professor of medicine at Göttingen, was joint editor, with Hufeland, from 1809 to 1814, of the celebrated German journal which bears the name of the latter.

[2] Mai, 1812.

[3] ' Principles and Practice of Homœopathy,' p. 36.

[4] ' Henderson,' p. 113.

both Masius and his children were preserved by attending to
the same precautions. We are rather amused at the manner in
which M. Masius is prepared to meet any objections which may
be offered to his very paltry evidence. " J'aime beaucoup," he
says, "un scepticisme raisonnable, mais je déteste l'aveugle
incrédulité de notre siècle." We shall have more to say by-
and-by of the " hazard " to which M. Masius is aware that some
at least may be inclined to ascribe his preservation, and this,
evidently, because the narrative favours the author's own
purpose.

Gumpert, a physician at Posen, commences a contribution
quoted in ' Hufeland's Journal ' for July, 1818, in very much
the same way as medical men have written during the last few
years; he did not, and they have not, given belladonna before,
because they wanted " faith," or " confidence," in the discovery
of Hahnemann. Gumpert, who was happy in the possession of
four children, of the respective ages of thirteen, eleven, seven,
and two years, administered belladonna to each during a period
of three months, when scarlet fever prevailed as an epidemic in Posen. At one period the disease existed in the same
building as his family lived in, on the floor below his own house,
and when in every house in the same street there were persons
affected with the disease. The elder children attended a public
school. The younger and elder children were alike preserved.
Gumpert, at the same period, employed belladonna in upwards
of twenty families which he attended, and always with success.
The preservation of his patients, even in the hands of this
most sanguine doctor, was not, however, universal. One person
took the disease during the first week of prophylactic treatment,
and another, a child, after taking the belladonna for two weeks.
We are left to conclude that these were the only two who contracted the disease after taking the belladonna; but we are
directly informed that Gumpert never had a case of scarlatina
in which the specific had been employed for more than two
weeks. We are, moreover, told, that in one family, consisting
of six, to which the second exceptional case belonged, one took
the disease, and two a few days thereafter became affected with
sore throats and slight fever, without having eruption or
desquamation.

In his synopsis of Gumpert's report, just as in that of Himly already referred to, Bayle does not adhere to the strict letter of the observer. This is perhaps pardonable in Bayle, because within the four corners of his book the statement of Gumpert is given *in extenso ;* but what are we to say of Dr. Black, who has evidently never read the statement of Gumpert, either in ' Hufeland's Journal,' or *in extenso,* as given in Bayle ;[1] or if he has read either, has contrived to ignore both.[2]

Gumpert père appears to have been the only one in the same district as his son who employed the belladonna. The latter records his father's success, during some years and in several epidemics, as well as the fact of the confidence of the inhabitants of the district in which he resides being so firm in the belladonna, that the druggists dispensed it without the form of a medical prescription :—"et qu'il y a la même confiance qu'en la vaccine."

Gumpert père further mentions that in no case in which the belladonna has been administered, at the proper time and in the approved manner, has scarlatina declared itself; and that those few cases of the disease which have occurred owing to the belladonna not having been administered during a sufficiently long period, have invariably been of a very mild type. This is no doubt the evidence of Gumpert père ; but we profess ourselves entirely at a loss to discover how Bayle, from it, is able to assert that Gumpert, by the timely and judicious use of belladonna, prevented the introduction of scarlatina "*into several villages.*" In this statement Dr. Black of course follows. After this our readers will scarcely require our advice as to the necessity of reference to the original quarter for information regarding the experience of German physicians.

M. Berndt[3] observed an epidemic which occurred at Cüstrin in 1817, 1818, and 1819. The following are the results of his observations :

1. Of 195 children daily exposed to contagion, and to whom

---

[1] Taken from Marc's translation in the ' Biblioth. Méd.,' tom. lxv, p. 114.

[2] It is not Gumpert who says he preserved eighty individuals, it is Bayle who supposes most gratuitously that each of the twenty families contained four individuals.

[3] Berndt's paper in ' Hufeland's Journal ' for 1820 is entitled, "Bestä-tigende Erfarungen über die Schutzkraft der Belladonna gegen die Ansteckung des Scharlachfiebers, von Dr. Berndt."

I administered the belladonna, there were only 14 who, not-withstanding the remedy, contracted the disease, whilst the other 181 were preserved.

2. The same experiments, made with a solution of three grains of the extract of belladonna, upon a large number of individuals, equally exposed to the influence of contagion, resulted in the preservation of the whole number.

3. The 14 who did suffer had the disease less severely than those who had not been similarly subjected to the influence of belladonna.[1]

Muhrbeck,[2] Dusterberg, Behr, and Méglin are all cited by Bayle as confirming in their own experience the peculiar virtue of belladonna. He quotes on this occasion from Martini's paper in the ' Revue Médicale ' for 1824. Muhrbeck speaks in the highest terms of its efficacy, having employed it for about seven years, and always with success. In regard to its action he makes the following remark—that vaccination and bella-donna differ in the preservation effected by the former being lasting, that of the latter temporary merely. The experience of Dusterberg is important; we shall, therefore, quote it at length from Bayle.

"Pendant trois épidémies consécutives de scarlatine, j'ai employé la belladone avec un succès tel, que je regarde ce remède prophylactique comme aussi efficace que l'inoculation de la vaccine. En effet lorsqu' en 1820 la fièvre scarlatine menaçait la population de la ville Warbourg, je me décidai à vérifier les expériences connues jusqu' alors sur la vertu prophylactique de la belladone. A cet effet je fis prendre aux enfans confiés a mes soins, 10, 15, ou 20 gouttes, suivant l'âge, d'une solution faite avec trois grains d'extrait de belladone et trois gros d'eau de cannelle. Cette solution ainsi administrée deux fois par jour, et durant plus d'une semaine, eut pour effet que tous les enfans ayant fait usage du préservatif furent préservé de la contagion, malgré leur contacte intime avec les individus atteints de la fièvre scarlatine. Pour mieux faire ressortir l'effet de la belladone et en écarter celui du hasard, j'ai choisi dans chaque famille un enfant, lequel fut excepté de ce mode de traitement. Or, tous les enfans auxquels l'usage du préservatif était

---

[1] We shall shortly have occasion to refer to the strength of the dose of the remedy employed by Berndt and others.

[2] The title of Muhrbeck's paper is " Die Schutzkraft der Belladonna gegen das Scharlachfieber." The same paper, with the author's name changed into Muhskbech, is rendered into French in the ' Nouveau Journal de Médecine,' tom. xii.

demeuré interdit, furent attaqués de la contagion. Plusieurs enfans, à la vérité, n'ayant usé du préservatif que pendant quatre ou cinq jours furent atteints également de la scarlatine; cependant, presque chez tous, la maladie fut si peu grave, que l'on ne s'aperçut de sa présence que lors de la desquamation." (p. 404.)

The following is the experience of Behr, at Bernbourg, during an epidemic which prevailed in that town in 1820, and which, though at first not of a formidable character, speedily acquired a more fatal aspect. Among forty-seven individuals, including children and adults, to whom the belladonna was given, only six were attacked by the disease, *and in nearly all the six* the disease was of a benign character.[1] After concluding his account of the experience of Behr, M. Bayle refers to that of Méglin,[2] at Colmar, who found, during an epidemic which continued during the autumn and winter of 1820, and the following spring, and which at times (*assez souvent*) assumed a severe and fatal character, that all those who, before the invasion of the epidemic, had taken the specific, were preserved.

---

[1] The paper of Behr is one of the most interesting, if not the most so, of all those published in 'Hufeland's Journal' upon this subject; it contains a table, giving the name, age, date of the commencement of the disease, &c., in forty-seven cases.—'Hufeland's Journal,' Stück ii, August, 1823.

In Dr. Black's account of this physician's experience, he says, the six alluded to above " were attacked in an almost insensible manner." This is certainly not Behr's own account, as our readers may satisfy themselves by referring to the paper of Martini in the 'Revue Médicale' for 1824. We confess to feeling a very strong dislike to the frequent discrepancies which we find between the different writers' own accounts—which surely are the accurate ones—and those furnished by Dr. Black; and as Dr. Henderson has rested satisfied by always referring to the latter, and has, in a footnote to p. 115 of his own work, recommended the English reader to the same source, we take this other opportunity of directing him from so unworthy a quarter. It may be, and in most instances is, very true that the important facts in regard to the question at issue, as given by the German writers, are fairly enough rendered in both Dr. Black's and Dr. Henderson's pages; but we have a right to expect more than that; and from those who ask us to believe experiences in which they put faith, we require that these experiences should be by them truthfully and accurately presented to us, otherwise let them furnish their readers with a simple reference to the authorities, to which, it appears to us, Dr. Black has never once turned for himself.

[2] See 'Nouveau Journal de Médecine,' &c., Paris, for November, 1821, under the head Variétés, the passage which M. Bayle quotes, and which we have rendered above.

M. Méglin administered the root of the belladonna in powder, with a little sugar, according to the following prescription: R. Pulveris radicis belladonnæ, gr. ij, Sacchari albi, ʒij, Misce: et divide in 60 partes æquales. From one to five doses to be taken, according to the age of the patient, and to be repeated four times daily.

M. Koehler, physician of Cercle, records the following:—A child, one of seven, was attacked with scarlet fever well-marked; the other six took a very small dose of belladonna, and were preserved, though remaining in the same apartment as the sick child.

Dr. Beeke, among other experiments in favour of the peculiar virtues possessed by belladonna, mentions that the physician of the district, Wolf, in Silesia, encountered an epidemic of scarlatina in the village of Staedtel; 120 persons were already affected; the specific was administered, and thereafter there occurred thirty-nine mild cases. In two other villages, where 132 individuals made use of the same extract, only six were attacked. In 1820, at Siegen, the son of a merchant was attacked with scarlet fever. His aunt, who had paid him a hurried visit, was also seized. She was the mother of three young children; they took the belladonna, and, though they were always beside their mother, they were preserved. Dr. Bénédix employed belladonna with success against the contagion of a malignant fever in the island of Rugen. His paper, a short and interesting one, follows Behr's in 'Hufeland's Journal' for August, 1823: and after it come two notices, one by Dr. Wesener, of Dülmen, in Westphalia, the other by Dr. Zeuch, practising in the Tyrol. The former appears to have thought little of the power of belladonna till he administered it to his own children, and finding them preserved from the contagion of prevailing scarlatina, he changed his views. The latter, in the military hospital for children, had the following experience. Twenty-three children out of eighty-four became affected; to the remaining sixty-one belladonna was administered during twenty consecutive days; only one of the sixty-one took scarlatina, although the disease continued to prevail in the neighbourhood of the hospital. Dr. Suttinger reports that before belladonna was administered several persons had died during an epidemic of scarlatina which occurred at Miaskowo, but

that after recourse was had to belladonna no other case
happened.

Hufeland, the learned editor, commences the November
number of his journal for the year 1825 thus:

"Es ist mir grosse Freude, die schützende Kraft der Belladonna gegen
das Scharlachfieber durch neue Erfahrungen zu bestätigen. Es sind
nun fünf (dreizehn?) Jahre vergangen, dass in diesem Journal die erste
Aufforderung zu der Anwendung dieses Schutzmittels erging, und jedes
Jahr hat seitdem eine Menge günstige Erfahrungen geliefert. . . . . . .
Ich selbst habe das Mittel mehrmals in meiner Praxis angewendet, und
nie gesehen, dass eines von denen, welche dasselbe gehörig gebraucht
hatten, angesteckt worden wäre."[1]

Having passed this panegyric on belladonna, the observations
made in the Frederick Institution at Berlin, to which he is
physician, by Kunzmann (whom Bayle calls Kunstmann, and
of course Black does so also), are detailed. He had remained
doubtful as to the efficacy of the remedy till, in January, 1825, he
became, from his experience in the institution already referred
to, satisfied as to the protective virtue of belladonna. In it there
were about seventy children of both sexes, from four to fourteen
years of age. On the 25th December, 1824, scarlatina manifested itself in the person of the director's son, and three days
later two young girls, one of four, the other of seven years,
became affected. The sick children were separated, but, adds
Kunzmann, it was impossible to cause a complete isolation.
The sound children then received a mixture, composed of two
grains of the extract of belladonna in an ounce of distilled
cinnamon water, of which each child took as many drops twice
daily as he or she had years. From that time to the 23rd of
January, a period of four weeks, no case presented itself, but on
that day a little boy of ten became affected, but only very
slightly, proving that the contagion still existed in the house.
A second son, however, of the director of the institution, who
had not taken the mixture, suffered a severe attack of the

[1] "It is a great pleasure to me to be able to confirm, by new observations,
the prophylactic power of belladonna in scarlet fever. It is now five
(thirteen?) years since, in this journal, the first mention was made of the
employment of this preventive, and each year since that time has brought
with it a large number of corroborative facts. . . . . In my own practice I
have on several occasions used this remedy, and I have never seen one of
those who used it in the proper manner affected by the disease."

disease. During six weeks the remedy was persevered in, and no cases occurred. The table furnished by Gelnecki, of Stettin (with whose name also Bayle, and Black after him, take great liberties, manufacturing it into Gencki), succeeds Kunzmann's report, and is a remarkably interesting one. His experience was obtained in Glasgow. There were in all ninety-four children. Of these, seventy-six appeared to be preserved from the contagion by the use of the belladonna, while fifteen, who had not employed the remedy, became affected with the disease, three who had employed the belladonna took scarlet fever, and two of the three died. Of the fifteen who took the disease without having made use of the prophylactic, four died.[1]

Maizier,[2] district physician of Burg, made use of belladonna in the village of Nigripp, and not one of the 170 children to whom he administered it became affected with scarlatina. The treatment was continued for fourteen days, and then the epidemic disappeared, though in the neighbouring village of Detershagen, where no belladonna had been employed, it continued to prevail, and some children died. This physician had previously obtained similar results with belladonna in 1821 : an epidemic of a fatal character prevailed at the village of Grabow, and its cessation followed the use of the prophylactic. In the districts of Riesel and Ziegelsdorf, where some children had been already seized, the belladonna was employed, and no other case occurred. Also in Burg, the place of his own residence, among from sixty to seventy children, there were only three or four who became affected with scarlet fever (when epidemic) after the use of the specific. Hufeland mentions Dr. Wiedemann, of Wolmirstedt, as bearing like testimony.

---

[1] The inexcusable blunder which both Bayle and Dr. Black, in copying him, have committed, in quoting the testimony of Gelnecki, is also observable in the table which Bayle has prepared, but which, from the inaccuracy we allude to, is rendered useless. Dr. Black, in a footnote to p. 39 of his book, says, " there is an error here as to the number, also in the tabular list ;" but he had not the ingenuity to correct the mistake into which Bayle had fallen, although in Bayle's own work the opportunity for so doing was afforded him.

[2] 'Hufeland's Journal,' November, 1825. For his account of Maizier's experience Bayle (and it is singularly inaccurate) quotes from a French journal. 'Journ. des Prog.,' tome i, p. 242.

Dr. Randham,[1] in the Orphan Hospital at Langendorf, on the occurrence of two cases of scarlatina, gave the belladonna to the 160 remaining, from February (when the two cases presented themselves), so long as the contagion lasted. On the 21st of April, the disease had attacked none of the other orphans, not even two who shared the same apartment with the two previously sick children. Velsen,[2] physician at Clèves, reports that of 247 persons who used the belladonna, thirteen only contracted the disease, of whom four were children who had taken the remedy during several weeks, but not with regularity, one child who had taken it regularly during fourteen days, another during eight days, and the rest during forty-eight hours. In all the cases the disease was mild, milder than with those who had not taken the medicine. Among the facts mentioned by Velsen is the following :—A man, the father of four children, who had visited but only for a few seconds a friend labouring under scarlet fever, was seized, some days thereafter, with the same disease, and in a violent manner ; his wife and children, the youngest of whom was only three weeks, and the oldest four years, took with great regularity the extract of belladonna, and, although day and night were passed with the sick husband and father, and in a small and badly-ventilated chamber, none took the disease. M. Velsen adds: "Est ce là l'effet du hasard, ou le résultat de l'emploi de la belladone ?"[3]

Such are some—indeed, nearly all—of the testimonies borne by foreign—and more particularly by German—physicians to the prophylactic virtue of belladonna. We now proceed to consider the facts which have been advanced in this country; here we find the evidence neither so extensive nor on so large a scale. The following account is given by Messrs. Taynton and Williams, gentlemen practising at Bromley, in Kent, in 1829 :[4]

[1] 'Hufeland's Journal,' 1825.

[2] 'Journ. Complémentaire du Dict. des Sciences Méd.,' tome xxviii, p. 370.

[3] Did our space permit we might have quoted Wagner's report of the epidemic at Schlieben, of Dr. Peters at Leopoldshagen, of Dr. Reuscher at Stendal, and Dr. Cohen. For these we beg to refer the reader to 'Hufeland's Journal,' 1825, also to the 'Gazette de Santé' for the same year for the statement of M. Lemercier. These are all alike favorable to the theory of the prophylactic power of belladonna.

[4] The 'London Medical Gazette,' vol. iv, p. 297.

" During the months of April and May the scarlet fever was very prevalent in this town and neighbourhood, and in many cases it proved fatal. Our attention was called by a friend to a notice in the 'Lancet'[1] of the 2nd of May, "On the Prophylactic powers of Belladonna against Scarlet Fever," by M. Hufeland. We were at that time attending in a boarding-school where the disease had attacked twelve of the boys, many of whom had been most dangerously ill, but none had died. There still remained several boys (perhaps twenty) who had not taken the infection; also four young children of the master's, and several servants. We immediately commenced the use of the belladonna, in the exact manner and dose advised by Hufeland. Only six or seven persons in the house took the disease afterwards, and in every instance it assumed the mildest form.

" In another school we were called to visit a child about two years old, who had been attacked the evening before. The disease was of the most malignant character, and the child died on the following morning, the third day from the attack. The house is a very small one. There were in it three other young gentlemen and five boarders, and a servant-girl. The belladonna was faithfully administered, and not one individual took the disease. We will not offer any conjecture on the *modus operandi* of the belladonna, or whether it did or did not prevent the other members of these families from taking the disease. The facts are stated exactly as they occurred, and we entreat our professional brethren to make trial of the belladonna whenever a favorable opportunity occurs."

The following is the result of Dr. Black's[2] experience :

"Belladonna was administered to eleven children who had never had scarlet fever, and who were living in a house with two cases of scarlet fever, the one of them attended with sloughing sore throat, and in intercourse with these cases: all escaped, even one who was sleeping in the same bed with one of the patients. In another instance, we gave belladonna to four children, none of whom had the fever, and were directly exposed to the contagion; three escaped; one took the fever, but so slightly that we were inclined to regard the symptoms as those of belladonna.

[1] The following are the conclusions of M. Hufeland, contained in the paper which Messrs. Taynton and Williams refer to :

I. The proper use of belladonna has, in most cases, prevented infection, even in those instances where, by the continual intercourse with patients labouring under scarlet fever, the predisposition towards it was greatly increased.

II. Numerous observations have shown that, by the general use of belladonna, epidemics of scarlet fever have actually been arrested.

III. In those few instances where the use of belladonna was insufficient to prevent infection, the disease has been invariably slight.

IV. There are exceptions to the above three points, but their number is extremely small.—' Lancet,' May 2nd, 1829.

[2] 'British Journal of Homœopathy,' vol. i.

In another instance we administered the remedy to four children and an adult, who were living in the same house with two cases of scarlet fever. The adult and two children were seized with the fever; two had only taken the remedy for two days, and one for three days; the other two children escaped. The three cases were much milder than the two cases in which no belladonna had been given as a preservative, Out of the twenty cases, we observed the remedy produce headache, with increase of pulse, in one child; in another, there was slight redness of the skin, which lasted for eight hours, and unattended with fever."

Dr. Patrick Newbigging[1] writes as follows :

"Scarlet fever having prevailed in John Watson's Institution to so considerable an extent, and the cases having occurred in close succession, notwithstanding a system of separation as complete as was possible amongst inmates residing under the same roof, I felt desirous to try the effect of belladonna as a prophylactic against the disease. It was an opportunity such as rarely occurs for the investigation of the alleged virtue of this drug on a large scale. Having ascertained the number of children unaffected with scarlet fever, or who were uncertain as to ever having had it—making, in all, sixty-nine—I directed that belladonna should be administered to them, in the proportion of one-sixth to one-fourth of a grain twice a day, according to the age of each child, the first dose being given before breakfast, and the last dose at bedtime. This plan was adopted on the 16th of October. Three new cases occurred between that and the 20th. After that date no child was affected, nor has there been any instance of scarlet fever since that period in the institution. . . . . . I should now consider it my duty to lose no time in making use of this medicine on the first appearance of this disease, and I would strongly recommend the same plan of practice to those of the profession who are connected with similar educational institutions, with the view, not merely of attempting to ward off a malady so uncertain in its progress, and occasionally so fatal in its termination, but also with the object of accumulating information on a point of such paramount importance to the public health. The opinion I have adopted on this point has been greatly strengthened by a similarly beneficial result produced some time afterwards in another case. I was requested to visit a young gentleman at a large educational seminary. I found him labouring under scarlet fever, with profuse eruption, an aphthous and very painful condition of the throat, accompanied by all the usual symptoms exhibited in the acute stage of a smart attack of this disease. I caused my patient to be removed, a few hours after first seeing him, to the house of a relative, and placed his brother, who continued to reside in the seminary, upon belladonna. This treatment was adopted on the other members of the family, consisting of nineteen, who had not previously been affected with scarlet fever. No other case occurred."

We might easily multiply the quotation of experiences such

[1] 'Monthly Journal of Medical Science,' September, 1849.

as the three now adduced. We believe such a procedure, however, to be unnecessary, the facts in favour of the employment of belladonna being as strongly elicited in these three as in any other recent accounts we have met with.

Our readers, after having followed us in the production of these various facts and opinions of authors in favour of the prophylactic action of belladonna, will naturally expect us to advance the facts and opinions of a contrary bearing. And if we now limit ourselves to the quotation of a few of the former, and to a mere glance at the general nature of the latter, it must not be supposed either that the facts are wanting or are even limited in number, or that silence has prevailed over the expression of opposite views. Such is certainly not the case; there exist, if not so many facts as in favour of the prophylactic action of belladonna, at least stronger, and altogether more reliable ones, on the inefficiency of its employment; while the expression of opinion in regard to its inefficiency —not always formed on the justest grounds, we allow—have undoubtedly been neither few nor uncertainly declared. Among German writers who have adopted this view is Lehmann, the staff-physician of the garrison at Torgau. Dr. Black makes it appear as if Bayle objected to the evidence of Lehmann, on the score of its being " supported by no facts." Such is not the case. Bayle never could have made such a mistake with the paper of Lehmann before him, and when he writes,—" Nous ne pouvons apprécier à leur juste valeur l'opinion de ces auteurs, parcequ'elle n'est appuyée d'aucun fait, et que la maladie n'est point décrite," Bayle means this to apply to the opinions advanced by Raminski[1] and Teuffel,[2] as quoted by Barth. Any reader, however, of either Black or Henderson, will come to the conclusion, that by Bayle the evidence of Lehmann was held in the same estimation as that of the two other observers just named—affording another proof of the danger of trusting to second-hand reading, and of the propriety of consulting in all cases, where possible, the original statements of every author. Had Dr. Black not rested satisfied by quoting the

---

[1] Raminski is mentioned by Barth to have lost his own son, and to have afforded many proofs of the augmentation of the disease after the employment of belladonna.

[2] Teuffel's observations, says Bayle, are to the like effect.

mere *résumé* of Bayle, he would not have fallen into this error; for at page 417 of his same volume, Bayle devotes a paragraph of nearly half a page in length to Lehmann's observations, entitling them, 'Observations du Docteur Lehmann :[1] Épidémie de Scarlatine dans laquelle la Belladone ne prévint pas la Maladie.' The title of the paper itself, in 'Rust's Magazin' is different; it is given below.[2] What Bayle says of Lehmann's experience is in every respect fair, and when he expresses his opinion in the following words, " Il n'a jamais pu parvenir à empêcher la contagion chez eux qui y étaient disposés, ni à modérer la gravité de la maladie chez eux qui déjà en étaient atteints " (p. 417), he says *no more than* Lehmann's accurately observed and precisely stated facts required.

Now this paper of Lehmann's is both a very interesting and a very important one. His experience was large ; his attention to the mode of preparation and the manner of administering the belladonna were alike exact—(" en le donnant," Bayle himself says, " suivant toutes les règles indiquées par ceux qui ont préconisé ce moyen ")—and lastly, his memoir has the advantage of almost all others which we have perused, while it is inferior to none in exhibiting the precision of its author's observations. We shall quote four of these :—

1. In a family consisting of three boys, the eldest was attacked with scarlet fever. The two others were immediately removed from the sick boy, and were confined to the floor of the house below that on which his room was. They got, at the same time, every morning and evening, the belladonna solution. After this boy's recovery, and at the end of one month from the first appearance of the disease, he was restored to the society of his two brothers. Four months later the youngest brother was seized with the disease in a severe form ; he recovered, and then the third (in respect of years, the second) brother, who remained on this occasion in proximity to the patient, but at the same time took the belladonna regularly, contracted the disease on the tenth day, and fell a victim to it.

---

[1] 'Magazin für die gesammte Heilkunde,' Herausgegeben Von Dr. Johann. 'Nep. Rust.,' vol. xxi, 1826 (at p. 42).

[2] Die Unwirksamkeit der Belladonna als Schutzmittel gegen das Scharlachfieber, nebst einem Impfungsversuche dieser Krankheit. Von Dr. Lehmann.

2. In a family consisting of five brothers and sisters, a boy of five years was first attacked with scarlet fever. To the other four the belladonna was immediately given. After eight days a little girl of four years old was seized, and on the third day of the disease died. The following day a sister of three years of age took the fever mildly, and recovered; another sister, of eleven years, was almost immediately afterwards affected, and on the fourth day of her illness died. The eldest brother, long a sufferer from bad health, and particularly from a chronic affection of the heart, remained free from the disease. It is of importance to know that the four patients together occupied a small and extremely damp room, on the ground floor; and this, indeed, was accepted as the probable cause of the early deaths.

3. A boy of five years, an only son, contracted scarlet fever after having uninterruptedly, during several months, taken belladonna. The fever assumed a cerebral character, and on the fourth day the little patient died.

4. In a family of four children, the eldest (who was five years) became affected with scarlet fever. The remaining three were immediately put on the belladonna; two of these, on the twenty-first day of the employment of the drug, became affected with the disease in a severer form than the first child, who had taken no belladonna.

Along with other facts of a like nature, Lehmann mentions that, in his own experience, whole families (one in particular, consisting of seven children), altogether escaped the disease, though epidemic in the place where they resided.

At Stralsund, writes Barth (quoted by Bayle, p. 419), Dr. Mierendorf observed that the children to whom belladonna was administered became more seriously affected, and died in much greater proportion than those for whom the drug was not prescribed. Dr. Schmidt, writes the same authority, lost two children who had taken the so-called prophylactic. Of 100 children so treated, fifteen became affected with scarlet fever, and one died.

Dr. Raminski, who lost his own son, had so many proofs of the exacerbation of the disease during the employment of the belladonna, as to make him altogether doubt its efficacy as a remedy.

Mr. Benjamin Bell, in the course of an article on "Scarlet Fever as it appeared in George Watson's Hospital in the spring of 1851,"[1] writes as follows :

"Conceiving that no means for arresting the disease ought to be neglected, and that a favorable opportunity now offered itself for testing the alleged prophylactic virtue of belladonna, I determined to give it a full and fair trial.

"Accordingly, on the 21st of February, upon the appearance of a second case of scarlet fever, the fifth part of a grain of the extract was given, morning and evening, to each of the boys. The dose was found, in a few days, to be too large, from the dilated state of the pupil and impaired vision which it occasioned in several instances. It was accordingly diminished, and then administered without interruption, to all the boys, who continued well until the 7th day of June, a full month after the last case of scarlet fever had occurred. It is important to remark that the second case already referred to had been in the sick-room, separated from the rest of the boys, for more than a week before the symptoms of scarlet fever appeared, and that no additional case occurred until the 21st of March, an entire month after the belladonna had been regularly administered. There was thus ample time for the manifestation of its virtue as a prophylactic; but the subsequent occurrence of so many cases seems to throw considerable dubiety over the existence of any such power. No experience of a merely negative character can be regarded as of much weight, when contrasted with this positive experience now detailed. It is by no means unusual to meet with only two or three cases of scarlet fever in a large assemblage of children without the belladonna having been used at all; and therefore we are not called upon to give it the credit of securing a similar exemption in cases where it has been administered ; but surely the occurrence of twenty-three cases out of fifty-four boys, who might be legitimately reckoned liable to the disease, is an overwhelming evidence on the opposite side."

In reference to the prophylactic action of belladonna, we find Dr. Elb, a homœopathic practitioner at Dresden, writing as follows :[2]

"I must add, that in general I did not find the prophylactic power of belladonna by any means so generally borne out, although cases have come before me, in which I gave belladonna as a preventive, and the children to whom I administered it remained free from scarlet fever. But just as often have I found that children have been attacked by it, notwithstanding the use of belladonna for several weeks, and that this long previous use of the belladonna had not even the power of diminishing the violence of the disease."

[1] 'Monthly Journal,' August, 1851.
[2] See 'British Journal of Homœopathy,' 1849, vol. vii, p. 33.

4

The interesting experiments of Dr. Balfour, conducted at the Royal Military Asylum at Chelsea, are thus alluded by Dr. West :[1]

"I cannot do better than relate the experiment in the words in which Dr. Balfour was good enough to communicate it to me. Scarlet fever having broken out in the visitation, Dr. Balfour determined to try the virtues of belladonna. 'There were,' he says, '151 boys, of whom I had tolerably satisfactory evidence that they had not had scarlatina. I divided them into two sections, taking them alternately from the list, to prevent the imputation of selection. To the first section (76) I gave belladonna; to the second (75) I gave none; the result was, that *two* in each section were attacked by the disease. The numbers are too small to justify deductions as to the prophylactic power of belladonna; but the observation is good, because it shows how apt we are to be misled by imperfect observation. Had I given the remedy to all the boys, I should probably have attributed to it the cessation of the epidemic.' To these remarks," continues Dr. West, "I need add nothing. They convey a most important lesson, but one which, I fear, we are all too apt to forget in the study and in the practice of medicine" (p. .600)

Dr. Andrew Wood's experience in Heriot's Hospital is thus mentioned by Dr. Simpson :

"In Heriot's Hospital my friend, Dr. Andrew Wood, placed half of the boys in each ward, or sleeping division, on belladonna, and left the other half without any such protection. The disease did not spread much, but at least as many of those using the belladonna as of those not using it were attacked; and the only fatal case out of forty which occurred during that epidemic was that of a boy who had been using belladonna in doses of one eighth of a grain twice a day for three weeks previously to his being attacked."[1]

---

[1] 'Lectures on the Diseases of Infancy and Childhood,' 3rd edition, 1854.

[2] Through the kindness of Dr. Wood and of Dr. Simpson we are enabled to give the experience of the former a little more in detail. The plan Dr. Wood adopted was an excellent one, and the result of his experiments, taken in connection with Dr. Balfour's and Mr. Bell's (somewhat differently performed), to our mind appears conclusive: "The plan that I proposed to myself," says Dr. Wood, "was this, viz. whenever scarlatina appeared in any particular ward, and not till then, I immediately made inquiry, and having ascertained the boys who had previously had the fever these I left out of the question. I then divided the remainder into two nearly equal sections: to one I gave one eighth of a grain of belladonna twice a day, to the other no belladonna was given. This experiment was continued for several weeks, and the reason why it was then discontinued was simply this, that a fatal case occurred in the person of a boy (J. B) who had been taking the

In drawing this article to a close, we have to consider, first, whether or not the prophylactic action of belladonna against scarlatina, as claimed, promulgated, and practised by Hahnemann and his followers, has stood the test of experience, and is now to be regarded as a reality; and second, whether, in regard to the employment of belladonna for a like purpose, in larger doses than those recommended by the former, experience and observation lead us to embrace the practice as a real boon to humanity, or to abandon it as inefficient and absurd.

At the outset, let us exactly understand what Hahnemann did, and his followers do now, claim for belladonna as a prophylactic, and what was the manner of its exhibition which he advised and required. This inquiry is not unnecessary, when we consider that in the numerous instances of failure of the belladonna reported to Hahnemann himself, he invariably attributed the want of success to the prophylactic having been employed in cases of a fever different from scarlet fever;[1] or the *Miliaire pourprée,* which was, according to Barth, imported

belladonna for nearly four weeks. Taking alarm I resolved to discontinue the experiment." The following is a brief analysis of the trial:

First ward—containing 11 boys. Case occurred April 17th. 5 already had scarlatina; 5 boys got belladonna; 2 got no belladonna. One of the 5 took scarlatina June 2nd and died on the 7th. No other case.

Eighth ward—containing 20 boys. Case occurred April 25th. 7 already had scarlatina; 5 got belladonna; 3 got no belladonna. No subsequent case.

Fourth ward—containing 25 boys. Case occurred May 9th. 4 already had scarlatina; belladonna given to 10; no belladonna to 10. On 19th May, J. G—, who had accidentally slept in the same room as a boy who had scarlet fever, and had been taking the belladonna since the 28th April became affected with the disease in a moderately severe form; he recovered. On 4th June a boy who had taken no belladonna contracted the disease in a very mild form. No subsequent case.

Fifth ward—containing 18 boys. Case occurred May 23rd. Had had the disease, 4; took belladonna, 6; took no belladonna, 7. No subsequent case of fever.

Seventh ward—containing 36 boys. Case occurred May 28th. Had had scarlet fever, 6; took belladonna, 18; took no belladonna, 11. No subsequent case.

[1] Hahnemann also speaks of the introduction of this Fièvre Miliaire Pourprée—(or, in German, Rothe Friesel, Purpurfriesel, Roodvonk)—purple rash—as having been introduced from Belgium in 1801. See 'Reine Arzneimittellehre,' von S. Hahnemann, vol. i, p. 15.

from Holland, in the month of January, 1801. It appears to
us that in all probability the limitation of the use of the
drug to the cases of scarlet fever, as described by Sydenham[1]
and Plenciz,[2] was an after-thought, and that, notwithstanding
the allusion made by Hahnemann to the similarity borne by
the epidemic of scarlatina at Königslutter to the disease
described by Plenciz; for, unquestionably, in the whole length
of the article "On Scarlatina," as translated by Dr. Dudgeon,
there does not occur a single expression whereby we are to
understand that his proposal of belladonna as a prophylactic,
or as a remedy strictly so called, was to be confined to cases of
the same nature as those which occurred in that epidemic.[3]
Were any further proof of this (than the absence of any
restriction) required, we think it supplied in the fact of Hahnemann, in his first publication, expressing his belief "that a
similar employment of belladonna would also preserve from
measles."[4] Now, no one will pretend to urge that a closer

[1] 'Processus Integri' (Sydenham edition of works), vol. ii, p. 242.

[2] 'Tractatus de Scarlatinâ,' Autore Marco Antonio Plenciz, sectio ii.
Vienna, 1772.

[3] Dr. Henderson argues that Hahemann has the advantage of Jenner in
not claiming universality of exemption from scarlatina after the use of
belladonna, as he says Jenner did after vaccination, from smallpox. To us
it appears that if Hahnemann had adhered to his original opinion—from
which he at the time allowed no exception—he would have been both more
honest and more entitled to our attention. We can, however, see no paral-
lelism either between the discoveries of Jenner and Hahnemann, or between
their subsequent histories.

[4] Hahnemann, in adverting to the subject of the treatment of scarlet
fever as recommended in the works of various authors, makes this singular
admission: "Here we often see the *ne plus ultra* of the grossest empiricism; *for each single symptom a particular remedy* in the motley, mixed,
and repeated prescriptions; a sight that cannot fail to inspire the unpre-
judiced observer with feelings at once of pity and indignation." We think
"the cap fits" most exactly here, and even pinches, though Hahnemann,
with strange perversion of observation, does not appear to feel it. The
proposal and employment of belladonna in scarlet fever is as apt an illustration as could be imagined of the fitting remedy to symptom. Belladonna
produces a scarlet rash; therefore, concludes Hahnemann, it will cure
scarlatina, or is homœopathic to it. But *scarlet rash* is not scarlet fever, it
is only a symptom of it; and if we were to give belladonna as often and as
long, and in whatever doses we chose, we might kill our patients, but we
never could contrive to give them scarlet fever. The question of the
power of belladonna to produce the rash which is so universally believed to

resemblance subsists between measles and scarlatina than between that disease and the *miliaire pourprée*, which, if it were really not a variety of scarlatina, must have very closely approached it in character, before so many observant physicians could have been deceived. In our opinion, then, the plea of want of success on the ground of dissimilar diseases being treated under the belief that they were alike examples of scarlatina epidemics does not hold good; for, first, there is no proof of the diseases treated by Raminski, Teuffel, and other physicians, not having been a true scarlatina; and second, Hahnemann himself did not confine the virtues of belladonna to scarlatina, but extended them to a disease whose characters are by a still longer way removed from it than the *miliaire pourprée*—namely, measles.

It has been contended, and this argument is referred to by Professor Henderson, that in instances of failure another drug than belladonna, dulcamara for example, may have been used. Now, we beg to submit that if this idea is allowed to have any weight, it must be permitted, in all justice, to affect both sides of the question; for we know no reason, and no experience, to justify such reason—why Hahnemann and his followers should have always hit upon the proper plant, and those who opposed his views have seldom or never done so. If Dr. Henderson insists upon this point, we are quite ready to allow that some physicians, who employed dulcamara, or some other member of the Solanaceæ, instead of belladonna, have failed (though not in consequence) to protect their patients from scarlet fever; but then, we must contend that certain other physicians, who administered these drugs instead of belladonna, have succeeded in the desire to have their patients preserved from the disease though not in consequence. Let it, however, be remembered that belladonna possesses a singular property—a property

follow its continual administration itself requires revision. For our own part we can say that, after giving belladonna for a long time, in more cases than one we have failed, though careful and repeated in our examination, ever to discern it. We do not mean to doubt the production of what may be called *spots* in some cases, but we altogether disbelieve the fact of even these following in any large number of instances. Schultz has justly remarked that similarity of symptoms, not of diseases, lies at the base of all the therapeutic proceedings of Hahnemann and his followers—a pity they do not see it.

almost peculiar to itself—and then we think it will be granted, that any physician entering on a careful investigation into its properties, by means of a given portion of its extract, will first establish the power of that individual specimen to dilate the pupil in the peculiarly marked manner which belladonna does.

Some singular discrepancies exist in regard to the frequency of the administration of belladonna as recommended by Hahnemann; for example, Barth, as cited by Bayle, says that "tous les six à sept jours" was the interval at which he advised the dose to be administered. Jahr[1] also says, as expressing the views of Hahnemann, "To this effect the smallest dose of belladonna ought to be[2] given every six or seven days." On the other hand, in his communication to Dr. Schenck, already quoted, Hahnemann says distinctly, on every fourth day the belladonna solution should be taken; and in his own pamphlet, as translated by Dr. Dudgeon,[3] he condescends to a greater particularity, and orders a dose to be given every seventy-two hours. It is not for us to reconcile these discrepancies, believing, as we do, that it certainly makes very little difference whether the $\frac{1}{432000}$th part of a grain of belladonna[4] be taken every seventy-two hours or every seven days. Some of his followers, moreover, take what we should have thought to be unpardonable liberties with Hahnemann's directions; of these we need only cite Dr. Black, who has the effrontery to double the Hahnemannic dose (making it thus $\frac{1}{216000}$th part of a grain), and to make the interval of its exhibition from ten to fourteen days.[5] Surely when Hahnemann's own followers, acting on their own responsibility, double the strength of his remedial measures, and fix their own time for their administration, Dr. Henderson[6] need not be so very indignant at Mr.

---

[1] Jahr's 'New Manual of Homœopathic Practice.' Edited by A. G. Hull, M.D. Article, Belladonna, in 'Symptomatology,' p. 161.

[2] Dio von mir gefundene Schutzkraft der Belladonne in der Kleinsten Gabe aller, 6, 7, Tage gereicht, &c., &c., are Hahnemann's own words.

[3] Op. cit., p. 438.

[4] And this (for a preventive object) as a dose for a child of ten years is, according to Hahnemann's own experience, too large.

[5] Dr. Black in the 'Homœopathic Journal,' vol. i, p. 138.

[6] I am persuaded, says Dr. Henderson, Mr. Bell will pardon me for asking if he made himself acquainted, before he began his researches, with Hahnemann's instructions as to the proper dose, and the interval that should

Bell likewise choosing the amount of his dose, and for himself determining when and how often to employ it.

But leaving the adherents of Hahnemann's system to reconcile these differences, we come to a point in the argument concerning both him and them, which we shall take the liberty of settling for ourselves. Hahnemann distinctly says (as we have already quoted) that the peculiar action of belladonna *does not last above three days*, and the repetition of the dose of the prophylactic at the end of every seventy-two hours is, therefore, strongly insisted upon, and (though he has mentioned longer intervals) appears always to have been acted upon. He never allows seventy-two hours to pass without the administration of a dose, though, if the epidemic of the disease be very violent, he counsels the safety, if children could bear it, of giving the second dose twenty-four hours after the first, the third dose thirty-six hours after the second, and the fourth forty-eight hours after the third; thereafter to let the subsequent doses be taken every seventy-two hours until the end, in order that the system may not at first be taken by surprise by the miasm.[1] Now, if we inquire the reason of the period of interval of the doses being at all events limited to seventy-two hours—never allowed to exceed that period—we are met by the (homœopathically speaking) very sensible answer, that "the peculiar action of this plant does not last above three days." Now, if that was Hahnemann's opinion—and these are his *ipsissima verba*—we should like to know what believer in the homœopathic action of medicines has any right to dispute it? Besides, Hahnemann first proposed belladonna as a prophylactic in scarlatina, and—to use the argument adopted by Professor Henderson, in addressing himself to Mr. Bell's experience—therefore try his way of it, and adopt his theory regarding it, else leave it altogether alone. But we do not require to do this; all the followers of Hahnemann acknowledge that the period of the duration of the effects of the "divine" remedy

elapse between the successive repetitions of it? If he did not, why try the medicine at all, since there was no other discoverer of the alleged preventive power of belladonna than that same Hahnemann, who also says that the dose ought to be very small, and ought not to be repeated above once in two or three days? We should prefer Dr. Black's answering this question.

[1] See Dr. Dudgeon's translation, p. 439.

never exceed seventy-two hours. "Vis per 56 horas ad mini-mum, per 72 horas ut plurimum durat," says the founder of the homœopathic school; and it makes very little matter if Hahnemann's ignoble editor, Dr. Quin, daring to attempt to improve upon what he has said and done, adds, in a note, "Aliquando belladonna ad diem vigesimum primum et ultra (most convenient) vires retinet;[1] or that Jahr still further improves upon both by saying that the duration of the action of belladonna extends "from one day to eighteen months."[2] If, then, Hahnemann's idea be correct, that the action of bella-donna as a prophylactic against scarlatina is exerted only, at the farthest, for a period short of seventy-two hours, we are fairly entitled to conclude that all these instances of preserva-tion from the disease in which the drug was exhibited at intervals exceeding that space of time, and which have been attributed to its prophylactic action, are just as likely due to any one of the many other causes which may be presumed to have acted beneficially in contributing to the exemption, and to some of which we shall presently allude. We shall, assuredly, not insult our readers, nor these pages, by inquiring if the exhibition, according to Hahnemann's direction, of the $\frac{1}{432000}$th of a grain of belladonna, at intervals not exceeding seventy-two hours, can, or ever has, preserved those exposed to the con-tagion of scarlet fever; we can unhesitatingly answer the question we put to ourselves in the negative. And now we pass on to the second. It may, perhaps, have occurred to our readers, that if we proposed to ourselves the settlement of this question by reference to the numbers of the facts and illustra-tions we advanced, that we were not doing ourselves justice, but that, on the contrary, we were assigning to the believers in the prophylaxis of belladonna an easy triumph. We beg to remind our readers of our expressed determination to give our opponents fair play; and further, of our own acknowledgment that we have been content to adduce a few of the many instances of failure of the drug in the hands of experienced and competent observers. Now, we are ready to acknowledge that, in attempting

[1] 'Fragmenta de Viribus Medicamentorum positivis sive in sano corpore humano observatis,' a Samuele Hahnemann, M.D. Edidit F. F. Quin, M.D., p. 21.
[2] Hull's 'Jahr,' p. 161.

to determine for ourselves the right of the question we have proposed, we escape from none of those difficulties which all are
ready to acknowledge perplex the path of him who, by a
reference to the experience of several or of many, endeavours
to determine a question in therapeutics. We do most entirely
agree with Dr. Alison, who, in the course of an article in this
journal,[1] replete with valuable information and the soundest
reasoning, writes:

"We do not mean to deny that questions occur in therapeutics, likewise, as to which large numbers of cases may be compared with advantage, and the 'numerical method' applied, ... but we think it is
reasonable and right for practitioners to build their opinions, as to the
powers of a remedy, on observations of very different kinds besides the
mere enumeration and statement of ultimate results of the cases in
which it is given; or, as it is shortly and justly expressed by a practical
author, that in order to make up our minds as to any such question, it
is better, in general, to watch than to count."

Now, the great objection we have to the evidence which has
all along been adduced in favour of the employment of belladonna in scarlatina is precisely, that "counting" has taken
the place of "watching." Numerous circumstances in the
particular epidemics, and in the particular cases occurring in
these epidemics, have either been altogether passed over, or, at
least, have not been awarded the importance they deserve. If
100 children have been exposed to the infection of scarlatina
(the degree of exposure is seldom noticed, or, at all events,
is very inadequately described), and belladonna has been
administered, and of the 100, if either all or a very large proportion have remained free from the disease, the *post hoc ergo
propter hoc* has been, in every instance, adopted; and, apparently,
as if there could be no objection offered to its adoption; because
belladonna was taken and the 100 children preserved—*therefore*
the belladonna preserved them. Again, and irrespective of the
necessity of attention being paid, in such investigations, to the
minutest particulars, to which we shall presently refer, let it be
held in remembrance that the great majority of facts which
have been advanced in favour of belladonna are entirely of a
negative character, while those we have brought forward in
opposition to it are positive.

[1] January, 1834.

"I conceive," writes the lamented Dr. Pereira on this point, "twenty cases of failure are more conclusive against the opinion than one thousand of non-occurrence are in favour of it. . . . . The cases which I am acquainted with are decidedly against the efficacy of the remedy."[1]

Let us very shortly glance at some of the foreign cases, and then more particularly consider what Dr. Henderson calls the "Edinburgh experiments." Now as regards the former, there is not one favorable to the belladonna theory which in the least degree approaches to the "experimentum crucis," and not one of *any weight* at all, if, perhaps, we except the experiment of Dr. Dusterberg at Warbourg, the principal features of which have been already detailed. The choice of an individual in each family to whom the drug was not administered, and the subsequent infection of the *whole* so excepted, is, we acknowledge, a startling circumstance. *Still* we are not satisfied, even supposing the statements of Dr. Dusterberg to be perfectly accurate, that the mode of experiment was a good one. The exemption from the belladonna treatment of one half of each family would have been much fairer; the exemption of only one in each family would undoubtedly serve as predisposing the ones so exempted to contagion in another and very marked manner, which is not even alluded to by the experimenter; the mental influence exerted over the exempted child of each family, we hesitate not to say, would be very decided, and all in favour of his or her contracting the disease. But apart from this consideration, there are points in the narrative of Dr. Dusterberg which make us very sceptical as to the reality of his experiments. Unlike most authors, he speaks of a *"contact intime"* between those who had taken the belladonna and those who were affected by the disease. And further, he asserts that in most instances of those subjected to the belladonna treatment, at the end of some days there appeared *"a general eruption resembling that of measles,"* and that all who presented this appearance remained free from the disease. We take leave to doubt the reality of the above altogether; indeed, as we have previously stated, it is *exceedingly doubtful* if any eruption over the skin of any kind whatever follows the internal employment of belladonna. Some of the other experiments, whose results appear in favour of the prophylactic action of belladonna, seem, as far as numbers are

[1] ' Elements of Materia Medica,' 2nd edit., vol. ii, p. 1233.

concerned, to tell well. Of 195, 14 attacked, 181 preserved (Berndt's experience). Of 525, 522 preserved, only 3 attacked (Schenck's experience). Out of 20 families, 2 attacked (Gumpert's experience). But apart altogether from any favorable circumstances which, it is not unreasonable to suppose, may have existed in these cases, and of which the exemption of so large a number as 181 out of 195, and of 522 out of 525, renders all the more likely, are not facts of this kind allowed every day to pass under our eyes, and to attract our attention, while they only, and very properly too, elicit the remark that these are unusual, or, at the most, remarkable coincidences? The truth is, in regard to scarlet fever, as well as many other infectious diseases, that an amount of capriciousness so evidently attends their progress, indeed, if we might so speak, regulates their progress, as to make it a very difficult matter to decide if, at any time, or in any degree, their occurrence is at all affected or moderated by external circumstances; and if this be true, as undoubtedly it is, how far more difficult must it be to decide if the exhibition of any prophylactic means does good?

Vaccination in its effects made itself at once recognised, and the contrast between the ravages of smallpox at the commencement of this century, and the almost entire immunity from that disease in an epidemic form which now prevails, are facts so plainly recognisable, and so appreciable, as in the instance of that disease entirely to remove the difficulty referred to. It is altogether otherwise with scarlatina; notwithstanding the introduction of belladonna, and its extensive employment both in this country and abroad, as a prophylactic against scarlet fever, we are not aware that the mortality in either has been reduced; a circumstance which in itself militates very strongly both against the prophylactic and the remedial efficacy of belladonna.[1] But let facts like the following be, moreover, taken into consideration.

[1] The total number of deaths in England and Wales from scarlatina alone during 1847 was 19,816, and in London during 1848, out of a total mortality from all causes of 57,628, there died 4756 of this disease. It may be said that belladonna was only very limited in its employment, but so far as we have been able to learn there are very few medical men who have not, at one time or other, employed it in their practice ; it follows that they have abandoned it on account of its inutility, or, as is the case with several, on account of its injurious consequences.

During the prevalence of scarlatina in Edinburgh and its vicinity, the writer of this article was requested to visit a young gentleman of twelve years of age, a boarder in an educational establishment at a little distance to the west of the city.[1] He was found to be labouring under well-marked scarlet fever, the characteristic eruption of which had made its appearance the day previously. In the room in which this boy lay there were other eight boys, only two of whom had suffered from the disease; and of sixty-five boys who lived under the same roof, there were thirty-eight who were in similar circumstances. The sick boy was immediately removed to the hospital at a little distance, the room he had occupied was well aired, and the bed-clothes removed from his bed; but, with these exceptions, no other means were adopted; the eight boys continued to tenant the same room, and no other case of the disease occurred.

A few months before this occurrence, the writer visited a young lady, one of a family of eight, whose ages were from six to twenty-four, occupying a comfortable, but neither very large nor very well-ventilated house, in the new town of Edinburgh. She passed through a severe attack of scarlet fever, having in particular very severe cynanche, and afterwards very profuse desquamation. None of her sisters or brothers, nor her mother, who nursed her, nor any of the domestics, contracted the disease. In the same street—not a very large one—there were, at the same time, at least two other houses in which the disease existed. These are not singular instances, nor are they recorded here in that belief; on the contrary, we know that the experience of every practitioner could amplify such a catalogue. But from such cases we do learn not a little; and this in particular, that the disease we have to deal with is a very fickle one, and that at times, in circumstances in which we should feel disposed to look with certainty to its diffusion and spreading,

---

[1] At the same time cases of scarlet fever had been known to have occurred in one of the houses nearest the place of this boy's residence, and but a few days before the attack we are presently to notice, the writer had been consulted in regard to the adoption of any measures which it might be expedient to put in force, seeing the disease, for which all directors or governors of such institutions stand in great awe, was then visibly within a few hundred yards.

it will, why or wherefore we cannot tell, pleasingly disappoint us. Had belladonna been employed in either of these two instances, or in any of the numerous similar ones which have occurred, we do not doubt the exemption of the thirty-eight boys in the former, and of the eight individuals (exclusive of domestics, who were comparatively little exposed) in the latter example, would have been attributed to its prophylactic action.

As regards the "Edinburgh experiments," we attend to them here for this reason particularly, in order to notice a remark of Dr. J. D. Gillespie, who observed and described an epidemic of scarlatina which prevailed in Donaldson's Hospital.[1] Dr. Gillespie did not employ belladonna, because "had belladonna been administered, the experiment would not have been decisive without allowing the healthy children to mingle freely with the infected." This Dr. Gillespie did not deem warrant-able, as very great facilities were afforded for keeping the children separated. Fifty-two children of a hundred who had not previously had the disease, took scarlet fever. Isolation of the sound from the sick, and removal of the sick from the part of the hospital occupied by the sound children, was, under Dr. Gillespie's judicious management, effective, to the extent of pre-serving forty-eight of the hundred children.

In criticising the accounts of the Edinburgh experiments, and contrasting, in particular, the experience of Dr. Gillespie in Donaldson's Hospital with that of Mr. Bell in George Watson's, Dr. Henderson, while assuming that some of the boys in the latter institution were protected by the belladonna, speciously endeavours to account for (what appears to us) the entire failure of the drug in Mr. Bell's hands, by urging the greater liability of the boys to contract the disease on account of the amount of belladonna taken. This argument, though ingenious, is most fallacious. We shall not go back to the Hahnemannic view of the action of belladonna in scarlatina, further than to point out this fact, and it is a very striking one, that though Mr. Bell's care and attention, and evident determi-nation to let the experiments in his hands have fair play, led him, "*in a few days,*" owing to the dilatation of the pupil and impaired vision, to lessen the amount of belladonna the boys took, yet he never in any instance for months noticed either

[1] 'Monthly Journal,' 1853.

the *sore throat* or the *rash over the skin of the body*, which Hahnemann described, and which he asserts led him to recognise in belladonna at once the prophylactic against, and the remedy in, scarlatina. Will it be contended that the small dose produces these symptoms, and the larger those which Mr. Bell has so faithfully described? If so, we can only add that after repeated attempts we have failed to produce any rash by the employment of very small doses of belladonna.

Dr. Henderson makes no objection to the experience of Dr. Newbigging, in John Watson's Hospital, yet his boys received *larger* doses than Mr. Bell's, for he gave the extract in the proportion of *one-sixth to one-fourth* of a grain twice a day, and *never* diminished it, continuing its use for five weeks. Mr. Bell began with *a fifth*, and finding, in a few days, that dose to be too large, he diminished it. Seeing that the injurious effects which led to the diminution of the dose by Mr. Bell were discernible in a few days, and that Dr. Newbigging continued the employment of the belladonna in some cases, in even larger doses than Mr. Bell had ever administered, we do think that a fairer statement of the case may be put than the one by Dr. Henderson. If *large* doses of the belladonna are to be regarded at once as exposing to the contagion of scarlatina, and as freeing from that contagion, there must be an end to all argument, for such a proposition tends in no small degree to the *reductio ad absurdum*.

Now, we do not mean to say that Dr. Henderson wishes this to be believed as his opinion, yet his words undoubtedly admit of this interpretation : for when he consigns Mr. Bell's cases to the ready action of the scarlatinal poison, owing to the *largeness* of the doses of belladonna which they have consumed, and attributes the freedom from infection which Dr. Newbigging's enjoyed to their having had the belladonna administered—he in reality says nothing less—for *during five weeks* Dr. Newbigging continued to dose the children at John Watson's Hospital with *a fourth, a fifth, and a sixth* part of a grain, while the second of these was found by Mr. Bell, in the course of *a few days*, to be too large. It will not do to say that the continuance of the drug in Dr. Newbigging's experience for a few more weeks might have caused the children to take the disease; for, most assuredly, if such effects as Mr.

Bell has described were produced with smaller doses than Dr. Newbigging for the most part employed, in the course of a few days, it is only reasonable to conclude that their continuance for a period far short of five weeks would have produced all those effects upon the boys which Dr. Henderson imagines caused Mr. Bell's boys to fall an easy prey to the contagion. Dr. Henderson determined to leave no stone unturned, having already, in regard to other experiments, suggested that some other drug than belladonna was used, conjectures that the extract of belladonna used by Dr. Newbigging was not so strong as that used by Mr. Bell. We venture, however, to remark that just on account of the variation in the strength of the extracts of belladonna, both gentlemen would satisfy themselves of the potency of the specimens they obtained.

The very accuracy which attended Mr. Bell's experiments, the evident care and attention he paid to all the particulars in connection with them, makes his experience one of peculiar value; and we have little hesitation in saying that his "excellent" paper will continue to be regarded alike an authority condemnatory of the so-called prophylactic action of belladonna, and on the general treatment of the disease. It is our opinion that experience has altogether failed to recommend the employment of belladonna, and that now we should be prepared to abandon the practice, as not only insufficient but absurd.

We sum up our disbelief in the prophylactic action of belladonna on account of the following reasons :

1. Numerous facts attest its want of success.
2. All those facts which apparently testify in its favour admit of other and ready explanations.
3. These explanations are, in themselves, perfectly satisfactory and philosophical.

In conclusion: we have thus seen that it is impossible to accept the facts which have been advanced (with as strict a regard to impartiality as possible) as establishing the prophylactic action of belladonna; for though, at first sight, not a few of them seem to give countenance to that view, these do not so in reality, and very many directly oppose it. It may be that a prophylactic against scarlatina exists, but, assuredly, it yet remains to be discovered; meantime, our knowledge of what affords the best protection against that disease cannot be said to

have advanced far beyond what was known to Frank, in whose
words, equally truthful now as when written, we shall not
inappropriately close :—" Salus igitur in solâ fugâ contagii
quæri debet, cui scopo regulæ adversus febres contagiosas jam
traditæ, præcipue vero cura severa scholarum et ambulacrorum
publicorum infantilium inserviunt.

IV.

SHORT ACCOUNT OF THE CASES

TREATED IN THE

CHOLERA HOSPITAL, SURGEON SQUARE,

DURING THE LATE EPIDEMIC.

(Read to the Medico-Chirurgical Society of Edinburgh, January 3rd, 1855.)

In 1848 Edinburgh acquired the by no means enviable distinction of being "the first part of the United Kingdom attacked by cholera."[1] In 1853, the disease, after an absence of little more than three years, made its re-appearance at Newcastle-on-Tyne on the 30th day of August, and before the close of the following month cholera had again broken out in this city. But, though for the third time very early in the list of places in the United Kingdom in which cholera appeared, we have nevertheless to congratulate ourselves, that the duration of the epidemic in Edinburgh, on the last occasion, has not been lengthened, nor its effects very fatal. The hospital in Surgeon Square, which, as the members of the Society are aware, was, during the epidemic of 1848-49, set apart for the reception of cholera patients, in September, 1853, was again opened for the same purpose, and at the request of the Sanitary Committee of the City Parochial Board, I undertook the duties of its visiting physician. From the circumstance of my having occupied that position, I have felt it incumbent upon me to offer

[1] Dr. Sutherland's report to the Board of Health, page 123.

5

to the Society a short account of the cases treated in the hospital. To this subject the following remarks will be confined, as I am neither desirous nor able to give an account of the epidemic as it prevailed throughout the city generally. During the late epidemic the hospital in Surgeon Square was originally opened on the 16th of September, 1853; it was temporarily closed about the commencement of June, 1854, to be again opened on the 24th of August. It was finally closed a little more than a fortnight ago; the last admission being on the 30th of November, and the last dismissal on the 11th of December ultimo. During the whole period there were admitted, in all, 243 patients, of which number only 45 were brought to the hospital during the earlier period, viz. from September, 1853, to May, 1854, and 198 during the period which intervened between the end of August and the commencement of December, 1854. The idea that the whole of the cases which occurred were somewhat equally distributed over these two distinct periods must not, however, be entertained, the Sanitary Committee having very wisely on both occasions kept the hospital open and retained the services of a medical staff, for what appeared a safe period, during which, probably for weeks, there were not admitted more than one or two cases at most. The proper impression will be conveyed, when I mention, that during the first period, as many patients were admitted during October and November as during all the other months, and that from October 3rd to 30th inclusive, 15 out of the whole 45 were admitted. Again, during the latter period, of the 198, no less than 168 were admitted during September and October, and in September alone 97. From the 22nd to the 26th of September the average of the cases under treatment in the hospital daily exceeded 25; on the 23rd of September there were 28 cases in hospital. Placing the numbers occurring during the two periods together, we find that the experience of the hospital has been roughly as follows:—Total number admitted, 243— of these, *males*, 97; *females*, 145; *total recoveries*, 126; *total deaths*, 117. *Deaths among males*, 43; *deaths among females*, 74; *recoveries among males*, 54; *recoveries among females*, 72. The total recoveries thus exceed the total deaths by 9, while the mortality among female patients exceeds by 2 the recoveries; and among the male patients falls short of the recoveries by 11.

Among these cases, however, it must be remembered, that not a few are included which were not cases of genuine cholera; thus, the number of recoveries will shortly be found to suffer a fall, and we shall also have to diminish the fatal catalogue by reason of a few deaths having occurred from other diseases than cholera, for during an epidemic it is by no means uncommon for patients labouring under severe disease in many different forms to be found occupying beds in a cholera hospital. Accordingly, we shall have to notice two fatal cases of peritonitis, and more than one death from other causes, dysentery, &c. In several instances the age, owing sometimes to the condition of the patient, was not ascertained. The following table gives in decennial periods the ages of the cholera patients which were correctly noted:

	Males.		Females.		Total.
Under 10 years	4		4	......	8
From 10 to 20 years ...	13		9		22
„ 20 to 30 „ ...	21	......	30		51
„ 30 to 40 „ ...	20	......	24		44
„ 40 to 50 „ ...	20	......	27		47
„ 50 to 60 „ ...	8		16		24
„ 60 to 70 „ ...	7		11		18
Above 70 „ ...	1		3		4
	94		124		218[1]

As regards the *habits* of the patients before admission, it was ascertained that of the little more than 200 adults, 95 were notoriously intemperate, and, with the exception of 51 who were reputed sober, there was reason to believe that the habits of the remainder were more or less irregular. Forty-seven adults were removed to the hospital from houses dirty and overcrowded; not a few of these had, in addition, darkness and dampness to afflict them. Many were in an enfeebled state of body, in privation, wanting the necessaries of life, alike as regards food and clothing. Several found in open stairs were

[1] A glance at this table will show the uniformity, as regards age, which exists in the seizure of males and females. Of the 124 females, 81 were between the ages of twenty and fifty; and of the 94 males, 61 were within the same periods of life. Adult age seems the one at which attacks of cholera are most frequent; for, keeping all the circumstances in view necessary in such an inquiry, it does appear that neither in youth nor in advanced age is the disease so common.

brought to the hospital by the police; one woman had for
many years slept, save at intervals when a tenant of the gaol—
without shelter of any kind—she recovered. Of 53, however,
it was affirmed that the houses from which they were brought
were clean, and of other 20 that their houses were *tolerably*
clean and comfortable.

The following are the streets and parts of the city, new and
old, from which patients affected with genuine cholera were
brought to the hospital, the asterisk indicating the localities
from which several cases were brought :

*Canongate.	St. Mary's Wynd.	Burnett's Close.
*High Street.	Big Jack's Close.	Horse Wynd.
*Lawnmarket.	James' Court.	Fishmarket Close.
*Grassmarket.	Alison Square.	Maconochie's Close.
*West Port.	Advocate's Close.	Carlton Street.
Trunk's Close.	Anchor Close.	Duncan Street.
Fleshmarket Close.	*Leith Wynd.	William Street.
Chalmers' Close.	Hyndeford's Close.	India Street.
Bailie Fyfe's Close.	Fountain Close.	Rose Street.
St. Leonard Street.	Monteith's Close.	Little King Street.
Hastie's Close.	Stevenlaw's Close.	*Canonmills.
*Candlemaker Row.	*Crosscauseway.	Thistle Street.
Baxter's Close.	Greenside.	Jamaica Street.
*Hume's Close.	*Hope's Land.	Water of Leith.
Blackfriars' Wynd.	Potterrow.	Poplar Lane, Leith.
Pleasance.	Craig's Close.	Canal Court, Leith.
Drummond Street.	Cholera Hospital,	*Holyrood.[1]
Castle Hill.	Surgeon Square.	

One case was brought from the prison and one from the
Magdalene Asylum. The former was a remarkable case in
more than one particular. He was the only prisoner who on
this occasion suffered from the disease—had been confined for
twenty days before he was attacked, and had he survived one
other day, his period of imprisonment would have terminated.
The elements are certainly wanting in this case to constitute

---

[1] The influence of locality in relation to cholera, and of elevation (a point
which has been most ably handled by Mr. Farr), I did not possess the means to
investigate, but these are subjects of great interest, and well deserving
attention ; it is to be hoped that in Edinburgh they will not be lost sight of ;
indeed, it were well that those who are charged with the supervision of
districts, should keep them in view, as bearing on the origin and progress of
all epidemic diseases.

any very probable theory of its having originated by contagion. It was, further, a very rapid case—from seizure till death only thirteen hours intervened. On looking over the table of localities from which patients were removed to the Surgeon Square Hospital during the epidemic of 1848-49, as given by Dr. William Robertson in his very interesting paper, I have been much struck by their very nearly exact sameness with those I have just read. In some particulars, indeed, the correspondence is most remarkable, the same localities in Leith are noted, and the parts of the High Street, Canongate, Cowgate, Lawnmarket, and West Port of Edinburgh are almost identical. Only one case of genuine cholera originated in the hospital during the epidemic. It occurred during the first period, and was that of an elderly female of very intemperate habits and broken-down constitution. She was connected with the laundry, and had no occasion to enter the wards, nor, so far as I am aware, had she ever done so; but she washed during several successive days the clothes of patients who were ill, or had died of the disease; a means, very potent, I have been led to believe, in the communication of the disease, and one which it becomes medical men to be very careful in advising regarding. During this period diarrhœa was common among both medical men and attendants. During the latter period, when, too, there were many more patients in the hospital, there originated no case of genuine cholera, and diarrhœa was not frequent among doctors or nurses. Dr. Robertson's experience in 1848-49, contrasts with this—five nurses contracted the disease, and three of the five died.

Of the 243 cases, the following were *certainly* not cholera, and these I enumerate in order to indicate the cases which are sometimes admitted to a cholera hospital :

1.   A female, aged 20, tubercular peritonitis.   Died.
2.   A man,   aged 30, acute peritonitis.   Died.
3.   A woman, aged 70, severe gastralgia.   Relieved.

| 4. 5. 6. 7. 8. 9. 10. 11. | Cases of intoxication brought by the police during the night, having either vomiting or diarrhœa, and not unfrequently cramps. | Recovered. |

12. A male child, aged 2, hydrocephalus.   Died.
13. A woman,   aged 20, delirium tremens. Removed to Infirmary.
14. A man,   aged 40, epilepsy.   Dismissed.
15. A female,   aged 25, hysteria.   Dismissed.
16. A female,   aged 50, dysentery.   Recovered.
17. A man,   aged 60, dysentery.   Died.

The 243 cases are thus diminished by seventeen, and the 226 are further to be reduced by those cases which were *evidently* more or less severe bilious diarrhœa; this done, there will still remain a few *doubtful cases* among the genuine cases of cholera; these, however, it is impossible from obvious reasons to separate, and all we can decidedly affirm of them is, that to the best of our knowledge, though they did not pass into the second stage of the disease, collapse at one time appeared more or less imminent. Of cases of diarrhœa which were easily cured, and never presented any threatening symptom of cholera, there were 18, and this further reduction leaves 208 cases of genuine cholera. Of 68 cases of genuine cholera, in which the condition of the patient on admission was accurately noted, 42 were in a state of either *profound* or *decided* collapse, or in a state *approaching* to collapse, and 26 were affected either with the characteristic discharges from the bowels and stomach, or, these having been arrested, with some other combination of symptoms distinctive of the disease. Of the 42, 28 were females and 14 males. Of the 26, 12 were females and 14 males. Of the 42 admitted in collapse, 36 died and only 6 recovered. Of the 26 who had not passed into collapse, 4 died and 22 recovered. The former experience does not appear to me to militate against the success of hospital treatment, so much as against the removal of patients to hospital in whom the disease has advanced to the stage of distinct collapse. The latter statement appears to favour the propriety of removal in the case of patients whose symptoms, though unequivocal, have not advanced to the stage of collapse.

A few other facts of interest may be noticed here. Of 35 fatal cases whose period of first seizure appeared to have been accurately noted, in 25 it occurred during the night between 9.30 p.m. and 5.30 a.m. In 10 during the day. In 14 of the 35, admission to the hospital took place during the night, and in 21 during the day. In these 35 fatal cases,

the period which elapsed between admission and death was as
follows :

In	1	.	.	.	.	4 hours.
In	1	.	.	.	.	5½ hours.
In	3	.	.	.	.	12 hours.
In	2	.	.	.	.	13 hours.
In	3	.	.	.	.	14 hours.
In	1	.	.	.	.	15 hours.
In	2	.	.	.	.	18 hours.
In	1	.	.	.	.	21 hours.
In	11	.	.	.	.	1 day.
In	1	.	.	.	.	27 hours.
In	3	.	.	.	.	2 days.
In	1	.	.	.	.	3 days.
In	1	.	.	.	.	4 days.
In	2	.	.	.	.	5 days.
In	1	.	.	.	.	7 days.
In	1	.	.	.	.	8 days.

35

Thus, fourteen survived less than twenty-four hours, and
only ten a longer period than one day.

In connection with some of these cases, there are a few
points of particular interest. It has been stated that "pregnancy is a predisposing condition to a fatal attack of the
epidemic." Whether pregnancy does or does not predispose
to cholera, I do not feel prepared to answer; but it is abundantly evident, that the risk of the disease proving fatal is
increased by the co-existence of that condition. Of patients
in this state brought into the hospital, the following facts were
noted :

1. A female, æt. 30, seven months pregnant; died in consecutive fever after being nearly four days in hospital; did not
miscarry.

2. A female, æt. 26, six months pregnant; died in consecutive
fever on the fourth day in hospital; miscarried two days before
death.

3. A female, æt. 30, five months pregnant; died in consecutive
fever on the third day in hospital; miscarried day before death.

It is to be remarked that all three passed from collapse into
the stage of fever, that in that state two of the three miscarried,
and that all died.

Two nursing mothers were admitted; one recovered, the other died. The facts observed in the hospital appeared to confirm the opinion that the weak and the cachectic are not peculiarly liable to cholera. None of the persons labouring under other forms of disease who were admitted contracted cholera, and, with few exceptions, the cholera patients themselves appeared to be free from lesions of importance. Neither did the existence of previous extensive disease seem, as might be at first imagined, to cause a fatal complication; at least, two patients, both females, suffering from advanced phthisis, struggled through very severe attacks of cholera.

One of the points, to the elucidation of which my endeavours were always directed in the hospital, was, whether or not cases of cholera are preceded by a premonitory diarrhœa. Certainly, in most of the cases, this question received an affirmative confirmation; still there were not wanting cases in which the most careful inquiry failed to elicit any evidence of such affection. In regard to the statements either of the patients themselves, or of the friends who accompanied them to the hospital, it must be borne in mind that an habitual state of looseness of the bowels is by no means uncommon among the lower orders—a circumstance which may explain the little attention being given in the first instance to a slight or even decided increase of it. Of fifty-three cases in which I imagined that a pretty near arrival at truth was made, there were twenty-one in which there existed no evidence of premonitory symptoms, and thirty-two in which there was certain evidence of their occurrence.

Of these thirty-two—

Six had diarrhœa for some hours.
Six   „   „   one day.
Three „   „   two days.
Four   „   „   three days.
Two   „   „   four days.
Two   „   „   five days.
Two   „   „   six days.
One   „   „   seven days.
Three „   „   eight days.
One   „   „   a few days.
One had sickness for two days.
One had vomiting and cramps for four days.

Other cases there were, in which careful examination failed

to elicit any evidence of the occurrence of premonitory symptoms. One of the most remarkable of these was that of the lad from the gaol, previously alluded to. At 11 p.m. he was seized with a feeling of sinking, having up to that time been quite well: had only one stool, and shortly afterwards passed into collapse, in which state he died within thirteen hours from his first seizure.[1] For days previously his bowels had been regular, and during the whole course of his fatal illness he had only one stool. There were not wanting other cases in which the *small* number and quantity of the discharges from the bowels bore a marked contrast to the sunken condition of the patient; in all such, however, it was easily ascertained that the matters lodged to a very considerable amount in the intestines. In not a few, in whom diarrhœa had not occurred for several hours, a copious discharge took place shortly after death.

Bloody stools were observed in several cases; in almost all these the patients were old. This symptom was invariably a very alarming one, and no patient recovered on the last occasion who had suffered from it. In regard to the occurrence of *consecutive fever*—in almost all the cases of recovery from severe collapse, the patients became affected with febrile symptoms; in but few cases, however (compared to what occurred in the previous epidemic, and with the accounts I have read of the experience of other practitioners), did these symptoms run so high as to deserve the name of consecutive fever; or did the condition of the patient become again imperilled. Of thirteen cases in which a severe form of consecutive fever did supervene, eight died and five recovered. Of these seven were males and six females. Of the eight deaths four were in complete coma, three of the four with complete suppression of urine. One from whose bladder urine in considerable amount had been drawn off for three days before death; and notwithstanding the tendency to coma, had continued to increase. Three patients died after recovery from collapse, more from acute pulmonary affection—in two bronchitis, in one pneumonia—than from cholera. Twenty-seven deaths, nineteen of females and eight of males, took place in profound collapse; two others, a man and a woman, both in collapse, perished suddenly. Both had

[1] For this fact I am dependent not merely on the testimony of the patient, but on that of the medical officer of the prison, Dr. Simson.

become violently delirious, and had been with great difficulty retained in bed : in a moment the delirium appeared to cease; both became quite sensible, but both were perfectly blind, and continued so till death, which did not occur in either for some hours.

The appearances of the body after death, and, in particular, the occurrence of the peculiar movements, "due to the coincidence of contraction in different muscles," were just such as have been frequently observed and recorded. I have no particular observations to offer on the morbid appearances found on dissection of the fatal cases. During the first period, the bodies of nearly all the cases proving fatal were examined; the appearances found confirmed the now generally received opinions in regard to the condition of the alimentary canal, namely, the prominence of the intestinal glands, both aggregate and solitary, especially the latter, in the lower part of the ileum, the distension of the gall-bladder with bile, the absence of urine from the bladder, the dry state of most of the serous membranes, and existence of ecchymotic spots on some of these. I must here record my grateful sense of the kindness of my accomplished friend, Dr. Haldane, pathologist to the Royal Infirmary, under whose immediate superintendence nearly all the dissections were conducted. During the latter and longer period of the hospital being open, we were unable to avail ourselves, on account of certain sufficiently good reasons, of the privilege we enjoyed in the former time, in having the use of the *post-mortem* theatre of the Royal Infirmary. The dissections were therefore performed in the Cholera Hospital itself, being, however, limited, by the wish of the Sanitary Committee, to those cases in which permission was given by the friends.

The remaining observations I have to make concern treatment. When the desperate condition of many of our patients on admission is held in remembrance, it will be seen that, in a considerable proportion of cases, our efforts were necessarily confined to relieving the sufferings of the victims; in very few with but little hope of anything further—in most with no such hope at all.[1] Even in the most desperate cases, however, their

[1] Of not a few of such, it may be affirmed, that had they been visited at home on the first occurrence of symptoms, the result would have been

reception into a warm and comfortable ward, with a nurse ready and anxious to administer to any want (and I cannot speak too highly of the faithful manner in which the nurses of the hospital discharged their onerous duties), and those appliances at hand by which we can relieve, though we fail to cure, I have just reason to believe that the hospital proved a blessing. In treatment, some general principles regulated our procedure. In every case we endeavoured to make the poor sufferer as comfortable as possible,—and here I may, once for all, remark, in the words of another, " It is notorious, that for this disease the best remedy is an indefatigable and skilful nurse." To the truth of this observation all who have had any experience of cholera will bear testimony. *Warmth*, by various different means, was applied ; by the aid of the ordinary hot bottles ; by the adaptation of a gas-lamp to the bed, the heated air being conducted through a tube under a cradle, over which the bedclothes were arranged ; an apparatus for which we were indebted to the ingenuity of Mr. Smith, of the City Parochial Establishment. We found few patients who were capable of enduring the application of the heated air after this plan for a longer period than twenty minutes. By packing in the hot damp sheet, after the fashion of Dr. William Gairdner, of the efficiency of which, in cases of early collapse, I entertain a high opinion ; by the hot bath, which, in early collapse, and particularly if the patient be young, and easily carried, is a most valuable adjuvant to every kind of treatment. By *friction*, we endeavoured to allay the cramps, which in many cases were excessive, and of themselves, in some, endangered the life of the patients. This was done either with the dry hand by an attendant, or with some stimulant or anodyne liniment, of which turpentine and tincture of soap and opium were the chief ingredients. By friction along the course of the spine, diligently performed for nearly an hour at a time, I have seen reaction brought about, warmth and pulse restored, when, too, the application of heat alone had altogether failed. I found no

different. The system of " house to house visitation," which has been fairly tested by Dr. Sutherland and others, appears to me one of the most powerful means we possess of combating the disease. It is a plan which, in the event of another visitation of the disease, should be organised in all large towns. (See Dr. Sutherland's Report, formerly referred to.)

means, however, so successful in controlling the violence of the cramps as one I have now to mention, and for which I have to thank a distinguished member of this Society, Dr. Wyse— namely, the application of the ordinary *tourniquet*, or *tourniquets*, over the limb or limbs chiefly affected.[1] The relief I have seen afforded from this simple means has been very great. The tourniquets require to be tightly screwed down; and seeing that, as a general rule, the patients are unable to bear their application for more than ten minutes to a quarter of an hour at a time, their removal and re-application is invariably required before sufficient relief is obtained. I can scarcely say too much in favour of this expedient; in several cases where the violence of the cramps in the limbs was so great as to threaten life, I have regarded the employment of the tourniquets as eminently conducing to the recovery of the patients. The exhibition of *stimulants* was, in many cases, along with some of the means just mentioned, really all that remained for us to do. I have become quite satisfied, that when the exhibition of stimulants is required, and it often is in the more hopeful class of cases, they should be administered very cautiously, and in small quantities. There is no doubt, that the tendency to the occurrence of fever after recovery from collapse is much increased by the exhibition of stimulants in large quantities during the stage of collapse. I confess the temptation to give large quantities of brandy, or wine, or ammonia, in one or other form (which is in reality safer), is sometimes very strong—irresistible, it would appear; but experience of such cases has tended to prove, that it is even doubtful if the recovery from collapse is secured by them; while if that does happily occur, the tendency to fever with cerebral

---

[1] Dr. Wyse, I am aware, is inclined (and from experience) to attribute more decided effects to the employment of the tourniquets than the mere arrestment of cramps. His theory is, that, by the pressure of the tourniquet on the femoral and brachial arteries, the blood is shut off from the extremities; and the circulation being confined to the viscera, reaction is more easily brought about. I can answer for the pressure over the arteries being quite unnecessary for the removal of cramps; all that is required is firm pressure over the body of the limbs. There are very evident objections to Dr. Wyse's theory; but any suggestion in practice from him, more especially when the best effects have been observed to follow, must always command our attentive consideration.

symptoms is undoubtedly increased. What even more than the liberal exhibition of stimulants, during collapse, leads to this untoward result, is the habitual indulgence in spirituous liquors. I have never seen a drunkard recover from cholera without passing through a marked stage of the post-febrile excitement.[1]

There is no doubt that the suppression of urine, and particularly the non-elimination of urea,[2] has to do with the development of this febrile condition, but it is not alone its cause. Several patients in the hospital had passed urine in abundance before it occurred, and continued to secrete it, with a due amount of urea, while the state of fever lasted. Two of these, notwithstanding, died in coma. In such cases we must of necessity look for the retention in the blood of some other poison than urea.[3]

Before quitting the subject of the suppression of urine in cholera, I may mention, that in some cases in the hospital we had every reason to believe that the abstraction of blood from the loins by cupping, or that dry cupping over the same region, did good, and appeared to hurry on the secretion of urine. I scarcely know whether to attribute any good effects to the exhibition of diuretics. We gave such remedies a fair trial in the appropriate stage of the disease; and of all these we were inclined to attach most remedial virtue to the acetate of potash in scruple doses; largely diluted and frequently repeated, it never caused nausea or sickness. In all cases recovering from collapse I have practised and counselled the employment of the catheter;[4] in most cases, a little dirty urine will be thus

[1] It is very common to hear Indian practitioners contrast the disease, as seen in India, with that witnessed in this country; and in no respect do they look upon this contrast as better marked than in the occurrence of the so-called consecutive fever in the cholera of the latter. That the prevalent use, or rather abuse of alcoholic drinks, has much to do with this result, we do not entertain any doubt. Even on the continent of Europe the occurrence of consecutive fever, in cases of cholera, seems to have been much rarer than in Great Britain. On this point see *Cases of Cholera*, collected at Paris, by James Jackson, junior. Boston: 1832.

[2] The chief morbid characters of the urine in cholera are the presence of albumen, and a very great diminution in the proportion of urea.

[3] Probably not an ingredient of the urine at all, but most likely of the bile.

[4] Upon this point Dr. George Burrows writes, "The catheter was some-

removed, while in three or four I have been agreeably astonished to find urine to the amount of six, eight, and even twelve
ounces flow through the instrument, the consequent relief to
the patient being evidently great—in all such the bladder was
firmly contracted on its contents.

Without attempting further subdivision of remedies into
classes, I shall merely indicate those from which in our experience in the hospital in Surgeon Square we imagined benefit
to accrue.   For the arrestment of urgent vomiting no remedy
seemed more effectual than the *mustard emetic.* A tablespoonful of mustard carefully mixed in a small pint of warm
water was the dose we generally administered—it was occasionally repeated. The immediate effects were distressing enough,
but as a general rule, and more particularly when the mustard
was retained for a few minutes, the result was most beneficial.
All other remedies, even *ice,* a most grateful boon to the patient,
have fallen short of the mustard.   In less severe vomiting, *ice,
bismuth, naphtha, chloric ether,* a few drops of *chloroform,
calomel,* in scruple doses, and *sinapisms,* have all appeared to
do a certain amount of good.   Some cases, I need scarcely add,
have resisted all these means, and the establishment of severe
blisters over the epigastrium as well.   One poor man who survived in collapse for nearly three days, had the most urgent
vomiting I ever witnessed.   He had been fearfully intemperate,
and whisky, for which he loudly called, and which in small
quantities was allowed him, was the only thing which his re-
bellious stomach would for more than a few seconds retain.
For the control of the *severe diarrhœa* in such cases as those
formerly noticed, we were in the habit of prescribing the
ordinary *lead and opium pill,* in which I placed very great confidence.   *Opium,* too, uncombined, may in such cases be given
freely,—in an after stage scarcely so freely, with safety; at
least, symptoms of the same class, as stimulants appear to
increase, opium appears to cause.   The treatment of diarrhœa
by *sulphuric acid,* I did not find so successful in hospital practice as I had at one time hoped.

When the stools are characteristic of cholera, the great aim
of treatment, while undoubtedly to arrest or diminish the
times introduced, and urine drawn off, although its presence was not
suspected."—Dr. Gull's 'Report,' p. 219.

exhaustive drain upon the system, is also to alter the character of those peculiar discharges—indeed, the latter is an element of the former; hence the folly and danger of making the latter the only object, and by purgation with castor-oil, or any other means, hurrying our patients to their end. It is not my desire to uphold any plan of treatment as superior to all others. We are unfortunately so ignorant of any very successful plan as to make such a course alike inexpedient and unprofessional. When, therefore, I name the exhibition of calomel in small doses, sometimes combined with a small quantity of opium, more frequently without,[1] I would not appeal to the successful results of the practice so much as to the clinical observation of the individual cases. It is right, however, that I should state, that in twenty-seven cases of cholera, in all of which collapse to a greater or less extent occurred, there resulted a nearly equal division of recoveries and deaths.[2] In all these the plan of treatment was rigidly adhered to, and only interfered with to the extent of the employment of stimulants in those cases where a fatal termination appeared to threaten. Calomel in scruple, in ten- and in five-grain doses, with greater or less proportion of opium, was exhibited in other cases. Three out of the ten recoveries under the first-mentioned plan were salivated severely; the treatment in these was in force regularly for sixty hours. So far as careful observation of these cases went, fatal as well as recovered, we attributed good effects to the calomel.[3] In the latter, the restoration of bile to the stools

[1] One grain of calomel, with or without one-eighth of a grain of opium, every hour.

[2] Dr. Ayre, who has expressed very great confidence in the efficacy of calomel, given in two-grain doses every five minutes, records 365 deaths out of 725 unequivocal cases treated with calomel.—Dr. Gull's 'Report,' p. 176.

I have a very great objection (founded on observation of the very disagreeable and often lamentable results) to giving medicines too frequently in cholera. True, a great deal may be done *about* a cholera patient—as, for example, by friction—but the exhibition of medicine every five or ten minutes is undoubtedly very exhausting to the patient, at a time, too, when the conservation of all his strength is required.

[3] If the pathological view indicated in regard to the retention of the bile in the gall-bladder and its absence from the bowels be correct (for notwithstanding what has been said as to its existence in very minute quantity in the stools—in most instances it is entirely absent)—then it follows that the employment of calomel in cholera rests not merely on empirical grounds, but

appeared to be uniformly quickened, and before urine in any quantity was secreted, its manifestation appeared critical. In some of the fatal cases the stools had become bilious before death—in two, bloody. We have alluded to the condition of the gall-bladder after death, and more especially to the fact of its being filled with bile—a circumstance which undoubtedly militates to a certain extent against the supposition that the non-elimination of bile has any very important part to play in the pathology of cholera. It is, however, just possible that a hurried secretion of this fluid may take place in the first hours of the disease (or, when cholera supervenes on diarrhœa, an increased secretion of bile having we know occurred) ; that the gall-bladder being distended, and the passage of bile into the intestines in some manner interfered with, its non-elimination then takes place until the disease is arrested and overcome.[1] However this may be, the presence of bile in the stools is even more than the presence of urine in the bladder (which, too, I have twice in cases of cholera, both rapidly fatal in collapse, found distended with urine evidently pre-secreted but retained) —an indication of a critical beneficial change. In several cases of severe diarrhœa (choleraic diarrhœa), we found benefit from the persesqui-nitrate of iron, in doses of twenty and thirty drops every hour or two hours; the same remedy was useless in genuine cholera. Dr. Cappie has employed the tincture of the muriate of iron in the same circumstances, with, I believe, rather better results. When bile has been restored to the stools, it is well in most cases to keep up the action of the liver and bowels by the substitution for the calomel of some other suitable medicine—the former, if continued, causing salivation, probably an unnecessary evil. Rhubarb, in ten-grain doses, with a double quantity of the bicarbonate of soda or potash, given once, twice, or thrice daily, were those generally used.

Venesection was practised in two cases when the occurrence of head symptoms after recovery from collapse was threatened.[2]

that, from its well-known action on the secerning power of the liver, calomel does fulfil a really important indication.

[1] See on a subject connected with this, a paper by Dr. John Smith, in the 'Edinburgh Medical and Surgical Journal' for 1834.

[2] These were the only two cases in which the lancet was employed ; for notwithstanding the strong advocacy for the treatment of cholera by bleeding, the results of the practice, even in the hands of the best informed

One recovered; the other passed into coma, and died. *The saline injection of the veins*—for which, after Dr. Robertson's experience in the hospital I possessed no favour—was performed in three cases by Dr. Asher and Mr. Falconer (according to Dr. Robertson's formula). All the patients died—two within twelve hours after the operation; while the third, in whose case it was practised three times, survived for two days. The *injection of warm water* into the cellular tissue in various parts of the body, repeatedly tried, did no good. *Galvanism*, carefully employed in all the various stages of the disease, appeared more hurtful than useful. The *saline powders of Dr. Stevens*, when retained, which was not often the case, appeared inefficient—a philosophical plan of treatment in theory, I do think, but one from which it is singularly difficult to obtain any satisfactory result in practice.

In regard to the cholera hospital in Surgeon Square, Dr. Sutherland, in his very able and interesting Report to the General Board of Health on the epidemic of 1848–49, has remarked, "that it was by far the best establishment of the kind in any of the districts under my inspection,"—no small meed of praise, when it is remembered that Dr. Sutherland's "inspection" extended to Glasgow, Manchester, Liverpool, Sheffield, and Hull, besides numerous other towns and districts in England and Scotland. It is to me a great gratification to be able to state in this meeting of the profession, that the Sanitary Committee of the Board of Managers of the City Parish, on the late as on the former occasion, most faithfully and efficiently carried out the duties entrusted to them, in providing not only hospital accommodation (in which they were aided by the Managers of the Royal Infirmary), but also every needful appliance and remedial means which ingenuity could suggest or devise.[1] I cannot close without bearing a willing testimony to the faith-

and most observant, has not been such as to recommend it. Mr. Hamilton Bell strongly advises bloodletting, but the successes even of his practice is not encouraging. In the Castlehill hospital at Edinburgh, in 1832—

44 cases in the first stage were bled—7 died.
6 verging on collapse,   .   all died.
9 in collapse,   .   .   7 died.

[1] To Mr. Smith, the energetic and benevolent Governor of the City Poor House, all who had to do with the hospital—physician and [patient alike—were much indebted.

6

ful and excellent manner in which all the gentlemen with whose assistance I was favoured performed their arduous and most important labours. I truly feel that much of the relief which the hospital in Surgeon Square afforded to the suffering poor was due to them.[1] I have purposely refrained from noticing the spread of the disease throughout the city generally, chiefly on account of my inability to do that subject justice, and further, because we may reasonably look to the various district medical officers in connection with the different boards for the most accurate and complete information. One thing, however, I feel bound to notice, because my position as hospital physician gave me an excellent opportunity of witnessing these, namely, the excessive labours which the gentlemen to whom I have just alluded underwent. I do believe that the profession generally entertains a very inadequate idea of the duties performed by district medical officers during epidemics of cholera. I have some right to speak of the indefatigable, disinterested and generous manner in which, during several months, the visitation of cholera patients was daily and nightly performed by the gentlemen connected with the City Parish. It is proper that the Society should have an independent testimony to the zeal with which they were always animated, the more so that one of their number,[2] and a member of this Society, in the very midst of his labours, fell a victim to the disease.

[1] These gentlemen were, Dr. Lauder Lindsay, Dr. J. M'C. Cowan, Dr. Asher, Mr. Falconer, Mr. Clarke, and Mr. Wilson.

[2] Dr. John Mackay, in whom, to a most amiable character and an excellent knowledge of his profession, was added an enthusiastic desire to dispense its benefits to the suffering poor, and who by reason of his unwearied labours, there is too much reason to fear, fell an easy prey to cholera.

V.

CASE OF CHRONIC HYDROCEPHALUS

CONNECTED WITH

CANCER AT THE BASE OF BRAIN.

WITH AN ACCOUNT OF THE MORBID APPEARANCES.

BY D. RUTHERFORD HALDANE, M.D.,

PATHOLOGIST TO THE ROYAL INFIRMARY.

(*Reprinted from the 'Edinburgh Medical Journal,' February,* 1856.)[1]

THE subject of this case, aged (at the time of his death) 11 years, was admitted into the Royal Infirmary, upon the recommendation of my friend Dr. Foulis, on the 26th September, 1855, and died on the 12th of November. The following history, the chief features of which I obtained from the mother of the patient, shortly after his admission into the hospital, but many of the more minute particulars from various sources since his decease, I beg, in connection with the very accurate account of the remarkable appearances found upon dissection by Dr. Haldane, to offer to the Society, in the belief that the record of a case, in many points of view so instructive, is likely to interest its members.

J. N— was born in the Parish of Duddingstone. His father is an agricultural servant, now aged 50, his mother aged 45, both healthy persons, and belonging to families, some of the members of which have attained a remarkable longevity,

[1] Read before the Medico-Chirurgical Society of Edinburgh, December 19th, 1855.

and have apparently been free from any hereditary disease.
The original number of the immediate family was *seven*, and
of this *five* survive, at the ages of 18, 16, 13, 8 and 5,
all ruddy, healthy looking boys and girls. The only other
death which has occurred being that of a sister, aged five years
—and now seventeen years ago—from convulsive fits, which
were supposed to result from a severe blow sustained upon the
head some time previously. At the birth of J. N—, two peculiarities were noticed, *one*, it may be presumed, of no interest
or importance in connection with the case, a ranula, which,
within a few days, was appropriately treated and discussed;
the other of very different signification and import, namely, the
left eye being very perceptibly smaller than the right, while the
latter was of the ordinary or natural size; besides being smaller
it appeared more deeply set in the orbital socket, and very
frequent lachrymation gave evidence of its being weaker. In
a note, with which I have been favoured by Mr. Hill of
Portobello, who carefully watched the progress of the case
throughout, he says, "the expression and appearance of the
left eye was always different from the right, and in early infancy
its total want of vision was obvious." It is probable that want
of sight in the left eye was congenital, though the determination
of its absence was not settled before the age of three, when Mr.
S—, upon whose farm the father of the patient was employed,
ascertained that he could not distinguish a watch and certain
other objects with which he was familiar, when the right eye
was closed. At birth nothing peculiar was noticed in regard
to the size of the head; and with the exception of the frontal
region being thought broad, nothing abnormal in its conforma-
tion. The mother is satisfied that the fontanels were not longer
in closing than in the heads of her other children. Between
the ages of three and four, and after the blindness of the left
eye had been determined, the following remarkable changes,
which I shall first notice in the words of Mr. Hill, occurred:—
"Both eyes became more prominent, and the left one projected
in an extraordinary degree, so as to become at one time
completely pushed out of its socket, the eyelids constricting it
behind, and giving rise to the most extreme suffering. With
some difficulty I was enabled to place it within the eyelids
again, and shortly after a large quantity of pus was dis-

charged, which had been collecting behind the eyeball, and the eye gradually assumed the appearance it afterwards retained." The discharge appears, from the testimony of his parents, to have continued during about eight days. About the same time he began to complain of pain, always referred to the back of the head, and a perceptible increase in the size of the cranium occurred. At five years of age he had measles severely, being the only febrile ailment he ever suffered from, with the exception of a very mild attack of scarlatina, about twelve months before his death. The sight of the right eye, which, in his fifth year, had been becoming gradually impaired, was, in his sixth, totally lost. During these years, besides the kind care of Mr. Hill, the little patient was seen by several eminent medical men in Edinburgh, who concurred in believing, that the remarkable appearance presented by the left eye, and the want of vision in both eyes, depended on the existence of a tumour within the cranium. All further concurred in a most gloomy prognosis. In his seventh year, with his head gradually enlarging, and now manifestly abnormally large, he enjoyed good health—his bodily frame developed proportionally more than in his earlier years—he played about, joined heartily in the games of other boys—was seldom noticed to be taciturn—and with the exception of the not unfrequent attacks of severe pain in the back part of the head, had no complaint. These headaches were noticed by his mother to be very sudden in their occurrence—he would join his companions at play, and unexpectedly return to the house, complaining of severe pain always in the same locality, when, after rest for a short period in the horizontal posture, he would rise and again join in play or amusement. At a little more than seven years of age, his health was so good, that, acting under the advice of some kind friends, his parents entered him as a boarder at the " School for Blind Children " in Gayfield Square. Here he continued to reside till very nearly the time when he came under my care in the Infirmary last September. At the Blind School he was frequently seen by Dr. Foulis, who very prudently enjoined upon the teachers the propriety of not forcing him on too speedily in his instructions, and particularly cautioned all with whom he there came in contact, to avoid all possible injury to his then too evidently abnormally enlarged cranium.

Upon making inquiry at the Blind School, the teacher, Mr. Haig, very kindly favoured me with the following particulars regarding the progress J. N— made while there. He entered the institution in September, 1852, when the teachers and servants of the school were much struck by the appearance of his head. He occasionally complained of pain; but during the three years he spent there, his health was as good as that of any of the other children. He took the same amount of exercise. He was rather selfish and stubborn in his disposition. His education was begun in the school, from the alphabet. It very soon became evident that he was a boy of good abilities —decidedly above the average of the boys who have been scholars there. He made rapid progress; and agreeably to the advice of Dr. Foulis, he was kept back, rather than encouraged, as would have been the case with another boy. For reasons which will appear, when Dr. Haldane reads his account of the dissection, I made very special inquiry regarding the integrity of the other senses, as well from Mr. Hill, as from the parents of the boy, and his teacher in the Blind School. All agreed in stating that hearing was perfect; but Mr. Haig felt quite certain that, for some time past his sense of smell had become materially impaired. This was opposed to the belief of Mr. Hill and the boy's parents; but it must be remembered that during the last three years of his life, the teacher in the Blind School had a better opportunity of forming an opinion upon this point than even his parents, from whom, with the exception of a few weeks' holidays, he was absent during the whole of that period. Moreover, the illustration which Mr. Haig gave me of the manner in which he determined the impairment of this sense, is very striking. It has frequently happened, he informed me, that when the children have been taking walking exercise, they have, as the blind are, of course prone to do, placed their feet in dirt, or otherwise come in contact with offensive matter, and, on many occasions, J. N— has done so; while any of the other children who might have done this would have made the discovery for themselves, and remedied it accordingly, this boy never did so; and even after the circumstance was mentioned to him, it was difficult to impress it upon him, owing to the deficiency of smell. Occurrences of this kind, and of a similar nature, led Mr. Haig to regard his sense of smell as decidedly impaired. In opposition to this view, it is right, however, to mention, that both the boy's parents, within a few months of his death, saw him smelling an apple, at least holding it to his nose, while they heard him speak of its odour being pleasant. The few weeks of vacation, during last autumn, J. N— spent with his parents; during the earlier part of it, they thought him looking well, though quite certain that the size of his head had very materially increased. Both parents had always regarded him as the cleverest child they had, and, on his return from the Blind School on this occasion, they were much gratified to find that his education had been very considerably advanced. He could now read the Bible with its raised character for the blind, while in know-ledge of arithmetic and geography he had made very consid-erable advancement. During the month of August, he played about with his companions, being overjoyed to find his way round about his father's cottage and the farm offices in its vicinity—an occupation in which the blind boy was without a rival. In September, the headaches, from which he had never been entirely exempt, occurred with greater frequency and severity; and being rendered additionally anxious regarding him, on account of a strange drowsiness which frequently overcame him, his parents requested me to admit him into the Infirmary.

The following was his condition at that time. The great enlargement of the head was at once noticed, and the measure-ments were found to be—*over the vertex, from ear to ear*, 1 *foot* 2 *inches; circumference of head*, 1 *foot* 11½ *inches*. The left eye was very prominent, but had a dull vacant expression, indicating the absence of sight—so also the right which was not prominent. Both pupils were large, but their size did not vary. Pressure over the prominent eye, even to a slight extent, caused much suffering; over the right eye, pressure could be borne. Hearing acute, no complaint of want of smell, nor any evidence of the failure of that sense existed. It was not, how-ever, tested in the way that I now wish it had been done. Face full and somewhat florid. Head plentifully covered with a peculiar woolly-looking, sandy-coloured hair. No imperfec-tion in the osseous development of the cranium could be detected; on the contrary, everywhere the bones felt of the usual hardness and firmness. Frontal region broad and prominent. Articulation distinct, and voice loud in replying to questions. Body well-covered; fingers and hands smaller than the size and age of the boy would have indicated. Perfect freedom in locomotion. Only complaint that of severe pain in the occipital region. Sleeps well, occasionally moaning. Appetite good. Bowels regular. Dejections and urine healthy. Respiration and circulation free from any evidence of disease. A few days after admission, the hair of head was removed, and a blister applied to the back of the neck, with some relief to the pain ; but owing to its return, and on account of a degree of somnolency, accompanied by slowness of the pulse, he was cupped about the middle of September, and another blister applied, while he took small doses of calomel, until salivation was produced. This resulted in a severer form than was intended, and he suffered a good deal from the irritation it produced. Unquestionably, a considerable degree of relief from the headache followed this treatment, and no further measures of importance were adopted, save keeping up, in a very mild degree, the action of the mercury, and the renewed application of blisters to the neck. The remarkable intelligence of the boy was a matter of daily observation in the ward, and he very speedily got reconciled to his hospital life, and became a particular favourite with the other patients. The special sense of touch was in him finely developed, as it generally is in the blind, and he frequently astonished gentlemen in the ward by the readiness with which he distinguished the different sizes of some keys which I carried in my pocket, and gave to him for that purpose.

The action of the bowels was always carefully attended to, and laxative enemata were frequently administered. He had never any sickness or vomiting. Occasionally he complained of giddiness as well as of pain in the head. For a week previous to the fatal event, he had been more than usually cheerful and happy, had expressed a desire to walk about the ward, and one day mentioned that his parents, who believed him to be now greatly better, wished him to return home.

On Sunday, the 11th of November, he was, to all appearance, in the same state as during the previous week. I saw him that day, and had a little conversation with him. In the early part of Sunday night he was noticed to be restless; but as his nights had formerly been disturbed, less attention was paid to that circumstance than might otherwise have been the case. About five a.m. on Monday, the 12th November, he was seized with a violent convulsive fit, and became quite insensible. During two hours he had a succession of fits, then he became quiet, though never sensible. After a recurrence of another convulsion of great severity, about ten a.m., he expired. He was seen, before death, by my friend and house physician, Dr. Moore.

Before the Society is put in possession of the very remarkable appearances found upon dissection by Dr. Haldane, I would beg, very shortly, to direct attention to the few following points which appear to me of interest in the history of the case:

1st. The evidence of *congenital* disease within the cranium, as marked by the peculiar aspect of the left eye, and by the want of sight in it, which, though not positively determined till the boy was in his third year, in all probability was absent from birth.

2nd. The enlargement of the head, and distension of the cranial bones, was first noticed at the same time as the changes took place in the eyes, *i.e.* between the third and fourth years, and very evidently point to the intimate connection existing between the tumour and the fluid, which thereafter continued to accumulate. "Chronic hydrocephalus," writes Dr. West, "is a morbid condition met with in children at various ages, and coming on under a great variety of circumstances. Sometimes it is congenital, and is then often, though by no means invariably, associated with malformation of the brain. In subsequent childhood, an excess of blood in the brain, or its deficiency, or the existence of some impediment to the circulation through the organ and conditions, all of which have been found to give rise to the effusion of fluid into the cavities of the brain, or upon its surface." Admitting, as it indeed appears necessary to do, with Rokitansky and Vrolik, and with Dr. West, that chronic hydrocephalus is not, in many instances, a mere passive dropsy, but that it may be the result of a slow kind of inflammation of the arachnoid, especially of that lining the ventricles; in the case now detailed, it is, I think, very evident that the effusion into the ventricle arose from the impediment to the venous circulation caused by a tumour, the nature and exact relations of which will be described by Dr. Haldane. It is rare, says the lamented Dr. Valleix, that chronic hydrocephalus, coming on a certain time after birth, is not found in connection with an organic lesion, which accounts for the collection of serum. Such are, for the most part, tumours of different kinds, cancerous, tubercular, cystic. Dr. Robert Whytt, a former distinguished professor of medicine in the University of Edinburgh, seems to have been the first physician who directed attention to the possibility of dropsies of the brain being produced by the pressure exerted on the circulation from the presence of tumours. In his 'Observations on the Dropsy in the Brain,' published in 1768, the following passage occurs :—" A scirrhous tumour of the glandula pituitaria, or in any part contiguous to the ventricles of the brain, by compressing the neighbouring trunks of the absorbent veins, will prevent the due absorption of that fluid which the small arteries constantly exhale, and occasion a dropsy in the brain ; in like manner, as a scirrhous liver, spleen, or pancreas, are often the cause of an ascites." As a proof of this, we may observe that M. Petit often found the glandula pituitaria scirrhous in those who died of a dropsy in the ventricles of the brain. In one case I met with a hard tumour within the right " thalamus nervorum opticorum."

One of the most frequent causes of chronic hydrocephalus, according to MM. Barthez and Rilliet, is the development of a tumour within the cranium, ordinarily tubercular, but sometimes also cancerous, or of some other nature. Of chronic hydrocephalus so produced, both these authors and M. Legendre have recorded instances.

3rd, and lastly. It is important to note the great intelligence possessed by this boy, the full interest of which will, however, be better appreciated when the details of the *post-mortem* appearances have apprised the Society of the amount of destruction done to the cerebral substance.

Sectio Cadaveris fifty-one hours after death.

External appearances.—No commencement of putrefaction. Head enlarged ; forehead prominent. The measurements corresponded to those taken during life. The left eye was prominent, but otherwise appeared natural. The neck was a little fuller than usual.

Head.—When the scalp was removed, the ossification of the

bones of the cranium was found perfect. The anterior fontanelle was quite filled up; there was a marked depression in that situation. The sutures (particularly the coronal and sagittal) were more marked than natural, but there were no ossa triquetra. The skull-cap was very thin, this was particularly the case in regard to the frontal, the anterior part of the parietal, and the squamous portions of the temporal bones. The bone was generally diaphanous, and in places was scarcely more than a line in thickness. The dura mater having been removed, the surface of the brain was found to be drier and paler than natural. The convolutions were much flattened out, and the intervening sulci were very shallow; this appearance was most distinct on the left side. There was an evident difference in the size of the cerebral hemispheres, the left being markedly the larger. Over the left hemisphere fluctuation was distinct, the right felt soft but solid. On slicing the brain, the left lateral ventricle was very soon reached, its upper wall being under half an inch in thickness; when opened into, a golden yellow-coloured serum began to escape. The upper layers of serum were quite clear, the lower were dark and bloody. There was considerable difficulty in removing the fluid from the deeper portions of the ventricle, as the orifice of the pipette became obstructed by what appeared to be a membranous substance. The whole amount of serum in this ventricle was about sixteen ounces. On fully laying open the ventricle, it was found to be very much dilated; its anterior and internal part was occupied by a yellowish, red, soft mass, on the surface of which lay several small, loose, undecolorised clots of blood. This mass, which was partially enclosed in a loose but tolerably strong membrane, appeared to arise from the floor of the ventricle; it was bounded, posteriorly, by the corpus striatum, but extended along the inner margin of this body, and went so far back as to press upon the optic thalamus. As the tumour bulged inwards in the direction of the right hemisphere, the anterior portion of the third ventricle, the septum lucidum, as well as what could be seen of the longitudinal fissure, were pushed over to the right side. The left corpus striatum, and the optic thalamus, though pressed upon by the tumour, were not involved in it. The whole lining membrane of this ventricle was thicker and tougher than natural.

On examining the right lateral ventricle, its anterior cornu was found very small, evidently from the pressure of the tumour; the posterior cornu was dilated, and, along with the middle cornu, contained about two ounces of serum, chiefly clear, but mixed with a little blood in its lower layers. The parts contained in this ventricle were quite natural. The foramen of Monro was about the size of the tip of the little finger, but appeared partially closed by a portion of the investing membrane of the tumour. The choroid plexus, in either ventricle, was natural. The third ventricle was scarcely enlarged.

The brain having been removed, a mass was found to project from the anterior part of the base, chiefly on the left side. This mass was of a yellowish-red colour, and presented a nodulated appearance, some of the nodules being of the size of filberts or small walnuts, but projecting little above the general surface of the tumour. The tumour was accurately bounded, externally and posteriorly, by the fissure of Sylvius of the left side, towards the mesial line it extended as far back as to the corpora albicantia. Anteriorly it reached nearly to the extremity of the anterior lobe. It had not involved the anterior part of the right hemisphere, but had extended towards it, so that the longitudinal fissure was pushed over fully an inch to the right. Farther back, however, the tumour had involved the angular portion of the anterior lobe, situated between the fissure of Sylvius and the longitudinal fissure. The anterior part of the left lateral ventricle had pushed aside the right hemisphere, and so appeared to constitute a part of the base of that division of the brain. Small clots of blood were found along the margin of some parts of the tumour, particularly in the left fissure of the Sylvius. Connected with the posterior edge of the mass, about an inch from the commencement of the left fissure of Sylvius, was a small tumour attached to it by a membranous pedicle. It had the appearance of a cyst growing from the investing membrane of the tumour. It was of the size of a large filbert, was of a reddish-brown colour mottled with yellow, and had a close resemblance to the polished surface of some agates. Several small blood-vessels could be seen to run along its surface.

The mass of the large tumour, as it appeared at the base of

the brain, had a firm, almost gristly feeling, the lobules, however, felt soft, almost fluctuating.

The crus cerebri of the left side appeared longer than the other, and the pons was twisted upon itself, being pulled down on the left side towards the cerebellum.

On examining the base of the brain, the olfactory nerves, the left optic nerve, and the optic commissure, could not be made out, they appeared to have been involved in the tumour. The right optic nerve where it lay upon the crus cerebri was natural.

All the other cranial nerves were uninvolved.

On cutting through the tumour it was found to extend from the base of the brain upwards into the left lateral ventricle. Its lower surface was firm, and of a greyish-pink colour, but the surface which appeared in the ventricle, as well as the nodulated portion, was soft. On gently squeezing the latter portions a milky juice escaped. The cystic tumour connected with its margin contained about two drachms of thin bloody serum. The cerebral matter immediately surrounding the tumour appeared natural. The pituitary gland was flattened out, and appeared a little enlarged, but its structure was healthy.

The dura mater lining the base of the skull, as well as the bones themselves, were healthy. The left orbital plate of the frontal bone was not thicker than card-board.

The left eye was taken out and examined; the opening of the optic nerve into it was very small, the nerve itself was almost entirely atrophied. The cellular tissue behind and around the eyeball was condensed and firm. The structure of the eye, lens, vitreous humour, &c., seemed natural.

The *neck* was not examined, but the thyroid gland was evidently a little larger than natural.

On opening the *thorax* the thymus gland was found to occupy the anterior mediastinum; its inferior extremity rested upon the right auricle of the heart. It consisted of two lateral halves (the left being a little the larger) connected together by loose cellular tissue. It was softish, and presented the normal appearance of the unatrophied gland. Its greatest length was 3¾ inches, breadth 1¾ inches, its weight was 227 grains. The heart was quite healthy. The lungs were normal; they were not congested; their weight was 15 ounces. The bronchial glands were natural. The liver, spleen, and kidneys were quite healthy. The supra-renal capsules were no larger than natural. The mesenteric glands were a little enlarged, but contained no abnormal deposit. The intestines were perfectly healthy, the follicular and agminated glands were distinct but not enlarged. The bladder, prostate, and testicles were natural.

Microscopic examination.—On examining a drop of the milky juice squeezed from the tumour, it was found to consist chiefly of round and oval nuclei, either loose or embedded in a very soft transparent substance. These bodies were about $\frac{1}{10000}$th of an inch in diameter, and contained one or two nucleoli and a little granular matter. In addition to these, though much less numerous, were cells of a round or oval form. These were from $\frac{1}{1500}$th to $\frac{1}{1000}$th of an inch in diameter, and each contained a nucleus exactly similar to those floating about. On the addition of dilute acetic acid the cell walls became a little paler and more transparent; no change was produced upon the nuclei. The denser portions of the tumour contained much fibrous tissue, combined with a smaller proportion of the cellular elements. The tumour was found to be abundantly supplied with blood-vessels, arranged in some places in loops and tufts.

On examining the fluid contained in the ventricles only blood-corpuscles could be detected.

On examination of the thymus gland, abundance of the ordinary corpuscles were seen, with a considerable intermixture of fat.

Remarks.—From the external appearances, as well as from the microscopical structure of this tumour, there can be no doubt as to its cancerous nature. It consisted, however, of two portions, one of which was much harder and firmer than the other. It is, I think, very possible that the growth was originally of a non-malignant nature, a circumstance which would account for the slow progress it made during the first years of life. This tumour was pretty accurately circumscribed; it was generally perfectly limited, and though it had involved a portion of the other hemisphere, this was rather due to simple extension than to cancerous infiltration. As was formerly mentioned, it presented no tendency to involve the dura mater or the cranial bones. It is also worthy of remark that the tumour in the brain was the only local manifestation of the cancerous diathesis. According to Dr. Walshe, the cases in which cancer in the brain is unassociated with the same disease in other organs, are about equal in number to those in which it is so associated. Judging from the history of the case, there can be little doubt but that the disease was congenital; it probably commenced in the internal and posterior part of the anterior lobe of the left hemisphere, consequently in the immediate neighbourhood of the left optic nerve. Hence the blindness which appears to have existed from birth. For a long time the tumour increased very slowly, a circumstance explained by the structure of its lower part being firm, and almost cartilaginous. The right optic nerve did not become affected for a period of at least five years. Previously to this, however, the head had been gradually enlarging. The hydrocephalus, which produced this enlargement, was evidently secondary, and was due either to obstruction to the return of the blood, produced by the pressure of the tumour, or depended upon a gradually increasing amount of fluid, the result of repeated congestions. The complete ossification of the skull proves that the observation of the boy's parents was correct.

The most doubtful point connected with the case is as to the condition of the sense of smell. From the situation of the tumour the left olfactory nerve must, I believe, have been affected from birth, the right, in all probability, not for some years later. Reasoning from the *post-mortem* appearances smell must for some time previous to death have been utterly impossible. And it must be remarked here that the loss of smell might very readily have escaped the attention of the patient's friends; for, granting that the special sense was destroyed, common sensation of the mucous membrane of the nostrils unquestionably remained. The circumstance of the boy taking pleasure in holding an apple to his nose may have been the result of agreeable associations.

Judging from the history the tumour must have begun to enlarge more rapidly within the last few months; this is explained by the soft structure of the recent growth. The immediate cause of death was, I apprehend, hæmorrhage from one or more of the blood-vessels, with which the growth was abundantly supplied; the appearance of the blood in the ventricle and elsewhere indicated that it had been recently extravasated, while the occurrence of convulsions fixes the exact date, it being well known that, in the case of children, hæmorrhage into the substance, or upon the surface of the brain, far more frequently gives rise to convulsions than to par᠎ ysis.

᠎ e unimpaired condition of the boy's mind is highly interesting, as illustrative of the great amount of lesion of the deeper portions of the brain, which is compatible with perfect integrity of the intellectual faculties. The mere flattening out of the convolutions appears not to prevent their grey matter from performing its functions.

In the account of the *post-mortem* appearances, I have alluded particularly to the condition of the thymus gland, as it has been noticed that in cases of sub-acute and chronic hydrocephalus, this body does not undergo its normal involution. In this case the thymus was considerably larger than is usual at the age of eleven years, and its fatty transformation had made comparatively little progress.

VI.

CASE

OF

PERSISTENT SARCINA IN THE URINE.

(Read to the Medico-Chirurgical Society of Edinburgh, 18th February, 1857.)

Since its discovery in 1842 by Professor Goodsir in the matters vomited by a patient, sarcina has been frequently recognised by various observers under the same and also in very different circumstances. It has been found in the fæces, chiefly in cases of chronic diarrhœa, in the stomach of the rabbit and other animals, in the urine, in pus removed from gangrenous abscesses, in the lung by Virchow, in the fluid of the cerebral ventricles by Dr. Jenner,[1] and adhering to the external surface of the capsule in a case of cataract for which extraction had been performed, by MM. Robin and Sichel.[2] But though familiarly known, as far as its appearance is concerned, the peculiar conditions under which sarcina occurs cannot be said to be as yet thoroughly understood. In a case at present under my care, I have noted its persistent presence in the urine. In this secretion, sarcina has not been so frequently observed as to make its occurrence other than a subject of interest. Heller, of Vienna, in 1848, when examining the urine passed by

[1] 'British and Foreign Medico-Chirurgical Review,' 1853.
[2] Nysten, 'Dictionnaire de Médecine,' &c.; Article, Sarcine.

7

a young girl of eight years, discovered sarcina in the sediment;
since that time he has met with it on two other occasions.
Twice respectively it has been seen by Dr. George Johnson and
Dr. Lionel Beale of London;[1] by the latter, in one of the two
instances, in connection with Mr. Brown of Lichfield.   The
late Dr. John Mackay, of this city, also discovered sarcina in
the urine as early as 1848.   A specimen of this urine was seen
by myself, and also by Dr. W. T. Gairdner, at whose suggestion it was shown by Dr. Mackay to Mr. Goodsir.   From what
is stated in the second and last editions of his ' Introduction to
Clinical' Medicine, this appears to have been the only instance
in which Dr. Bennett has seen sarcina in the urine.   I do not
know if, in any of these cases, the presence of sarcina in the
urine was persistent, but this appears to me one of the chief
points of interest in the case which has fallen more particularly
under my own observation.

On the 10th of November, 1856, my advice was requested by
a gentleman about sixty years of age, of studious and somewhat
sedentary habits, on account of the following symptoms.
Severe lumbar pain, felt chiefly upon exertion being made, and
for some time after meals, with a frequent desire to pass water,
though the demands did not appear to arise from the quantity
of urine discharged.   This brief outline of the case was communicated to me by letter.   As these symptoms appeared to
arise from renal or vesical affection, I requested to make a
careful examination of the urine.   On the 12th, a specimen of
the urine was sent to me for this purpose—it had been passed
the same morning.   On the 13th, I examined it at the Infirmary, in company with my friend and house physician, Mr.
William Hill.   It was of pale straw colour, with a distinct
mucous sediment; odour faintly urinous; of neutral reaction.
Sp. gr. 1·025; depositing phosphates on the application of
heat; not coagulable.   Under the microscope numerous sarcinæ, smaller in size, but otherwise precisely similar to the
sarcina ventriculi, were at once detected; there were also
present a considerable amount of epithelium, and a few small
crystals of the ammoniaco-magnesian phosphate.   The day after
the examination of the urine was made I saw the patient for
the first time.   He was of a stout, rather corpulent frame, and

[1] ' The Microscope, and its application to Clinical Medicine,' p. 176.

his appearance did not indicate failing health. He informed me that for many months he had been subject to various dyspeptic symptoms, including want of appetite, foul tongue, with unpleasant taste in the mouth, flatulency, uneasiness in the stomach after meals, and confined bowels. In addition to these, there had been urinary and nervous symptoms : the former comprehending the lumbar pain, and the frequent calls to void water, to which reference has already been made; the latter, some degree of despondency of spirits, and incapability at times for mental exertion. At an earlier period, symptoms of a more precise character, as regards the urinary organs, had been present. He had on one occasion suffered very suddenly and unexpectedly from retention of urine; the assistance of an eminent surgeon had then been sought, and the catheter passed. About the same time the bladder was sounded, under the impression that a calculus might exist. No stone was detected, but since then two small concretions had been passed along with the urine. Regarding the case as one of dyspepsia, connected with a tendency to phosphatic deposits in the urine, I endeavoured to enforce such attention to the ordinary rules of health, particularly as to diet, bodily and mental exercise, as we know to be so generally useful in such circumstances. For the regulation of the bowels, small doses of rhubarb and bicarbonate of potash were prescribed; and I further ordered the use, firstly, of the diluted phosphoric, and then of the nitro-muriatic acid, in doses of twenty drops, thrice daily; the latter, not so much from the known effect of the continued administration of acids in causing the disappearance of phosphatic deposits, as on account of the general tonic virtues possessed by the combined acid. On the 22nd, that is, in the course of ten days, I again saw the patient, and was pleased to receive a favorable account of his state. He felt a material improvement as regarded the dyspeptic symptoms; and though the uneasiness in the back and the frequent calls to micturate continued, he was by no means discouraged, and readily yielded to my desire that he should continue the plan of treatment prescribed. On the 21st, the day previously, I had the second opportunity of examining the urine : its condition and characters were almost exactly similar to what were found on the former occasion, the sarcina. in particular, being present in very considerable amount. On the 27th, I examined a specimen of the urine passed on the previous day. Colour pale straw, clear, with a small amount of white mucous sediment; odour faintly urinous ; reaction neutral. Sp. gr. 1·028; phosphates deposited on the application of heat; not coagulable ; no trace of sugar ; presence of chlorides and sulphates determined. Urea existed in considerable amount. Under the microscope, sarcina, and crystals of the triple phosphate, as on former examinations. On the 10th of February, I examined a specimen of the urine of the 9th : the condition and characters were precisely the same as formerly, with the exception of the sp. gr., which was 1·026 instead of 1·028. On that day I saw the patient still suffering from the lumbar pain, though in less degree; but as regards his other ailments, decidedly relieved. On the same occasion I examined a specimen of the urine immediately after it was voided, and found it to contain the sarcinæ in as great number as when the urine had been kept for one or more days ; the reaction of the urine, when thus examined, was faintly acid, and it did not contain crystals of the triple phosphate. It does not appear to me necessary to make any further remarks at present in regard to the case itself, which, except from the occurrence of the sarcina, has no point of special interest ; at the same time, the short detail of its nature and progress which I have given, seemed to be required.

The observations in respect to the occurrence of the sarcina in this case may be stated as follows :

1st. *Its persistent presence :* including the examinations I have specially alluded to, and others, I have in a period of a little longer than two months examined the urine on ten different occasions, and have always found the sarcina present.

2nd. *Its being present in the fresh urine immediately after micturition :* an observation made on two separate occasions.

3rd. *The sarcina being unaccompanied by torulæ :* as is generally the case in the vomited matters, the evidence of a fermentative change.

4th. *The sarcina being present in urine, the reaction of which, though acid, very speedily became neutral and alkaline.*

5th. *The sarcina being distinctly visible in its perfect form for many days after the urine became highly alkaline.*

M. Robin[1] prefaces some most interesting historical remarks on the subject of sarcina, by observing that it seems to have no important pathological signification—that, in fact, it is innocuous; an opinion which seems to be the one generally entertained, and appears to receive some degree of confirmation from the case I have detailed, in which amelioration of symptoms has not been accompanied by any decrease in the amount of the sarcina. The addition of acids and alkalies produced no sensible .effect on the sarcinæ, except that it rendered some which possessed a slight yellowish hue decidedly paler. Though the sarcinæ could be distinctly seen, and apparently quite unaltered for days after the urine in this case had become intensely alkaline, I observed that by degrees, as the decomposition advanced, the cells became broken up, and at last it became impossible to recognise them. Dr. Beale has made a somewhat similar observation in regard to one of the cases which fell under his notice. From what I saw, however, I am disposed to think that he attributes too much importance to the alkalinity of the urine in effecting the destruction of the cells. In connection with peculiar changes in the system, whether vital or chemical, it is interesting to note that by Virchow, who has very carefully investigated the whole subject of sarcina, it has been found in two cases of what he terms Pneumono-mycosis Sarcinica. In the one case, originally published in Froriep's 'N. Notizen,' 1846, Mai, No. 825, and which Virchow has again produced in his own 'Archiv' for June 1856—that of a man aged seventy, who had suffered reverses of fortune, and died from exhaustion eight days after admission to hospital in a state of complete marasmus, with diarrhœa and cough, with but little expectoration—sarcina in large numbers were found in part of the left lung, which had evidently undergone gangrenous disintegration; and in the second case, which is published in the last number of the 'Archiv,' that for November, 1856, the subject of which was a young man of thirty-three years, affected with tubercular phthisis, Virchow observed, on the dissection of the body, a part of the middle lobe of the right lung apparently affected in the same way as in the former case. In it, too, microscopic examination revealed the presence of sarcina in large amount.

[1] 'Histoire Naturelle des Vegetaux Parasites qui croissent sur l'homme et sur les Animaux Vivants.

As yet, we cannot be said to be thoroughly informed in regard to the circumstances in which sarcina occurs. On other points, however, which were long regarded as doubtful, we can now speak with greater confidence. Its development has been carefully studied by Frerichs; its vegetable nature scarcely admits of question. Yet though first described by Goodsir, in 1842, as a vegetable parasite, it was regarded by Professor Link and Busk, in 1843, as of animal structure, an infusorial animalcule of the genus Gonium. In 1844, its discoverer reasserted its vegetable nature. In 1847, Schlossberger described sarcina as portions of disintegrated primitive muscular fibre, a view which the experiments of Hasse, Virchow, and Robin, and the recent observations of the different circumstances in which it occurs, have completely exploded. Its vegetable nature is now almost universally conceded, and it is classed under the genus Merismopœdia of Meyen, the species Merismopœdia ventriculi of C. Robin. It has been contended that sarcina is a product of decomposition, an opinion which Virchow holds not to have been demonstrated, and which, in the instance I have related, it would certainly be difficult to establish. It has also been attempted to prove that sarcina plays some part in the act of fermentation;[1] but neither with fermentative change in the system, or other abnormal symptoms, does the formation of sarcina appear to be at all intimately associated.

It is very possible that further researches may throw additional and very important light on those parts of the subject which must be still regarded as obscure. Towards this end, nothing will tend more directly than placing on record the circumstances connected with any additional observation; such is the motive which evidently animates our distinguished brethren on the Continent. And as Virchow has recently published a single case in which sarcina was found in the dead body, I trust that the present contribution towards the elucidation of this peculiar parasite, as it occurs in the living, will be accepted by the Society.

[1] See "Clinical Lectures" by Dr. Todd. 'Medical Times and Gazette,' 1854, vol. xxx.

VII.

CASE OF ANEURYSM OF THE AORTA,

WITH LARYNGEAL SPASM,

IN WHICH TRACHEOTOMY WAS PERFORMED,

WITH REMARKS.

(Read to the Medico-Chirurgical Society of Edinburgh, November 18th, 1857.)

In June, 1851, on the occasion of Dr. William Gairdner bringing under the notice of the Medico-Chirurgical Society a case of aortic aneurysm simulating laryngeal disease, there occurred an interesting discussion, bearing chiefly on the question of the propriety of performing tracheotomy in certain cases of thoracic aneurysm, as a means of affording temporary relief. Since the publication of the views then expressed, more particularly by Professor Miller and Dr. Gairdner,[1] Dr. Stokes' original and complete work on 'Diseases of the Heart and the Aorta' has appeared, where, at page 596, he expressly states, that in his opinion there may be circumstances in which the justifiableness of the operation does not admit of doubt. At the same place, Dr. Stokes mentions, however, that he is unable to give the results of any experience of his own on the subject. Dr. Walshe, in his work, makes a nearly similar remark.[2] A case of aortic aneurysm, presenting several features of interest, having recently been under my care in the Royal Infirmary, in

---

[1] See 'Monthly Journal of Medical Science' for 1851.
[2] 'Diseases of the Lungs and Heart,' p. 774.

which, after much anxious deliberation, I considered it necessary
to authorise the performance of tracheotomy, I am anxious now
to submit the details connected with it to the judgment of the
members of the Society.

W. C—, æt. 41, a shoemaker, of very irregular and intemperate habits,
was admitted on the evening of September 4th, 1857. Partly from
himself, but chiefly from a near relative, who subsequently visited him
in the hospital, we received the following details as to his previous history. He had enjoyed good health till within the last twelve months.
During that period has been affected with cough, and
Previous uneasiness in the breast, though not with actual pain.
History. For three months has felt his strength falling off; and
his friends have noticed his appearance during the same
time become materially altered. Three weeks ago he went to Fifeshire,
in the hopes of being benefited by a change of air. In Kirkcaldy he
consulted a medical man, who advised him to return home. On the
day of his admission to the Infirmary, he applied at the New Town
Dispensary, where, on account of the peculiarity of his voice, the
medical officer on duty, without further examination (as he appeared to
be much exhausted), recommended him for admission to the hospital as
a case of laryngeal ulceration. The patient was first seen, and carefully
examined by me, on Monday, September 7th, at noon.

He is a slight man, but without any appearance of emaciation. Face
pallid; countenance remarkably anxious. Is now suffering greatly
from dyspnœa, amounting to orthopnœa; respirations are very frequent;
expiration certainly prolonged; and during the rapidly
Symptoms recurring and very severe paroxysmal exacerbations of the
on Admission. dyspnœa, from which he has suffered since his entrance
to the hospital, it is also accompanied by marked laryngeal stridor. Voice evidently considerably altered, being suppressed in
character, and husky. Cough, which is also frequent, is short and
imperfect; expectorates a very small quantity of viscid mucus; has
never spat blood. The veins of the neck, especially on the right side,
are considerably distended. The trachea in its lower third recedes, and
is evidently subjected to pressure, being with difficulty moved by the
fingers. Slight degree of fulness over upper sternum, and at the right
sterno-clavicular articulation. Pulsation visible above the sternum, at
root of neck, and very distinctly felt, especially to the right side.
Fremitus perceptible over upper sternum and a little to the right. On
percussion, there is impaired resonance—amounting over the sternum
itself to decided dulness—from below the middle of the right clavicle to
the left sterno-clavicular articulation. Over the sternum the dulness
extends lower than in the sub-clavicular region, and is continuous with
the cardiac dulness. Over the upper sternum, and at sternal extremity
of right clavicle, there is a distinct prolonged systolic bruit, which is
immediately followed by a heavy, almost metallic sound. The bruit is

audible in the carotids, most distinctly in the right. Apex of heart beats at sixth left rib, and a little to the outside of the nipple—the impulse is considerable. Area of cardiac dulness is increased. Over the base of heart the normal cardiac first sound is partially heard, while the second is obscured by a distinct blowing murmur, which continues to be audible over the ventricle. Pulse small and frequent; equal in both radials. Pupils natural, and uniformly equal. Respiratory murmur much less pronounced than usual, but equal over both sides. On the previous day the patient had been bled to ten ounces, with considerable relief to the dyspnœa.

September 8th.—Diagnosis formed after the examination of yesterday, was, aneurysm of the arch, very probably involving

Diagnosis. the innominate, causing direct pressure on the lower portion of the trachea, so inducing a considerable share of the dyspnœa. From the frequent and severe paroxysmal exacerbations, I thought it likely that the recurrent, probably on the right side, was also involved in the pressure caused by the dilated vessel. The heart enlarged somewhat, and incompetence, to a certain extent, of the aortic valves.

Having failed to perceive any degree of relief to the spasm by the exhibition of several remedies, including the inhalation of chloroform, before leaving the hospital this afternoon I instructed my able and attentive resident physician, Dr. Brydon, that, in the event of a very severe and apparently likely to prove fatal attack of dyspnœa supervening, the operation of tracheotomy should be performed. I communicated the nature of the operation to the poor patient, and explained to him exactly what we expected might be the result in the event of its being performed or otherwise; he entreated that it might be done. During the afternoon he became quiet, and slept for a short time; but a little before 6 p.m. was suddenly seized with most severe spasm, when a modification of the operation of tracheotomy was performed by Dr. Inglis, one of the resident surgeons. No

Tracheotomy. unusual difficulty was encountered, and there was little hæmorrhage. The operation, according to my directions, was performed higher in the trachea than ordinarily, owing to the pressure exercised upon the passage below, and to avoid all possible risk of wounding the dilated vessel. The cricoid cartilage and two upper rings of the trachea were cut. The patient remained in the sitting posture during the operation, and upon its completion immediately manifested the greatest relief. All the resident physicians and surgeons witnessed the operation; and they agreed in stating that when seen before the operation the patient appeared to be "*in extremis;*" and, further, that a remarkable freedom from dyspnœa followed its performance. This improved condition continued. He was seen frequently during the evening; and at night there was no recurrence of the spasm, and his breathing appeared greatly relieved. He was able to lie with the head lower; and, what is most satisfactory to me, he indicated most clearly that he was sensible of the relief afforded by the operation. Most unfortunately, a little after 4 a.m., he was permitted to rise to stool, and returned unaided to bed. No increased embarrassment of the respiration occurred; but he appeared to sink quietly and rapidly. At half past four he was dead, having survived the operation about ten and a half hours.

The body was examined on September 11th; and from the careful and accurate report of Dr. Haldane I now give the following particulars:

"The heart was enlarged; the left ventricle, in particular, being dilated and a little hypertrophied. The aortic valves were **Post-mortem** incompetent. The ascending aorta was slightly dilated **Examination.** (its internal circumference half an inch above the valves was 3·4 inches), thickened, and atheromatous. An aneurysm of a spherical form, as large as a good sized orange, arose from the arch of the aorta, just at the junction of the ascending and transverse portions. The anterior wall of the sac adhered to the back of the sternum, and to the external end of the right clavicle and first right rib. The aneurysm projected upwards into the root of the neck. The innominate artery arose from the upper wall of the sac near its posterior border; it was much shortened (not more than half an inch in length), its commencement being involved in the aneurysmal dilatation. The sac contained some fluid and loosely coagulated blood, as well as several concentric layers of decolorised fibrine. When the contents were removed it was found that anteriorly the sac had partially given way, and that the wall was here formed by a portion of the back of the sternum (which was very slightly eroded), and the right sterno-clavicular articulation; the joint, however, not being opened into. The opening by which the aneurysmal sac communicated with the aorta was rather larger than a crown piece. The remainder of the transverse portion of the arch of the aorta, as well as the first three inches of the descending aorta, were considerably but uniformly dilated; just beyond the origin of the left sub-clavian artery, the external circumference of the aorta was five inches. Both of the brachiocephalic veins crossed the sac, and were considerably stretched and compressed, the compression being greater on the left than on the right side. The trachea was pushed backwards, and was situated fully two and a half inches behind the top of the sternum; its lower part and the commencement of the right bronchus were somewhat compressed. The nerves on the right side were not at all interfered with; the left pneumogastric and recurrent were slightly stretched over the dilated aorta. On examining the larynx, the rima glottidis was found to be much diminished in size, owing to considerable œdema, so that the inferior vocal chords were almost in contact, and the ventricles of the larynx appeared nearly obliterated. There was no congestion of the mucous membrane of the larynx or trachea. No other important morbid appearances."

Only **two** points in this account of the dissection call for present remark:—1st. The freedom of the right recurrent and pneumogastric. Judging from the position of the pulsation and dulness on percussion, I had thought that the nerves of the right side would be involved; they were, however, free, and those of the left, as is certainly more commonly the case, were stretched. 2nd. The œdema glottidis, if not altogether a new pathological condition in connection with aneurysms at the root of the neck, is certainly a most interesting circumstance. That it did not result from any inflammatory exudation is indeed most probable; and I quite agree with Dr. Haldane in ascribing its production to the compression of the veins at the root of the neck, by the aneurysmal dilatation.

The occurrence of the severe laryngeal spasm may now probably be best explained, partly by the affection of the rima, and partly by the stretching of the left recurrent.

This case, then, was one of laryngeal stridor, while, at the same time, the trachea was compressed by an aneurysm. In such circumstances, I need scarcely say, the performance of tracheotomy can of course be only expected to give a present relief.

Accepting the division of aortic aneurysms with reference to the performance of tracheotomy—or the modified operation of the present case—into three classes—1st, aneurysms directly compressing the air-passage; 2nd, aneurysms exciting laryngeal dyspnœa by pressure, or other interference with the recurrent nerves; 3rd, in which both conditions existed—the case I have detailed belonged to the third class; and, partaking as it did of the nature of both of the others, the question as to the performance of tracheotomy in it must be judged by a consideration of all the circumstances connected with it. Had the direct pressure on the trachea been more marked than it was, I am inclined to think that I should not have counselled operating; but while, no doubt, a certain amount of the dyspnœa resulted from it, I felt sure the greater part, paroxysmal in character, was the consequence of other interference. It was on that account the operation appeared to me expedient as a "*dernier ressort*;" and we have this consolation, that it changed into a quiet death what would otherwise, in all probability, have been attended by great suffering. The case was rendered still more unfavorable by the existence of enlargement and valvular disease of the heart; to which, indeed, I think the death is to

be directly ascribed. Unfavorable as it was, I fully believe
that life was prolonged by the operation for the ten and a
half hours.

VIII.

NARRATIVE OF A CASE

IN WHICH

MALFORMATION OF THE PULMONARY VALVES

GAVE RISE TO

REMARKABLE CARDIAC SOUNDS.

(From Dr. Beale's ' Archives of Medicine,' No. V, 1860.)

At a meeting of the Medico-Chirurgical Society of Edinburgh on the 16th of November, 1859, Dr. Haldane, Pathologist to the Royal Infirmary, exhibited a heart which had been removed by him from the body of a patient on the 14th of the same month. In examining this heart, the valves of the pulmonary artery were tested by a stream of water, and were found to be slightly incompetent. There were four valves, three of about the ordinary size, the fourth much smaller than the others, and imperfectly separated from one of them. The other valves of the heart were healthy, and the organ was of its natural dimensions.[1] The heart, the description of the abnormal appearances in which I have given very nearly in Dr. Haldane's words, was that of a young man, who for a period of nearly three years had been under my observation, whom I had, times without number, occasionally alone, more frequently in the presence of a clinical class in the Infirmary, examined; and from the date of the first examination, at the commencement

[1] " Proceedings of Medico-Chirurgical Society," 'Edinburgh Medical Journal,' December, 1859.

of 1857, had believed to labour under some abnormal condition of the arterial valves on the right side of the heart.

W. W—, æt. 18, consulted me in the very early part of 1857, chiefly on account of a slight degree of difficulty in breathing, aggravated on making any forced exertion. In reply to my careful inquiry he stated that he had always considered himself to be "touched" in the breathing, having observed, from his earliest recollection, that he could not run with the same facility as other boys, and that on lifting heavy weights he was very soon fatigued and caused to "pant."

At eighteen, when I first saw the patient, he had no appearance of suffering from bad health, was then able for the duties of a light porter, and admitted that he applied for medical advice from no feeling of increase in the difficulty of breathing and slight palpitation which from boyhood he had suffered, but in the hope that his old symptoms might be subdued.

When W—, removed his clothes to permit a careful examination of the chest, I was struck by the peculiar appearance of the right arm; it was much shorter and thinner than the left, a condition which he stated had existed from birth. The left arm was well developed. He was, it is scarcely necessary to add, left-handed. On inspection of the chest a more ample clothing by the pectoral muscles over the left than the right front was at once apparent. Besides this, there existed a decided prominence in the cardiac region. Impulse of the heart, without being decidedly exaggerated, was readily appreciable. Rhythm of heart natural. Apex beat was detected in the normal situation, and there existed no increase of precordial dulness. A very decided thrill accompanied the systolic action of the heart, when the hand was applied over the base. On more careful examination, the thrill was found to be almost entirely limited to the situation in which a loud systolic murmur was heard with the greatest degree of intensity. That was at the left border of the sternum, over the cartilage of the third rib. The systolic murmur thus distinguished was blowing in character and of an unusual loudness; in the same situation it was followed by a diastolic murmur of much less intensity.

The systolic murmur was readily distinguished over the whole upper part of the chest, but with much facility the seat of its greatest intensity was determined to be that already indicated.

The diastolic murmur was limited or almost limited to the same situation. Over the aortic valves something like the normal second sound was from time to time audible. The loud systolic murmur was not propagated in the course of the systemic circulation, for though loudly heard over the upper sternum, it was scarcely appreciable in the carotids. The radial as well as other superficial pulses were normal, no jerking character or trace of visibility distinguished them. The strength of pulse good, average frequency 74. Respiratory murmur of both lungs was feeble, otherwise unaltered. Patient had never suffered from rheumatism, had never spat blood, had little or no cough, and no expectoration. Complained occasionally of drowsiness. Had no appearance of lividity of the countenance. Subsequent to this, my first examination, he was on three occasions under my care in the Infirmary, once in 1857, and twice in 1858. Repeatedly examined, the physical signs underwent no change, so that in the notes of his case I frequently find this remark, " physical signs precisely as before." The slight breathlessness he suffered was always relieved by the care and comfort of hospital residence, and the palpitation, which seemed in great degree functional, was always mitigated by attention to the state of the bowels, proper regulation of diet, and on one or two occasions, when more severe and lasting than usual, by the application of a belladonna plaster. By iron and henbane, which he took for a lengthened period, both when in the hospital and out of it, he stated that he always felt himself benefited.

He left the Infirmary for the last time on the 5th of October, 1858. I had then been successful in obtaining employment for him of a light nature; at this he continued for a considerable period. I saw him frequently thereafter; there was up to the very last occasion on which I accidently met him in the early summer of 1859, no change in his appearance, and he always expressed himself as feeling as well as on any former occasion. For several months I had not seen him, when on Sunday the 13th of November, on visiting the Infirmary, I was startled by the announcement from the nurse—under whose charge in the hospital he had been on the occasions alluded to in this narrative—that his body was then lying in the dead-house. On inquiry I was grieved to learn that during the afternoon of the

preceding Friday, when in a state of intoxication—to habits of
which he had only lately become abandoned—he had fallen
down a stair and had been brought to the surgical hospital,
where, upon examination an extensive fracture at the base of
the skull was detected.   He died the same evening in a state
of complete insensibility.   It was in the performance of the
post-mortem examination to determine the precise nature of
the injury of the head, that the opportunity occurred for observing the state of the heart.

This interesting case may be almost left without any com-
ments, on one or two points only I am tempted to make a few
remarks :

1. The physical signs seemed to me from the very first examination to indicate a lesion of the pulmonary valves, one which
offered some obstruction to the flow of the blood outwards from
the ventricle, and at the same time permitted the reflux of
blood backwards to a limited extent.   The obstruction I argued
could not be very great, as there existed no evidence of hypertrophy of the right ventricle, nor any signs of imperfect supply
of blood to the lungs.   The loudness of the systolic murmur
seemed to bear out the doctrine of Dr. Hope, that pulmonary
murmurs, from the greater nearness of the pulmonary artery to
the surface of the chest, are likely to be louder than aortic
murmurs.   Equally strong indications of the pulmonary origin
of the murmurs, as the precise situation in which they were
most clearly heard, were the want of propagation in the aortic
and large vessels, or along the sternum, and the absence of any
peculiarity in the superficial pulses.   The incompetency of the
pulmonary valves I considered to be only to a limited extent,
from the faint character of the diastolic murmur and the absence
of any marked pulmonary symptoms.

2. The history of the patient's case, the fact very specially,
that throughout life his breathing had been slightly affected ;
that he had never suffered from rheumatism, and his appearance,
with the shortened right arm, made it not improbable that the
cardiac lesion whatever it might be was of fœtal origin.

3. Lastly, the absence of any other form of valvular disease,
in this case, may reasonably be considered as having materially
simplified the diagnosis, though its interest cannot be considered
as on that account in any degree diminished.

IX.

CASE OF FATAL CROUP IN THE ADULT;

WITH REMARKS.

(Read to the Medico-Chirurgical Society of Edinburgh, March 6th, 1861.)

No feature in the etiology of croup is more interesting than age. It is essentially a disease of childhood. Not only so, but an extended experience in all countries, and by many observers, has distinctly pointed out that the period for the maximum occurrence of croup is between the second and the seventh year. "Disponunt ad croup," writes Joseph Frank in his wonderful 'Repertory of Medical Knowledge,' "ætas infantilis, et ita quidem, ut primum vitæ mensibus haud communis sit, frequentissimus inter primis et septimum annum."[1] "In no part of Britain, I imagine," remarks Dr. Cheyne, "is croup more prevalent than in Leith and its immediate neighbourhood; yet in the course of nearly fifty years of extensive practice, in which he has attended many hundred cases of this disease, my father has not seen one instance of croup occurring after puberty."[2] Although, however, the ages now mentioned do include the season in which croup is infinitely most prone to occur, it is of importance to know that the disease has been observed during the period of lactation, also after puberty, and in adult as well as even senile life. Bretonneau, for example, records the case

[1] 'Praxeos Medicæ Universæ Præcepta.' "De Croup."
[2] 'The Pathology of the Membrane of the Larynx and Bronchia.' By John Cheyne, M.D., p. 27.

8

of a child of a fortnight old, very feeble and small, who died of
well-marked croup;[1] Molloy, the case of a child who died at
the age of one month ;[2] Desessart, a third case fatal at the age
of three months.[3]   As to the occurrence of croup in the adult,
on the other hand, Louis, in 1826, on the occasion of the publication of his well-known and important memoir on the subject,
was no doubt justified in stating that croup is so rare after
puberty, and in adult age, as to have escaped the notice of many
practitioners, who indeed doubt its existence at that period of
life : the recorded observations of croup in subjects who have
passed the age of puberty are rare, and such, continues Louis,
that the annals of medicine do not contain more than three or
four well-authenticated instances during the last fifteen years.
Louis himself, in the memoir now referred to,[4] recorded eight
instances of croup in the adult, all of which had been observed
under the care of different physicians in the Charité, Necker,
and Salpêtrière Hospitals at Paris.   To some points of interest
in these cases, and in Louis' "resumé," I shall have occasion
to allude in the sequel.   Within a more limited period, other
examples of croup occurring in the adult have been placed on
record by different observers ;—by Charcelay, among French
writers, in 1839, in the 'Gazette Médicale,' and in this country
by Dr. Gillespie, whose interesting case, read to this Society
in 1850, and published in the 'Monthly Journal' for the same
year, as well as one recorded in the 'Lancet' for 1838, and
referred to by Dr. Gillespie, have perhaps escaped attention
somewhat, from the circumstance of their having been entitled
cases of "Laryngo-Tracheitis :" that they were, however,
instances of croup occurring in the adult, is just as certain as
is the one the particulars of which I now communicate.

Alexander Hamilton, employed in the North British Rubber Manufactory, æt. 39, but having the appearance of being ten years older, was
admitted to the Royal Infirmary, under my care, in the month of June,
1860. He was then, and had been for some months previously, affected
by diabetes. On his admission, he was considerably emaciated, had

[1] 'Des Inflammations spéciales du Tissu Muqueux, et en particulier de la
Diphthérite,' &c., p. 36.
[2] and [3] Frank, loco citato, p. 114; "De Croup."   See also Valleix 'Guide
du Médecin Practicien,' vol. i, p. 159.
[4] 'Mémoires ou Recherches Anatomico-Pathologiques,' p. 203.   "Du Croup
considéré chez l'Adulte."

great thirst, and was passing from 220 to 280 ounces of urine in the course of the day. There was no hereditary tendency to the disease to be discovered in this man's family, and the origination of it in his own case is probably to be ascribed to the extremely intemperate habits in which he had for years indulged. He was a slight-made man, of sanguine temperament, possessing bright red hair and light blue eyes. Under a duly regulated diet, consisting chiefly of animal food with gluten bread, a limited allowance of sugar (which in several instances lately I have found useful), and a restricted indulgence in fluids, the patient, for some time after the commencement of his hospital residence, decidedly improved. He gained flesh, and acquired some measure of strength; the amount of his urine gradually diminished to 160 ounces, and its density from 1·045 steadily fell to 1·034. During this time he had a fair trial of the alkaline plan of treatment; bicarbonate of soda and magnesia being the remedies employed, as well as the Vichy water. Arsenic, in the form of Fowler's solution, he also took; and it was while so doing that the most decided improvement in his appearance, and the greatest increase in flesh, were observed. A pint, and afterwards two pints, of London porter *per diem* were allowed him.

During the extremely cold weather of December, Hamilton had been noticed to have fallen off in appearance. He was in the habit of leaving the hospital occasionally for a walk; he did so on the 30th of December. On the following day he felt some symptoms of cold, but made no complaint till the evening of January the 1st. Dr. William Anderson, my resident physician, then found him suffering from sore throat, but without any distinctive character, and by no means violent in degree. Some simple remedies were prescribed; among others, warm poultices of bran to the throat and the inhalation of steam. On January 2nd the pain in throat had increased considerably, being referred to the larynx and trachea, and slight pressure over both caused great uneasiness; he had difficulty in swallowing, barking cough, with noisy croupal respiration, and was only able to articulate in a whisper. Early in the morning, after a fit of coughing, he had expectorated, along with some thick mucus, a portion of greyish-coloured tough membrane (an inch and a half long by an inch broad). At visit, a careful examination of the mouth and throat was made. The tonsils appeared a little swollen; the uvula elongated, and at its termination œdematous; the upper part of pharynx of a red colour, but no trace of pellicular exudation could be discovered; the nostrils also were quite free. On passing the forefinger down to the epiglottis, it was felt to be raised and tumid. Pulse 120, and small. The application of the warm cloths was ordered to be continued with diligence, and a little wine of ipecacuanha to be administered at short intervals. In the course of some hours, another, but smaller, portion of membrane was expectorated.

In the afternoon of the same day, the dyspnœa had not increased, and no attacks of spasmodic difficulty of breathing had occurred; voice was still more suppressed; a very distinct thrill was communicated to the hand when placed over both fronts of the chest; and on auscultation the vesicular murmur, especially over the left side, was very imperfectly heard. Pulse more feeble. Wine and a little brandy were adminis-tered.

At 2 a.m. of January 3rd Dr. Anderson was summoned suddenly, to find the patient evidently sinking. He could only with difficulty count the pulse, but noticed no increased embarrassment of the respiration, no lividity of countenance, or appearance of gasping for breath. In the course of a few hours he died. It may be mentioned as interesting, that during the last two days of the patient's life the amount of urine voided was greatly diminished; the density, however, remained as before, and the chemical indications of sugar equally distinct.

On the 5th January the body was examined by Dr. Haldane, to whom I am indebted for the following account of the morbid appearances. The mucous membrane of the fauces and pharynx was reddened, but there was no exudation over its surface. The epiglottis was swollen, and of a red colour; the lower half of its inner surface, and the whole of the lining membrane of the larynx, was coated with a tenacious adherent false membrane of a dirty yellowish-grey colour. This mem-brane extended downwards to the upper part of the trachea, then it ceased abruptly, the lining membrane of the trachea being of a bright red colour, though coated by a thin soft layer of lymph. At the lowest part of the trachea, false membrane, similar in all respects to that found in the larynx, existed, and extended into both bronchi—into the left more decidedly than into right. Traces of false membrane existed in the very small bronchial ramifications of left lung.

On microscopic examination, the false membrane was found to con-sist essentially of fibre and cells, but at some places there was an abun-dant deposit of spores and filaments of the oidium albicans. On examining the portion of membrane expectorated, the presence of the the same vegetable parasite had been detected.

There was slight œdema of both lungs, but no other morbid appear-ance in the thoracic or abdominal organs.

As a termination of diabetes the occurrence of croup in the case now briefly detailed appears to me of some interest; such a termination, indeed, must be regarded as extremely rare. I am not aware of its having ever been previously noticed. Comparatively few of the recorded cases of croup in the adult were examples of the disease occurring as a primary affection; in the great majority, as in the one just read, the croup was a secondary affection, coming on in the course, or immediately on the termination, of some other severe disease, by which the strength of the patient had already been greatly reduced. Only one of the eight cases recorded by Louis is entitled simple croup; but the subject of his seventh observation, a woman of thirty-two years, although exhausted by misery and imperfect nourishment, had not suffered from any other malady. In the remaining six cases of Louis, croup was a complication of typhoid fever in two; in other two, of an inflammatory affection of the gastro-intestinal mucous membrane; in óne it occurred in the last stage of phthisis; while in another, it supervened on an attack of chronic pleurisy. In a case communicated by Dr. Rollo to Dr. Cheyne, and the particulars of which are given by the latter in his work,[1] the patient had, previous to the attack of croup, suffered from a severe catarrh; in his youth, too, he had been more than once ill with croup. This was a gunner in the Royal Artillery. A preparation from the case is preserved in the Museum of the Royal College of Surgeons (Catalogue 1293, xxvi B). The case recorded by Dr. Gillespie, already referred to, and the one published in the 'Lancet' for 1838, are two well-marked examples of primary croup in the adult. It is worthy of remark that in both subjects pregnancy was far advanced.

With one exception (the seventh observation), the existence of a distinct false membrane in Louis' cases was not limited to the air-passages properly so called—larynx, trachea, and bronchi—as in the case of Hamilton; but the uvula, the tonsils, and pharynx—in some the œsophagus and posterior nares, were likwise involved. To the absence of false membrane over the mucous surface of the pharynx in the exceptional instance, special attention is directed by Louis; and he remarks, that, having in the six cases previously detailed, observed that the membranous concretions are propagated from above downwards, the question suggests itself, whether the malady in this instance may possibly have had a different course; or, supposing it to have originated, as in the others, by implication first of all of the pharynx, whether the false membrane formed there may not have been detached, so as to permit its subsequent only very incomplete re-formation. M. Louis himself does not answer this question; it would therefore be presumptuous in me to do so. In 1818—that is, some years before the publication of M. Louis' cases—M. Bretonneau had read to the French Academy his original observations on "Diphthérite;" and in 1826 his remarkable treatise on that subject, as well as

[1] Loco citato, p. 115.

the memoir of Louis, simultaneously appeared. That some of
the cases of croup in the adult recorded by the latter, as well
as others which have been published by different French physicians since, partook to a considerable extent of the nature of
the affection first accurately described by Bretonneau, there
can, I think, be little hesitation in concluding. But in connection with this particular question there is a point which
appears to me one of very considerable importance, namely,
how far is the disease which is familiar to us as croup (whether
affecting the adult or, as is so much more common, the child),
and which at the hands of various English writers has received
a full illustration (let me instance Home and Cheyne among
the older, and Drs. West and Charles Wilson among recent
authors), to be regarded as identical with the croup described
by French physicians. I am surely not mistaken when I state
that the very circumstance of the implication of the pharynx to
any considerable extent—especially if it becomes distinctly the
seat of the adventitious deposit, still more if it be the earliest
part affected by it—in the opinion of English physicians generally, would lead to the conclusion that the case is one of
diphthérite, and not of our true English croup. I remember,
as I have before observed in this Society, on the occasion of
my first seeing cases of croup in the French hospitals, to
have been struck by noticing the great care exercised in the
examination of the mouth and throat of the child; and when
instances of the disease were described by Trousseau or by
Guersant, I failed to recognise the distinguishing features of
the disease as familiar to me in the writings of British physicians. Croup, as the distinguished physicians now named
taught us, was a disease commencing in the pharynx. This is
indeed the doctrine of the French school; let me refer to what
M. Trousseau has stated in his recently published work,
' Clinique Médicale de L'Hotel-Dieu de Paris.'[1] You will hear
it remarked by men of undoubted experience, that they have
often seen children die of croup in whom the pharynx has not
been involved. Before M. Bretonneau had read, in 1818, to
the Academy his earliest observations on " Diphthérite," before
the publication in 1826 of his treatise, the fact was generally
admitted that membranous croup commenced in the larynx.

[1] P. 327. 'Angine Diphthérique et Croup.'

M. Bretonneau has caused a revolution in science by maintaining and demonstrating that almost always, at least nineteen times out of twenty, it was not so, but that the malady commenced in the pharynx. Guersant, his friend, and for a lengthened period physician to the Children's Hospital, after having supported the former opinion, when his attention was directed to the point, adopted the view of Bretonneau. Trousseau then goes on to observe that, as regards himself, having perhaps seen more of croup than any other physician of the capital, from the circumstance of his connection during eighteen years with the Children's Hospital, and from having been very frequently consulted in regard to the operation of tracheotomy in the treatment of diphthérite—"I assure you," he says, "that the proposition announced by my venerated master is the true one, and that in most cases the croup begins in the pharynx." "I do not deny," he observes, a little further on, "that croup may first affect the larynx, any more than I hesitate to admit that in very rare circumstances it may have its first seat in the bronchial ramifications. Croup commencing in the larynx is a rare and exceptional fact." The maintenance of a different opinion Trousseau explains on the ground, first, of the insufficient attention which has been paid to the examination of the mouth and pharynx; and, secondly, because, in most instances, the early symptoms of the malady are comparatively trivial, and, before the larynx and trachea have become involved, the distinct traces of the pharyngeal affection have passed away.[1]

[1] Croup occurring in the adult runs, in the opinion of Trousseau, a similar course. The derangement of health and febrile disturbance are at first very slight, the pain in the throat trivial, and the existence of false membrane in the pharynx may be found in patients whose only complaint is that of a little difficulty in swallowing. Here, however, the danger is greater than in the child. The adult having the opening of the larynx proportionally larger than in the latter, the calibre of the trachea being also greater, the air finds a sufficient passage even after the deposition of false membrane on its walls has commenced; and when the symptoms of croup become confirmed, the false membrane has already occupied, to a great extent, the bronchial ramifications.

These phenomena, says Trousseau, have for a long time attracted my notice. I first observed them in the epidemic of Sologne, where I was sent with Dr. Ramon in 1828 to study the disease.

Let me give, very much in Trousseau's own words, the following case of

I turn now, very briefly, to notice the statements of two of the most accurate observers in our own country. "The cavity of the mouth and the fauces do not present," remarks Dr. West, "any invariable alteration in cases of croup. Congestion about the fauces and soft palate is of frequent occurrence, sometimes coupled with a scanty deposit of false membrane in those situations, or the tonsils are found in a state of ulceration."[1] Dr. Wilson, who perhaps of all English writers on croup has treated most fully of the condition of the pharynx, tonsils, and palate in the early stage of the disease, and speaks of the fauces being always affected "to an extent which indeed varied considerably, but which was in every instance sufficiently obvious, and always characteristic"—having described the red and congested appearance of the parts—observes, "Along with this, though only in a small minority of instances, there may be observed traces of exudation on the amygdalæ or pharynx."[2]

Like the French physicians, and Dr. Wilson in our own country, I feel inclined to insist upon the importance of making, whenever possible, a careful examination of the mouth and croup in the adult, which he has most graphically recorded:—I was one day —it was a day too memorable for me ever to forget it—dining with M. de Bethune, whose château is situated at a little distance from Selles, in the department of Cher, when a peasant came for me in a great hurry to see his wife, who he said was suffocating. I went immediately to the patient. I found a woman of 26 years, still attired in her holiday garb—it was Whit Sunday. She had attended morning mass, at about a quarter of a league distant; after walking home she had dined as usual, and was again prepared to go to vespers when she was suddenly seized with a sense of suffocation, so violent that her husband feared it might overpower her before we arrived. The unfortunate woman was indeed expiring when I saw her. Examining immediately the throat, I discovered a dense false membrane stretching across the pharynx. The nature of the malady was thus sufficiently shown; and the poor woman being at her last extremity, tracheotomy alone appeared able to avert immediate death. Without any delay, I forthwith had recourse to it, with no assistance but that of the husband, and with no other instrument but a knife with convex blade, which fortunately I had with me. I was compelled, moreover, for want of a proper tracheal canula to make a clumsy one out of a leaden ball, which I flattened with a hammer, and fashioned like a tube. Unfortunately, the false membrane had already penetrated into the smaller bronchi, and on the following day my patient died."

[1] 'Diseases of Infancy and Childhood,' p. 358.
[2] 'Edinburgh Medical Journal,' 1855-6.

pharynx in every case where the suspicion of croup may be reasonably entertained; but, from the remarks now made, I think it must be obvious that, in the experience of physicians in France, the pharynx is more seriously, if it be not more frequently, involved in croup than is the case in Great Britain.

In bringing this case under the notice of the Society, I have not thought it necessary to refer in any special manner to the treatment which was pursued during the eight and forty hours the patient survived the attack of his fatal disease. The croup found him greatly exhausted from the long continuance of another grave disorder, and seemed to tell more distinctly by causing further depression of the system generally than by determining that great difficulty of breathing which, in other circumstances, is so distinctive a feature of its invasion. Laryngeal dyspnœa there was undoubtedly, and truly croupal in character; but it was modified in degree, and, in particular, not characterised by the occurrence of those sudden spasmodic attacks or exacerbations of dyspnœa (the accès of French writers) which so frequently, in ordinary croup, prove the immediate cause of death. As the patient had spat up some portion of false membrane before I saw him on the 2nd January, I considered it advisable to aid the further expectoration of such by the employment of small doses of ipecacuanha. This was not long persevered with, for the tendency to sinking clearly showed that the only safe plan to be pursued was as long as possible to maintain by stimulants the patient's fast ebbing strength. Tracheotomy in such circumstances was surely altogether inadmissible; but, at the same time, I should have derived little profit from the study of the able and complete observations of Mr. Spence on that subject, so familiar to the members of this Society,[1] had I not on the one hand carefully and anxiously considered whether this operation could reasonably be expected to effect any good, or, having so considered, hesitated to decide that it could not. The presence of the vegetable parasite, the oidium albicaus, in the exudation matter is not without interest; and perhaps there are some who from the fact of its existence may feel disposed to regard the case as one more closely allied to diphtheria. Such is not the opinion I entertain. With the development of that disease the pro-

[1] 'Edinburgh Medical Journal,' February, 1860.

duction of a vegetable parasite has, I believe, no intimate connection; it is not an epiphitic disease, and in many circumstances
we meet with the oidium albicans, and kindred vegetable
parasites, when the mucous surfaces of various parts of the
body are the seat of inflammatory action.   It is certainly more
nearly allied with the Muguet of French writers, the aphthous
disorders of children, and ailments of like nature; but I see no
reason why its presence may not at times be determined in the
exudation of true croup.   Possibly the morbid condition of the
system previously in existence—I mean the glucogenic—may
have had some influence in its generation.

X.

ON ICHTHYOSIS;

WITH SPECIAL REFERENCE TO THE PARTICULAR FORMS IN WHICH IT OCCURS.

(Read to the Medico-Chirurgical Society of Edinburgh, June 5th, 1861.)

THE term Ichthyosis has for a long period been applied to an affection of the skin, characterised by the formation of scales, peculiar in their nature, and bearing a resemblance, more or less marked, to those of a fish.

In several of the older writers, descriptions of cases, designated for the most part as rare and remarkable, will be found, which are, no doubt, examples of one of the now recognised forms of ichthyosis. Panarolus,[1] who flourished as professor in Rome about the middle of the seventeenth century, gives a curious description of a woman who was otherwise free from disease, but whose skin was everywhere covered with scales. ("Mulier in cute squamas undique repræsentans citra morbum.") Stalpartius Vander Wiel,[2] physician at the Hague, and the contemporary of Panarolus, under the head of " Squameus, ac veluti Phocæ pelle contectus puer," records a remarkable case. It is curious, moreover, as illustrating the notion which was entertained regarding the origin of the disease at the period

---

[1] Dominicus Panarolus Romanus. 'Iatrologismorum seu Medicinalium Observationum Pentecostæ Quinque, &c.' Hanoviæ, 1654. See p. 146.

[2] Cornelius Stalpartius Vander Wiel. 'Observationum Rariarum Medic. Anatomic. Chirurgicarum Centuriæ posterioris, Pars prior, &c.' Leidæ, 1727. Observation 35. See p. 374.

in question. The case, indeed, is adduced by Vander Wiel as an example of the power which the imagination exerts over the body, and specially in the instance of pregnant women. In the year 1683, says the author, a boy, about 10 years of age, by name Bernardus, and born in the kingdom of Naples, was seen at the Hague. The hands and feet, legs and arms, of this boy were covered with rough scales; also the whole body, the head alone being unaffected. His maternal aunt, under whose care he was, accounted for the occurrence of the deformity of the skin by the mother, when washing linen at the shore, having seen in the river many scaly animals and shell fishes, by which her imagination had been so occupied, that, not long afterwards becoming pregnant, the fœtus acquired the character described. In this opinion Vander Wiel concurred; and he refers to other instances of a similar kind detailed by different authors. Those interested in the early history of ichthyosis should consult the writings of the physicians now named, as well as those referred to by Vander Wiel. In the treatise, 'De Medica Mirabili Historia,' of Marcellus Donatus,[1] who lived in the preceding century, some interesting allusions to skin affections of the same nature will be found. I must pass, however, to a brief notice of more recent accounts. Plenck,[2] of Vienna, the earliest to publish anything like a detailed cutaneous nosology, placed ichthyosis in the class of Squamæ, the seventh in order of his arrangement, following in his definition the description of the disease offered by Sauvage in his ' General Nosological Method,' which had appeared some years previously. By Willan, writing in 1798, ichthyosis was placed in the sixth of the eight classes into which he divided cutaneous diseases; and in the same order, Squamæ, it remained in the modification of Willan's arrangement adopted subsequently by Bateman. Alibert, in 1810, attempting to form his cutaneous nosography by grouping together diseases which presented distinct analogies, made a separate class, "Ichthyoses." Into this he admitted many varieties dependent on a fancied resemblance to different fishes, or the barks of different trees. Some among the more recent classificators of cutaneous diseases have apparently experienced much

---

[1] A physician of Mantua, died in 1600. His work, referred to above, was published at Mantua in 1586.

[2] ' Doctrina de Morbis Cutaneis.' 1783. See p. 89.

difficulty in assigning a proper place in their arrangements to ichthyosis. Thus, the late Dr. Anthony Todd Thomson, in his edition of the 'Practical Synopsis of Willan and Bateman,'[1] objecting to its being included, as these writers had done, in the order of Squamæ, placed ichthyosis under the head of Tubercula, though evidently with some degree of hesitation; for he observes: "notwithstanding the minuteness of the morbid papillæ, it certainly is more allied to the tubercula." Mr. Plumbe,[2] whose treatise was first published in London in 1824, includes ichthyosis, with lepra, psoriasis, and pityriasis, under the head of diseases marked by chronic inflammation of the vessels secreting the cuticle, producing morbid growth of this structure; constitutional causes or influence uncertain. Cazenave retains ichthyosis among the Squamæ; but his English editor, Dr. Burgess, regards the disease as being both misnamed and misplaced. "There is nothing," remarks Dr. Burgess, "scaly about it. The term warty disease would be much more appropriate than that of fish skin."[3] The German synonym for ichthyosis is Fischuppenkrankheit; and by Hebra, so highly esteemed as an authority on diseases of the skin, it is included along with pityriasis and psoriasis in his third class, that of scaly eruptions, "Die Shuppichten Hautausschläge," Efflorescentiæ Squamosæ.[4] On the other hand, Dr. Parkes has placed ichthyosis by itself, as a disease of doubtful position.[5] Rayer,[6] the well-known writer on cutaneous diseases, describes it under the head of Hypertrophies; and, still more recently, Dr. Neligan,[7] following Gustav Simon, also removes ichthyosis from the Squamæ, and includes it with molluscum and other disorders in a class of Hypertrophiæ. Other opinions might be

[1] See p. 377.
[2] 'A Practical Treatise on Diseases of the Skin.' By Samuel Plumbe, &c. See p. 330.
[3] 'Cazenave.' Translated by Dr. Burgess. See foot-note, p. 220.
[4] 'Diagnostik der Hautkrankheiten in tabellarischer Ordnung nach Dr. Hebra's Vorlesungen.' Von Dr. Benedict Schulz. Wien, 1845. See p. 36.
[5] 'Dr. Anthony Todd Thomson's Practical Treatise on Diseases affecting the Skin.' Edited by Dr. Parkes. See p. 347.
[6] 'Traité Théorique et Pratique des Maladies de la Peau,' tome iii, p. 614.
[7] 'A Practical Treatise on Diseases of the Skin.' Dublin, 1852. See p. 257.

quoted, but these statements will probably suffice to indicate the different views which exist in respect to the nature and proper classification of ichthyosis. Whence, then, arises this difference of opinion? My own observation of the disease has led me to regard it as essentially a scaly or squamous disorder, and therefore correctly associated with lepra and psoriasis; but this applies to what, by way of distinction, must be called the true form of ichthyosis, and to it alone; for—and in this is the explanation of the different views which have been expressed to be found—unfortunately, under the one head, Ichthyosis, cutaneous affections possessing no real resemblance have been included. There are two among the most recent writers upon diseases of the skin who have done much to clear away the confusion which has arisen from the cause just adverted to. These are Mr. Erasmus Wilson and M. Devergie, more especially the latter. Mr. Wilson[1] treats of ichthyosis under the general head of "Diseases affecting the Special Structure of the Skin;" Diseases of the sebiparous glands. He has noticed augmentation of secretion, and the opposite condition, diminution of secretion, which he denominates Xeroderma (from the Greek ξηρὸς, aridus, dry), simply dry skin, and then he describes a xeroderma ichthyoides, for which ichthyosis vera, true ichthyosis, is a synonym. Mr. Wilson, in the opening sentence of his account of this affection, accurately explains the origin of the great confusion in the writings of different authors. This, he says, arises "from the want of a distinction between two obvious forms which the disease is apt to present. In one of these, to which I have given the term xeroderma ichthyoides, and which may very properly be called ichthyosis vera, the epidermis is the seat of the morbid alteration; while in the other, which I have named ichthyosis sebacea, and which may also be denominated ichthyosis spuria, the morbid appearances are due to the presence of the sebaceous secretion, altered in its quantity and quality, and deposited on the surface of the skin." M. Devergie,[2] retaining this disease among the Squamæ—affections squammeuses, distinguishes three principal forms of ichthyosis. These are—Ichthyose blanche, Ichthyose brune, and Ichthyose porc-epic. The first of these is the true ichthy-

---

[1] 'On Diseases of the Skin.' Fourth edition. See p. 587.
[2] 'Traité Pratique des Maladies de la Peau,' p. 493. Deuxième edition.

osis, and is to be regarded as a different affection altogether from the remaining two. Of the white, or true ichthyosis, Devergie describes three varieties, distinct in themselves. One of these, which at first sight is scarcely appreciable, is named, "ichthyose blanche farineuse;" it is characterised by the skin presenting a farinaceous or mealy aspect, from which, when rubbed in different directions, a mealy powder is detached. In the second form of white ichthyosis, named "ichthyose écailleuse," the skin is covered with scales or epidermic laminæ, pearly in appearance (lames épidermiques nacrées), and possessing a size and arrangement which certainly give to the skin thus affected an appearance resembling the skin of fishes. It is, however, seldom that the whole surface of the body presents a similar aspect. The forearms, the legs, and, less frequently, the arms and thighs, are apt to exhibit these pearly scales. The third form of white ichthyosis occupies a position between those already described, the shades of difference, however, being very various. Of it, M. Devergie mentions two varieties—ichthyose nacrée serpentine, and ichthyose nacrée cyprine. The grand distinguishing feature of these three forms of white ichthyosis in their different degrees of pronunciation—in other words, the most important feature in the recognition of true ichthyosis—is the colourless aspect of the epidermal productions. In true ichthyosis the whole surface of the body is habitually more or less affected, not excepting the face. This general character of true ichthyosis is specially insisted upon by Devergie. He does not recognise what various authors have described under the name of local ichthyosis. True ichthyosis is always a general malady of the skin, not presenting itself in circumscribed patches, as psoriasis and lepra vulgaris do; it is always diffused; and when one member, in its whole extent or partially, is found affected in a more or less considerable degree the three other limbs will appear in a nearly similar condition. Such is a somewhat detailed account of the description of true ichthyosis offered by M. Devergie.[1] This is the affection with which clinical experience, more especially in the hospital, has made me familiar, and has afforded me the opportunity of corroborating the views and so establishing the accuracy of Devergie's descriptions. Before passing, however, to a brief consideration of the clinical experi-

[1] Loco citato, p. 495.

ence of true ichthyosis, I have to notice very shortly the other
affections of the skin included under the same name. These
are, in the division of M. Devergie, brown ichthyosis (ichthyose
brune), and porcupine disease (ichthyose porc-epic). Brown
ichthyosis has no real resemblance to the white or true ichthyosis. The epidermal production which distinguishes it is of a
greyish-brown colour; and, on passing the hand over the
affected surface, it is found to be hard like a wart, or even horn—
portions breaking off, or irregularly splitting, on any pressure
being applied. Unlike the true ichthyosis, this is not a general
disease; it is found occurring around the knees, over the popliteal space behind, in front of the ankle, at the elbows and wrists;
its most frequent situation by far is in the neighbourhood of
the knee, anteriorly and posteriorly. I have twice seen brown
ichthyosis, in a very well-marked form, between the leg and
foot, in front of the ankle. Like true ichthyosis, this affection
may occur in the earlier months of life. Generally speaking,
however, it becomes developed at a later period. Lastly, the
porcupine disease—ichthyose porc-epic. This affection, styled
by Mr. Erasmus Wilson ichthyosis sebacea spinosa, only differs
from the other form of sebaceous ichthyosis he describes, in the
shapes assumed by the hardened sebaceous matter when it has
become effused. Several well-known examples of this form of
ichthyosis are on record in recent times; and there can be
little doubt, from the descriptions of older writers, that some of
the instances observed by them were of this nature. In 1710
a Suffolk man was known under the name of the " Porcupine
Man," owing to the whole surface of his body, with the exception of the face, palms of the hands, and soles of the feet, presenting an appearance of short, hardened spines. The disease
appeared in this man two months after birth. He enjoyed fair
health, married, and had six children, who were all similarly
affected. Two brothers, of the name of Lambert, suffered from
the same disease. In this family, ichthyosis of the nature in
question was hereditary—appearing, however, only in the male
branches. These and other instances[1] are referred to in all
works on diseases of the skin. The beautifully-executed model
which I show, is illustrative of this disease as occurring in a

[1] See 'Medico-Chirurgical Transactions of London' (vol. ix, 1818) for Mr.
Martin's well-known " Case of Hereditary Ichthyosis," p. 52.

man 45 years of age, who enjoyed good health and suffered no inconvenience from his unseemly disorder. The disease appeared to be hereditary, but as in the case of the Lamberts, through the males, the females always escaping. This man had one child, happily a female, who was quite free from the disease. There appears to me no good reason for separating the brown ichthyosis from that form of the malady now described. Both are included by Mr. Wilson[1] under the head of Ichthyosis Sebacea; in the one the affection is localised, in the other it is more diffused; but evidently in both the essence of the disease consists in an increased as well as altered secretion of sebaceous matter. It is the sebiparous cutaneous glands which are primarily at fault. Neither is there any real distinction to be sought between the sebaceous ichthyosis when the hardened matter assumes the form of flattened plates, and when, on the other, its comparison to the quills of the porcupine more correctly distinguishes it. These are essentially the same disease—forms of ichthyosis spinosa, as Mr. Wilson has well named them. It is certainly to be regretted that a disease, or the two forms of a disease, bearing no resemblance whatever in their external characters to the appearance of a fish, should have been thus named, and for a lengthened period familiarly recognised; but this cause for regret will be in great measure removed, by the adoption of correct views in regard to the nature of the two different diseases included under the one name. It is altogether erroneous to say that the term ichthyosis, when used, is always misapplied. This, however, is the statement of Plumbe,[2] as well as of Dr. Burgess, in the passage already noticed. There is a cutaneous disease of general diffusion, characterised by the formation of altered epidermal scales, sometimes more correctly styled plates, which are colourless, or nearly so, and which on some parts of the affected surface bear the closest possible resemblance to the scales on the sides or back of certain fishes. In this disease it is the epidermis which is affected; the secreting glands of the skin are wholly uninvolved. There is no increase of sebaceous matter; on the contrary, the skin is unusually dry, and as a consequence of that alone, it is rough. This is the ichthyosis vera, true ichthyosis—the ichthyose blanche of Devergie. A short account of my clinical experience of this disease will con-

[1] Loco citato, p. 596.   [2] 'Diseases of the Skin, p. 331.'

9

clude these observations. Several instances of true ichthyosis
have fallen under my notice since I first became familiar with
its appearance in the Saint Louis Hospital at Paris, and chiefly
in the wards of M. Devergie. Of those observed in the Infirmary
I select two for more particular notice :

R. H—, æt. 15, bookbinder, a native of Edinburgh, entered the
Infirmary in January, 1857, suffering from a very severe attack of acute
bronchitis. A peculiar condition of the skin was immediately observed
to exist; it was very dry, and over the trunk, harsh. On the upper
and lower limbs the surface was much smoother though equally dry.
Epidermal scales, closely resembling in appearance, and more especially
in their relation to each other, the scales of a fish, were seen over the
limbs, particularly over the thighs and calves of the legs, also over the
whole of the lower part of the abdominal surface. The remarkable
smoothness of some parts of the affected skin allied it to the so-called
ichthyosis nitida; in others, the distinctly shining aspect of the scales
established the appropriateness of Alibert's appellation, ichthyose
nacrée. The skin of the face was very slightly affected. The morbid
condition of the surface had existed since infancy. Maternal grand-
father was stated to have the same disease. This lad had a very narrow
escape from death in his bronchitic attack. No diaphoretic remedy
had the very slightest effect. He did, however, recover, and thereafter
was treated for the cutaneous affection. He was undoubtedly benefited
by arsenic, and the continued use of the warm bath, more especially
when sulphur was added; but when the former remedy was omitted,
the disease, never altogether removed, returned; and lately I found him
quite as much affected with ichthyosis as before.

Upon this case I may remark, that, owing to the serious
aggravation of the chest inflammation caused by the cutaneous
disease, I was especially anxious, on the recovery of the lad
from the former, to adopt the treatment most likely to be
serviceable in removing the skin affection. Arsenic did
influence it, but only for a time; the disease returned. This
is a special character of ichthyosis; it is little amenable to
treatment. Devergie remarks, "Ichthyosis is generally an
incurable malady."[1]

In the second case recently under my care in the Infirmary,
the patient, a young boy of 14, who has had the disease nine
years, without any hereditary history, has been decidedly
benefited by the arsenic; but still the morbid condition
remains, and I believe will remain. In this boy the fishy scales
are tolerably well marked on both lower limbs, as distinctly

[1] Loco citato, p. 497.

above as below the knees. The warm bath, the use of the flesh-brush or a rough towel, and oleaginous applications, which may be considered as requisite adjuvants in treatment, have been employed in his case.

The late Dr. Anthony Todd Thomson, in his edition of 'Bateman's Synopsis,' mentions a case of ichthyosis as having been materially benefited by the internal use of a decoction of the rumex acutus. Dr. Parkes, again, in his edition of Dr. Thomson's own 'Treatise on Cutaneous Diseases,' refers to his successful employment of the rumex obtusifolius.[1] "If," remarks M. Devergie, "there be anything capable of effecting a cure, it is arsenic; but arsenic has failed in nearly all the instances in which it has been used." There is little risk of confounding true ichthyosis with any other cutaneous malady; but from the remaining scaly affections, for one or other of which it might possibly be taken, there are two characters which will readily distinguish it. First, as already insisted upon, its diffusion—ichthyosis is always diffused; secondly, the condition of integrity in which the subjacent skin is always found when the thickened and altered epidermal scales are removed. By both of these characters is ichthyosis to be distinguished from lepra or psoriasis and pityriasis, but especially by its general diffusion, from the latter—by the absence of any inflammatory indication, from the former.

In ichthyosis vera there is never any complaint of heat, itching, or uneasiness in the skin; nor, among the several instances of the affection which have fallen under my own notice, do I remember to have seen one person to whom the disease was more than a matter of curiosity. The existence of this form of ichthyosis in a marked degree may, however, prove serious in the way of aggravating, or at least complicating, other maladies. That the severity of the acute bronchitis in the first instance briefly related, was to a certain extent determined by the condition of the skin, there can, I think, be no reasonable doubt; while, unquestionably, the very harsh and dry cutaneous surface stood directly in the way of those febrifuge and specially diaphoretic remedies, upon whose beneficial operation in the treatment of that disease we are accustomed to place very considerable reliance.

[1] Page 349.

XI.

ON PARTIAL AND COMPLETE LOSS OF SIGHT IN DIABETES;

WITH A

NOTICE OF TWO CASES OF DIABETIC CATARACT.

(*Reprinted from the ' Edinburgh Medical Journal,' June,* 1861.)

AMONG the frequent, though by no means invariable, symptoms of advanced diabetes may be reckoned dimness of vision, amounting in some instances to complete loss of sight. By several of the more recent writers on this affection, the morbid phenomenon in question has been particularly noticed; while, as is now well known, a careful inquiry has determined its dependence, in several examples, on a special form of disease within the eye. Why failure of sight should occur in some cases of diabetes, and not in others which have reached the same stage, and why the experience of different observers on this point should vary very considerably, are questions which undoubtedly merit a careful consideration.[1] It is not, however, to this particular inquiry that I now desire to direct attention,

[1] Dr. Watt, Dr. Craigie, Dr. Prout, and Dr. Watson, among British writers, have noticed dimness of vision as a symptom of diabetes. In France two able writers have done so, MM. Bouchardat and Mialhe. On the other hand, M. Contour, whose experience of the disease cannot have been very limited, has never observed enfeebled sight (affaiblissement de la vue) among its attendant phenomena.

but briefly to the causes upon which dimness of vision or more decided loss of sight, when it does occur in diabetes, depends. One cause of defective vision in diabetes, and the first I shall notice, is cataract. This association had been at least casually observed by various writers[1] before the able and satisfactory elucidation of the subject by Mr. France, in the 'Ophthalmic Hospital Reports' for January, 1859, and more recently in 'Guy's Hospital Reports' for 1860. Among the former, Dr. Mackenzie,[2] the distinguished oculist of Glasgow, and Dr. Matthews Duncan,[3] of Edinburgh, had specially observed certain instances.[4] Mr. France has himself seen four cases, and from different sources has collected others, so as to raise the number to about twenty. To this list I am now able to add two cases which have recently fallen under my observation in the hospital, through the kindness of my colleague, Mr. Walker; both patients having, in the first instance, applied at the ophthalmic wards for advice in regard to their failure of sight. It is unnecessary to furnish minute details of these cases; the following summary of facts in each, from the more extended notes of my clinical clerk, Mr. Wilson Moore, will suffice. It is somewhat remarkable that both cases fell under observation at the same time:—   •

CASE 1.—Elizabeth R—, æt. 32, married, admitted February 1861, mother of two children. A maternal aunt died of diabetes. For nearly two years this patient has suffered from the same complaint. About three months after she first noticed the occurrence of excessive thirst, and the passage of an unusual amount of urine, her sight began to fail; it has gradually become more and more impaired, and for some months has been so bad that she has required to be led about. During last summer she suffered much from the occurrence of obstinate boils on different parts of the body. Latterly she has had cough, with purulent expectoration and frequent attacks of diarrhœa.

[1] See Valleix, 'Guide du Médecin Praticien,' tome iii, p. 552. 1850.
[2] 'Diseases of the Eye,' p. 747, under the head of "Remote and Predisposing Causes of Cataract." 1854.
[3] His translation of 'Braun on Puerperal Convulsions,' foot-note, p. 15. 1857.
[4] That, as Mr. France has conjectured, several other instances of diabetic cataract have been observed, cannot admit of any doubt. Lately, Dr. Cadenhead, of Aberdeen, informed me that he had seen, at all events, three such. Professor A. Von Graefe, of Berlin, regards their occurrence as far from rare.

On admission, she presents the marked aspect of a diabetic patient —greatly emaciated; skin very dry; much hair of head has fallen, it is now very thin; has double lenticular cataract, evidently symmetrically developed, and, from their colour and bulk, of soft consistence. The amount of urine passed in twenty-four hours varies from 180 to 220 ounces; of density 1·036, and highly saccharine. Physical signs of tubercular deposit exist in the apices of both lungs. The chest affection made rapid progress; signs of extensive softening and excavation in the pulmonary substance on the right side became developed; and the diarrhœa resisted all endeavours to check it. This poor woman died at the close of March. An examination of the body was made within thirty hours after death. Putrefaction had advanced very rapidly; so that a careful examination of the eyes, which Mr. Walker had proposed to make, was defeated. The lungs were the seat of extensive tubercular deposition; several cavities existed in the right. The pancreas was small.

The subject of this observation is still under my care in the Infirmary.

CASE 2.—Jane W—, æt. 37, married, admitted March, 1861. Has had four children. Has been suffering from diabetes for nearly eight months. During the last three months her sight has rapidly failed; that of the right eye became earliest affected. For a few weeks she observed that she could see best during the dusk; lately, however, she has lost sight entirely.

On admission, is thin and emaciated, with dry skin, constipated bowels, and much thirst. Urine has a density of 1·038 to 1·040; amount passed has not exceeded, on any occasion, 200 ounces in the twenty-four hours. Trommer's, the bismuth, and Liquor Potassæ tests show the presence of sugar in very characteristic degree. Has double lenticular soft cataract, precisely similar in appearance to that of the former patient.

Under treatment this patient has very considerably improved. Her strength has increased, and she has gained weight. The amount of urine is diminished to seventy ounces, and has been as low as fifty-five; the density is now uniformly 1·031. Her thirst is easily controlled. Animal food, gluten bread, Vichy water, a moderate allowance of sugar, and London porter, have constituted the dietary. Sensible benefit has resulted from the employment of the combined tinctures of the sesquichloride of iron and nux vomica. By doses of twenty drops of each, administered thrice daily, her thirst has been entirely removed.

In both of these cases the development of the cataracts occurred somewhat earlier in the progress of the general disease than has been observed in other instances; still, there can be no hesitation in concluding that the diminution or entire loss of sight dependent on opacity of the crystalline lens, when it does occur in diabetes, is a phenomenon of its advanced stage. Mr. France has pointed out—to which the cases now briefly related form no exception—that in every example the cataracts have been symmetrically developed on both sides, and have also been of the soft variety. For a further interesting and accurate account of the eye-disease, I must refer to Mr. France's last communication on the subject.[1]

The importance of the connection subsisting between cataract and diabetes is greatly increased by the results of certain experiments performed by an American physician, Dr. Weir Mitchell,[2] as well as those more recently instituted by Dr. B. Richardson, of London.[3] Dr. Mitchell determined that in the frog "the formation of a peculiar variety of cataract is one of the most curious and striking symptoms attendant upon the sugar poisoning;" while the investigations of Dr. Mitchell and Dr. Richardson have demonstrated that, in the instance of several of the lower animals, when sugar, in one way or other, in considerable amount is introduced into the system, the formation of lenticular cataract is the result.

But it is very apparent that all instances of defective vision in diabetes are not dependent on the formation of cataract. There is a diabetic amaurosis as well as a diabetic cataract. Without depreciating the difficulty of determining between these two affections in their early stages, even by a very careful examination of the eye—a difficulty which the introduction of the ophthalmoscope has greatly removed—there are particulars in the instances of diabetic amaurosis which have fallen under my own observation, serving to distinguish it from those cases in which the failure of sight is due to the morbid condition of the lens:—1. In the former, the dimness of vision has occurred at an earlier stage of the disease. 2. It has been accompanied by pain, or at least uneasiness, in the eyes; or by peculiar noises in the ears; or by general headache. 3. The failure of sight early noticed continued to exist, making very gradual advance; and in some instances, after being stationary for a time, lessened.

---

[1] "Additional Notes on Diabetic Cataract," 'Guy's Hospital Reports,' Third Series, vol. vi.

[2] 'The American Journal of the Medical Sciences,' January, 1860. "Production of Cataract in Frogs by the Administration of Sugar."

[3] 'Journal de Physiologie' for July, 1860.

I am disposed to think that these peculiarities, taken in connection with the careful inspection of the eyes themselves, will be found to establish the diagnosis; for, in the case of cataract— 1, the failure of sight is not an early phenomenon of the diabetic state; 2, impaired vision is not accompanied by ocular pain, and still less by pain in the head generally; 3, instead of making slow progress, the sight, once affected, never improves, but becomes rapidly worse; and, when so, the cataractous appearance will assuredly be marked.

In one case of diabetes which fell under my care about five years ago, and which terminated fatally by coma, the condition of enfeebled sight had existed for many months, without the least appearance of cataract; and in that instance, as well as another, seen since, severe headache and tinnitus aurium were not unfrequent symptoms. In such instances the nervous system generally must be held as being injuriously affected through the altered condition of the blood. Precisely similar symptoms occur in the progress of renal disease.

It is not necessary, I think, to ascribe the failure of sight, as M. Mialhe does, to a milky state of the blood (*latescence du Sang*), caused by the presence of what he styles his modified albumen, altering the transparency of the humours of the eye;[1] for, firstly, there is no distinct proof of the existence of such a substance in the blood of diabetes; and, secondly, the phenomenon in question is really best explained by the operation of the blood—altered, impoverished, or poisoned—on the retina itself. In the so-called Diabetes Insipidus, a failure of sight, if not of precisely the same nature, nevertheless closely allied to it, occurs; also in anæmia and chlorosis, and in various other affections.

Failure of sight, then, occurring in diabetes is not necessarily to be ascribed to the existence of cataract, but may be truly of the nature of amaurosis. I have thought it expedient to direct attention to this point, specially at the present time, when, through the interesting observations of Mr. France, and the important experiments of Dr. Mitchell and Dr. Richardson, the subject of diabetic blindness is being discussed.

[1] 'Chimie Appliquée à la Physiologie et à la Thérapeutique,' p. 164.

XII.

LEAD IMPREGNATION

AND ITS

CONNECTION WITH GOUT AND RHEUMATISM.

(*Reprinted from the 'Edinburgh Medical Journal,' August,* 1862.)

THE symptoms which manifest the injurious operation of lead upon the system have long been familiar to physicians, and have, more especially of late, been carefully studied. Epidemic Colic was described by Baillou and Riverius in the sixteenth, while in the succeeding century the same disease was with much accuracy delineated by Francis Citois, a physician of Poictou. The observations of Dr., afterwards Sir George Baker,[1] of Drs. Warren, Hardy, and John Hunter, besides other English physicians in the eighteenth century, satisfactorily determined that the peculiar form of colic noticed by the earlier writers, as well as the endemic disorder of Devonshire and Derbyshire, of Surinam, and other localities, was due to the same general cause, namely, the introduction of lead into the system. Since that time, under the names of Lead Colic, Saturnine or Painter's Colic, Colica Pictonum, and various other less distinctive

---

[1] 'An Essay Concerning the Cause of the Endemial Colic of Devonshire,' 8vo., London, 1767. Of this inquiry it has been truly remarked that it presents "one of the best examples modern times have afforded of the method to be pursued in medical inquiries, and constitutes a model for all who are labouring to extend the boundaries of medical science."—Dr. Munk's 'Roll of the Royal College of Physicians of London,' vol. ii.

appellations, the severe abdominal pain, usually the earliest in its appearance of the characteristic symptoms of lead impregnation, has been known and described. From a very early period, likewise, the peculiar and interesting form of local paralysis which occurs in connection with, for the most part succeeding, the colic had been noticed; the loss of power over one or both hands is well represented by Citois, for example, in the following words:—Manibus incurvis, et suo pondere pendulis, nec nisi arte ad os et cæteras supernas partes sublatis." More recent observation of lead impregnation has shown, that the nervous system in this disorder is apt to be affected in two, though not in two separate and distinct ways; firstly, the nerves in particular parts of the body suffer; and, secondly, the nervous centres themselves become affected; the latter event occurs only in the severer forms of the disease, and, succeeding the paralysis, affords evidence of the contamination being more than usually powerful; this is shown in general convulsions attended by loss of consciousness. A very important corroborative proof of such symptoms as those now mentioned being due to lead impregnation, was first pointed out by Dr. Burton—namely, a blue or bluish line seen along the free margin of the gums, but absent where a tooth or stump is wanting. This blue colour Mr. Tomes has proved to result from a chemical action exerted by the lead which has entered the system upon the tartar of the teeth. In addition to these particulars of interest and importance relating to the diagnosis and pathology of lead impregnation, Dr. Garrod, first in 1854,[1] and again more fully in 1859,[2] has satisfactorily demonstrated that lead exerts a remarkable influence as a predisposing cause of gout. The general characters of lead impregnation are very well exhibited in the two cases, a short notice of which succeeds, while the relation of this disorder to gout is in them also very strikingly evidenced. These cases have occurred in the ordinary course of hospital experience, and are among several of the same nature of which I have preserved the record. I cannot confirm the statement made by a very eminent authority, Dr. Christison, that " poisoning from protracted exposure to lead is a very rare occurrence in Edin-

---

[1] 'Medico-Chirurgical Transactions,' vol. xxxvii, 1854, p. 181.

[2] 'The Nature and Treatment of Gout and Rheumatic Gout,' p. 281. London, 1859.

burgh,"[1] any more than my hospital experience leads me to
regard "gout as occurring very rarely." That both disorders
are more frequently met with in the hospitals of London than
in our city does not admit of doubt, and, in explanation of this
circumstance, reasons altogether satisfactory have been afforded ;
but, on the other hand, neither of them can, according to my
own experience, be looked upon as at the present time of so
unfrequent occurrence as the observations of Dr. Christison,
just quoted, would tend to imply.

CASE I.[2]—W. B—, æt. 30, a house-painter, admitted to Ward V.,
6th May, 1862. Has followed the occupation of painter since he was
thirteen, always mixing his own colours. For many years his habits
have been intemperate. He has consumed porter and ale freely, but
has very rarely indulged in whisky.

About four years ago, suffered for the first time from colic. This
attack was slight; but in the course of twelve months was succeeded by
a second, much more severe, and attended by great constipation. Since
then he has suffered repeated attacks of colic, till thirteen months ago,
when the earliest indications of paralysis appeared; the fingers of the
right hand being first affected. The paralysis gradually increased, and,
ten months ago, both hands were disabled. During this time he has
had several severe convulsive seizures, attended by complete loss of
consciousness. *On admission*, the patient presents a well-marked
example of wrist-drop in both arms, and is quite unable to extend the
hands. He can flex the latter, but not firmly or completely. The
muscles of the upper-arm and shoulder are quite unaffected; the exten-
sors of the fore-arm are evidently considerably wasted, and the muscles
of both thumbs still more so. There is a good deal of tremulousness
visible when movements of the upper limbs are made. There is no loss
of power in the inferior extremities, and the patient voids water without
any difficulty. The amount of urine is considerable; it is of pale colour,
acid reaction, having a density of 1·010, with a very faint trace of
albumen. The bowels are now no longer confined. A distinct blue
line exists along the free margin of the gums, and the teeth are much
discoloured. Was ordered as follows :—

℞ Potassii Iodidi, ʒij.
Aquæ Destillatæ, ℥xij.—*Solve.*
Sign. Sumat cochlearia duo ampla bis indies.

May 10th.—Complains of severe pain in the ball of the great toe of
right foot, and also in the right ankle-joint. The former is considerably
swollen and tender; the cutaneous surface is also reddened. Patient
states that he has suffered greatly from pains in different joints, and that

[1] Dr. Garrod on ' Gout,' p. 284.
[2] Reported by Mr. Thomas Walker, B.A., clinical clerk.

on three former occasions the joint of the right great toe now affected has become of a bright red colour, much swollen, and exquisitely painful.

In addition to the iodide of potassium, the following prescription was ordered:

> ℞ Extracti Nucis Vomicæ, Extracti Colchici Acetici, ā ā, gr. vj.
> Alöini, Lupulinæ, Extracti Hyoscyami, ā ā, gr. xij.—M.
> Fiat massa in pilulas æquales duodecim dividenda.
> *Sign.* Una mane et vespere quotidie sumenda.

To have white fish and fowl, in addition to the common diet of hospital, withdrawing the boiled beef.

14th.—An improvement in the power of extending the hands, especially the left, has been noticed during the last few days. Gouty affection of foot has almost entirely disappeared. There exists very evidently, however, a chronic enlargement of this articulation, as well as of the corresponding one of the left foot, in which he also admits he has not unfrequently experienced severe pain. Is to-day suffering from a feverish attack. Ordered to keep bed, and omit the medicines prescribed.

19th.—Quite recovered from the febrile indisposition. Former treatment resumed.

From this date to 1st June continued to progress favorably. On the latter day was again feverish, and complained of palpitation, with pain, in the region of the heart. On auscultation, a bruit, following rather than accompanying the ventricular systole, was audible, most distinctly heard near the xiphoid cartilage. Pulse 120; pains felt in joints of arms and legs; tongue coated; breath foul. The iodide of potassium and pills were again omitted, and, after the operation of a purgative, the following mixture was commenced:

> ℞ Potassæ Nitratis, ʒij.
> Potassæ Acetatis, ʒvj.
> Aquæ, ʒviij.—*Solve.*
> *Sign.* Sumat cochleare magnum ex aquæ cyatho sextâ quâque horâ.

June 3rd.—Feverishness continuing. Bruit audible as before.

5th.—Heat of skin and frequency of pulse somewhat diminished. Bruit very distinct, heard along the whole sternum, but most clearly a little to the left of the xiphoid cartilage. Precordial pain recurs from time to time. Was dry-cupped to-day.

From this date to the 10th was still feverish. Occasionally slight delirium occurred by night. On two or three occasions manifested a tendency to faint, becoming pale, and with the pulse at the wrist very feeble. The urine more albuminous.

11th.—Decidedly improved. Bruit over heart less distinct. The abnormal sound has now more the character of slight roughness with the first sound. Pulse 108.

14th.—Iodide of potassium restored in three-grain doses thrice daily. Galvanism to muscles of forearm for a few minutes daily.

18th.—Completely recovered from arthritic attack. Ordered as follows:

> ℞ Extracti Colchici Acetici, gr. iv.
> Extracti Nucis Vomicæ, gr. vj.
> Ferri et Quinæ Citratis, gr. xviij.
> Extracti Gentianæ, q.s.—M.

Fiat massa in pilulas æquales duodecim dividenda; quarum sumat unam mane et vespere quotidie.

23rd.—Very rapid improvement in the condition of the wrists. Can now extend the hands, though not as yet perfectly. A small blistered surface has been produced over the back of both wrists, and to it half a grain of strychnine applied a few times.

July 1st.—Making rapid progress. Believes himself quite able to resume his employment, and is very anxious to do so. No longer complains of articular or muscular pains. Appetite good. Urine of higher colour, density 1·012, still very faintly coagulable. Rhythm, sounds, and action of heart normal. Pulse 74.

In this case we have the usual succession of the phenomena indicative of lead impregnation—the attacks of colic gradually increasing in severity, then the development of the characteristic form of local paralysis, speedily followed by the epileptic seizures, which emphatically proclaim its gravity; finally, the patient, after repeatedly suffering from gout in the ball of the great toe of right foot, becomes, while under our observation, the subject of an acute arthritic attack, in which the pericardium is evidently involved.

CASE 2.—J. H—, æt. 37, admitted to Ward V., June 8th, 1862. Has worked as a house-painter for more than nineteen years, generally mixing his own colours. For a lengthened period has suffered from pains in the belly, attended by sluggishness of the bowels. Three weeks ago these symptoms increased so much as to compel him to quit his work. Nausea and vomiting occurred about the same time. Has had no passage from the bowels for eight days. The belly is now considerably distended and hard. He suffers much pain, bending forwards and doubling himself up in the endeavour to obtain its mitigation. Has also pains, which he calls rheumatic, in the head, shoulders, and limbs. The patient states that, during the last eight or nine years he has had three distinct attacks of severe pain, attended by much swelling and redness, in the ball of the great toe of right foot. He has been accustomed for a lengthened period to drink pretty freely; and, while whisky has been his ordinary beverage, he admits that he has partaken more commonly than his fellows of both porter and ales. The gums present an unusually distinct blue line. There is no paralysis, and no muscular atrophy. He has never had any fits.

Ordered a warm bath, and thereafter to take as follows:

> ℞ Tincturæ Opii, ♏xv.
>> Olei Ricini, ʒvj.
>> Aquæ Cinnamomi, ʒij.—M.
>> Fiat haustus: statim sumendus.

June 9th.—Bowels have been moved. Colicky pain, however, continues. The draught to be repeated. Has passed forty-five ounces of urine in the twenty-four hours. It is of normal colour, acid reaction, and of density 1·022, not coagulable.

10th.—Was ordered the iodide of potassium in ten-grain doses twice daily.

During the next few days the abdominal pain gradually diminished. The castor-oil was repeated daily, or on every alternate day.

16th.—Was discharged to-day at his own request, the pain in the belly having entirely ceased, but still feeling rheumatism pains. Advised to continue the use of the iodide of potassium for some time, but in smaller doses.   .

This case, much less severe in its nature than that of W. B—, being in fact one of simple lead colic without paralysis, still illustrates equally with his the association of lead impregnation and gout, and I beg to remark in connection with it, that in all its particulars it may be regarded as an apt example of cases which, to the number of nearly a dozen, have fallen under my observation during the last seven years—cases of lead colic, the sufferers from which have always complained of pains either in the limbs generally or in particular joints. Lately, I have seen a young man, J. M—, house-painter by occupation, and presenting the characteristic blue gingival line, who passed, three years ago, through a very severe attack of rheumatic endo-pericarditis, specially interesting in this particular, that, although there had been much complaint of flying pains through the limbs for many weeks before the true febrile accession occurred, the inflammation first attacked the heart, and, for several days before a single joint had suffered, there were the signs of effusion into the pericardium, as well as those of implication of the mitral valve. The patient now presents the undoubted signs of mitral insufficiency, and some among the less reliable indications of an adherent pericardium.

I have already observed that it is to Dr. Garrod we are indebted for pointing out the really intimate connection which subsists between lead impregnation and gout. The curious fact had struck him that a very large proportion, at least one in four of the gouty patients who had come under his care in University College Hospital, had at some period of their lives been affected with lead poisoning, and for the most part followed the occupations of plumbers and painters. Keeping this subject prominently before his mind since 1854, the date of his earlier observation, Dr. Garrod has satisfied himself that persons following the trades referred to, are very frequently attacked with gout, much more so than other workmen in the same station of life.[1] In directing attention to this interesting inquiry Dr. Garrod has not lost sight of the bearing which other predisposing causes of gout may have in connection with lead impregnation, and chiefly the free use of fermented liquors. I am disposed to regard the difference in this respect which exists between the workmen in the south and in Edinburgh as of very great importance in determining the varied experience which physicians have had. Of the powerful predisposing influence exerted by fermented liquors there cannot exist any doubt, and it is equally well-ascertained that indulgence in distilled liquors does not create anything like the same proclivity to gout. In Edinburgh, whisky is the liquor ordinarily indulged in by the intemperate of the class from which our hospital patients are derived. Accordingly, while we see the injurious effects of such habits in the production of diseases of the nervous system, and specially in the frequency of delirium tremens, of hepatic, renal, and other visceral disorders, it is beyond doubt that gout is with us much less common than in the London hospitals, though, as I have already remarked, by no means so unfrequent in its occurrence as many have supposed. It will probably, I believe, be found that the association of lead impregnation with indulgence in fermented liquors gives a very strong predisposition to gout; and that, in the case of painters, those most subject to be injuriously affected by lead, the latter part of the required predisposition holds good, may, I venture to think, be true in London, for unquestionably as a class in Edinburgh they are not distinguished by sobriety. It is interesting to observe that in the two instances of lead impregnation with gout which I have

[1] See his 'Treatise on Gout,' p. 282.

10

now recorded, the patients, contrary to what ordinarily obtains
with us, had indulged in *fermented* drinks; both were intemperate men; one had used porter and ales alone, the other,
while usually taking whisky, had consumed more of the
former than his comrades.   The ale and porter drinker, though
the younger man, has suffered more severely from gout than
the consumer of distilled liquor as well as fermented drinks;
and when lead impregnation in him was established, it presented itself in a form far more serious and unequivocal than
in the latter.   I cannot see that the greater attention to ablution after work, which has been assigned as a reason for the
Edinburgh painters suffering less frequently from lead impregnation than the like artificers in London—the former living
nearer their homes in most instances, and readily returning
from work to meals—can adequately explain the difference
which has been supposed to exist in respect to the frequency of
the disorder in the two cities.   In the Government works the
greatest possible attention has been paid to ablution, thereby,
however, nothing like immunity from lead impregnation has
been attained.   But, as already observed, I conceive the
disorder to be of far more common occurrence in Edinburgh
than has been stated.

Some very interesting observations have been made by Dr.
Garrod, with the view of determining the particular manner in
which lead acts as a predisposing cause of gout.   He has carefully examined the condition of the blood and urine of patients
under the influence of the saturnine poison; and he has likewise ascertained the effect which lead, when administered
medicinally, has upon the secretion of uric acid.   The important results generally obtained are now well known to the
profession : the blood has been found to be rich in uric acid,
or, at all events, abnormally charged with it, while this
ingredient has been correspondingly deficient in the urine.
Relying on the accuracy of Dr. Garrod's experiments, in
neither of the cases detailed did I subject the blood to examination for uric acid, but in both it was ascertained that the
amount of uric acid discharged from the system was very
greatly diminished.   In the case of W. B— the urine was
carefully examined by Dr. Murray Thomson on two occasions :
the first within a day or two after the patient's admission to

the infirmary—he was then passing upwards of four pints in
the twenty-four hours, and the amount of uric acid per pint
was found to be 0·56 grain. On the subsequent examination,
the flow of urine having increased, and a marked improvement
in the symptoms of the patient having occurred, the amount of
uric acid in the pint was determined to be 1·63 grain, or nearly
three times as much as on the former analysis. In the case
of the second patient, the sufferer from lead colic without
paralysis, the urine was also examined by Dr. Murray Thomson.
The whole quantity passed in twenty-four hours being forty-
five ounces, yielded 2·80 grains of uric acid. One or two other
particulars in respect to the urine in these cases call for remark.
In the second case, though the amount of uric acid was greatly
deficient, the density of the urine was as high as 1.022, the
average amount of urea being excreted. Thus we have a proof
of the lead impregnation interfering with the uric-acid excreting
function of the kidneys, and with it alone, as well as of the fact
that the elimination of uric acid by these organs may be at
fault, while the integrity of the urea excretion remains unaffected. In the case of W. B— the urine has been of low
density, and continues so; it is further very slightly coagulable;
and although no microscopic element of importance has been
detected, these are untoward indications, which must affect the
prognosis we now entertain, seeing that with gout a particular
form of renal disorder is very intimately connected, which form
is likely to show itself at an early period by just such changes
in the urine as those now noted. As respects the operation of
lead taken medicinally on the system, Dr. Garrod has found
that by it the amount of uric acid in the urine is decidedly
reduced. Reference has already been made to a case of acute
rheumatism with endo-pericarditis, and resulting in valvular
disease. Its subject, a young painter, was of regular and sober
habits, but for some time before his severe illness had been
suffering from derangement of the stomach and bowels, and
from articular pains. That the partial lead impregnation by
which he was affected, played a part in predisposing him to the
rheumatic seizure is, I am disposed to think, not unlikely, for
I can call to remembrance two other cases in all essential
particulars similar; and for several years, before, indeed, I had
become aware of Dr. Garrod's valuable observations and ex-

periments, I had noticed the invariable occurrence of severe
articular and muscular pains in all subjects suffering from lead
impregnation whom I had had the opportunity of seeing. The
fact appears to me significant in this and other cases of the
same kind, that there had been no predisposition to gout
acquired by indulgence in fermented drinks : had it been otherwise, then I submit as likely that gout and not rheumatism
would have been the general disorder which followed.

I conclude with a single observation in respect to treatment.
In these cases, as in several others, I have employed the iodide
of potassium, as originally proposed and strongly recommended
by M. Melsens. The urine was very carefully tested by Dr.
Murray Thomson both before and after the administration of
the remedy in the former case, and lead was not discovered.
Granted that the kidneys are instrumental in effecting the
removal of the poison, and that under the operation of such a
remedy as the iodide of potassium its discharge is quickened
—facts established by the observations of Dr. Fletcher of
Dublin,[1] and those of Drs. Sieveking, Malherbe, Œltingen, and
Dr. Parkes[2]—still the efficiency of the cutaneous surface as
the more powerful emunctory, in some cases at least, must not
be lost sight of. This is probably more likely to hold true in
those instances in which the warm bath has constituted a
special part of treatment, and in such as, like W. B—, suffer
from some renal affection which may antagonise the removal of
the lead by the latter channel. The employment of colchicum
and iron in such cases as the former, and the judicious use of
galvanism in all cases of saturnine paralysis have much to
recommend them.

[1] 'Dublin Medical Press,' January, 1848.
[2] Dr. Parkes on the 'Composition of the Urine,' p. 164.

XIII.

ON CHYLOUS URINE.

(*Reprinted from the 'Edinburgh Medical Journal,' August,* 1862.)

By "chylous urine" is understood urine which presents a white or milky appearance, and undergoes a more or less decided spontaneous coagulation. Other terms have been employed to distinguish it. By Dr. Prout such urine was styled chylo-serous, by Dr. Willis oleo-albuminous; it is the "urine albumino-graisseuse et laiteuse" of Rayer and other French writers. Of rare occurrence in our own and other temperate climates, the disorder of which it is the striking characteristic, is by no means unfrequent in certain countries, particularly in the West India Islands among the native population, in Brazil, and in the island of Mauritius. With the exception of an interesting case recorded by Dr. Priestley, I am not aware of any instance of chylous urine observed of late years in Edinburgh, and during a lengthened period the example which has fallen under my own notice is, I believe, the only one which has been seen in the Royal Infirmary.

CASE.—T. R—, born on the 5th of January, 1834, at Meerut in the East Indies. Arrived in Scotland in 1838, and has continued ever since to reside in this country. Since 1847 has followed the occupation of a shoemaker. Till 1850 enjoyed good health, but in that year became subject to derangement of the stomach and bowels, and began to suffer very frequently from severe headaches. Shortly after this he acquired great irregularity in his habits, taking whisky to excess, being often drunk, and in consequence much exposed to cold and wet. In 1855 had a long-continued attack of gonorrhœa, and thereafter suffered greatly from weakness in the back and limbs. After the gonorrhœa, he first observed the urine to be altered in colour, usually white in appearance, though passed without any pain or uneasiness. Such continued to be the character of the urine till June, 1857, when it became much thicker, having at times the consistence of curds when it was passed. This thickness of the urine lasted for a few days together, and was again succeeded by a discharge of the white and thin urine: when the thick water was voided there was always more or less of pain, and frequently very great suffering. In June, 1857, he again contracted gonorrhœa, and in the following month had an inflammation in the left eye. During this year he frequently noticed that the urine after standing a short time became quite firm. In January, 1858, states that on one occasion he suffered from retention of urine for several hours, but that the attack was relieved by the passage of a dense substance very similar in size and appearance to an oyster. During 1859 and the two following years his habits have been somewhat steadier, and he has suffered less pain in the back, and only occasionally from uneasiness or difficulty in voiding urine. Came to Edinburgh in December 1861, and commenced work, but owing to general weakness had soon to abandon it. It was at this time that he was seen by my friend Mr. Traquair, and recommended to apply for admission to the Infirmary. The patient is short in stature, and has a somewhat sallow and unhealthy appearance. There is no emaciation, but the muscular development of body and limbs is feeble. Complains of a nearly constant sense of weight and often of dull pain in the lumbar region. This is relieved rather than aggravated by pressure. The appetite is good, tongue clean, pulse normal, skin rather dry; suffers from thirst, and generally has confined bowels.

The patient continued under observation in the Infirmary for several weeks, during which time the appearance of the urine varied very greatly, and frequently from day to day. At one time there was scarcely more than an opalescence, at another the urine was very thick and milky, but whether slightly or highly chylous, always rendered clear upon being treated with sulphuric ether. After exposure for a short time in glass vessels, a whitish sediment, varying in amount in different specimens, but at no time very copious, was deposited. Different specimens of urine were subjected to careful chemical analysis, and, as has previously happened in similar cases, with very different results as respects the amount of fatty matters present. Dr. Murray Thomson found in one sample the amount of fat per 1000 grains to be 2·075, and in another only 0·76 was discovered; both were the urines of the forenoon, passed shortly after the hospital morning meal of tea and bread. Mr. Arthur Gamgee found in one specimen of very milky urine the amount of fat as high as 10·32 in 1000 parts. The following is the result of a more detailed analysis by the same gentleman; the sample of urine in this instance was by no means so chylous in appearance as that portion which rendered the former result:—

Quantity of urine passed in twenty-four hours . 41 ounces.
Specific gravity 1020; reaction, acid,

Water in 1000 parts	965·90
Urea	10·15
Uric acid and vesical mucus . .	1·52
Animal extractive, and ammonical salts	6·02
Albumen	1·70 } 34·10
Fat	2·00
Fixed alkaline and earthy salts . .	12·71

On the application of heat, and on the addition of nitric acid or of nitro-hydrochloric acid to this patient's urine, a very partial coagulation always occurred; the degree varied considerably in different specimens and on different days, but was never great. Microscopic examination revealed the presence of blood corpuscles, few in number, and of fatty matter in large amount, the latter always in the condition of so-called molecular division. On one or two occasions my house-physician, Dr. James Grant, called attention to the presence of a very few oil globules; such were always easily produced by the previous addition to the urine of a few drops of sulphuric ether.[1] Besides these ingredients there existed a good deal of bladder epithelium, and in nearly every specimen examined a number of distinct fibres. The latter abounded in such urine as after standing for a short time exhibited small coagula, sometimes coloured pink, at other times colourless; consisting of the spontaneously coagulable ingredient in chylous urine, namely, fibrine. Casts of the renal tubules were never found. Only on one occasion while the patient was under our observation did the urine acquire, after standing a couple of hours, in part the consistence of "blancmanger."

In the case of this patient, as of others previously described by different observers, the chylous condition of the urine could be readily increased or diminished at will. Rest operated very strongly in determining a diminution of the fat and albumen, while a brisk walk, or even moving about in the ward, on the other hand, as powerfully increased both. The patient maintained that stimulants lessened the milky appearance of the urine, but, with the exception of a limited allowance of gin, under which the urine was for several days clearer, we determined that they really increased it. Many remedies were administered, but with very little benefit. Gallic acid, which Dr. Bence Jones has found most useful, failed to effect any change; the salts of iron seemed more serviceable, particularly the persesqui-nitrate. A proper regulation of diet I consider

[1] Simon found oil globules in chylous urine, but the observation has hitherto scarcely been confirmed. See 'The Microscope in Medicine,' by Dr. Lionel Beale, p. 314.

to be of most consequence; for although an increase of the
chylous condition of the urine was observable after partaking
of all kinds of food and after every meal, even when rest had
been previously indulged in for a considerable time, yet the use
of such articles of diet as caused a feeling of indigestion, speedily
and seriously increased the morbid state of the urine.

In this patient's case there is no reason to apprehend the
existence of organic renal disease, such as occurred in the
instance recorded by Dr. Priestley.[1]

The affection is undoubtedly an obscure one. This much
may be considered as ascertained, that in all cases of chylous
urine, occurring of course to a much greater extent in some
than in others, the abnormal constituents of that fluid, the fatty
matter, the albumen,[2] and fibrine with blood globules, when
they occur, are diverted from their proper channel and being
removed at the kidneys—whether owing to change in the lymphatics of these organs, or in their capillaries, is not known—
prevent the due nutrition of the system, to which they are
properly subservient. The debility and cachectic appearance
soon manifested by some sufferers, and the look of indifferent
health which before long all more or less acquire, confirm this
view. Dr. Prout[3] has in our own country had by far the
largest experience of this peculiar disorder, and by him and
Dr. Bence Jones[4] the subject has been carefully investigated.
On the Continent, the most extended inquiry regarding it has
been made by M. Rayer.[5] From time to time individual cases
are being placed on record; of one such a very interesting and
detailed account has lately been given by Dr. Beale.[6] I may
mention that the patient whose case I have related is at present
engaged in his old occupation, and is freer from pain and inconvenience than for some time past.

[1] 'Edinburgh Medical Journal,' p. 945, 1856; and 'Medical Times and
Gazette,' April 18th, 1857.

[2] Probably in the condition of the peptone of Lehmann, or albuminose of
Mialhe.—(See Parkes on the ' Urine,' p. 300.)

[3] 'On Stomach and Renal Diseases,' p. 116, fourth edition.

[4] 'Medico-Chirurgical Transactions,' 1850; and ' Philosophical Transactions of London,' p. 651, vol. cxl.

[5] ' Traité des Maladies des Reins,' vol. iii; ' Hæmorrhagies Rénales Essentielles (endemique),' p. 373.

[6] ' Archives of Medicine,' p. 10, vol. i.

XIV.

MALIGNANT DISEASE OF THE ŒSOPHAGUS

SUCCEEDED BY

SUDDEN PERICARDITIS, AND ULTIMATELY BY PNEUMO-PERICARDIUM WITH EFFUSION.

(Reprinted from the ' Edinburgh Medical Journal,' October, 1862.)

SYSTEMATIC writers on diseases of the heart have, for the most part, acknowledged three different ways in which an accumulation of air in the inflamed pericardial sac may be determined. 1st. Gas may be the direct product of the irritated membrane itself. It is admitted that occasionally air is produced in the cavities of the pleura and peritoneum when these are the seat of inflammatory action, and if so, there can be no reason why the same formation, or pneumatosis, should not occur within the pericardium. Dr. Stokes has recorded a case of this nature,[1] to which, in connection with a brief discussion of the physical signs of pneumo-pericardium, I shall again allude.

2nd. Gas may result from the decomposition of fluid within the pericardium. Laënnec[2] and others have not only pointed out the physical signs which indicate this lesion, but—the former more particularly—have in all probability greatly exaggerated the frequency of its occurrence. The effusion of air

[1] ' Diseases of the Heart and Aorta,' p. 21.
[2] ' Traité de l'Auscultation Médiate.'—" Du Pneumo-Pericarde."

and fluid into the pericardium was, in the opinion of Laënnec, a phenomenon likely to occur in the last stage of all diseases, and its existence he was wont to determine both by percussion and auscultation. "L'épanchement liquide et aëriforme à la fois du péricarde peut avoir lieu dans l'agonie de toutes les maladies. Il m'est arrivé quelquefois de l'annoncer à une résonnance plus claire du bas du sternum, survenue depuis peu de jours, ou à un bruit de fluctuation déterminé par les battements du cœur et par les inspirations fortes." In a case recorded by M. Bricheteau—to which reference will be found in Bouillaud's work (Traité des Maladies du Cœur), as well as in a note by Andral to his edition of Laënnec's treatise, and which is also noticed by Dr. Stokes and Dr. Walshe—the diagnosis of air as well as fluid existing in the pericardium was made during the life of the patient, chiefly from the presence of a peculiar sound with the heart's action, compared by Bricheteau to that produced by a water-wheel (l'eau agitée par la roue d'un moulin), while on examination after death the pericardium was found occupied by a purulent fluid of very fetid character, air escaping with a whistling sound when the sac was opened.

3rd. Gas may reach the pericardium from a distance through perforation, and this again may be the result of direct injury or of disease. Further, in such circumstances the source of the air may be various. A remarkable case is mentioned by Dr. Walshe in which a communication was established between the œsophagus and pericardium, in an attempt to swallow a long blunt instrument, a juggler's knife—the case terminated fatally. The physical signs in this instance, to which I shall refer, were of great interest and clearly established by Dr. Walshe.[1] A case of traumatic pneumo-pericardium, unattended by inflammation and resulting in complete recovery, is given by Dr. Flint, to whom it was related by Dr. Knapp of Louisville. The patient was stabbed with a knife, which penetrated the pleural cavity and perforated slightly the pericardium.[2] After the operation of paracentesis pericardii and injection of iodine, physical signs precisely similar to those met with in traumatic cases have been discovered. Such resulted in the memorable

---

[1] 'Diseases of the Heart,' pp. 46 and 271.
[2] Flint on 'Diseases of the Heart,' p. 357.

instance recorded by M. Aran, under the title, "Pericardite avec épanchement, traitée avec succès par la ponction et l'injection iodée,"[1] Of communication established between the pericardium and neighbouring organs through the progress of disease, and permitting the entrance of air into the cavity of the former, cases have been already recorded by different writers. Dr. Graves, in his 'Clinical Medicine,' has furnished a remarkable example of communication by fistulous opening between the stomach and an hepatic abscess on the one hand, and the pericardium on the other. Dr. M'Dowel exhibited to the Pathological Society of Dublin the morbid appearances in a case of communication established between a cavity in the left lung and the pericardium.[2]

When the close anatomical relationship of the œsophagus to the pericardium—the former lying in the posterior mediastinum in contiguity with the posterior portion of the pericardium for nearly two inches—is held in remembrance, it will be seen how, in their conditions of disease, likewise, the one is very apt to influence the other. The pressure exerted on the œsophagus by a distended pericardium, may unquestionably determine dysphagia, a symptom of pericarditis, which, though recognised by Testa, has only been duly insisted upon by Dr. Stokes, by whom, however, it is regarded as less a mechanical than a vital effect of pericarditis. The case I am now to record is one which illustrates the intimate connection to which reference has been made—disease of a cancerous nature, primarily affecting the œsophagus, subsequently involved adjacent organs, in particular giving rise to pericarditis with effusion, and ultimately, by perforation to pneumo-pericardium.

CASE.—Mrs. W—, æt. 43,[3] mother of seven children, admitted to Ward XIII, 29th July, 1862. She had for several months previously been under the care of Dr. Hislop, of North Berwick, from whom, at the time of her admission, I received the following brief account:—"She had been suffering from increasing difficulty in swallowing, at first considered to arise from spasm in the muscles of the œsophagus—

[1] 'Bulletin de l'Académie de Médecine,' Séance du 6 Novembre, 1855. See also Trousseau, 'Clinique Medicale de l'Hôtel Dieu de Paris,' p. 720, vol. i.

[2] For both cases, see also Dr. Stokes's work, pp. 23, 25.

[3] Report subsequent to patient's entering the Hospital, furnished by Dr. James Grant.

an opinion which was strengthened by the relief she experienced after passing the probang on several occasions. A month or more ago, in attempting to pass the probang much greater difficulty was experienced, and its use was finally desisted from. She suffered much about the same time from vomiting, and once brought up some blood with mucus." Dr. Hislop added, " From the pain she feels in the back, the increasing difficulty in deglutition, and the general features of the case, I fear that the morbid deposit is of a malignant character. I have for some time been doing nothing but supporting the system."

State on admission.—Patient presents an anxious expression of countenance, is very anæmic, without history of hæmorrhage or renal disease. No albuminuria. As far as can be determined, the only cause for her present condition is defective alimentation, on account of dysphagia, which, coming on gradually, had existed more or less for nearly two years. She has almost constant vomiting, or rather there occurs immediate rejection of the food before it has reached the stomach. Has little or no pain. On careful examination of the chest, no abnormal indication is furnished either by the lungs or heart. Abdominal organs apparently free from disease.

From the time of admission the opinion gradually gained weight that the patient laboured under malignant disease of the lower portion of the œsophagus.

August 22nd.—Under a careful regulation of diet some improvement has resulted. The dysphagia and vomiting have greatly abated. *Vespere.*—Has this evening complaint of headache and pain in the chest.

23rd.—After the application of a sinapism the pain in the chest was relieved. On auscultation, a distinct to-and-fro pericardial friction sound is audible over the region of the heart. There is no increase of precordial dulness. In the evening the patient fainted, losing consciousness for a very brief period; but on her recovery from the swoon remaining cold and collapsed in appearance, with almost imperceptible pulse. Brandy was administered, and warmth applied externally.

24th.—Remained very much sunk during the whole night; the surface of body covered with clammy moisture; at times becoming almost pulseless; when perceptible, the pulsations at wrist numbered 120. Brandy and aromatic spirit of ammonia were given freely. She is now—*Noon*—a little stronger, free from pain and without dyspnœa. The friction sound over the heart has lost nothing of its distinctness.

25th.—Has continued in much the same state. The attrition sound with the heart is not quite so distinct, and now there exists a little increase of dulness on percussion, with appearance of slight fulness in the fourth and fifth left intercostal spaces near the sternum.

26th.—More sunk in appearance. Physical signs have undergone no change.

27th and 28th.—In much the same state.

29th.—On auscultation to-day at visit, a very remarkable character of the heart's sounds was noticed. The friction is replaced by a gurgling noise, a *churning splash*, audible over the whole cardiac region, and rendered more distinct when, for an instant, the patient holds her breath. This sound is not distinguishable at a distance from the chest. The dulness on percussion over the heart has vanished, and now a clear and nearly tympanitic note prevails, with increased fulness in precordial region. The patient's extreme weakness forbids any attempts to alter her position in bed; the effect of change of posture on the percussion note cannot therefore be determined.

30th.—Physical signs remain as yesterday.

31st.—Patient died at 9 a.m.

In endeavouring to explain the remarkable physical phenomena connected with the heart, which presented themselves during the closing days of this poor woman's life, I considered it probable that the pericarditis, of which, on the 23rd of August, the signs were perfectly distinct, was determined by the progress of the cancerous affection of the œsophagus to the posterior wall of the pericardium; and when, on the 29th, the friction sound over the heart was replaced by the gurgling râle, limited to the cardiac region, and altogether unlike any sound connected with the heart's action previously familiar to me; and when, in addition to the evidence thus afforded, there had occurred an unmistakable alteration in the percussion note over the heart, dulness having yielded to clearness, I concluded that perforation of the œsophagus had taken place, and that, besides the presence of lymph and fluid in the pericardial sac, there was also air. The diagnosis then formed and expressed was as follows :—Cancer, affecting the lower portion of the œsophagus where in contact with the pericardium ; pericarditis with effusion from extension of disease in the former ; finally, rupture of the œsophagus and passage of gas into the pericardium. The *post-mortem* examination, conducted on 1st September by Dr. Haldane, determined the correctness of this opinion in all essential particulars.   I subjoin Dr. Haldane's report.

"The body was much emaciated : the surface very pale.

" When the chest was opened the pericardium, marked by the pressure of the ribs, bulged forwards, and on being punctured air escaped. There were no adhesions of the pericardium, but in its cavity were about three ounces of a dark-brown fetid fluid. Both surfaces of the serous membrane were coated with lymph of a yellowish-grey colour, of leathery appearance, and evidently of some standing; there was also some softer and more recent lymph, which could be readily scraped off with the nail. When the heart, which was of natural size and structure, was removed, an irregularly circular opening admitting the point of the finger, and communicating with the œsophagus, was found in the posterior wall of the pericardium. On examining the œsophagus, its upper part was found healthy, but the whole of the lower part from about the middle of the thoracic portion was in a cancerous condition; about two inches and a half of its anterior wall was completely gone, and its cavity was here bounded by the back of the pericardium and by the inner margin of each lung. It was here that the pericardium was perforated, and the pleuræ covering the lungs in this situation was dull and of a brownish colour, but the lungs were not opened into.

"While the liver was being removed, it was found that the back of its left lobe was adherent to the anterior wall of the stomach in a space about the size of half-a-crown. On separating the adhesions, an opening with sloughy margins was found in the stomach, but the firm connection with the liver had prevented communication with the peritoneum. The whole of the lower part of the œsophagus, the cardiac extremity of the stomach, and the adjoining portion of its anterior wall were cancerous; the cancer was soft and fungating, and in several situations was in a sloughy condition. The intestines were contracted. There was no other lesion."

I conclude with a very few remarks on the physical signs of Pneumo-hydro-pericarditis. Laënnec, who, as already observed, probably exaggerated the frequency of the occurrence of gas in the pericardial sac, speaks of three signs upon which dependence is to be placed in the diagnosis of air and fluid in the pericardium. 1. Unusual resonance over the lower part of the sternum. 2. Fluctuation sound (*bruit de fluctuation*) audible with the action of the heart, and on deep inspiration. 3. As specially relating to the diagnosis of pneumo-pericardium, the circumstance of the heart's sounds being heard at a distance from the chest. Upon this sign Laënnec placed very considerable reliance. He states, indeed, that his observations respecting it were made some time after those already referred to as *one* and *two*, and that he had not been able to determine whether it existed in connection with these. Dr. Stokes, whose observations on pneumo-pericarditis are most instructive, noticed the fact of the heart's sounds being heard at a distance in the case which he has recorded. He remarks, however, that this sign was not present in either Dr. Graves' or Dr. M'Dowell's cases already noticed. I have mentioned that it did not occur in the instance now recorded, and Dr. Walshe has no doubt correctly observed that Laënnec's expressed conviction, that in almost all cases (for he uses the expression *presque tous les cas*, and not simply *occasionally*) when the heart's action is heard at a distance from the body, the cause of the phenomenon is a temporary development of gas in the pericardium (often readily absorbed, and whose presence does not give rise to any serious result), cannot at the present day be received.[1] In the remarkable case of pneumo-pericarditis related by Dr. Stokes, the following signs were observed. I give them in Dr. Stokes' own language :—" On examination a series of sounds was observable which I had never before met with. It is difficult or impossible to convey in words any idea of the extraordinary phenomena thus presented. They were not the rasping sounds of indurated lymph, or the leather creak of Collin, nor those proceeding from pericarditic with valvular murmurs, but a mixture of the various attrition murmurs with a large crepitating and a gurgling sound, while to all these phenomena was added a distinct metallic character. In the whole of my experience I never met so extraordinary a combination of sounds. The stomach was not distended by air, and the lung and pleura were unaffected, but the region of the heart gave a tympanitic *bruit de pot fêlé* on percussion, and I could form no conclusion but that the pericardium contained air in addition to an effusion of serum and coagulable lymph."[2] The phenomena on auscultation and percussion thus recorded will receive further value as indicating the existence of hydro-pneumo-pericarditis, if in addition there be noticed, as was done by Dr. Walshe in the " singular case of traumatic communication between the œsophagus and pericardium," referred to in his work on ' Diseases of the Heart,'[3] a dull or tympanitic sound elicited over the precordial region according to the position assumed by the patient. The extreme weakness of the patient in the instance I have recorded alone prevented our determination of the existence of this important sign : from the appearances presented after death I have little doubt that, had it been in our power to alter the patient's position after the development of the peculiar auscultatory phenomena, we should have had this last indication also to guide us. Without it, however, and in default of a metallic

---

[1] ' Diseases of the Heart,' p. 269.
[2] ' Diseases of the Heart,' p. 22.
[3] Page 46.

character of the cardiac sounds, as noticed by Dr. Stokes, the diagnosis of pneumo-pericarditis with effusion may I think be made from observing a gurgling or churning splash sound with the heart's action limited to the cardiac region, with which more or less of tympanitic precordial resonance is associated. Still more reliable as signs will these phenomena be if, as in the instance now recorded, the gurgling has succeeded, after its continuance for a few days, a distinct friction sound, and the tympanitic replaced a dull percussion note.

XV.

THE DIAGNOSTIC VALUE

OF AN

ACCENTUATED CARDIAC SECOND SOUND.

(*Communicated to the Hunterian Medical Society, March 27th,* 1863, *and reprinted from the 'Edinburgh Medical Journal,' June,* 1863.)

It is now universally admitted that the second sound of the heart is produced during the act of closure of the semilunar valves in the orifices of the aorta and pulmonary artery. The sudden tension of the membranous structure of which these valves are composed is a sufficient, possibly the *only*, cause of the sound. It is, however, probable that, as generally held, the recoil of the blood against the valves contributes to its production.

Careful clinical observation has materially aided the direct experiments which, at a former period, were made regarding the heart's sounds. As respects the second sound, it may indeed be concluded that, by the former means of research, much left unfulfilled by the latter has been supplied. For example, I may refer to one or two particulars of importance, which have a special bearing on the subject of this paper. When the second sound is entirely replaced over the base of the heart by a murmur, it is not audible over the ventricles, and is not to be detected at the apex of the organ. In other words, when the murmur of aortic regurgitation is so loud as to drown all

11

normal second sound, preventing, by its very loudness, the recognition of the pulmonary second sound over the pulmonary valves, or in their immediate neighbourhood, where the second sound originating there is most readily heard, it cannot be detected even in small part over any other portion of the heart. Here, however, there are some points worthy of special observation; they concern what may be called exceptional cases of aortic insufficiency. A diastolic murmur may largely obscure, but not obliterate, the second sound over the aortic valves, a portion of it remains ; and in such cases, the pulmonary second sound being either readily appreciable or at least audible, the murmur diminishing in loudness as the stethoscope is placed over the ventricles, the normal second sound, pulmonary in origin, or the portion of aortic second sound which remains, is with greater readiness discovered there, or even at the left apex, than at the base. In endeavouring to account for this circumstance, it must be held in remembrance that the murmur of aortic regurgitation is not conducted with anything like the same distinctness over the ventricles as it is down the course of the sternum to the very limit, in some instances, of the ensiform cartilage itself. I have found not unfrequently that the second sound, greatly obscured by murmur at the base, and having precisely the same character at the end of the sternum, has been partially unclouded at the left apex, and over the ventricles a little less so. In such instances, it has not been difficult to determine that the more ready recognition of the sound in the latter situations has been due to the loss in distinctness sustained by the murmur.

Dr. Walshe has noticed " a distinct sound at the left apex in more than one case, while at the aortic base the ordinary regurgitant murmur alone existed."[1] So also in cases in which the second sound at the base is only feebly heard—no murmur existing—there may be, if not a loud, at all events a more readily recognised second sound near or at the apex. To such instances Skoda has directed attention, and they have likewise been fully considered by Dr. Walshe. In explanation of their occurrence it may be, as Skoda has suggested, and Dr. Walshe is disposed to allow, that some of the phenomena occurring during the diastolic action of the ventricles, which are properly

[1] 'Diseases of the Heart,' third edition, p. 65.

or rather naturally, soundless, become attended by sound—in other words, produce a second sound of their own; or it is equally conceivable—although perhaps not fully established—that certain diseased states in existence may determine a sound bearing a resemblance, more or less exact, to the normal diastolic sound of the heart.

These few observations I have made by way of preface to the statement of great practical value which I now wish to consider,—That an accentuated condition of the heart's second sound is heard in connection with one or other of two conditions of disease—aneurysm of the aorta, or dilatation of the aorta. It is hardly necessary to say, that no account is taken here of the by no means uncommon phenomenon of an accentuated pulmonary second sound. All careful auscultators know of how much value that phenomenon is in relation to the condition of mitral valve constriction. In describing the heart's second sound as accentuated in the instances of aortic aneurysm and aortic dilatation upon which the present observations are based, it is perhaps necessary to explain that the expressions, intensified, or greatly pronounced, would equally well indicate the character of the sound which has been found to exist. When occurring under the circumstances referred to, the accentuation of the second sound is always well-marked. I have frequently observed that early auscultators have, unaided, noticed the peculiarity, while very rarely indeed has there been difficulty attending its recognition by such, when their attention has been called to the subject. In a case of aortic aneurysm under my care last summer, there existed so accentuated a second sound over the base of the heart as to arrest the notice of all who examined the patient by auscultation. Several students, merely tyros in the art, readily recognised the *booming* character of the sound.

When the accentuated second sound occurs in connection with aortic aneurysm or aortic dilatation, it may be presumed that the semilunar valves are competent. Their insufficiency and the occurrence of an accentuated second sound are inconsistent; if the former lesion be in existence, a diastolic murmur is the necessary result. The influence of valvular disease in the production of murmurs in cases of aortic aneurysm is a point of the greatest importance for consideration. There may be, of course, associated mitral valve disease, or tricuspid disease, and, if so, murmurs may be thus originated; but such association is to be regarded rather in the light of an accidental coincidence, and not by any means of the same importance as the occurrence of disease of the aortic valves. Judging from cases of aneurysm which have come under my own observation in hospital, I conclude that it is very common to find aortic valve insufficiency in connection with aortic aneurysm; while in such cases the diastolic murmur, usually a very loud or at least very distinct one, so characteristic of the former lesion, is the most prominent auscultatory phenomenon. The cases now referred to are very evidently not cases of valvular disease in the first instance, and subsequently of aneurysm; in none has there been any foregoing attack of rheumatism, in none any distinct rheumatic history. Neither are they examples of a mere accidental association. The relation of the valvular imperfection to the aneurysm is, I believe, of the greatest interest and importance, and in all, its occurrence has been subsequent to the disease of the vessel. If an aortic aneurysm attain to any considerable dimensions, and affect the ascending portion of the arch, the aortic valves are rendered incompetent; and being so we shall find the auscultatory phenomena connected with the latter lesion in existence, and likewise the other physical signs which afford such evidence, especially the well-known peculiarities in the pulses, as pointed out by Dr. Corrigan and Dr. Henderson. I never remember to have seen an instance of aneurysm of the aortic arch within the pericardium of any considerable size unattended by diastolic murmur—the diastolic murmur of aortic valve insufficiency. On the other hand, the prominent physical signs of aortic insufficiency have led me—and no doubt the same error has been committed by others—to overlook the existence of aneurysm altogether. Dr. Haldane has in his possession a preparation of a large aortic aneurysm removed from a patient who had been under my own observation, as well as at different times under the care of three hospital physicians. In this case the signs of insufficiency of the semilunar valves were of unusual distinctness, and so, during the patient's life, the existence of that lesion was recognised, while the aneurism escaped detection till after death. The fatal event occurred suddenly, not from rupture of the aneurysm, but after the mode in which a very sudden termination not unfrequently takes place in cases of aortic insufficiency. With these facts before us, how necessary is it to make a careful use of the other means of diagnosis, in addition to auscultation, which we possess.

There is no diseased condition within the chest which gives rise to so many and different auscultatory signs as aneurysm. I have no intention at present of making any detailed reference to these. My remarks will be limited now to one peculiarity— the *accentuated* second sound. Here I purposely avoid making any mention of the systolic cardiac sound. Of course, in all cases, it is of importance to determine its true state, whether pure, or itself accentuated, or attended by murmur; any of these it may be, while the accentuated character of the second sound prevails. Now, as the result of careful observation and continued attention, I have found that, excluding the accentuated pulmonary second sound, and the intensified aortic second sound in some cases of hypertrophy and dilatation of the left ventricle, the accentuated second sound in the aorta is an indication of aortic aneurysm, or of dilatation of the aorta associated with atheromatous degeneration. If it be the former, the aneurysm probably does not arise within the pericardium, and probably does not affect the ascending portion of the arch, but has most likely its seat in the transverse portion; it may, however, arise at an earlier part of the aorta, as was found in the following case :—

Aneurysm of the Aorta, pointing externally, bursting through the Lung into the Left Pleura.

S. M—, æt. 36, under my care in the Infirmary, Ward V, during August and September 1862. Between the second and third left ribs, near their cartilages, a pulsating tumour was detected on the patient's admission. On auscultation a soft bruit was audible over the tumour; and at the base of heart, as well as over the upper bone of sternum, a very loud ringing second sound. The latter phenomenon never varied during the patient's six weeks' residence in hospital. He died suddenly, after expectorating a little blood. On examination of the body after death, serous fluid and coagulated blood, to the amount of more than half a gallon, were found in the cavity of the left pleura; the heart was pushed downwards and backwards; it weighed fourteen ounces. *The valves were perfectly healthy.* An aneurysm was found commencing

abruptly an inch and a half above the semilunar valves—the whole
vessel suddenly dilating to a point immediately beyond the origin of
the left carotid, where the dilatation as suddenly ceased. The pouch
so formed was six inches in length; it passed behind and was applied
to the back of the manubrium sterni, and made its appearance externally
between the second and third left ribs. The left extremity of the sac
was intimately united to the left lung, the edge of which had become
thinned by pressure, and the pleura having then given way, allowed the
escape of the aneurysmal contents into the pleural sac.[1]

In the foregoing case the peculiarity of the second sound
was of comparatively little value in leading to the recognition
of the aneurysm, other and still more distinctive signs, especially
the visible pulsating tumour, of that condition being in existence ;
but the accentuated sound led to the diagnosis of the competency
of the semilunar valves, which post-mortem examination confirmed. In the following case the accentuated second sound was
the earliest noted reliable sign of aortic aneurysm.

W. M'A—, æt. 35, a hawker, was first seen by me in March, 1862,
complaining of slight chest symptoms, particularly cough and expecto-
ration of a little phlegm. Had not been a sober man.
Condition on first examination.—Has a slight bronchitic affection.
Heart's second sound markedly accentuated over the aortic valves.
No other auscultatory phenomenon connected with heart or great
vessels.
I had frequent opportunities of seeing and examining this man up to
November 6th, when he entered the Infirmary, becoming a patient in
Ward IV. During this time his general health had failed considerably;
he had become thinner, feebler, less able for his occupation, though still
moving about and doing something as a traveller.
On 6th November the following notes of his condition were made :—
Has been suffering from dyspnœa, which has seized him on a few
occasions suddenly, and without any previous effort or exertion having
been made. Cough is somewhat clanging in character. Has some pain
and peculiar sense of weight in region of sternum. Over the left portion
of manubrium there is visible pulsation—the latter readily distinguished
on palpation. Left radial pulse is feebler than right. Murmur of soft
blowing character accompanies first sound over the seat of pulsation,
and is heard less distinctly over the base of heart. The second sound
at base is of a loud *booming* character. Respiratory sounds in upper
part of left lung, feeble. Posteriorly there is a little bronchial stridor.

---

[1] The post-mortem examination was performed by Dr. Haldane, at that
time Pathologist to the Royal Infirmary, and the account given above has
been abbreviated from his record of dissections.

This man, so far as I know, survives: he left the Infirmary about eight weeks since. With such signs as those detailed, the existence of aneurysm becomes unquestionable, they have become gradually developed in succession to the accentuated second sound, the earliest noticed of all.

Of this kind I might furnish other examples, several are known to me; and the opportunity has occurred for directing the attention of students to these, in the ordinary course of clinical instruction.

I have further to remark, that a similar condition of the second cardiac sound may be caused by dilatation of the aorta, associated with more or less of atheromatous degeneration. To distinguish between the two—in other words, to know when the accentuated second sound is due to aneurysm and when to dilatation of the aorta, is not always easy. Reliance is chiefly to be placed on the associated physical signs in the former case, more particularly prominence, pulsation, extended percussion dulness, and the signs of internal pressure. If atheromatous dilatation exist, and that is the special condition, independent of aneurysm, which gives rise to the accentuated second sound, there will probably be more or less pulsation in jugular fossa, atheromatous condition of superficial pulses (radials, temporal arteries, &c.) noticeable, and probably the arcus senilis.

The following points appear to me to be of importance in endeavouring to explain the mechanism of an accentuated second sound, under the circumstances now considered :

1. The condition of the vessel both in cases of aneurysm and of dilatation with atheromatous degeneration, being such as greatly to diminish, if not to destroy, the support given to the circulation by the artery, there results an increased recoil of blood on the closing or closed valves.

2. It is possible that a morbid condition of the valvular apparatus itself heightens or intensifies the sound. The valves are not incompetent, but in such cases they are sometimes found thickened, and even presenting a hard surface at parts.

3. Something may, I conceive, be due to the increased calibre of the vessel, in connection with the altered condition of its internal tunic, in causing the peculiarity of sound.

But in whatever way the phenomenon is to be correctly explained, there can be no doubt of its existence being entitled

to very considerable value as a clinical fact. I have noticed
that the accentuated second sound is most readily appreciable
over the aortic valves in both conditions.   In the cases of dilatation of the aorta it has, however, been more decided in character
over the manubrium sterni than in aneurysmal cases.   I may
add, that in the majority of cases observed by myself, in which
the accentuated second sound has existed under the circumstances now detailed, the expression, *booming* second sound, or
second sound with *ringing boom*, has best described the acoustic
character of the sound itself.   I have known the booming sound
continue for many weeks, and in one remarkable case of aneurysm lately observed (Walker, in Ward V, and afterwards in
Ward IV), for months, and thereafter become at first obscured,
and ultimately entirely replaced by a loud diastolic murmur,
telling plainly that the semilunar valves had become insufficient
owing to the extension of the disease towards the heart.

XVI

VASCULAR BRONCHOCELE

AND

EXOPHTHALMOS.

(*Read to the Medico-Chirurgical Society of Edinburgh, 1st July, 1863, and reprinted from the 'Edinburgh Medical Journal,' September, 1863.*)

THAT an affection characterised by so remarkable a tetrad of symptoms as palpitation of the heart (often violent in degree), notably increased pulsation of arteries, prominence of the eyes with peculiar startled expression, and enlargement of the thyroid gland, should, when once accurately observed and definitely described, have attracted a large share of professional attention, is by no means surprising. This odd form of disease,[1] as a recent distinguished writer has called it, is certainly not new—it has only remained for a lengthened period unobserved or unappreciated; its history in this respect not differing from that of several other ailments which recent research has alone brought to light; as, for example, Bright's disease of the kidneys, leukæmia, and the rheumatic inflammation of the cardiac structures. That the association of two, and even of all the symptoms referred to, had, moreover, been occasionally noticed,

[1] "Cette maladie si *bizarre*, pardonnez-moi cette expression," &c. Trousseau, in the report to the French Academy.—'Bulletin de l'Académie Impériale de Médecine,' tome xxvii, p. 996.

long before any proper conception of their importance had been formed, is abundantly clear from the cases recorded by Flajani,[1] by Dr. Caleb Parry,[2] and certain anonymous writers, particularly in the Medico-Chirurgical Journal and Review.[3] By Dr. Graves, the cardiac affection and enlargement of the thyroid gland were accurately noted and described in 1835; and, subsequently, Dr. Stokes particularly alluded to the enlargement of the eyes in relation to the other features. In 1839 the disease was carefully observed by Dr. Begbie; and, in the course of the succeeding ten years, again and again recognised—till, in the form of a memoir, his observations, comprehending a theory as to its origin, the proof of its amenability to treatment, and important suggestions as to the means to be employed were brought before this Society in 1849.[4] Meantime, both in this country and on the Continent, the disease had attracted the attention of physicians—earliest in Germany, that of Basedow, who, under the apellation of "cachexia exophthalmica," described it.[5] It is for Basedow that Hirsch and others have claimed a priority of observation, and, conformably to a practice which finds favour with many, have sought to identify his name with the disease; Basedow's disease (Maladie de Basedow) is the title under which these writers have presented their observations and recorded instances of the malady in question. Trousseau, on the other hand, whose high admiration for the character and writings of the distinguished and lamented physician of Dublin, Dr. Graves, is well known, and can only be most agreeable to us, has determined that the disease shall be recognised as Graves's disease (Maladie de Graves); and thus he has styled it in the recently published volume of the 'Clinique Médicale de l'Hôtel Dieu de Paris.' It is, however, only fair to Dr. Stokes to observe again, that the first distinct reference by the Dublin physicians to the enlarge- of the eyeballs, in connection with palpitation of the heart and enlargement of the thyroid gland, was made by him when communicating the particulars of a case to Dr. Graves.

---

[1] 'Collezione d'Osservazioni e Riflessioni di Chirurgia,' tome iii.
[2] 'Unpublished Writings of the late Dr. Caleb H. Parry,' vol. ii.
[3] For February, 1816.
[4] 'Monthly Journal of Medical Science,' 1849.
[5] 'Caspor's Wochenschrift,' 1840.

Of the actual existence of such a disease as that described by Graves, Stokes, Basedow, Begbie, Trousseau, there can be no question ; whoever has had the opportunity of seeing and care- fully studying a single well-marked instance of the phenomena referred to, must admit the entity of the disorder whose cha- racteristic features they are. The case brought before the Imperial Academy of Medicine at Paris in April 1860, by M. Hiffelsheim, and that produced by the late M. Aran, when engaging the attention of the Academy with the same subject in the December following, are admirable illustrations of the disease, and wholly satisfactory as proofs of its separate and distinct nature. In the very important discussion in the Im- perial Academy which succeeded the reading of these cases by MM. Hiffelsheim and Aran, only one speaker attempted to throw discredit on the observations—to challenge the correct- ness of the view which assigned to the assemblage of symptoms under discussion the dignity of a specific morbid state or disease. "There does not exist," concluded M. Piorry, on 22nd July, 1862, "a morbid unity called diathesis, cachexia, or neurosis, constituted by a triad, or a tetrad, or a pentad, or a polyad of symptoms, and which merits the name of exophthalmic goitre." I am not aware of any other expressed opinion in accordance with that of M. Piorry, while a subsequent speaker in the same discussion, M. Bouillaud—not less than M. Piorry himself— has thrown some fresh light on the real occasion of the extra- ordinary statement just quoted. M. Bouillaud's parole, on the 5th of August, commences as follows :—" Gentlemen, before proceeding to the subject of discussion, I desire to pay a just tribute of praise to the two eminent colleagues (MM. Trousseau and Piorry) who, during the two former sittings of the Academy, have occupied the tribune. Happy the Academy, if, renouncing certain notorious antecedents, these two orators had in some sort extended the fraternal hand, and had afforded us the edifying and agreeable spectacle of a reconciliation which science would not have failed to applaud. The hour for the consumma- tion of so desirable an event is not yet arrived." But, not only is there a disease mainly characterised by the features adverted to, the malady in question is very far from being uncommon in its occurrence. From the period when Dr. Graves wrote, there is scarcely a country in Europe in which the disease has

not been met with and described; while, in our country, in
France, Germany, and other parts of the Continent, it has
formed the subject of many interesting, and some extended,
observations.   In America, likewise, it has not been overlooked.
I am satisfied that in this city the disease is of frequent occurrence, and, in hospital practice, have often encountered it.   No
session has passed since my appointment as physician to the
infirmary during which the opportunity has not been afforded
me of directing the attention of a clinical class to the remarkable phenomena the disease presents ; while, as a general rule,
my experience has been that of the last session, several cases
having come under our notice.   Up to the time when Dr. Begbie
wrote, the instances of this disorder which had been recorded
were merely isolated examples—or were, at all events, related
as illustrations of what was properly regarded as a remarkable
combination of symptoms, without any attempt being made to
explain their occurrence or production.   Thus, Parry, to whom
undoubtedly credit belongs for having early and independently
noticed the association of two of the symptoms, observes :—
" There is one malady which I have, in five cases, seen coinci-
dent with what appeared to be enlargement of the heart, and
which, so far as I know, has not been noticed in that connection
by medical writers.   The malady to which I allude is enlargement of the thyroid gland."   It is perhaps scarcely correct to
affirm that Dr. Parry attempted no explanation of the coincidence
he had been shrewd enough to observe; but, as regards the
causation of the enlarged thyroid, all he remarked was as follows :
—" One can scarcely avoid suspecting that the thyroid gland,
of which no use whatever has hitherto been hinted at by physiologists, is intended, in part, to serve as a diverticulum in order
to avert from the brain a part of the blood, which, urged with
too great force by various causes, might disorder or destroy the
functions of that important organ."   And so also, in a way
equally accidental, Dr. Graves wrote—" I have lately seen three
cases of violent and long-continued palpitation in females, in
each of which the same peculiarity presented itself—namely,
enlargement of the thyroid gland ; the size of the gland, at
all times considerably greater than natural, was subject to
remarkable variations in every one of these patients."[1]   Equally

<hr/>

[1] ' Clinical Lectures on the Practice of Medicine,' vol. i, p. 193.

true is it that no explanation of the phenomena was, in the first instance, offered by Pauli or Basedow in Germany, or by Dr. Macdonell or Sir Henry Marsh in Ireland, by whom, meantime, interesting cases had been observed, and, in considerable detail, recorded.

When Dr. Begbie, in 1849, brought his observations on enlargement of the thyroid gland and eyeballs before this Society, he regarded these appearances as the consequences of anæmia, and this substantially is the view he still entertains.[1] A similar opinion has since that time been expressed, specially respecting one of these symptoms—namely, the prominence of the eyes—by several distinguished oculists. Dr. Mackenzie of Glasgow, for example, styles this condition "anæmic exophthalmia." Mr. White Cooper and Dr. Robert Taylor have respectively described it as "protrusion of the eyes in connection with anæmia, palpitation, and goitre," and "anæmic protrusion of the eyeballs." The anæmic theory as to the origin of the malady has, therefore, found much favour with ophthalmologists; it has likewise been adopted by physicians who have had the opportunity of devoting attention to the consideration of the whole phenomena. Among such may be mentioned the late Dr. Bellingham of Dublin and Dr. Isaac E. Taylor of New York. The former able writer thus expressed himself:—"The affection may be regarded as one of the rarer results of anæmia, as first pointed out by Dr. Begbie; indeed, the subjects of it present the ordinary characters of anæmia; they are generally pale and chlorotic looking, and often labour under amenorrhœa, leucorrhœa, and menorrhagia; they suffer from indigestion, impaired appetite, disturbed sleep, short cough, coldness of the extremities, headache, ringing in the ears, and palpitation; while various nervous or hysterical symptoms, as intercostal neuralgia, or spinal irritation, are occasionally present."[2] But, while all observers of this disease have recognised its connection with anæmia, there are several—and among these some of the best of recent writers—who have hesitated to assign to a simple blood impoverishment the important rôle which, in the view of the other writers named, it is considered to play. Anæmia is confessedly present in a large proportion of cases; but inasmuch

---

[1] 'Contributions to Practical Medicine, p. 176.
[2] 'A Treatise on Diseases of the Heart,' p. 532.

as.that condition did not precede the development of the characteristic features in some instances, while in others it only
became manifest after. these had been in existence for a considerable period, it cannot, they argue, be regarded as an adequate
explanation of their production.   Unable to recognise the existence of anæmia in connection. with the palpitation, the enlargement of the thyroid.gland, and remarkable appearance. of the
eyes, some observers, more particularly on the Continent,
having noticed the association of these symptoms with a condition of the general system more or less depraved, have described
the disease under the by no means definite or distinctive apellation of a caehexia.   Thus, Basedow in Germany, to whom
reference has already been made, uses the expression Cachexia
exophthalmica (Glotzaugencachexia, literally, large staring eye,
or goggle-eyed cachexia) ; Withusen, that of Cachexia exophthalmica ; and Hervieux, with Fischer and other French.writers,
terms precisely similar—as, Cachexie exophthalmique, L'exophthalmos cachectique.   In the former of the two valuable
papers on the subject recently read by Dr. Laycock to this
Society, it is implied that certain German writers have identified
the so-called exophthalmic with the strumous cachexia.[1]   In
the descriptions of Romberg and Henoch, whose contribution
bears the title, " Herzkrankheit Struma und Exophthalmos,"[2]
and in the observations of Schoch, entitled, " De Exophthalmo
ac Struma cum Cordis Affectione,"[3] I have, however, been
unable to find any warrant for this assumption ; they have
merely employed the word "struma," as it is often used by
German writers, in a sense synonymous with bronchocele, and
having no reference to that bad habit of body which English
and other writers designate as the strumous.   I have said.that
the term cachexia is by no means a definite one ; the meaning
attached to it by different writers varies considerably; as we
meet with it in medical literature, it is not in all circumstances
possible to ascribe a uniform, exact, or clear signification to it.
While, by certain physicians, the word cachexia, and, perhaps
still more, cachectic, is used to denote the existence of some
profound, indeterminate, and irremediable vice of the organism,

[1] 'Edinburgh Medical Journal,' February. 1863.
[2] ' Klinische Wahrnehmungen und Beobachtungen,' 1853.
[3] ' Dissertatio Inauguralis.' Berlin, 1854.

by others the term is not understood in so formidable a light. Trousseau, who has evidently the most serious view of a cachexia, sees none in the " maladie de Graves ;" and, again, by Basedow and others, who have employed this word in their descriptions of the disease under consideration, it has very evidently been used as precisely synonymous with chlorosis, anæmia, or hydræmia. This is very clearly shown in the able observations of M. Beau during the discussion in the French Imperial Academy of Medicine.[1] Lieutaud, he reminds the Academy, was the first to employ the term anæmia, though long antecedent to his time the characteristic features of anæmia had been with accuracy observed—to wit, pallor, swelling, feebleness, and flaccidity, which most readily arrest attention—and to the same assemblage of symptoms the word cachexia has also been applied. M. Beau further quotes from Felix Plater a passage, in which, under the name of cachexia, precisely the symptoms of anæmia, as now generally understood, are included —to use M. Beau's own language, "the ordinary symptoms of our modern anæmia." Every feature of anæmia is indeed noticed in this description of cachexia by Plater, if we except the important auscultatory phenomena, the discovery of which was reserved for Laënnec and his successors. " Cachexia," he says, "is a disease accompanied by discoloration of the skin, in which the florid hue is lost, and, for the most part, the proper appearance of the body is changed ; hence the term cachexia. In this disease the skin becomes white, or grows pale, or acquires a livid hue, or turns to a leaden aspect, while the surface of the body acquires a swollen appearance. The affection is generally accompanied by dyspnœa, which chiefly attacks the sufferers in walking, or ascending heights, with palpitations of the arteries in the neck, and of the heart, and with weakness of the limbs. While (Plater concludes) all may suffer from this disease, it is peculiarly apt to affect young women." The cachexia, then, which is thus defined, or a condition nearly identical with it, is evidently the state or appearance of body with which the more remarkable features of the disease under consideration are held by some writers to be associated. And this cachexia is surely nothing more or less than an anæmia. In such a depraved condition of body as either of these terms may be held to express

[1] 'Bulletin de l'Académie Impériale de Médecine,' tome xxvii, p. 1101.

there is noticeable—pallor of the tissues, muscular feebleness, softness or flaccidity of flesh, and not unfrequently œdema. Associated with these well-marked features there exist, usually in a distinct form, the peculiar auscultatory phenomena connected with the heart and arteries, and with the veins, chiefly those in the neck, which have been generally supposed to result from an impoverished condition of the blood, as well as palpitation of the heart and pulsation of the arteries, and many other less important, because not constant, symptoms. Dr. Laycock has objected to the value usually attached to the hæmic murmurs as evidences of anæmia; nevertheless, I am thoroughly persuaded of their importance. In instances of marked anæmia, I have never failed to detect the systolic soft blowing murmur at the base of the heart, the arterial souffle in the arteries of the neck, and the humming-top sound—bruit de diable—in the jugular veins particularly, but not unfrequently in the femoral and brachial. For their production, in anything like perfection, I believe two circumstances to be requisite; firstly, a marked excess of water over the corpuscular elements of the blood, and, secondly, a considerably exalted action of the heart. When these conditions have co-existed, I have never failed to identify the cardiac and vascular hæmic murmurs. I have found all of these, though never well marked, in cases which presented little if any of the general features of the anæmia or cachexia already adverted to; and I have failed to distinguish them in some instances of sufficiently anæmic or cachectic individuals. In the former case there has probably been that excess of water over blood-corpuscles which is, I believe, required for their production, though the external characters of anæmia were not pronounced, and the absence of the sounds in the latter case was probably due to the feeble action of the heart. In ordinary examples of splenic leukæmia, I should not expect, and have not found hæmic murmurs, for the corpuscular element of the blood in them is far from being deficient, and I cannot agree with Dr. Laycock in regarding their usual absence in such cases as militating against such valuable information their presence in other circumstances affords. In chronic Bright's disease, if hydræmia has at the same time existed, and the heart's action been moderately strong, I have never failed to detect them. In the disease under consideration, I have always found these murmurs. The loudest hæmic murmur at the base of the heart, as well as the most distinct venous bruit in the neck I ever heard, were in a well-marked example of associated exophthalmos and bronchocele.[1] It must here be observed that, by those physicians who have in the strongest manner upheld the blood origin of the cardiac palpitation and arterial pulsations, the enlargement of the thyroid gland, and prominence of the eyes, the coincidence of remarkable nervous symptoms with these phenomena has not been overlooked. But while evidently impressed with a sense of their importance, their nature and even their occurrence being far from uniform, they have been viewed by such either as accidental or, as at most, accessory symptoms; and, even by those who have specially noticed them, have been ascribed, like the other phenomena of the disease, to the impoverished condition of the blood. More recently, several experienced writers and observers, in explaining the causation of the various symptoms, have attributed these to an affection of the nervous system, and have regarded the anæmic or cachectic appearance presented by the sufferers as resulting from the long-continued nervous disorder. Dr. Stokes, in his work on ' Diseases of the Heart and Aorta,' has styled the disease a special form of cardiac neurosis. "There are," he says, " strong reasons for holding that the disease is originally a neurosis of the heart, and, perhaps also of the cervical vessels themselves;"[2] and Withusen, the able Danish writer already referred to, has remarked, "We must, therefore, adhere to the opinion that we have, in such cases, to deal with a nervous

[1] The microscope affords important information in anœmia. I am satisfied that there may be the pallid appearance of countenance, and the other general symptoms of this condition, in cases in which the auscultatory phenomena adverted to have little or no existence. In such cases the microscope detects no deficiency of the red corpuscles; but they have an altered appearance, are much less coloured, are serrated in their borders, and rarely form rouleaux. This condition, as well as that of a true hydræmia, may exist in the advanced stages of renal disease. I have now under my care in the Infirmary, a sufferer from chronic Bright's disease, whose look is so sufficiently cachectic or anæmic as, in connection with infra-orbital œdema, to suggest at first sight the malady under which he labours. Auscultatory phenomena exist, but in feeble measure. His blood is not watery, yet it is certainly impoverished; it is deficient in colouring matter, and the corpuscles are unlike those of health.

[2] Page 293.

affection of the heart, which may indeed give rise to organic
cardiac disease, but does not necessarily do so; to attempt to
demonstrate the source of the affection would, as we cannot
find it in anæmia, with our present materials, be a fruitless
labour, and would lead us far into the region of hypothesis.[1]
It is now four years since Koeben expressed the opinion that a
lesion of the sympathetic best explained the entire phenomena;
and in 1860, the late M. Aran, having diligently studied the disease, and having brought the subject under the attention of the
Imperial Academy of Medicine, concluded that, in all probability,
the primary seat of the disease was in a lesion of the grand sympathetic.   M. Trousseau, who has of late had considerable clinical
experience of exophthalmic bronchocele, and whose views on the
subject may be found at length in the discussion before the Imperial Academy, in which, as "rapporteur," he took a very prominent part, as well as in the second volume of the Clinique
Médicale de l'Hôtel-Dieu de Paris, rejects the anæmic theory as
to its causation, and regards the anæmia as secondary to the
cardiac palpitation, the arterial pulsations, and the phenomena
connected both with the eye and thyroid gland.   "Anæmia," he
says, "is an epiphenomenon ; it is secondary, sometimes tardy in
its development.   The morbid cause acts primarily on the heart,
and it is not till the lapse of a certain time, more or less considerable, that the blood is modified in the constitution of its
elements.   The woman in bed 34 of the ward St Bernard
presents at this time the features of anæmia; these features
were not, however, in existence when she came under our care,
although the disease had then continued for nine months.   A
neurosis of the grand sympathetic had preceded the anæmia."
Again, the same distinguished physician observes, "The disease
is, in my opinion, a neurosis with local congestions, having its
proximate cause in a modification of the vaso-motor apparatus."[2]

There may, then, be said to exist, at the present time, two
theories respecting the origin of the singular and interesting
ailment we are considering.   The one, that it depends upon
anæmia, a blood impoverishment ; the other, that it results
directly from a disorder of the nervous system, is a neurosis

[1] "On the Cachexia Exophthalmica of Authors."   Translated by Dr. W.
D. Moore, ' Dublin Hospital Gazette,' July 13th, 1859.

[2] ' Clinique Médicale de l'Hôtel-Dieu de Paris,' tome ii, p. 645.

depending on lesion of the vaso-motor apparatus. I am strongly inclined to think that the true explanation of the pathology of the disease rests somewhere between these two propositions. Neither the state of the blood nor the condition of the nervous system, as the point of departure, "the primum mobile," is to be overlooked. It may be conceded that all the symptoms which go to constitute anæmia may result from disorder of the nervous system, and by such disorder will assuredly be aggravated; still, if it can be found that the features of the former malady were in existence before there was any evidence whatever of nervous disturbance, we shall feel entitled to consider that the blood alteration was first in the order of events. That in most, if not in all, of the cases of associated exophthalmos and bronchocele this holds true, is, I think, probable. No doubt this opinion will be controverted by some physicians, whose statements are entitled to respectful consideration, but having already pointed out that the anæmia of the writers who adopt the humeral pathology of the disease is in all probability identical with the cachexia of those who have rejected it, I feel there is some ground, even in their own statements, for the opinion just expressed. When, in addition, a careful study and analysis of the numerous cases recorded by different writers is made, there are undoubtedly afforded very strong reasons in favour of anæmia operating as their cause. The following particulars under this view of the subject must not be lost sight of. *First.* That the sufferers from the disease have, in a large proportion of cases, presented adequate causes for blood impoverishment. These causes have varied in different cases—the more frequent in their occurrence have been uterine hæmorrhage, hæmorrhoidal flux, long-continued leucorrhœa, amenorrhœa, prolonged lactation, lientery, and diarrhœa. While so suffering, the occurrence of the enlargement of the thyroid gland, or the prominence of the eyes, or both, have not unfrequently been preceded by some cause acting injuriously on the nervous system, particularly such as excited the emotions or passions—grief, fear, fright. *Second.* That the sufferers have themselves, in numerous instances, presented the characteristic features of anæmia, pallor of countenance, feebleness of limbs, and flaccidity of tissues, tendency to œdema, palpitation of the heart, and the peculiar auscultatory phenomena connected

with the heart and blood-vessels, to which reference has already
been made. And it is while these symptoms in succession to
some adequate cause of blood impoverishment have been in
existence that, either spontaneously, or apparently resulting
from some injurious operation on the nervous system, the bronchocele and proptosis have appeared. *Third.* That the remedial
means which have hitherto been directed to the relief of these
symptoms, with most decided effect, are just those which, in
the treatment of anæmia, are confessedly of the greatest service.
And *Fourth.* That the structural changes to which the central
organ of the circulation is subject are of the like kind with
those which result from its long-continued functional derangement in connection with anæmia when assuming its more ordinary characters.   There are, then, I repeat, very cogent reasons
afforded by clinical observation for associating blood impoverishment with exophthalmos and vascular bronchocele, and for
assuming that they stand to each other in the relation of cause
and effect.   A diligent study of the phenomena of the disease
must, however, satisfy all, that the anæmic theory, as thus
expounded, stops short of explaining all the peculiar features of
such cases, even when the anæmia is best marked, and, still
more, those instances in which, while a cachexia is certainly
present, there is a hesitation, an accountable disinclination, or
even an impossibility, in the way of pronouncing it anæmia, as
that condition is ordinarily understood.

This leads me to offer some remarks on the special and peculiar conditions which are met with, the cardiac palpitation, and
arterial pulsations, the bronchocele and prominence of the eyes.
That these are, one and all, to be regarded as symptoms of the
same disorder, does not, I think, admit of any doubt; and,
further, I believe that the essence of the disease may be in
existence without the association of all these symptoms.   With
the cardiac palpitation and arterial pulsations, and without the
bronchocele or prominence of the eyes, it occurs; and while
the latter symptom is absent, the enlarged thyroid may, in
some instances be found.   Clearly, and this view of the subject
has a very important bearing on treatment, the cardiac and
general vascular disturbance precede the thyroidal and ophthalmic symptoms, and, when properly recognised, by suggesting
the employment of appropriate means may be said to prevent

the appearance of the latter. The palpitation of the heart is, for the most part, the symptom which chiefly attracts the attention of the patient, and leads her to seek professional advice.[1] It is generally vehement, often it is tumultuous, always it is rapid, being precisely of the same nature, though usually more violent, as the palpitation with which we are familiar in ordinary instances of anæmia and chlorosis. That the excited action of the heart is, in the early stage of the disease, altogether independent of organic change admits of no doubt.[2] Again, the accounts of post-mortem appearances, in the fatal cases, which have been investigated by Sir Henry Marsh, Basedow and Dr. Begbie, satisfactorily prove that those changes which result from long-continued functional derangement of the heart are to be met with—chiefly permanent dilatation of its chambers, with more or less of hypertrophy. The cardiac disturbance being admitted to be among the earliest of the morbid phenomena in this disease, the question presents itself—upon what does this disturbance depend? That it is essentially neurotic in its nature may be admitted; such disturbed action of the heart as we thus find is probably best explained by interference with the cardiac plexus of nerves. That important network is formed by small branches from the pneumogastric, and by branches from the three cervical ganglia of the sympathetic; from the cardiac plexus styled great, and in which at least two ganglia are to be recognised, nerves proceed in intimate

---

[1] As is well known, the affection under consideration occurs more frequently in women than men; still, the observations of Dr. Macdonell, Dr. Begbie, Romberg, Henoch, and others, have shown that among the latter it can assume its most typical expression.

[2] I consider it quite unnecessary to advance any proof of the correctness of this statement. By some writers the heart affection has, indeed, been described as organic, and the sufferers from exophthalmos and bronchocele have likewise been regarded as the subjects of cardiac hypertrophy. Trousseau has specially addressed himself to the refutation of this error. But both Trousseau and Beau, the latter more especially, have admitted the existence in such cases of a temporary hypertrophy, "hypertrophic passagere," or rather a general dilatation of the whole cardiac chambers, such as the researches of Larcher, Ducrest, and Blot have shown to occur during pregnancy. Muscular relaxation with flaccidity is a characteristic feature of anæmia—the involuntary muscular structure of the heart is just as likely to suffer as the voluntary muscles from the contact of impoverished blood.

relation with the coronary arteries to the organ; into its substance they are to be traced, and they are there distinguished
by possessing in their course minute ganglia, or nervous
centres, which have not unreasonably been supposed to regulate
the rhythmical movements of the heart. I conceive that the
aberration of cardiac function, which interference with these
ganglia best explains, may as readily and probably, on the
whole, with greater probability of truth, be accounted for by
their originally impaired nutrition, through an impoverished
blood, than by the direct operation on them, or on more distant
nervous centres with which they are intimately connected, of
an injurious cause which cannot with any accuracy be defined,
—chiefly spoken of as emotional. Healthy blood is the proper
stimulus of the heart as well as of the vessels. Impure blood,
unoxygenated, returning to the left side of the heart paralyses
the organ, and venous blood, too, stagnates in the pulmonary
capillaries. This, indeed, is the primary phenomenon in
asphyxia; the depressing influence exerted by such blood on
the nervous centres succeeds its retardation in the lungs. A
less deteriorated blood tells on the cardiac nerves, and through
them the heart is excited to unrhythmical movements.

If now we turn to the consideration of the remarkable condition of the vascular system, I believe we shall there find,
likewise, satisfactory evidence of its hæmic as well as neurotic
origin. The palpitation of the heart is certainly not more
characteristic than the violent pulsations of the arteries; it is
chiefly in the neck that these are visible; the carotids beat
tumultuously, and yield a very loud "bruit de souffle." When
the hand is applied over the neck, or still more, when both
sides of the neck are held in the widely opened hand, the
vibratory thrill or purring tremor from the carotids is remarkable. Of the cervical pulsations the patient complains; they
are often most distressing to her, and are always greatly increased by muscular exertion. With them are associated a
sense of fulness in the chest and head, throbbing in the temples,
beating in the ears, vertigo, and dyspnœa. Severe dyspnœa,
paroxysmal in character, I have only seen in one case, in which
the bronchocele was of very large size, and must have in all
probability interfered with the recurrent branch of the pneumogastric. Unquestionably all these distressing symptoms are

likewise aggravated by emotional causes. Marked as the pulsation in the vessels of the neck, superficial as well as deep, is, it is not in these arteries alone that the movement is visible; if the larger superficial vessels at a greater distance from the heart are examined in characteristic examples of the malady, it will be found that they too are similarly affected—the brachial, radial, and ulnar of the superior, and the femoral, popliteal, and tibial arteries in the lower extremities. I have, moreover, known a patient to complain more of the *beating* in the belly than of either the cardiac or cervical pulsations, and have always found the abdominal aorta affected just as the other arteries of the body; distressing pulsation in the abdominal aorta is, indeed, of common occurrence in ordinary examples of anæmia and chlorosis. M. Beau has directed attention to the circumstance that, by writers generally on this disease, the radial pulse has been described as small, and states that he is unable to adopt a similar opinion.[1] The apparent smallness of the radial pulse is, however, due to the calibre of the artery; and, agreeing as I do with M. Beau in this observation, I believe that a juster view of the arterial pulsations will be formed if the whole superficial arterial system be examined. Something, indeed, may be ascribed to the ready way in which an increased pulsation in the superficial vessels of the head and neck is recognised. Hippocrates, who was probably unacquainted with the doctrine of the pulse, nevertheless had noticed pulsation in the temporal arteries, Σφυγμός εν τοις κρόταφοις. I have further, in attending to this particular, determined that the synchronism between the heart's contraction and the distant pulses is more exact than in ordinary circumstances, and in this phenomenon, as well as in the exaggerated vascular motion, have recognised the increased energy of the heart's action excited to overcome the loss of assistance afforded by the rhythmical contraction of the arteries. In anæmia and chlorosis, increased pulsations of arteries, particularly the arteries of the neck, are not absent,

[1] Dr. Stokes has said on this point, "In most instances we observe a want of proportion between the force of the pulsations of the arteries of the neck and those in other parts of the system. The carotid and thyroid arteries may pulsate with vehemence, so as to give the idea that all the vessels of the neck are enlarged and in a state of morbid activity, yet the radial pulse be small and weak, and only rapid or irregular according to the state of the heart's action."—' Diseases of Heart and Aorta,' p. 281.

and have long attracted attention. Felix Plater, whose description of cachexia has already been quoted, after speaking of various signs, remarks, "Accidente simul pulsatione arteriarum circum jugulum ;" and Rondelet observes, "Noscitur pallidus color virginum, ex arteriarum colli pulsatione, et ex cordis palpitationibus." These writers are cited by M. Beau; and both he and M. Bouillaud, in their paroles before the Imperial Academy, have expressed the common experience of physicians when they said, that every day chlorotic girls ask our advice for palpitation of the heart and pulsations in the arteries, who believe themselves to be affected with some serious disease of the heart, and have already lost hope of recovery. As we have found the cardiac derangement to depend on a hæmic as well as neurotic cause, so I believe in the same way may the pulsations of the arteries be best explained. Allusion has been made to the supply of nerves to the heart; it is by minute branches of the same system that the blood-vessels throughout their most distant ramifications are embraced. The muscular apparatus, with its contractile property, chiefly resident in the small blood-vessels governing their diameter, receives no other nervous supply than from the sympathetic. Careful experiments have demonstrated the influence of the organic nervous system upon the calibre of blood-vessels both large and small. Those of Valentin and others, by which irritation of the sympathetic and the roots of the cervical nerves produced contractions in the aorta, and the still more important experiments of Waller on the former nerve in the neck, section or ligature of which caused enlargement of the minute arteries, accompanied by elevation of temperature, while application of the galvanic stimulant for a brief period effected their contraction to the ordinary calibre. In the disease under consideration, there is first of all increased unrhythmical pulsation of blood-vessels, and ultimately permanent dilatation—the proof of the latter occurrence will be adverted to when I come to treat of the thyroidal enlargement and proptosis. That the influence of the vaso-motor nerves is perverted, and that from this cause results the irritation of blood-vessels, and ultimately the serious impairment of that structure in them by which through nervous energy the circulation is properly maintained, can scarcely be said to admit of doubt. The question is, whence arises this morbid influence? Is it, as Dr. Laycock has ingeniously endeavoured to establish, ganglionic, affecting certain central portions of the vaso-motory apparatus. There are certainly not wanting features in this most interesting disease which appear to lend support to this view; but it appears to me as still more probable that the influence is exerted chiefly on the nerves of blood-vessels themselves, and that just as in the affection of the heart already discussed, so in the blood-vessels, it is the blood which operates injuriously on them. It is true that there are no direct experiments to establish the correctness of the view, that blood-vessels may be stimulated to contraction, and if so, the subsequent changes may be imagined—directly through the medium of their own nerves. There are great difficulties in the way of such experiments, but at least there are no experimental observations which oppose the conjecture, and there are some facts which give it probability. Dr. Carpenter sees no reason to doubt that by the sympathetic the impression of imperfectly-arterialised blood circulating through the systemic vessels may be conveyed to the spinal cord.[1]

There remain for consideration the bronchocele and the remarkable appearance of the eyes. The enlargement of the thyroid gland, which is met with in such circumstances, varies very considerably as regards size, from a mere fulness to a bronchocele of no inconsiderable dimensions. In its nature, likewise, there exists some variety dependent in great measure on the length of time during which it has existed. At first, it is very evidently the so-called vascular bronchocele—the gland is occupied to a great extent by blood, the blood-vessels are distended, and the thyroidal arteries, like the carotids and other superficial trunks, pulsate more or less vehemently; the thrill or fremitus experienced when the hand is placed over the tumour is generally considerable. To the touch the bronchocele at this stage feels uniformly soft. Beneath the skin which covers it the superficial veins are seen unduly prominent and loaded. Suddenly, as in instances detailed by Dr. Robert Taylor, the bronchocele may appear, ordinarily the swelling occurs gradually, often with considerable rapidity, always in succession to the derangement of the heart and blood-vessels already described. The bronchocele may disappear suddenly; while yet recent its

[1] 'Principles of Human Physiology,' p. 273.

size is readily affected by treatment; it has entirely disappeared in not a few instances. Nevertheless there is a manifest tendency to the swelling continuing permanent; when so certain important changes are noticeable—it has generally somewhat diminished, has become less vascular, not so pulsatile, and of denser consistence. Hypertrophy of gland structure, perhaps cystic formation, and permanent dilatation of blood-vessels, have in these cases resulted. In endeavouring to explain the occurrence of the vascular pulsatile bronchocele under such circumstances, assistance is obtained from attending to the normal structure of the thyroid gland, and, particularly, to the size and distribution of its blood-vessels. All anatomical descriptions of this body have reference to the remarkable vascularity which distinguishes it. A ductless gland presumed to be concerned in the process of blood elaboration, it is invested by a thin layer of dense cellular tissue, by which it is connected with adjacent parts, receives support to its vessels, and is imperfectly separated into vesicles of small but varying size. As to its blood-vessels, the thyroid gland is distinguished by their number, large size, and free inosculation. "In fact," says a recent anatomical writer, "it appears to be composed of a tissue of arteries and veins."[1] It has two and sometimes three independent sources of blood-supply, and the veins are equally numerous and large, forming a plexus upon it. Having, as Dr. Begbie and other writers have already done, spoken of the bronchocele as vascular, and entertaining no doubt that the augmentation in bulk of the gland depends upon arterial and venous congestion, associated with dilatation of both sets of vessels in the more advanced stages of the malady, having witnessed sudden and very considerable increase in its size, and its visible pulsations redoubled in force, when the heart's action became excited, I explain the enlargement of the thyroid gland in such cases as are under consideration by a reference to the number and size of its blood-vessels. Dr. Laycock has, however, argued that, depending on nervous interference, the pathological condition is to be connected with a lesion of a special nervous centre. We know the sources of nervous supply to the thyroid gland : these are twofold—from the laryngeal branch of the pneumo-

[1] Holden's 'Manual of Dissection of the Human Body, p. 16.

gastric, and the cervical ganglia of the sympathetic. I do not know any circumstances in the cases of bronchocele we are considering which would certainly lead me to suppose that a particular definite portion of the nervous centres is the seat of lesion. On the other hand, recognising excited vascular action, and afterwards dilatation of arteries as well as veins, not limited to the thyroid gland, though well-marked in it, but seen more or less in the whole vascular system, I am led to believe that while the nervous system is certainly at fault, it is essentially the vaso-motor nerves in their intimate distribution to blood-vessels which are affected, that this is specially marked in the thyroid gland, because it is so extremely vascular; and again, that a hæmic origin as readily or better explains the phenomena than the direct operation on the nervous system of some obscure cause. It may be objected to this view that bronchocele is of less common occurrence in connection with anæmia than such observations seem to imply. Upon this point I would beg to remark that I have often noticed a moderate degree of vascular thyroidal fulness, in persons of both sexes, who, having lost blood, presented some appearance of anæmia. I lately saw a youth labouring under scorbutus, and who had suffered two attacks of epistaxis, one very severe; he was of anæmic aspect, had palpitations, general vascular pulsations, and a small bronchocele.

Anatomically, as regards its great vascularity and ductless nature, and physiologically, as in all probability concerned in the elaboration of blood, the spleen may be classed with the thyroid gland. An increase in size of the latter organ has been noticed in several instances of associated bronchocele and exophthalmos, and has been specially referred to by Sir Henry Marsh, Basedow, and Dr. Begbie. In one case the spleen weighed twenty ounces, in other two it was found enlarged. Heusinger has particularly directed attention to the condition of the spleen, which he found after death much increased in volume, and manifestly diseased. I have been able in two well-marked examples of the disease to satisfy myself that the size of the spleen was considerably augmented.

Passing now to the consideration of the remarkable appearance presented by the eyes—the so-called exophthalmos. It is well ascertained that in this disease there exists a degree

more or less marked of prominence of the globes ; that vision
is little, often not in the least degree, affected ; that the feeling
of fulness and tension, varying greatly as the heart's action, is
comparatively calm or much excited, is not ordinarily attended
by any visible redness or injection of the conjunctival or scle-
rotic membrane ; that, except in very advanced instances of the
disease, there is no interference with visual accommodation ; that
the eyes under gentle pressure can be caused to retreat into the
orbits ; and, lastly, that the pupils are, in their normal state,
contracting on exposure to a bright light.   Such has been the
condition of the eyes and of vision in all the cases of this disease which have come under my own notice, and this description
coincides with the statements of Dr. Begbie and Dr. Stokes, as
well as those of Mr. Walker, Dr. Mackenzie of Glasgow, Dr.
Argyll Robertson, and other oculists.   I have never seen in any
case the least degree of squinting, even to so slight an extent
as to depend on what may be called a want of tonicity of the
ocular muscles, never ptosis, never nystagmus or twinkling of
eyelids or eyeballs, or increased vascularity of the conjunctiva,
or any corneal affection ; nothing in short to indicate the existence of a lesion of the nervous centres, cerebral or spinal ; nor
have any of the patients who have come under my own care
suffered from orbital neuralgia of any kind or degree.   I seek,
then, in the condition of blood-vessels the cause of the prominence
of the eyes.   A distended state of the ophthalmic vessels in all
probability does exist.   Increased vascularity of the choroid has
been found by Graefe and Withusen, the latter of whom
expressly states that a high degree of congestion of the vascular
membrane of the eye is often combined with prominence of the
eyeballs.   The veins of the choroid are placed on the external
aspect of the membrane, and are arranged in drooping branches,
" vasa vorticosa."   The arteries are found within, and form a
very minute network, the " tunica Ruyschiana ;" but with the
dense sclerotica covering the choroid, it is inconceivable that
the distension of these vessels can give rise to any great amount
of ocular prominence.   Nevertheless, in their congestion, and
still more in that of the ophthalmic veins which, receiving many
branches in their backward course, terminate in the cavernous
sinus, it is not improbable that the cause of the proptosis exists.
The congestion, however, just as in the congestion of the

thyroidal vessels, is determined by a nervous lesion—not, as I have already observed, a lesion of nervous centres—but by injury done to the "vaso-motor" nerves themselves. Here, too, there appears to me no important objection to the view that the impoverished state of the blood is the original morbid cause acting on the nerves of blood-vessels; and it is remarkable with what uniformity the protrusion of the eyes has by oculists, at least, been regarded and styled anæmic. It is not fatal to this view that no congestion of the ophthalmic veins has been found invariably in such cases after death;—it has sometimes been found. Such an appearance does not continue long, the blood readily passes into other and larger trunks than the smaller veins which it had occupied before, and the adjacency of the veins to the sinus may account for its more rapid disappearance in the case of the ophthalmic veins. But the enlargement of veins has been frequently met with—the jugular veins, the thyroidal veins, the vena cava inferior, these are all mentioned in different cases as having been found greatly enlarged. The permanent dilatation is more likely to ooccur in veins than in arteries, for the former, while possessing essentially the same structure as the latter, have less of the true elastic tissue. That the dilatation of the veins in the neck, as well as in other parts of the system, may be in part due to the distending influence of an accumulation of blood in them, which in its turn results from a diminution in the influence exerted by the contraction of muscles on them is not improbable, we know that thereby the venous circulation is in considerable measure maintained, and if the blood be impoverished muscular energy will likewise suffer. This is, I think, a more probable view than that of Dr. Marshall Hall, that the protrusion of the eyes was due to pressure on the veins, exerted by the muscles of the neck. Mr. Walker has signified a modified assent to this view; but if the action of the muscles was moderate the venous circulation would be only maintained, and if violent, besides seeing the phenomenon, we should find, at least in some cases, the trachelismus of Marshall Hall produced;—this I never heard of. Dr. Laycock having adopted another theory of the cause on which the protrusion of the eyes depends, has endeavoured to strengthen his position by a reference to the important experiments of Budge and Waller, and of Claude

Bernard, on the sympathetic in the neck.[1] Interesting and important as these are, however, I do not see that they nor the more recent experiments of the last-named physiologists have any immediate bearing on the eye affection which is found in connection with bronchocele. It is, in the first place, true that the former occurs, though that is very rare without the latter, and therefore the pressure of an enlarged thyroid on the cervical sympathetic could not explain the relationship when it did occur. This, however, while at one time the view entertained by Dr. Laycock, has long been abandoned, and, founding on the experiments of the accomplished physiologists referred to, he has embraced the opinion, and ably supported it, that there is a definite tract of the cord intimately connected with the ganglionic nervous system, which is the seat of lesion, —a tract which maintains through the sympathetic and cerebrospinal ocular nerves a most important relation. This tract, too, is no doubt in connection with the heart and blood-vessels in the neck, and hence may be assumed to arise their disturbance. I have already attempted to show that this explanation of the cardiac and vascular excitement—and the latter includes the bronchocele—is unnecessary, and that the operation of an impoverished blood on the vaso-motor nerves of the sympathetic, at least as satisfactorily accounts for their implication; and I think, further, that there are grave objections to the view that a lesion of the cerebro-spinal system, acting through the cervical sympathetic, determines the proptosis which we meet with in such cases as those now under consideration. In the cavernous sinus the sympathetic is connected by branches with the third, fourth, fifth, and sixth nerves, besides this, has, with two of these, the third and fifth, other important connections, and

---

[1] The late M. Aran, in endeavouring to explain the etiology of the exophthalmos associated with bronchocele, and cardiac, as well as vascular disturbance, had made full use of the important experiments of M. Claude Bernard, very specially attaching importance to the influence exerted by the sympathetic on the orbital muscle of H. Muller, the action of which is to carry eyeball forwards. Dr. Laycock, availing himself of still more recent experiments by the same physiologists (" Recherches expérimentales sur les Nerfs vasculaires et calorifiques du grand sympathique," 'Comptes Rendus,' 18th Août, 1862), has ingeniously argued that heat is the proximate cause of the nervous and anæmic palpitations, pulsations, and thrills.—' Edinburgh Medical Journal,' July, 1863.

itself governs the radiating fibres of the iris. Now, were the cilio-spinal region of the cord, "regio cilio-spinalis," as Budge and Waller have styled it, or the sympathetic trunk in the neck, or any of its ganglia, the special seat of irritation, it may be inferred that some abnormal condition of the muscles, governed by the third, fourth, fifth, and sixth nerves, or an abnormal state of the pupil, which is under the control of circular fibres, receiving supply from the third pair and the fifth, and radiating fibres which filaments from the sympathetic govern, would have been found and described. Such, as already stated, has not been the case. Neither convergent or divergent squint, nor contraction, nor dilatation of the pupil, nor ptosis have been noticed. That such conditions have been observed in some instances of proptosis is certain, but not in instances of the disease with which we are occupied. Petit's shrewd discovery more than a century ago, that section of the united pneumo-gastric and sympathetic in the neck affected the pupil; the queer gropings of Testa, forty years ago, half in the dark;[1] the philosophical conclusions drawn by the late Dr. John Reid, respecting the influence of the sympathetic on the pupil; the brilliant experiments of Valentin, Budge, and Waller, and Claude Bernard, not less than the patient clinical observations of Dr. W. T. Gairdner, Dr. Walshe, Dr. Ogle, and many others, have shown that there exists no more certain result of irritation of the cervical sympathetic, and very probably of the spinal centre with which it is connected, than a modification of the pupil.[2] One other nervous phenomenon I have noticed in cases of associated exophthalmos and bronchocele, namely, an exalted temperature, of which the patient herself often complains, not of face, or neck, or chest alone, but of general internal heat, sometimes experienced greatly in the feet; the dilatation of minute blood-vessels most satisfactorily explains this condition.

[1] 'Delle Malattie del Cuore.' See chapter ix of second volume, entitled " Della cecità, che talvolta sopravviene ad. alcuni Cardiaci.

[2] It must be held in remembrance, as mentioned by Dr. Argyll Robertson, that Dr. Praël, of Brunswick, has found in three out of nine cases that the protrusion of the eye was unilateral, the right being the one affected—a circumstance which, while not directly lending support to the anæmic theory, does not, I admit, oppose the view of the proptosis depending on a lesion of nervous centres.

Before adverting to treatment, and mentioning certain general conclusions to which the foregoing observations seem to tend, I desire to communicate very briefly the history of two cases of vascular bronchocele with exophthalmos, which have recently come under my notice in the Royal Infirmary.

CASE I.—P. B., æt. 34, admitted into Ward 15, Royal Infirmary, 6th November 1862. Married nine years, and has had one child. Has for a long period suffered from scanty menstruation, with occasional intervals of total absence of the discharge. One of these intervals extended over a period of eleven months. Has enjoyed, on the whole, better health since her marriage than before it. For some months previous to February, 1862, suffered from profuse leucorrhœa, and, after recovering from this, continued in a very weak state. In June had several profuse bleedings from the nostrils, and these attacks, though lessened in severity, have continued to occur till the present time. While so suffering, about June she began to have palpitation of the heart, from the first accompanied by buzzing noises in the head, and severe headache. About a month after the palpitation had commenced she observed a fulness about her neck, and, after the lapse of another month, her friends had remarked an altered expression and prominent appearance of the eyes. Throughout the summer has had frequent looseness of the bowels, and has noticed that the stools often contained portions of undigested food. Has latterly become very nervous and depressed in spirits.

On admission, the patient has a decidedly anæmic appearance; the eyes have a prominent aspect, and peculiar wild expression (" expression sauvage" of French writers); the eyes feel hot and tense to the patient, but her sight is unaffected; there is no peculiarity about the pupils, or the muscular apparatus of the eyeballs or eyelids, no orbital œdema. There is a bronchocele of considerable size, more prominent to the right than left side of neck, and much pulsation in the thyroidal and carotid arteries; the jugular and thyroidal veins appear distended. With the stethoscope a loud blowing sound closely synchronous with the systolic action of heart is audible, and when the hand is applied over the tumour a distinct thrill is distinguished. The heart's action is much excited— the beats 120 per minute—the rhythm altered considerably and variously. Region of precordial dulness not extended; soft blowing murmur, with first sound at base; loud bruit de souffle in the arteries of neck, arms, and lower limbs; very loud in abdominal aorta, the pulsation of which is readily seen, and proves distressing to the patient. She is easily agitated, and now somewhat desponding.

In this patient's case I had the first opportunity of combining the general regimenal treatment and the use of iron, as recommended by Dr. Begbie, with the employment of belladonna.

After the application of a large plaster of belladonna, for a few days, a very marked diminution in the size of the bronchocele, and a sensible amelioration in the condition of the eyes, had resulted.

While the application of the plaster was continued, I prescribed atropia internally, in doses of one sixtieth of a grain, morning and evening, only interrupting its administration when a complete dilatation of both pupils had resulted, and the patient was unable to read.

Greatly improved in health, this woman left the hospital a little after Christmas. I have seen her twice since that time. On the last occasion, only a few days ago, when availing herself of an excursion by train from the part of the country where she resides, she came to town. I found the eyes normal; the bronchocele still existing, but not as a vascular bronchocele; a small firm tumour alone remained, while cardiac palpitation and vascular pulsations have vanished. Her appearance is no longer anæmic, and, twice since she left the hospital, menstruation has taken place.

This is in every respect a favorable case. Treatment was employed at an early period, and speedily produced a beneficial effect. In cases distinguished by the continuance of the characteristic symptoms for a much longer time, so successful a result is scarcely to be anticipated. That a relapse may possibly occur is not to be questioned; but familiar as I am with one of the earliest cases recorded by Dr. Begbie, in which a perfect cure has resulted, and now at the end of fifteen years continues, I am disposed to think that such an occurrence is unlikely.

CASE 2.—Mrs.—, æt. 37, mother of seven children, with her strength greatly reduced from nursing an infant of thirteen months, and repeatedly a sufferer from menorrhagia. Anæmic in appearance; has a considerable bronchocele, and in a marked degree the peculiar prominence and expression of the eyes. These symptoms have developed themselves within the last two months. Is not nervous. The beating of heart and arteries, and the auscultatory phenomena connected with these, are precisely as in the former case. This woman states positively that she never sustained any sudden shock, or mental distress of any kind.

After a few weeks' treatment the patient has greatly improved under the use of iron, with belladonna prescribed in the same manner as in the case already detailed.

The plan of treatment pursued in these cases and in others

13

which have come under my care has had reference, firstly, to
calming the excited action of the heart and blood-vessels;
and, secondly, to improving the evidently deteriorated condition
of the blood.   I believe that in order to remedy the disorder
both of these indications must be met, the one without the
other will fail.   Belladonna is a powerful excitant of blood-
vessels, acting on the unstriped muscular fibres in them.   The
experiments of Brown-Séquard upon animals have sufficiently
established this point.   Again, as a remedy, belladonna is known
and prized from its possession of this very property.   Acting
in all probability on the blood-vessels of the iris, it causes dilatation of the pupil; on the blood-vessels of the mamma it arrests
the secretion of milk; on the muscular coat of the intestine
action of the bowels.   Administered in the form of its extract,
in doses of one sixth or one fourth of a grain, or as atropia, in
doses of one sixtieth, or applied as a plaster over the enlarged
thyroid gland, I have found this remedy to produce speedily a
remarkable effect on the eye, in causing its retirement and in
removing the peculiar staring expression; on the thyroid gland
in leading to the rapid, or at all events speedy diminution in
its bulk; on the heart and blood-vessels in modifying and controlling their excited action.   I cannot doubt that in producing
these effects its special action is exerted on the dilated vessels,
stimulating them to rhythmical contractions, and thus overcoming congestions.   It is from its action in this way that the
late Professor Schroeder van der Kolk found belladonna so
useful a remedy in epilepsy,[1] and that Brown-Séquard has satisfactorily tested its claims to employment in cases of paraplegia
dependent on congestion of the cord or chronic inflammation.[2]
But while belladonna, and specially atropia, produce these effects,
and thus greatly modify the distressing symptoms in such cases,
unaided neither will accomplish a cure.   Iron, as the "summum remedium" in blood impoverishment, must be administered, and that steadily for a time.   Thus combined, I think,
in comparatively recent cases, the most desirable results will

---

[1] 'On the Spinal Cord and Medulla Oblongata, and on the Proximate
Cause and Rational Treatment of Epilepsy.' New Sydenham Society's
edition, p. 275.

[2] 'Lectures on the Diagnosis and Treatment of the Principal Forms of
Paralysis of the Lower Extremities,' 1861.

speedily be obtained. Dr. Begbie had found iron in combination with henbane, a plant belonging to the Atropaciæ, and exerting some properties similar to belladonna, most serviceable ; and before I was led to employ the latter, I always used the tincture of hyoscyamus with the tincture of the muriate of iron. Trousseau has employed digitalis, and speaks with confidence of the remedial virtues of cold compresses when applied over the thyroid gland. The operation of the latter is evidently directly on the vaso-motor nerves, and leads to a sympathetic contraction of blood-vessels in other parts. Iodine is not only useless as a remedy in this form of bronchocele, but, as M. Beau and others have shown, positively injurious. None of those means which are ordinarily employed with benefit in the treatment of blood impoverishment, associated with more or less of nervousness or hysteria, should be neglected,—advantage is certainly to be derived from change of air and scene ; but, on the other hand, the disease is emphatically one requiring for its relief the continued use of such remedies as have been referred to. It has been noticed by some writers that when a woman affected with this peculiar disease becomes pregnant, a manifest improvement in her condition occurs—a circumstance only to be explained by the change which takes place in the condition of the blood while pregnancy exists, and pointing, therefore, to the hæmic origin of this complex malady.

I am, therefore, disposed to conclude,—that the true pathology of the bronchocele and exophthalmos, found in connection with cardiac palpitation and vascular pulsations and dilatations, lies both in the blood and in the nervous system, but that the " primum mobile " is the former ;—that an altered state of the blood—for a time stopping short of what is generally known as anæmia,—but in many cases amounting to well-marked anæmia, acts directly on the nerves of blood-vessels, and on the nerves of the heart—" Sanguis moderator nervorum ;"—that, as a consequence, their rhythmical movements are seriously affected, and dilatation of the heart's chambers, and of blood-vessels, arteries, but chiefly veins, results ;—that for a lengthened period the bronchocele is truly a vascular enlargement and dilatation ; but that, in course of time, hypertrophy and degeneration of gland-structure result ;—that the exophthalmos, which is not a necessary consequence any more than the bronchocele of the disordered state of blood, and neurosis of blood-vessels, depends upon congestion and vascular dilatation of the ophthalmic vessels, with effusion of serum into the post-ocular cellular tissue;—and, lastly, that a plan of treatment directed to the improvement of the condition of the blood, and, at the same time, to the state of the nervous system,—is successful in effecting a cure, provided those organic changes in the heart, to which reference has been made, have not already been induced.

XVII

FAVUS (TINEA FAVOSA):

ITS TREATMENT BY DEPILATION.

(*Reprinted from the 'Edinburgh Medical Journal,' March,* 1864.)

This interesting form of cutaneous affection, the truly parasitic nature of which is now generally admitted, has been of frequent occurrence in the hospital wards during the whole period of my service as physician. I have nothing to add to the accurate as well as detailed accounts of the disease which are to be found in the writings of such authors as Devergie, Hebra, and Bazin, on the Continent, and of Mr. Erasmus Wilson and Dr. M'Call Anderson, in our own country. The experience I have had of Favus has convinced me of its intimate connexion with filthiness of the head and body, of its ready communicability when favoured by the pre-existence of dirtiness, the predisposing cause of most importance, in the person exposed; and, lastly, of its eminently satisfactory treatment by one plan, and by that one plan only. I contrast, very favorably for the process of depilation, the different means for the cure of Favus affecting the scalp, which have been formerly witnessed, at various times, and in various places—and likewise employed by myself; and now, having obtained results so completely satisfactory, by the employment of depilation,—practised very nearly as M. Bazin has recommended it, I have relinquished all other expedients for effecting the removal of this frequently loathsome disease, and can confidently recommend depilation as a most efficient remedy. Coupled with the depilatory process, however, must be, first of all, the thorough cleansing of the scalp, and then the employment of what are likewise styled *parasiticide* remedies, or still more strictly in relation to Favus, a disease dependent on the existence of a plant or vegetable-like parasite—*phyticides.* Of these a solution of the corrosive sublimate (one or two grains to the ounce of water, with the addition of a little alcohol or hydrochlorate of ammonia), the oleum juniperi pyrolignicum (huile de cade of the French), and the subsulphate of mercury (turpeth mineral), in the proportion of a scruple or half a drachm to the ounce of prepared lard, are the chief; and so long as the act of depilation is in progress, the diligent use of one or other of these parasite destroyers is to be enjoined. I have found the empyreumatic oil of juniper to be most serviceable; and from the year 1850, when I first saw it in use in the St. Louis Hospital at Paris, have been constantly in the habit of employing it in the treatment of the parasitic, as well as of the scaly, affections of the skin. The precise plan pursued in the treatment of all the cases of Favus recently under my care, is as follows :—On reception, the patient has at once a hot bath, and both head and body are as thoroughly as possible cleansed with the aid of soft soap ; the hair of the head is then cut to the level of the Favus crusts, and, as Bazin has directed,[1] the oil of juniper (before mentioned) is applied by means of a thick camel-hair brush. On the succeeding day, poultices of potato-starch are placed over the head, and diligently continued till the complete separation of the crusts is effected. This done, the juniper oil is re-applied ; and on the day following, the process of depilation commenced. While this is continued, the daily use of one or other of the phyticide applications is being made. Care should always be taken that the depilation is complete, and that it is persevered in until the growth of healthy-looking hairs over all parts of the scalp is observed. Thus the treatment may require *many weeks* for its thorough execution ; but when it is held in remembrance that the cure effected is radical, its lengthened duration may well be tolerated.

The following, one of the most recent examples of Favus under my care, in which the trunk as well as the scalp was

[1] ' Leçons Théoriques et Cliniques sur les Affections Cutanées Parasitaires.' Professées par le Docteur Bazin. Paris, 1858. (See p. 138.)

affected, will serve as a further illustration of the treatment now described :

E. S—,[1] æt. 17, single, living in her sister's house at M., near Edinburgh, admitted into Ward XV, Royal Infirmary, in November 1863, suffering from well-marked Favus of the head and upper part of the back, which she says has existed since infancy. By the application of poultices, and by washing with black soap, her head has frequently become so clean as to lead her friends to believe that they had effected her relief from this offensive complaint ; but in seven or eight days the scalp had again become covered with yellow crusts, emitting the peculiar and characteristic odour. The patient has on several occasions been under medical treatment, but with a like result. She has always been well clothed and properly fed, taking animal food three or four times a-week. She has no other ailment, and has always enjoyed good health. Till within the last two years the disease was confined to the head; but about that period a similar eruption began to show itself on the upper part of the back, and has since then extended over both shoulders. At present the scalp is almost entirely covered with dirty yellow crusts, and over it several patches of baldness exist. The eruption on the back possesses a brighter yellow colour than that on the head, extending on the left side from the top of the shoulder to the waist, and, transversely, from about the angles of the ribs to the spine ; the denser crusts being situated over the scapular region. The patient complains of much itching and uneasiness in the parts affected, but of no pain. The head and back having been carefully washed, while the hair was closely clipped on the former, the juniper oil was applied, and thereafter the removal of the crusts effected by poultices of potato-starch. This done, depilation was commenced, and at the same time the use of the following lotion, for both the head and back :

> ℞ Hydrargyri Sublimati Corrosivi, gr. xij ;
> Ammoniæ hydrochloratis, ℈i ;
> Aquæ fontis, ℥vj. Solve.

The first depilation in this case was completed in about three weeks ; it has been continued till nearly the present time (13th February), so as to effect the removal of all the unhealthy-looking hairs which have re-appeared. Latterly, the following application, which I can strongly recommend as a phyticide, has been employed for the head, instead of the corrosive-sublimate lotion :

> ℞ Saponis Mollis, ʒij ;
> Olei Juniperi Pyrolignici,
> Spiritus Rectificati,
> Glycerini, āā ʒiv. M.

[1] Reported by Mr. S. E. Roberts, clinical clerk.

The patient still remains in hospital; but the appearance of both head and back is eminently satisfactory, while the hair over the former is now appearing in a healthy and vigorous condition. I see no reason to doubt that in this case, as in many previous examples, the recovery will prove complete and lasting.

XVIII

HERPES CIRCINATUS (TINEA CIRCINATA) WITH FAVUS.

(*Reprinted from the 'Edinburgh Medical Journal,' March,* 1864.

THE association of Tinea Circinata, a parasitic affection frequently styled ringworm of the body,—to distinguish it from
Tinea (Herpes) Tonsurans, ringworm of the scalp,—with Favus,
has been noticed, more particularly by Hebra, who has delineated
the two eruptions as occurring at the same time in the same
subject.[1] The case I am about to relate appears to me of interest
—*firstly*, as an example of the co-existence of two affections
supposed by Bazin and others to be dependent on the presence
of separate and distinct vegetable parasites. In Favus it is the
well-known *Achorion Schoënleinii,* in Tinea Circinata the *Trichophyton tonsurans,* which is met with. *Secondly,* the case
is pre-eminently illustrative of the communicability of the
former disease by something short of actual contact. And,
thirdly, it exhibits the cure of both affections resulting without
the employment of parasiticides, or indeed of any remedies,—a
circumstance due, I believe, to the uncongenial nature of the
soil in which the parasite or parasites found themselves deposited.

M. Y—, æt. 40, widow, a washerwoman, resident in the country, was
admitted to Ward XV, on the recommendation of Dr. Junor, of Peebles,
in November 1863. She is the subject of sore throat and of a cutaneous

---

[1] See a plate in Hebra's 'Atlas of Cutaneous Diseases.' To be found also
in the earliest fasciculus, issued by the New Sydenham Society.

disorder resembling Rupia Prominens, but chiefly complains of severe
rheumatic pains of several joints, greatly aggravated during the night.
She was at once placed under a constitutional treatment, consisting
mainly of cod-liver oil, with iodide of potassium ; and speedily the cutaneous disorder underwent a very favorable change, when, the crusts
having been removed by poultices, a weak solution of nitrate of silver—
five grains to the ounce of water,—or the black wash was applied to the
different sores. The Rupia ulcers which required most attention were
situated on the back and on the upper and lower extremities. One, in
particular, was seated on the outer side of the ankle of left foot, immediately behind the external malleolus. This foot she exposed morning
and evening for the purpose of dressing the sore, removing a stocking
and bandage with which it was covered. The patient is a person of
cleanly habits, and the surface of the body indicates the attention
which she has paid to ablution. About the middle of December, the
patient's notice was attracted to the condition of the skin in the neighbourhood of the internal left ankle by feeling a considerable degree of
itching, and on examination, she found it red and inflamed in appearance.
Thinking that this part was about to become the seat of a fresh Rupia
crust, she said nothing about the circumstance for a few days; but
having by that time observed the circular form of an eruption which
had become developed, she directed my attention to the appearance at
visit on the 23rd of December. I immediately recognised a very characteristic circle, or rather circles, of Herpes Circinatus(Tinea Circinata).
Watching the progress of this eruption from day to day, I was much
interested to find, in the course of five or six days from its first recognition, the appearance of two or three—the number afterwards reached
seven or eight—most distinct, yellowish, cup-shaped crusts of Favus.
At this period I made a very careful inquiry into the whole circumstances of the patient since her admission to the hospital, and with the
following result. In the same ward, during the entire period of her
occupation of a bed, there had been two well-marked cases of Favus—
one of these being that of the patient E. S—, already briefly detailed at
page 199, the other that of a little girl, J. M'N—, æt. 8, who had
laboured under the disease, affecting the head only, since her second
year. This little patient, it was distinctly ascertained, was frequently
in the habit of visiting the woman M. Y—; and it is conjectured, with,
I think, every show of probability, that while so engaged, some of the
sporules of the Achorion may have fallen from her head upon the foot
of M. Y—, which she had at the time exposed, for the purpose of cleaning the sore on its external surface, and of applying to it the lotion of
nitrate of silver.

The precise relation of the Tinea Circinata to the Favus may
be difficult of explanation, but the intimate co-existence of these
two parasitic disorders is one of the most interesting features
in this very illustrative case. The parasite existing in the

former affection is believed to be identical with that found in Tinea (Herpes) Tonsurans—ringworm of the head,—and in sycosis (Mentagra)—ringworm of the beard—the so-called *Trichophyton tonsurans*. The microscopic differences between the Achorion and the Trichophyton are, however, confessedly not very remarkable. The former is composed of sporules, empty tubes (the mycelium), and tubes filled with sporules; the latter is characterised by the presence of spores, with very few if any tubes. It is, however, consistent with my own observation, that in the examination of some Favus crusts, sporules alone are to be detected, just as Mr. Erasmus Wilson states that mycelium is sometimes to be found in the Trichophyton.[1] Hence, probably, it results that so competent an authority as Hebra reduces the number of cutaneous fungi to one, conceiving the differences in the microscopical characters of the four usually recognised parasites—the Achorion, the Trichophyton, the *Microsporon furfur*, and the *Microsporon Audouini*—to be determined by the peculiarity in structure of the part of the skin which is their seat. However this may be, I had no difficulty, in the present instance, in detecting the Achorion, presenting the appearance of well-marked oval and round sporules, with very few tubes, in the small yellow crusts which appeared on the surface of the erythematous patch lying within the distinct vesicular circles of Herpes. And so, likewise, when the usual desquamative change had succeeded the earlier appearance of the Tinea Circinata, in the cuticular scales gently removed for microscopic examination by means of a blunt instrument, I observed numerous sporules, but neither empty nor filled tubes—precisely the same appearance as I have frequently seen before, and last witnessed in a case of ringworm which occurred this week in the hospital. The limitation of the two affections in this case to a very small surface of the skin—their appearance on no other part of the body separately —the immediate succession of the Favus crusts to the annular eruption of Herpes—the exposure of the patient herself to the contagion (or communication short of actual contact) of Favus, but not, so far as can be ascertained, to that of ringworm—and

---

[1] "On the Phytopathology of the Skin, and Nosophytodermata, the so-called Parasitic Affections of the Skin," 'British and Foreign Medico-Chirurgical Review,' January, 1864.

finally, the joint and complete disappearance of the two eruptions, all traces of which have now vanished—exhibit, I think it must be admitted, a very intimate connection between the two disorders in this particular instance. As an evidence of the communicability of Favus, the case, indeed, is one of very great value. It is also valuable, as showing that even that intractable disorder (well named *Tinea*) may come to a spontaneous termination. Essentially it is a disease of the hair-follicles. Developed in the situation in which it occurred in this case, the fungus speedily dies, as it were, a natural death. The same remark applies to Herpes Circinatus, which not unfrequently requires no decided treatment.

XIX.

—

ON PARACENTESIS THORACIS

IN THE TREATMENT OF

PLEURAL EFFUSIONS, ACUTE AND CHRONIC.

(*Read before the Medico-Chirurgical Society of Edinburgh, May* 2, 1866, *and reprinted from the 'Edinburgh Medical Journal' for June,* 1866.)

THE perforation of the thoracic walls, in order to give vent to purulent and other fluids, is an operation dating from the most remote antiquity. In the Hippocratic treatise, ΠΕΡΙ ΝΟΥΣΩΝ ΤΟ ΔΕΥΤΕΡΟΝ—*De Morbis, Liber Secundus,*—a work which there is good reason for believing, although not composed by the illustrious Father of Medicine himself, was written either by one or more of his contemporaries, or by some among his immediate descendents in the school of Cos,— there occur two most interesting and instructive passages, the one having reference to the method by which the existence of pus in the pleural cavity, or empyema, as the latter term is understood by the moderns, is to be recognised, while the other describes the operation by which that condition is to be removed. The order of procedure, both as regards the diagnosis and the treatment, is in these passages laid down with great exactness. Under the former head, it is directed that after the patient has been carefully washed with warm water,

he is to be placed iu a firm seat, and his hands held by an assistant, the physician meantime taking him by the shoulders
shakes him, and attentively listens in order to determine on
which side of the chest a sound is occasioned. Again, in treating of the means of cure, it is directed that recourse to the
operation is not to be had before the fifteenth day from the
commencement of the effusion ; where pain is chiefly felt, and
swelling is most conspicuous, the opening is to be made, while
a preliminary incision through the integuments precedes the
penetration of the pleura, effected by a sharper and more pointed
instrument than that which is required for the earlier incision,
the second instrument being protected by a piece of cloth. In
some instances, the perforation of the thoracic parietes was
made not through an intercostal space but through a rib. When
a sufficient quantity of pus has been permitted to flow, the
wound is to be closed by means of a portion of linen cloth
attached to a thread. Daily a similar quantity of pus is to be
evacuated. On the tenth day, when the whole of the collection
has been allowed to escape, a mixture of tepid wine and oil is
to be injected through the opening for the purpose of cleansing
the lung. This part of the operation is to be practised twice
daily ; the injection of the morning being withdrawn and replaced by a fresh quantity in the evening, and so on. At length,
when the purulent fluid has become clear and thin, a metallic
sound is to be introduced, the size of which is to be gradually
lessened as the fluid itself diminishes ; thus the wound is permitted to cicatrise.

In connection with the description which I have now epito-
mised, it is very interesting to note the expression by the
author of the treatise, of some shrewd observations relating to
prognosis ; for example, an empyema on the left side, he remarks,
is less dangerous than on the right. In modern times, as I
shall have occasion again to notice, the operation of thoracentesis has been more successful on the left side than on the right.
Again, the author mentions, that according to his observation,
when the pus was clear and studded more or less with small
sanguinolent threads, that appearance indicated the probability
of a satisfactory recovery ; but, on the other hand, if on the
first day of its removal the fluid possessed a colour like the
yolk of egg, while on the succeeding day it was thick, having a

pale green hue, and emitting a fœtid odour, it was likely that the sufferer would not recover, but shortly die. In Hippocratic times, the operation of thoracentesis was not invariably made with the knife, that is by division of the integuments and muscles in an intercostal space, and the subsequent penetration by means of a sharp-pointed instrument through the costal pleura; it was sometimes effected by means of the actual cautery.

The succussion of the chest, to which as a means of diagnosis reference is made in the treatise from which I have been quoting, occupies, as is well-known, to this day an important place in our recognition of hydro-pneumo-thorax, or, as it may be called also, of pneumo-thorax with effusion; and very appropriately it bears in our time the designation of *Hippocratic* succussion. The production of the fluctuation or splashing sound on succussion enables us to recognise the existence of that morbid condition, and as I believe of that condition alone. It cannot be said to diminish the interest of the statement in the Hippocratic writings concerning this sound, that the author supposed its production to depend on the existence of pus in the pleural cavity, in contradistinction to water,—he regarded it as a ready means of distinguishing an empyema from a hydro-thorax. Thus, he had overlooked, or rather had been unaware of the necessity there exists for the co-existence of air and fluid in the pleural cavity, in order that any sound should be produced. The writer had noticed and has placed that observation likewise on record, that when much sound is heard, there is less pus in the cavity than when the sound produced on succussion is feeble. The explanation of this accurate observation is now readily offered by us, although misinterpreted by the Hippocratic writer; but surely the misconception respecting the primary cause of the auscultatory phenomenon, which he has so faithfully described, need not lessen in any measure the tribute of respect and admiration for his amazing powers of observation, which a perusal of almost any portion of his writings is calculated to draw forth.

Other references there are in several of the Hippocratic works to the relief which an operation is capable of affording to the sufferers from empyema and aqueous collections,—for example, in the Book of Aphorisms—one of these, because expressing an opinion which I shall have to consider in another part of

this paper, may be quoted. It is the twenty-seventh aphorism
of the sixth book :—"The sufferers from empyema and dropsies
treated by incision, or by the cautery, certainly perish if the
pus or water is suddenly evacuated."

In the writings of Galen there is to be found little in addition
to the directions for the treatment of empyema which exist in
the pages of Hippocrates. It is not unlikely that the operation
of thoracentesis was performed by him at Pergamos, if not in
Rome; but that this means of cure was not held in any high
estimation by the professors of the healing art during the earlier
centuries of the Christian era, is rendered probable from the
little that has been written regarding it by Galen himself, and
by the nearly complete silence on the subject of Cælius Aureli-
anus and Celsus.[1] I need not particularly refer to the opinions
of the Arabian physicians concerning thoracentesis, some of
whom, Rhazes for example, undoubtedly practised it, much as
the Greek physicians had done, but none have added anything
to our store of knowledge regarding it. Nor do I propose to
trace at any length the history of thoracentesis during the
seventeenth and eighteenth centuries,—it had been again employed, although very rarely, in the sixteenth ;—such a task is
quite uncalled for, seeing that M. Trousseau, in the first volume
of the ' Clinique Médicale de l'Hotel-Dieu,' has already accomplished it in a most interesting and satisfactory manner.
Moreover, as the student of medical history is well aware, the
subject to which I have thus briefly alluded, is discussed at
great length by the erudite Kurt Sprengel in his ' Versuch

---

[1] As regards the last-mentioned renowned writer, it is no doubt true that
in book fourth, when treating of affections of the liver, he remarks—" Si
vero jecur vomicâ laborat, eadem facienda sunt, quæ in ceteris interioribus
suppurationibus. Quidam etiam contra id scalpello aperiunt, et ipsam
vomicam adurunt." And again, in the eighth book, and there having distinct reference to the chest, because writing "De Costis fractis"—" Si
suppuratio vicerit, neque per quæ supra scripta sunt, discuti potuerit ; omnis
mora vitanda erit, ne os infra vitietur ; sed, quâ parte maxime tumebit,
demittendum erit candens ferramentum, donec ad pus perveniet ; idque
effundendum ;" but notwithstanding these and a few other references to
the treatment of empyema,—that is, of internal abscesses, abdominal and
pectoral,—I repeat that Celsus is nearly silent on the subject of thoracentesis, which, on the other hand, as we have already seen, Hippocrates so
fully considers.

einer pragmatischen Geschichte der Arzneikundç." It is worthy of note, however, that in the seventeenth century Thomas Willis and Richard Lower, two names famous in connection with the progress of anatomy and physiology in England, had performed it. About the middle of the eighteenth century, when the employment of the cautery in thoracentesis had become entirely superseded by the knife, the latter method became in its turn supplanted by the trocar. M. Trousseau informs us that the use of the trocar was recommended in 1765 by Lurde, but that nearly a century before that time its employment had been proposed by Drouin. That the strong recommendation of its advantages by Lurde and others did not obtain for the trocar an immediate or even speedy adoption, is evident from the circumstance that surgeons of the eighteenth century so distinguished as Desault and Chopart objected to its employment, on the ground that the wound it inflicted was necessarily violent (pénétrer brutalement), and that there existed no small risk of injuring the intercostal artery or the lung.

As was to be expected, the great discovery of Laennec gave a decided impulse to the performance of thoracentesis, from the aid which auscultation afforded in the diagnosis of pleural effusions. The whole subject is discussed with that author's usual sagacity as well as brilliancy, in his work on auscultation; but, strangely enough, he witheld his recommendation of the operation, except in cases which were in their nature exceptional. He remarks, "There are two cases of pleurisy in which the operation should be performed. The first of these is when in acute pleurisy the effusion, very abundant from the beginning, increases with such rapidity that in the course of a few days it causes a general or local œdema, and threatens suffocation." To this Laennec gives the name of acute empyema (empyème aigu); and, on the other hand, he assigns the appellation of chronic (empyèmes chroniques) to those instances in which the effusion has from the outset been chronic, as well as to those which, in the first instance sufficiently acute, have afterwards become chronic. Now, regarding the employment of thoracentesis in the latter cases, he remarks,—"It is to be had recourse to as an extreme remedy, when there is œdema of the affected side, when the lengthened existence of the malady, the gradually advancing emaciation and feebleness of the patient, and the

14

failure of all other remedies to effect absorption of the effused fluid, seem to hold out little hope of any cure."

Laennec proceeds to state that the operation is rarely followed with success; and this he ascribes to causes which have not been sufficiently estimated. The first of these is the unhealthy condition of the lung, which is too frequently the seat of tubercles; but the chief cause which, in the opinion of Laennec, opposed the successful result in cases of empyema treated by perforation was the compression, amounting to flattening (aplatissement), of the lung against the mediastinum and vertebral column, and the dense nature of the false membrane coating the lung. "The lung," he observes, "subjected to pressure (refoulé) for a long time has lost its elasticity and expansive force; it allows with great difficulty the air to penetrate from the trachea, and only very slowly regains a size sufficient to fill something like the space which it occupied before the occurrence of the malady." The objection to the performance of thoracentesis from the entrance of air into the pleural cavity, which, as he remarks, has always attracted the attention of surgeons, Laennec does not overlook; but it is evident that the importance assigned to it has in his opinion been exaggerated, while the precise action of air upon the contained organs has also been misinterpreted. Notwithstanding the objections to thoracentesis thus alluded to by Laennec, and there are others, a reference to which will be made as I proceed, it is very satisfactory to find this great observer, near the conclusion of the article on the treatment of pleurisy, thus expressing himself:—
" I am persuaded that the operation for empyema will become more common and more extensively useful in proportion to the increasing employment of mediate auscultation."

Becker, a physician of Berlin, is quoted by Trousseau as having, in 1834, published five cases of chronic pleurisy treated by puncture of the chest, the operation having at his request been performed by the distinguished surgeon, Diffenbach. In the following year, Dr. Thomas Davies, in the London Medical Gazette, endeavoured to establish the value of the operation as a remedy in hydrothorax and empyema, while he objected to its employment in pneumothorax as useless. There are two particulars worthy of note in the observations of Davies,—the first is, the very successful results of paracentesis thoracis in cases of children. On this head I shall have something to say in another part of this paper; for my own experience of the operation in children, although by no means extensive, leads me to agree in the expression of opinion given by Dr. West, "that the impression left on my mind by each year's additional experience is more and more in favour of its comparatively early performance." The second particular in the lectures of Dr. Davies has reference to the exact method he pursued in operating. He used a small trocar, and adopted no special means for preventing the entrance of air; but,—and this procedure has undoubtedly something to recommend it,—he introduced a grooved exploring needle as a preliminary measure, seeking thereby to determine the nature of the effusion, its consistence, and if false membrane likely to interrupt the removal of the fluid existed. In short, as a means of establishing the diagnosis, Dr. Davies used the exploring instrument, and as giving confidence to the physician, I am prepared still to recommend its use; indeed, in practice I very generally employ it.

In 1841, there appeared a very valuable contribution to the subject of paracentesis thoracis in the treatment of pleurisy, by a well-known surgeon of Vienna, recently deceased, Schuh, and a still more distinguished physician of the same city, Skoda. This monograph was succeeded in 1844 by the important memoir read to the Academy of Medicine in Paris, by M. Trousseau; while in the same year there were published in our own country two papers well worthy of notice, both of which have had an important influence in extending the benefits which the operation of thoracentesis is capable of exerting. These papers are, first, "On Paracentesis Thoracis as a Curative Measure in Empyema and Inflammatory Hydrothorax," by Dr. Hamilton Roe;[1] and, second, "On Paracentesis Thoracis, with Cases," by Dr. Hughes and Mr. Cock of Guy's Hospital.[2] Since the period of publication of these memoirs, the attention of the profession has been called to the subject by the appearance from time to time of many successful instances of thoracentesis in the different journals. In America, of late years, Dr. Brady, of New York, and still more recently, Dr. Bowditch, of Boston, have done much to gain for the

[1] 'Medico-Chirurgical Transactions,' 2nd series, vol. ix, 1844.
[2] 'Guy's Hospital Reports,' 2nd series, vol. ii, 1844.

operation an established place in professional confidence. The latter physician employing a particular apparatus, for which we are indebted to Dr. Wyman, has had his method of operating, and his remarkable success in the treatment of pleurisy by that means, brought under the notice of the profession in this country, more especially through the writings of Dr. Budd, and Dr. W. T. Gairdner. In his work on Clinical Medicine, Dr. Gairdner has at some length discussed the propriety of operative interference in cases of pleurisy; and to some of his observations I shall have occasion in the sequel to refer.

So far as I am able to judge, it appears to me that there is a growing conviction in the minds of professional men, that, notwithstanding the reliance which is justly placed in the ordinary, and happily still more available remedies which we possess, the cases of pleural effusion, acute and chronic, are not few in which recourse to the operation of thoracentesis should be had; and in the instance of those who have employed it, a growing confidence in the remedy itself. Pleurisy, whether acute or chronic, is to be regarded as a serious, it is not unfrequently, however skilfully treated, a fatal disease. From time to time there appears to be an unwonted or remarkable prevalence of pleurisy, and it is specially at such times, as I have myself observed, that there are apt to be marked peculiarities in the nature of the cases which present themselves to our notice. Some are characterised by the violence of their onset, the very acute lateral pain, and the high pyrexia, which seem to call for speedy and very active treatment; others are unaccompanied by any marked degree of either—indeed the pain, wanting altogether the true characteristics of the typical pain of pleurisy, may be absent, and the constitutional disturbance for a time at least trivial. The latter cases are oftentimes, moreover, most insidious in their progress; and it is not of unfrequent occurrence to find a sufferer from pleurisy presenting himself at the hospital, or in some other way seeking professional advice, when, and not till then, one side—it is usually the left—is distended by effusion. There is, probably, much truth in the statement of M. Pidoux, that large or excessive effusions are apt to occur in one particular form of pleurisy very different from the ordinary disease.

Such experience is, I am persuaded, far from being unusual;

and I am equally satisfied that, in the opinion of all experienced physicians, the disease in its ACUTE FORM—for of that I wish now *in the first place* to treat—is one which tends in some cases, if not at times in many, to the unfavorable termination. M. Trousseau has very specially considered this question, and that in all its bearings. "To justify the employment of paracentesis of the chest in pleurisy with large effusion," he remarks, "it is necessary as a first step to establish, contrary to the opinion expressed by M. Louis, that pleurisy is sometimes fatal." Here let me briefly record not the earliest fatal case of pleurisy which I have witnessed, but one among the earliest. There were circumstances in connection with this case which necessarily led to its making a deep impression on my mind; to these I need not now refer, except to express the conviction which, with an increasing experience of the treatment of pleurisy, and, latterly, an assured confidence in the value of paracentesis, I do with confidence, that the use of that remedy *might* have availed to save life.

CASE I.—A lady, æt. 45, the mother of several children, had enjoyed uninterruptedly good health, till the occurrence of her fatal illness, now about twelve years since. That took place as follows :—After exposure to cold she was seized with severe pain in the left side, accompanied by short cough, and difficulty of breathing. A few leeches were applied over the seat of pain within a few hours from its commencement, and when the existence of distinct pleuritic friction sound had been discovered on auscultation, repeated small doses of Dover's powder, and a mixture containing acetate of potass, were also prescribed. On the following day, the lateral stitch was found greatly relieved—in fact, nearly removed—but extended dulness on percussion and considerable embarrassment of breathing were present. The pulse, previously sharp, was then very frequent and soft. The same treatment was continued, and shortly after a large blister was, in addition, applied to the side. In the course of a few days there was evidence of increased pleural effusion, afforded by still more extended dulness on percussion, by displacement of the heart to the right of the sternum, and by entire obliteration of vocal thrill and vesicular respiration sound over considerably more than the lower two-thirds of the left side of the chest. These indications were not in themselves alarming; but in the anxiety of countenance, and the frequent as well as somewhat feeble pulse, there *was* something to create anxiety. I requested Dr. Begbie to visit this lady with me. On that occasion, Dr. Begbie was so much struck by the anxious expression of her countenance, and by the peculiarity in the action of the heart and character of the pulse, consisting mainly in their feebleness, that he suggested the possibility of the pericardium being involved; that, in addition to pleural, there was possibly pericardial effusion. This suggestion appeared at the time very important; and although, from the feeble action of the heart, and the extended dulness on percussion in the neighbourhood of the organ, perhaps otherwise induced, we had unusually little to depend upon in the way of physical signs, still the implication of the pericardium, or possibly of the heart itself, seemed at the time adequately and satisfactorily to account for the alarming symptoms. From that time the patient had at brief intervals a little brandy or wine. Towards evening of the day on which the last report was made, there occurred a tendency to syncope, demanding the freer employment of stimulants. During the night an attack of fatal syncope took place, death resulting before—being hurriedly summoned—I had time to reach the house. On examination of the body, we found a large collection of serous fluid, with a few flakes of soft lymph floating through it, in the left pleural cavity, the left lung much compressed in its lower lobe, but only partially so in the upper, which was adherent to a limited extent in front. The surface of the lung, where free, was coated with a tolerably thick layer of recent lymph. The heart was considerably displaced to the right, but the pericardium and the interior of the organ were healthy; and, on careful microscopical examination, the muscular structure of the heart was found to be quite unimpaired. Neither in the aorta nor in the pulmonary artery was there found any clot, or any obstructive coagulum sufficient to account for the fatal symptoms; these, indeed, did not point to the likely occurrence of embolism, and certainly no embolism existed.

This, then, was a death in uncomplicated acute pleurisy; in a case, moreover, not characterised by the existence of any excessive effusion. It is worthy of remark, that the mode of fatal termination was purely that of failure of the vital function of the circulation—a syncope, threatening in its recurrence again and again during a brief period, and then ultimately causing death. Neither is this experience in pleurisy—remarkable as it is—very unusual; indeed, I feel persuaded, and in special view of the employment of paracentesis, would desire to urge this consideration, that in cases of pleurisy with considerable effusion we do well to regard a termination by syncope as one of the dangers which is to be if possible averted. Such a termination may occur suddenly, almost unexpectedly, or, as in the case now briefly detailed, may be threatened more or less imminently for a time, perhaps for days, and then unhappily take place. It is very specially in such circumstances that the performance of paracentesis is called for, and that the results from the operation are found to be so satisfactory. The following instance of acute pleurisy, treated by paracentesis and other remedial means, will best illustrate the plan which I have now frequently adopted, and invariably with the same gratifying success.

CASE 2.—A. T—, æt. 22, a servant, was admitted to the Royal Infirmary, under my care, in March, 1864. On the 5th of that month, after exposure in washing and drying clothes, she was seized with severe shivering and vomiting, and soon after had pain in the left side, with stitch. Thus suffering, she was confined to bed and under medical treatment till the 15th, when, with considerable difficulty, owing to her weak condition, she was removed to the Infirmary. On admission, the embarrassment of breathing was great; the face somewhat flushed; the countenance anxious; pulse 130, and feeble; there was little cough and no expectoration; she was unable to assume the entirely recumbent posture, but was supported in bed with pillows in the semi-erect position; she stated that for several days she had been unable to lie on the right side. Passed a very small quantity of high-coloured urine, with a copious deposit of pink urates. On percussion, the left side of chest, in front, in the lateral region, and posteriorly, was found absolutely dull, with the exception of a very limited space in the vicinity of the left-sterno-clavicular articulation and above the clavicle, where percussion elicited a partially tympanitic note. The vocal thrill over dull regions was absent; at the very summit of the lung, anteriorly, it was felt in an exaggerated degree. Distant bronchial breathing was audible along the left border of spine, but no vesicular murmur was to be heard anywhere. The timbre of voice posteriorly was ægophonic in character. The lower intercostal spaces in the left lateral region were extended, but there was an absence of any marked distension. There was no parietal œdema of the chest, and no œdema of arm or neck. The heart's impulse was perceptible to the right of the sternum and at the summit of the scrobiculus cordis, it was feeble, and so were the cardiac sounds, which otherwise were unaffected. The respiratory murmur over the whole right lung was greatly intensified. At visit of the 16th, the patient having passed a wholly sleepless night, and taken no food, I tapped the chest, introducing a small-sized trocar, without any preliminary incision, between the eighth and ninth ribs posteriorly, in a line drawn directly downwards from the lower angle of the scapula. A clear straw-coloured and highly albuminous fluid escaped. Of this twenty-five ounces were allowed to flow; certainly no air entered the chest, although no special means for effecting its exclusion was at the time adopted; and then the cannula being withdrawn, a small piece of lint, held in position by two short cross strips of diachylon plaster, was applied over the minute wound. A little brandy with water was administered to the patient during the operation, and after the withdrawal of the fluid she found that without any difficulty the recumbent posture could be assumed. Before leaving, directions were given for the application of a large blister over the left side of chest, and the following remedies were ordered :—

℞ Potassii Iodidi, ʒi;
Aquæ Destillatæ ʒvi. Solve.
Sign., a tablespoonful thrice daily.

℞ Pulv. Scillæ, gr. i;
Massæ Pilularum Hydrargyri;
Pulveris Ipecacuanhæ cum opio, āā gr. ij. M.
Mitte tales vi. Sign., one, night and morning.

On the 17th, we found at visit that the patient had passed a good night, and that she felt much more comfortable, breathing with little difficulty. She had taken some food. The bowels had been moved, and an increased amount of urine passed. On examination of the chest, the region of tympanitic percussion note in front was found to be considerably extended, and a similar character of resonance was for the first time noticed above the scapular spine posteriorly. After this there was no further anxiety about the case; the iodide of potassium, and diuretic pills were continued for a few days, and then, without the latter having produced any physiological action of mercury, a mixture containing the infusion of digitalis and scoparium was substituted for them. A second blister was also applied after the first blistered surface had healed. Gradually the dulness on percussion diminished, and the normal resonance became restored. Friction sound, very coarse in character, was audible in the left lateral region for a considerable period, but in time that also disappeared. The patient's convalescence was protracted, or rather delayed, by an attack of dry pleurisy, very distinct in its characters, on the right side; but having regained flesh, and with completely re-established health, and with very few, and these indistinct, signs of the malady which brought her under our notice, she left the hospital on the 15th June, after exactly three months' residence.

Now, in this case, the termination of which was so satisfactory, as, at all events, to imply that the remedial means employed were well suited for the treatment of the disease, the question presents itself, was thoracentesis really requisite? in other words, was the condition of the patient at the time when the single tapping was performed, such as to make it at least improbable that other, and these the ordinary remedies, would have availed to combat the disease? This is a question which I have invariably put to myself before using the trocar, in all of the now many operations in acute and chronic pleurisy which I have performed. In the instance of A. T—, the feebleness of the heart and pulse, taken in connection with the very considerable amount of dyspnœa, led me to conclude that it was necessary to afford relief to the patient as soon as possible ; that there was danger, imminent danger, in practising delay. I cannot certainly affirm that in this case, any more than in others, to some of which I shall immediately refer, recovery without paracentesis would not have taken place; but I had then, and still have, a strong impression that the unfavorable termination was, of the two events, the more likely to occur.

The recommendation has been given by some physicians to allow a *certain* period of time to elapse from the occurrence of the effusion, during which the diligent employment of the more ordinary remedies available for promoting its removal is to be practised, and that when this period, fixed by some at fifteen days, by others at three weeks, and as long as six weeks, has been permitted to pass, then, and then only, the operation, truly in such circumstances as a "dernier ressort," or with the proved failure of all other means—the confessedly "remedium anceps melius quam nullum," may be had recourse to. This I submit, as has already been done by many experienced physicians, is not giving thoracentesis a fair or even decent trial ; for if the remedy can be shown in careful hands to be itself free from any unusual hazard, clearly then we are entitled to claim for it an employment more dignified than is implied in its being looked to as a last resort, or at best a very doubtful means of cure. For myself, I am, in so far as this question of thoracentesis in acute pleurisy is concerned, entirely opposed to the plan of settling the exact occasion of its employment by any reference whatever to time or days. I agree in the criticism by Celsus of one of the Hippocratic doctrines, founded too exactly on the Pythagorean philosophy, " quum hic quoque medicus," says he, " non numerare dies debeat, sed ipsas accessiones intueri ; et ex his conjectare," etc. Nor do I conceive that a satisfactory answer to the many questions which crop up, on anything like a candid consideration of this subject, can be obtained from a statistical investigation—that certainly may aid, it has already aided our inquiry, as in the extended experience of Dr. Brady and Dr. Bowditch—but concur in the expression of Dr. Gairdner, " This question is one not to be answered by statistics, but rather by the careful consideration of individual cases," [1]

[1] 'Clinical Medicine,' p. 375.

There are, then, a few features of importance in the case now briefly detailed, to which I desire to call attention. The effusion in it was considerable, but certainly not excessive, for there was an entire absence of parietal œdema; and although the left side of chest was somewhat rounded, there existed no very marked bulging of the intercostal spaces. Moreover, the heart was not displaced to the extent I have often seen it in cases of very large effusion; and there still existed, at the time of the patient's entrance to hospital, a little, although that little was altered, resonance on percussion. But with a pleural effusion of fourteen days' existence, stopping short of being excessive, there was in this case a very feeble action of the heart, and a quick as well as feeble pulse. The dyspnœa was great; indeed, as orthopnœa existed, it may properly be styled urgent; but as I have witnessed larger pleural effusions than this case presented, accompanied, as might be inferred, by greater dyspnœa, and have not performed thoracentesis, but trusted to the use of ordinary remedies, so I desire here to impress the view, that the determination immediately to adopt the operation in this case was formed from a consideration of the impediment to breathing, coupled with the feebleness of the circulation. This consideration has guided me in all the instances of acute pleurisy in which I have used thoracentesis. I look upon it as the most important point to receive attention. There may be very considerable dyspnœa without marked depression of the circulation, and there may also be marked depression of the circulation without any very great dyspnœa; while these conditions may exist with a disproportionate amount of effusion. For I have a distinct impression, that in my own experience the cases calling most urgently for the employment of the remedy, the judicious use of which I advocate, were not characterised by the excessive amount of the effusion nor by an extreme degree of dyspnœa.

That the tendency to syncope, observable in some cases, is not directly due to the amount of the pleural effusion, I infer from what I have myself witnessed of pleurisy, both fatal and otherwise. In the case of the lady already described, which belongs to the former category, it will be remembered that the amount of fluid found after death was not very large, and further that the physical signs during life—and this holds true of cases belonging to the second category—did not indicate the occupation of the pleural cavity to any inordinate degree by fluid. Again, in seeking to arrive at the true cause of this tendency to depression of the vital function of circulation, it is further worthy of notice that the displacement of the heart, which at first sight might not unreasonably be regarded as explaining the different experience in different cases, does not in or by itself prove sufficient; for, although admitting that altered and probably depressed function will result from its dislocation, it is consistent with my own observation that the cases in which the position of the central organ of the circulation has been most altered have not been characterised by the occurrence of the syncopal tendency. And, again, that tendency, in a most marked and even in a fatal degree, has been exhibited in cases in which cardiac displacement has been by no means great. I have thought that possibly some such cases as the former had escaped this danger, from the very circumstance that the heart, yielding to the accumulating pressure, had had its position more decidedly altered. This explanation, however, is inadequate. The tendency to the occurrence of syncope—the actual occurrence of fatal syncope in pleurisy—has taken place when the effusion has had its seat in the right side as well as in its more frequent situation, the left. In the former, the implication of the heart by direct pressure has been comparatively slight. I apprehend that the cause of this really important, because serious, event in pleurisy is to be sought not in any merely mechanical or purely dynamical disturbance,—it lies, in all probability, deeper. We may not be able—rarely do I think we shall be able—to indicate at an early or at any precise period of the disease the cases in which the depression referred to is to be looked for as more than ordinarily likely to occur. It is, however, intimately connected with those vital changes, more especially of innervation, which we know to exist in all abnormal action within the body, and still more immediately with inflammation, changes, too little regarded by those whose pathological alterations must needs be seen by naked eye or microscope, but which nevertheless modify the progress, and probably largely determine the ultimate event in cases not of pleurisy merely, but of all fatal diseases. Dr. Walshe, who has been fortunate in very rarely meeting with a fatal termination in acute pleurisy, has stated, and the expression is borne out by my own observation, that asphyxia (pure), owing to the copiousness of effusion, he has never witnessed as a form of danger in the acute stage of the simple unilateral disease.[1] That such a termination as that now under consideration may take place in cases where the heart's structure has been previously unsound, is a proposition which it is unnecessary to consider at any length : that is self-evident; but the tendency is of much more frequent occurrence in pleurisy than in such comparatively rare instances. Besides, these are examples of complicated disease which do not call for consideration, as I am now treating of simple pleurisy. Already, as in the first case detailed in these observations, the occurrence of fatal syncope has been found in connection with a heart perfectly sound in structure, and only slightly displaced by an effusion far from excessive. It has indeed been suggested, as by Dr. Gairdner, that death in such circumstances may be considered to be due "to the severity of the diet, or to the treatment by depletion and digitalis, rather than to the disease." This explanation cannot apply to the cases already noticed, nor to others which I am now anxious to record.

In the following case, the operation of thoracentesis was performed on account of an acute pleurisy occurring in a man upwards of seventy years of age, the oldest subject of the disease, as well as of the remedy, who has fallen under my notice :—

CASE 3.—T. B— was a patient in the Royal Infirmary in October, 1862. He was seen at an early period of his illness, and judiciously treated by the late Dr. Andrew Pow; but owing to an increase in the severity of the symptoms, and some obstacles to his being properly cared for in his own house, on Dr. Pow's recommendation he was brought to the hospital. On admission, he had the ordinary signs of a large pleuritic effusion on the left side. The only exceptional point in his case regards the heart and arteries. He had evidently considerable degeneration of the arterial tunics; and the heart, displaced by the pleural effusion, was also the seat of disease. A bruit indicating some obstruction at the aortic orifice existed, and that obstruction was regarded as in all probability due to some atheromatous affection of the semilunar valves themselves, or to some deposition of a similar nature at the very commencement of the great vessel. These changes,

---

[1] 'Diseases of the Lungs,' p. 290.

incident to his advanced years, did not certainly improve the prospects of his recovery. I know that my late friend, Dr. Pow, regarded the condition of this old man as very critical, and did not hesitate to ascribe the satisfactory termination of his case to the treatment which was pursued. The patient, on admission, was extremely breathless, and quite unable to lie down in bed. His heart's action was feeble and a little irregular; and his pulse at the wrist, where the radial artery was distinctly visible as well as tortuous, possessed the same characters. Any exertion, even of the slightest description, aggravated the dyspnœa. The usual remedies had been employed before his admission—blisters, diuretics, and the external application of iodine. Three weeks had elapsed from the first occurrence of the malady. Looking upon this man's age and previous condition of health, as exerting a decidedly unfavorable influence on the therapeutic action of such remedies as might otherwise have received for a time at least a renewed trial, and believing that neither his age nor infirmities could be regarded as in any sense barriers to the operation, I introduced a small trocar between the eighth and ninth left ribs in the lateral region, and drew off nearly thirty ounces of pale, clear, albuminous serum, in which a fibrinous clot formed very speedily on cooling. The immediate result was most assuring, and the subsequent progress of the case such as to satisfy me that a right remedy had been used. As in the former case, the tapping was single; the use of the acid tartrate of potash, in the form of an electuary, with treacle, the application of a blister over the left side, with a moderate allowance of stimulants, were the only other means employed. Admitted on October 2nd, the old man was discharged with an expanded left lung, and healthy breath-sounds audible over its whole surface, on 22nd November.

I need not in this case again particularly inquire, Was the simple operation necessary? That question I have endeavoured to answer, in part at least, in the observations which succeeded the details of the former case; and I will only add here, that if " the end justifies the means," the case of this old man and the treatment he received are well worthy of attention. I might speak at length of the great relief he experienced on the withdrawal of the first few ounces of fluid, and of his unwillingness that I should, by the removal of the cannula, interrupt the flow. I do not do so, because present relief is one thing, certainly not unimportant, but permanent benefit and successful treatment are what I desire to establish as the results of a judicious employment of thoracentesis.

The record of this second instance of a single successful tapping in acute pleurisy leads me, however, to make one or two further observations. It will be observed, that in neither case

was thoracentesis employed until the ordinary treatment had
been put in execution, and had received a proper trial. I am
most happy to express my great reliance upon, and confidence
in, the remedies which are generally employed for the treatment of acute pleurisy in all its stages, including moderate
bloodletting, specially in the earliest stage, when lateral stitch
is very severe and inflammatory fever high; likewise in
febrifuge medicines, especially those exerting a sudorific or
diaphoretic action. When effusion has occurred and fever still
prevails, I use the salts of potash—the nitrate, acetate, or
bicarbonate; while in young and vigorous constitutions I sometimes select calomel and opium, or blue pill with squill and
digitalis,—remedies which I have often seen most useful; or if
a rheumatic or gouty taint be present,—as is very frequently
the case,—I combine with these remedies lemon-juice or
colchicum, or aconite, or actæa. When the more ardent fever
has subsided, I have recourse to blisters, large and frequently
applied, and to the internal administration of iodine, particularly of iodide of potassium, or the acid tartrate of potash.
Rarely disappointed in these remedies, there soon comes a time
when, with a steadily if not rapidly diminishing effusion, a
change to the use of the Liquor Iodi Compositus, or the syrup of
the iodide of iron, or one of the simple salts of iron, or of
quinine or cinchona, is found to be beneficial. Placing, therefore, great reliance in the use of these remedies, I do not wish
it to be supposed that the cases are otherwise than a small
minority in which the withdrawal of the fluid from the pleura
in part, or as nearly as possible in whole, is to be considered
desirable, or, to use more correct language, is called for.

During the period when the hospital cases already detailed
occurred, there were many cases of severe pleurisy successfully
treated by some one or other of the remedies named,—cases
which I should as soon have thought of treating by the trocar,
as I should now be willing to forego the use of that valuable
instrument in any case resembling those of the young woman
and the old man, already detailed. But, again, in both of these
cases, I wish it to be distinctly noted that a limited amount of
the fluid contained in the pleura only was removed; in both
instances a large quantity, probably a much larger quantity
than that withdrawn, remained. Now, I think there is a very

great advantage in this particular mode of procedure: for, *first*, while there are no doubt in different cases somewhat different reasons for having recourse to the operation, there is one reason common to all, namely, the desire to give immediate relief to the more urgent symptoms,—to make, if possible, the breathing easier, and the pulse, or rather heart's action, steadier. I believe that these important issues can, in the great majority of cases of acute pleural effusion, be secured by the removal of a limited—even a very limited amount of fluid; in the instances already recorded, twenty-five ounces, and about thirty ounces respectively were allowed to flow; and then the change in the condition of the patient to the better being conspicuous, the further abstraction was unnecessary; for, *secondly* experience shows, that not only are the urgent symptoms thus relieved, but that the apparently direct consequence of the operation is a busy action of the absorbents and secreting organs, by which the remaining fluid is speedily carried off. This result is in some instances really quite astonishing. In one case, for example, in which the symptoms of pleurisy were very severe, and the effusion excessive, but where for certain reasons I had wished not to have recourse to the simple remedy a day too soon, I was at length compelled to do so, from the extremely scanty secretion of urine, and the appparently entire failure of the foremost diuretics to stimulate the kidneys. I withdrew, by Bowditch's syringe, a very large quantity of clear fluid, and within twenty-four hours the patient passed a large chamberpotful and a-half of urine. This powerful diuresis continued for some days, and the pleural effusion had in that time completely disappeared. But, *thirdly*, the operation of thoracentesis, performed in the way and for the purpose described in the two cases which I have detailed, is really a very simple and an eminently safe means of treatment. There is no risk whatever in such circumstances of the entrance of air, and therefore a simple trocar and cannula are alone required; an exhausting syringe or valvular apparatus is quite unnecessary. Selecting a dependent position, and having with a little force depressed the intercostal space about its middle, you introduce the trocar boldly where dulness is well marked; and, as you remove it, the fluid passes through the cannula; the limited portion you desire to remove is, properly speaking, determined by the influence the withdrawal of the serum has upon the patient's condition. You carefully watch that, and whenever the breathing is decidedly relieved, and the pulse is improved in strength—for these events occur together—you remove the cannula. Thus operating, I have never known any air to enter.

While alluding to the possibility of the entrance of air during the performance of thoracentesis, let me say that the dangers of this occurrence have, in my opinion, been greatly exaggerated. I quite agree with an able American writer, the late Dr. Swett, that "experience proves that the admission of air into the chest in these cases is attended with no serious inconvenience." In operating in some sub-acute and chronic cases, and before I had the advantage of possessing the syringe of Wyman and Bowditch, occasionally a little air entered, but I never saw this give rise to any unpleasant consequence. The air was speedily absorbed, and the signs of a very limited pneumothorax, which were at first present, soon ceased to exist. No importance, I believe, is to be attached to the notion entertained by some, that the presence of air in the pleural cavity favours the decomposition of the contained fluid. No doubt, the fluid drawn off from the chest in cases of hydro-pneumothorax is sometimes fetid; but that that condition is not caused by the mere presence of air is proved by the circumstance that, on post-mortem examination in long-standing cases of hydro-pneumothorax, and of empyema with pneumothorax, it is not of unfrequent occurrence to find no fetor either of the air or fluid such as must have otherwise existed before death. I have satisfied myself that the fluid withdrawn from the chest by thoracentesis may be kept with little change for many days. I have kept it for a fortnight freely exposed to the air, and in contact with animal matter removed along with it from the pleura, without its undergoing any decomposing change. The considerable presence of chloride of sodium in such fluid may probably tend to its lengthened preservation of both normal appearance and smell.

Let it be granted, however, that the entrance of air should be if possible prevented,—and in the treatment of acute pleurisy requiring thoracentesis that can be done by the employment of the American syringe,—or if, as I believe in the vast majority of instances is alone necessary, it be intended to remove only a limited quantity, let the trocar be introduced in a dependent position of the chest, where the signs of effusion are unequivocal. I have of late generally, as Dr. Bowditch mentions is his usual practice, entered the trocar on the posterior aspect of the chest between the seventh and eighth, or eighth and ninth ribs, in a line leading directly downwards from the lower angle of the scapula. In acute cases of pleurisy, adhesions interrupting the proper performance of the operation rarely—in my experience never—exist in that situation. There is truth in the axiomatic statement of Hippocrates, that the sudden withdrawal of fluid from the shut sacs is attended by danger. I have seen a patient nearly faint—and at such a time a faint is a very dangerous event—when the fluid was rushing out quickly from the pleura through a pretty large cannula. We see this accident occur in paracentesis abdominis, if the patient be raised in the sitting posture, and the fluid be suddenly or very quickly withdrawn. It is prevented by keeping the patient in the recumbent posture, and using a small trocar; and these measures render the employment of substitute pressure by the broad sheet unnecessary. In the removal of a limited amount of fluid from the chest, I have never seen anything like faintness ensue, for generally, on the contrary, the strength of the patient immediately improves. Having given the particulars of the case of an old patient, the subject of acute pleurisy, I may briefly refer to a few other instances, and, first, to that of a young child.

CASE 4.—A girl, æt. 4, was tapped on an evening in the month of June, 1863. I had been asked to see her through the kindness of Professor Simpson, and on account of thoracentesis being in his opinion required, owing to the severity of the dyspnœa and great feebleness of the little patient. She had been suffering from pleurisy of the right side for several days, and the effusion had somewhat suddenly undergone increase, giving rise to considerable aggravation in the character of the symptoms. In the presence of Professor Simpson and Dr. Black the trocar was introduced between the seventh and eighth ribs in the lateral region, and by means of Bowditch's syringe nearly eighteen ounces of a clear serum, in which a coagulum of fibrine speedily formed, were drawn off. I saw the little patient on the following morning in a greatly improved state, and had afterwards the satisfaction of learning from Professor Simpson and Dr. Black that the recovery was complete.

I have already alluded to the generally very successful results

15

of thoracentesis in young children, and this remark applies to
cases of acute pleurisy and empyema as well as of chronic
effusion.   I have employed this remedy in the cases of several
children besides the one just recorded, particularly in a little
girl of three years, and in another little girl of five, both of
whom màde rapid and complete recoveries.   I should certainly
not be deterred from the use of thoracentesis by the consideration of the mere tenderness of the child; however young, if the
case itself called for the operation, I think it should be
employed.   Indeed, considering the difficulty of administering
ordinary remedies to very young children, it appears to me
that they ought specially to be regarded as suitable subjects for
the operation.

CASE 5.—Of all the cases of acute pleurisy, treated by thoracentesis,
which have fallen under my own care, the one in which I felt most
satisfied, not only as to the urgent necessity there existed for immediate
interference, but after the operation had been had recourse to, of the
remedy having truly availed to save life, was that of a youth admitted
to the Royal Infirmary, under my care, in October, 1864. He was
suffering from a large pleural effusion on the left side, the form of
which was greatly altered, being rounded, with obliteration of the
intercostal spaces, and great prominence. The side was uniformly
dull on percussion, and the heart much displaced to the right; there
was likewise a little parietal œdema over the affected side of the chest.
Orthopnœa, and great feebleness of the pulse existed.   Considering this
patient to be in imminent danger, a view likewise taken by my friends
Dr. Wilkinson, late of Tranent, and Dr. Alexander Robertson, of
Queenscliff, Australia, who happened to be in the ward at the time, I at
once introduced the trocar, and removed about forty ounces of highly
albuminous serum, which, as in other cases already detailed, only to a
greater degree, formed into a jelly on cooling. There was immediate
relief from the operation, the patient assumed the recumbent posture,
and fell into a tranquil sleep. Blisters and diuretic remedies were
subsequently employed, and the youth made an excellent recovery,
leaving the hospital within six weeks of his admission.

It will be observed that in this case, as in the others, a
single tapping was alone required : the practice pursued being
that to the excellence of which I have already borne a strong
testimony.   In this instance the pleura was packed with fluid,
and I believe in such a condition as to make it very unlikely
that any internal remedies—such had been judiciously used—
could act favorably, or indeed act therapeutically at all, until

the removal of a portion of the fluid permitted them to do so. Speedily the passage of an increased amount of urine followed the withdrawal of the effused fluid from the chest. Immediately on the performance of the operation, expansion of the compressed lung occurred, ascertained by the clear percussion note over the summit of the chest, anteriorly and posteriorly, as the lad sat in bed, and by the distinct though feeble respiratory sound on auscultation. The patient was disturbed by cough for a day or two, short in character, and attended by the expectoration of a little clear phlegm. This will generally, I believe, be noticed to succeed the performance of thoracentesis in both acute and chronic pleurisy, and more particularly in those cases where the lung, previously compressed, rapidly expands. The presence of a little catarrhal affection of the lung itself, certainly not to be wondered at, is probably the determining cause of the forcible expiratory effort. One other remark is called for by what we observed in this youth's case, as well as in other instances, indeed less notably in his than in others. The lung seemed to expand steadily, for a time even rapidly; percussion resonance, normal in character, returned to the anterior and upper part of the affected side, but in the dorsal region, and still more, the axillary and lower lateral regions, dulness continued marked. I have known this to hold true in cases of pleurisy thus treated for many months, indeed for years. It need, however, scarcely be observed that the same dulness on percussion, with diminished expansive power, impaired vocal thrill, and enfeebled respiratory murmur, are found long-continued, or lasting permanently, in many cases of severe pleurisy treated by ordinary remedies, and which have made a satisfactory recovery. In such instances a considerable deposit of lymph has in all probability taken place, and it is to the existence of that inflammatory product that the physical signs, as well as the physical change in the condition of the chest just noted, are to be ascribed. It is remarkable to how great an extent that dulness and those other signs may in course of time be found yielding, or even entirely passing away.

In at least four other instances of acute pleurisy, very similar in their character to those already detailed, I have thought it necessary to have recourse to thoracentesis. In one of these four, a young gentleman of twenty-four years of age, the pleural effusion was associated with a peculiar swelling of the corresponding limb, both in the leg and thigh. This swelling was not of an œdematous character, but firm, and resembling a good deal the condition of the extremity when affected by phlegmasia dolens. In two cases of typhus, and in one of enteric fever, one of the subjects being a gentleman of about twenty-five, and the other two females in hospital, I have witnessed a precisely similar affection; but Dr. Begbie informs me—and the observation appears to be very interesting—that in three cases of pleurisy occurring to him within a limited period of time, he has observed the swollen limb corresponding to the pleuritic side. In one of these the lymphatic disturbance in the leg—for such it would appear to be—preceded the pleurisy, in the others was consequent on it. To a few particulars in the history and treatment of one other example of acute pleurisy I shall now allude.

CASE 6.—A married woman, in very comfortable circumstances, was the subject of a very severe pleurisy. The disease occurred on the left side, and was ushered in by considerable constitutional disturbance and great pain. The distinctive signs of pleurisy were early discovered, and before any fluid effusion had occurred the patient had been placed under appropriate treatment. This, however, did not avail to prevent the serous accumulation occurring and augmenting, until the cavity was apparently completely occupied, and the parietes were much distended. Three weeks of employment of ordinary measures were followed by no improvement whatever. The condition of the patient had indeed now become critical; there was great fever, hot skin, very frequent pulse, much breathlessness, and general derangement of system. In these circumstances thoracentesis was performed; and with Bowditch's syringe I removed upwards of sixty ounces of straw-coloured serum. The whole fluid passed into the condition of a really firm coagulum within a few hours of its removal from the chest. From the day, I may say the hour, of its performance, this patient improved, and nothing occurred to retard her recovery, which has been rapid as well as perfect.

I shall conclude these observations, on the treatment of acute pleurisy, by a few remarks specially applicable to the condition of EMPYEMA, as it occurs in an acute form. When the effusion of fluid within the pleura is known or suspected to consist of pus, there is then much less room for difference of opinion as to the proper plan of treatment. Purulent fluid is far from being readily absorbed from the pleura, so that in such cases the advice of Dr. Watson will probably be found consistent with the view generally entertained by the profession, that "whenever (no matter how we ascertain the fact) the effused fluid consists of pus, it should be let out." If thoracentesis is not performed at an early, or comparatively early period, the probability is that the pus will find a way of exit for itself, either through the chest walls—when the opening is far more likely to prove fistulous and permanent than when incision or puncture is made—or through the lung, or less likely through the diaphragm into the cavity of the abdomen (case of Carroll, in Ward 7, Royal Infirmary, 1857), or in some other manner. The cases of acute empyema which are met with vary in their character and course not a little. Some are the result, after a time longer or shorter, of ordinary acute pleurisy; others, and these are, as a general rule, less promising, appear to have been attended by an effusion, which, from the very commencement, has been puriform or even purulent. In such there is little formation of lymph, and pleural adhesions rarely result to any extent. That the removal of pus in large amount from the pleura in cases of acute empyema may be followed by results as satisfactory as those which have already been described as succeeding the withdrawal of serous fluid, my own observation and experience have convinced me. It must, however, be held in remembrance that such cases as are from the first attended by purulent effusion, and those also, although in less degree, in which the fluid has soon become pus, are more serious in their nature, accompanied by fever of a truly hectic character capable of rapidly undermining the patient's strength, less amenable to treatment of all kinds, and are very frequently connected with disease of the lung. I am more suspicious of empyema on the right side being connected with pulmonary disease than when the effusion is seated in the more ordinary position on the left. Possibly this more frequent connection of tubercular disease of the lung with empyema on the right side may, in part if not wholly, account for the fewer recoveries after the operation of thoracentesis on the right side as recorded in the statistics of Dr. Brady. I will briefly relate the particulars of one remarkable instance of acute empyema treated by thoracentesis, and in doing so shall be led to offer a few observations on the special points of difference between this affection and the one we have already considered.

CASE 7.—Eight years ago, G. P—, æt. 25, a painter, became my patient in the Royal Infirmary, suffering from an extensive and recent pleural effusion on the left side. There was that about the appearance of this man which induced me to believe that the nature of the fluid was purulent; he had hectic fever, dusky countenance, and anxious expression. Moreover, he had suffered previously from cough, and had other chest symptoms at the same time; he had lost one brother from phthisis, and during his residence in the hospital another brother died of the same disease. In this case the effusion was very large, altering the form of the chest, giving rise to considerable distension, and to œdema of the thoracic parietes, as well as of the upper part of left arm. The heart was much displaced, and the left side of the chest universally dull. After fully a week's employment of ordinary remedies, there appeared a tendency to pointing in the lowest part of left lateral region, and in that situation I accordingly introduced a trocar, removing 120 ounces of healthy-looking pus, free from smell. The dyspnœa, which had been very great, was much relieved by the operation, and the condition of the chest not a little improved. In ten days the reaccumulation of pus necessitated the performance of thoracentesis for the second time, when about 80 ounces were withdrawn. So matters continued for several weeks, till I had myself, on nine different occasions, removed nearly 1000 ounces. About five months after the original perforation by the trocar, I made a pretty free incision through the parietes and into the pleura, between the eighth and ninth ribs in the lateral region : pus flowed freely into a soft sponge, and the sponge, made hollow in the centre, being reapplied, the pus was thus for many days collected. The patient thereafter left the hospital and resided for some weeks in the country. He visited me from time to time, and calculated that from the period of leaving the hospital fully another thousand ounces of pus had escaped. In the course of other six months the wound healed, and the patient was able to resume his occupation, at which he has continued ever since. The condition of his chest was for a lengthened period most satisfactory; from the time the opening closed until recently, the left lung was fully expanded, and occupied the pleural cavity so completely as to make it a difficult task—in which many educated students have failed—to say, from a simple inspection, on which side of the chest his empyema had existed.

To an interesting circumstance in connection with this case I may here allude. An aduncated appearance of the nails and distinct clubbing of the fingers on the affected side took place during the period the patient was under observation. This change became so marked and was so much more conspicuous in the left hand than in the fingers of the right that I had, through the kindness of Dr. Frederick Steell, a cast of the hand made, in which the peculiarity in question was well exhibited. A reference to the occurrence of clubbing of the finger ends on the diseased side in empyema is made by Dr. Walshe, and by other writers. Dr. Walshe remarks that this change " is sometimes strikingly marked." This, however, is not the point to which I have specially to call attention, which remains to be noticed, it is this, that after the lung underwent expansion, and the purulent discharge diminished, and still more decidedly, when the lung had fully expanded, and all passage of pus had ceased, the clubbing of the finger ends became much less marked, and for many months so continued. Latterly this man has had pulmonary symptoms, which have occasioned a little anxiety; he has repeatedly spat blood, although never in large amount, and the cough, which had entirely disappeared, has again returned. With these symptoms there have presented themselves signs of tubercular deposition in the summit of the right lung, and the fingers of both hands have become clubbed. Nevertheless, he has, with occasional interruptions, been able for his work as a carriage painter; and since his attack of empyema, he has married a wife and begotten one child, healthy, and in every respect well-conditioned.

I have spoken of collecting the pus in a sponge applied over the opening in the thoracic parietes. This plan answers well both in adults and in children, in whose cases it was first recommended by Dr. Brotherston, of Alloa, in a paper giving an interesting account of three instances of empyema occurring after scarlatina, treated by paracentesis.[1] Dr. Brotherston applied the sponge while the cannula was still retained; and this—following his suggestion—I have also done, and found most useful, keeping the instrument effectually in its place, which, owing to the alarm and restlessness of very young patients, is otherwise very difficult.

[1] 'Monthly Journal of Medical Science,' 1853. So interesting are these cases that M. Trousseau is found quoting one of them,—"Je vous demande la permission (he says, in the first volume of the 'Clinique Médicale de l'Hotel Dieu'), de vous lire un de ceux (empyèmes purulents scarlatineux), que le Docteur P. Brotherston a publiés dans le 'Monthly Journal.'"

The difference between cases of acute pleurisy, the effusion in which is serous, and cases of acute empyema, is not such as to make the rules which should guide us in the treatment of the former otherwise than applicable to the latter. I am prepared to recommend the employment of paracentesis in all cases where there exists such an association of symptoms—but very specially the tendency to failure of the circulation—as already has been so much insisted on, and that without any reference whatever to the nature of the effusion. In the fatal cases of acute pleurisy, which I have seen, and in almost all of the instances of acute pleurisy treated successfully by thoracentesis, either by myself or others known to me, the effusion has been still serous. This experience, however, it is quite possible, might readily undergo a change, for it is only probable that in cases of purulent effusion the symptoms which seem to call for the operation are as likely to be present as in those of the more simple serous effusion. Indeed, the hectic fever and more profound constitutional disturbance which accompany empyema, must be held as likely to cause a predisposition to their occurrence ; but with this preliminary statement, I do not consider it inconsistent very specially to urge the propriety of thoracentesis in cases of acute empyema. If the effusion is ascertained to be purulent I think the sooner it is removed the better. In effecting this, being desirous to prevent the entrance of air, it is well to employ the American syringe. That a satisfactory recovery may take place without the employment of that instrument the case of G. P—, now detailed, and the many instances of successful treatment of empyema by the ordinary operation of paracentesis which have been recorded, sufficiently prove ; but as no danger attends the use of the syringe, and as a conceivable source of accident is by its use removed, while the statements of Dr. Bowditch regarding its employment are so encouraging, I now prefer in all cases of empyema to remove the fluid by that means.

I have stated that we are not to look to statistics for an answer to the question when thoracentesis is to be performed ; but we may, on the other hand, with reason accept a satisfactory reply from that method of inquiry, on some points of no small interest bearing on the more general question, for example, how the quality, and how the quantity of the effusion, influence recovery after thoracentesis. The latter part of this query may be answered in a single word : when the effusion has been very large, when it has been excessive, recovery has often occurred ; but the success of the operation—and this has more particularly reference to empyema—is greatest in cases not marked by the largeness, but by the comparative smallness, of the effusion.

As regards the quality of the fluid, there is reason to believe that a more extended and careful investigation may lead to some important conclusions. Hippocrates, as we have already seen, attached a distinct prognostic value to the nature of the pus, and this has generally been done from his day down to the present time. The statements of authors are, however, so contradictory as to render renewed inquiry necessary. Dr. Brady, of New York, for example, gives the results of 132 operations collected from various journals as follows :—Pus in 52 cases, of which 37 recovered, 2 were relieved, and 13 died. Serum in 59 cases, of which 29 recovered, 12 were relieved, and 18 died. Sero-pus in 8 cases, of which 5 recovered and 3 died. In 13 the nature of the fluid was unknown, and of these 10 recovered and 3 died. Dr. Brady's results may be expressed in this way,—that of cases of empyema in which thoracentesis was performed, about 25 per cent. died, or 1 in every 4 ; while of the cases in which the effusion was serous, about 30 per cent. died, or 1 in little more than every 3.

But turn from this picture, which I cordially agree with Dr. Walshe would not justify us in regarding thoracentesis as "among the valuable gifts of surgery," to that presented by Dr. Bowditch. In 26 out of 75 instances serum was drawn, and 21 out of the 26 got well. Pus was found in 24 patients. Eight got well, 7 died, 9 were *relieved* one or many times, but they had either a very tedious illness, terminating usually in phthisis, or fistulous opening, or a "doubtful result." I am unwilling, with my present limited experience, to refer to statistics at all, but there can be no impropriety in mentioning that in no case in which serous fluid was found, has the result been other than a satisfactory recovery. The little girl to whose case I alluded as having been visited by Professor Simpson, is now, as I have understood, at the distance of nearly three years from the operation, sinking from disease of another nature altogether, and seated in a different part of the body.

One young gentleman, on whom I operated nearly a twelve-month ago, is still far from strong, but his want of strength—and I am happy to think he is regaining strength—is not so intimately connected with his attack of pleurisy as to forbid me stating his recovery from that disease to have been satisfactory. In the remaining cases, and they exceed a dozen in number, in which serous fluid has been removed, there has been no untoward termination.

It is otherwise where pus has been found. In cases of acute empyema, in which there has been great reason to believe that the lung had been involved in tubercular disease, I have witnessed a fatal termination within a day or two, or a few days, after the operation. In these instances, I do not believe for a moment that the performance of thoracentesis accelerated the fatal event. On the contrary, having seen the wonderful degree of relief to most urgent symptoms experienced by the patients, and having heard their own expressions of thankfulness, I am disposed to think that in such circumstances, although a doubtful, as regards ultimate recovery, it was the best remedy to employ, and that, consequently, it was demanded. For as a palliative remedy, I am indeed prepared to recommend the operation in the circumstances now adverted to, as well as in cases of hydrothorax, the result of organic disease. In two cases of this kind, the remedy afforded great relief. In one of these I tapped the pleura ten times, in the other twice. The former case has been published in Dr. Beale's ' Archives of Medicine.'[1] The latter was seen by Dr. Begbie and Sir James Simpson, with whose concurrence thoracentesis was performed. The fluid which escaped was sanguinolent—dark red in colour. Thus, the nature of the case, which had been conjectured, was established. On three occasions I have witnessed such fluid escape, and all of the three patients have died. I must, however, add, that the presence of a little blood, which after the fluid has been for some time in repose, falls to the bottom of the containing vessel, and leaves the great body of the fluid clear, is not by any means an unfavorable index. In such case the blood has escaped from the parietal or pleural wound. Neither do I think the presence of a little blood is to be regarded as serious, where a free coagulation of the mass of fibrine entang-

[1] Vol. ii.

ling the blood corpuscles takes place; it is the thin watery fluid of low density, and wholly as well as uniformly coloured, that I should dread to find; for that marks the case as one of malignant disease, either of the pleura alone, or of the lung and mediastinum as well.

I have now to direct attention to the employment of thoracentesis in cases of *chronic pleurisy*, and this I shall do by relating in the first place the history of one or two cases.

CASE 8.—W. H—, æt. 28, by occupation a tanner, became affected in March, 1864, with difficulty of breathing, hard dry cough, night sweats, loss of appetite, and great loss of strength. In the course of three months he was so much reduced in strength, and so breathless, that he could scarcely walk more than a few yards without taking a rest. During the summer there was for a time a diminution in the severity of these symptoms, but as winter advanced he felt himself getting worse than ever, had great difficulty in lying down, and could not maintain the recumbent posture except on the left side, with the head and shoulders much elevated. At this period, and up to the time of my seeing the patient, he suffered greatly from palpitation of the heart on the right side. He continued to lose flesh and strength, although taking, under medical advice, cod-liver oil, and having his chest rubbed with the same. This man came under my notice in the month of August, 1865. Calling at my house, which he was able to reach only with great difficulty, and with the assistance of his brother, I was struck by his emaciated and worn-out appearance. He was very breathless, and gave me the impression, as I looked at him, that he was labouring under phthisis in an advanced stage. Upon proceeding to examine his chest, however, the cause of his symptoms was found to be a large accumulation of fluid in the left pleura, displacing the heart to the right to an extent I have never seen surpassed, depressing the left lobe of the liver, and causing great prominence of the intercostal spaces, entire immobility of the chest on the affected side, absolute dulness on percussion, and total suppression of all respiratory sounds. A slight degree of œdema of the chest on the left side existed. I learned from the patient that up to the commencement of his present illness he had uniformly enjoyed good health; that his immediate relatives were all healthy. Further, that during his illness he had been repeatedly blistered, and had taken from first to last a large amount of medicine. He had the impression, and this was shared by his brother, who accompanied him, that the disease under which he laboured was consumption; he had been so frequently told so that he could not doubt it; still, he thought it strange that he should have no spit, and no constant cough.

Having formed my own opinion of his case, I expressed it to him, and on the following day commenced the treatment by drawing off, with a small trocar and cannula, about twenty ounces of clear, dark straw-coloured serum, having a density of 1.030, highly albuminous, and containing a large amount of chlorides. This limited tapping greatly relieved the breathing, but it was far more useful than that; it convinced me that although the effusion had been in existence from March, 1864, to August, 1865—nearly eighteen months—the compressed lung was still capable of expansion, for upon careful examination of the chest after the removal of the fluid, I found improvement in the percussion note, near the sterno-clavicular articulation, and, on auscultation, heard a distinct though distant murmur of breathing. Accordingly, being assured, by this simple preliminary tapping, of the expansibility of the lung, I drew off, within a day or two thereafter, upwards of one hundred ounces of fluid. This was done with a common trocar, but no air was permitted to enter. The opening was made posteriorly between the eighth and ninth ribs. This operation, performed in my own house, and without assistance, gave immense relief, and for the first time the patient slept on his right side, and with the head raised in bed only to the usual extent. A blister was applied over the side, and a little iodide of potassium and acid tartrate of potash prescribed.

In five weeks there was an accumulation of fluid to such an extent as to make it desirable to repeat the thoracentesis. That was done, and about sixty ounces of fluid were removed. The patient now desired to go home to Stirlingshire, and this I permitted, after receiving his promise to return in the course of a few weeks. He did so; I again tapped him, removing about forty ounces. Again he returned home, and again came back in six weeks according to promise, having meantime begun work as a shoemaker. I tapped him for the fourth time, drawing off about thirty ounces. At intervals, varying from five to seven weeks, I have tapped him three times since; the last occasion was on the 21st April, when, with Bowditch's syringe, I could only get away eight ounces. There was no more to come; and I have every confidence that another tapping will not be required. The man has gained nearly four stones in weight, eats well, sleeps well, has walked several miles without fatigue, and his breathing is, to use his own words in a letter I lately received from him, "as good as ever it was." This is a most satisfactory case, and yet I believe it would be far from being remarkable, if physicians placed that confidence in the efficiency of thoracentesis as a remedy in chronic pleurisy which, in my opinion, it justly deserves.

Let me ask attention specially to a few features of interest suggested by this case, as now briefly recorded.

1st. The fluid was still serous, at the distance of sixteen months from the commencement of the illness, and it continued so, changing a little in colour, becoming pale, and losing in density, till twenty-five months after the attack commenced, when its formation may be said to have ceased. I have known the fluid to remain serous for a much longer period, indeed, for several years. It did so in the case of a sailor, who was under my care in the hospital eight years ago. I tapped this man's chest on three occasions, removing between fifty and sixty ounces of serum at each time, dark in colour, and free from any smell. The first quantity removed was found to contain cholesterine in considerable amount. The man, finding himself much relieved, insisted, greatly to my regret, on leaving the Infirmary, and so the subsequent progress of his case is unknown to me. That the right lung—his was a pleural effusion on the right side—had expanded to such an extent as to make it hopeful that the case might terminate as favorably as the one now related, I was convinced; but I am equally sure that, after a time, and for a considerable period, the fluid would slowly reaccumulate, rendering repeated tappings necessary.

2nd. I have mentioned that blisters were used, and that diuretic as well deobstruent remedies were employed after the performance of thoracentesis. Such cannot be expected to act with the same degree of energy as when used in like circumstances in the acute effusions; but, still, I believe their action to be far from wholly inert; used independently of tapping they are useless. Again and again I have seen them employed in cases of chronic pleurisy, diligently and for a lengthened period, but never can I say that any decided benefit resulted.

3rd. The tapping earliest performed in W. H—'s case was tentative. I ask attention specially to this expression—for had the lung not given evidence of expansibility after its employment. I should either have adopted a different practice, as in other cases, or on subsequent occasions used the measure as one purely palliative. The lung did, however, expand, affording evidence that after many months of compression the return to a healthy condition is quite possible. To attempt either in the case of a chronic serous effusion, or in that of an empyema, the removal of other than a moderate quantity of the effused fluid, until the capability of the lung undergoing expansion has been ascertained, is, I think, a dangerous practice. True, it is only by strong suction power, which in such circumstances is not safe, that we are able to remove any very considerable amount; but, I repeat, a safer and better plan is to watch carefully the extent to which pulmonary expansion occurs, and repeat the operation according to circumstances. This also was the method pursued in the following instance.

CASE 9.—D. B— was a patient in the Royal Infirmary in 1863, suffering from chronic pleurisy on the right side, of several months' standing. After the repeated application of large blisters, and the use of iodine and mercury without appreciable benefit, a tentative thoracentesis was performed, and the lung having evidently undergone expansion, the operation was repeated. This plan was pursued for some months, thoracentesis being performed by means of a small trocar at varying intervals, and blisters, as well as iodide of potassium, being likewise used. The result was most satisfactory: the patient, after nine months' residence in hospital, was dismissed with a lung greatly expanded, and in a state of health permitting him to return to the performance of his duties as a warehouseman, from which he had for many months been compelled to desist.

It is not, however, in all cases of chronic pleurisy, and certainly less frequently in empyema than in instances of simple serous accumulation, that results so satisfactory follow. I have twice, in cases of chronic empyema, found death to ensue after repeated tappings,—the patient gradually becoming more and more hectic, and ultimately sinking through a gradual asthenia; and in a third case, a permanently fistulous opening having been established, the same train of events occurred. This was, however, a case of empyema complicated with serious pulmonary disease on both sides of the chest.

I have had too little experience of the influence of injections into the pleura to be able to express any confident opinion regarding their value. In one case of empyema, with very offensive fetid discharge, the injection of a little chlorine water, freely diluted, had certainly a good effect in controlling the fœtor. In another case of very chronic empyema, limited in extent, I injected, after the manner of the late M. Aran, a little tincture of iodine. The immediate effect seemed to be satisfactory; but the patient, a man in hospital, requested his discharge a short time after the treatment was put in execution, and the result was alike imperfect and unknown. Both Aran and Trousseau, however, as well as other physicians, have borne testimony to the efficacy of injections with iodine.

Another expedient, of which, although I have no personal experience, it appears much may be made, is the drainage tube.

In the hands of Dr. Goodfellow, of London, and more recently of Dr. Banks, of Dublin, Dr. George Kidd,[1] and other Irish physicians, the introduction of a drainage tube, by permitting the fluid in the pleura to run off as soon as formed, has, undoubtedly, in acute cases of pleural effusion—and also in chronic empyema with fistulous opening, in which the tube has favoured the freer escape of pus—rendered eminent service.[2]

I have not thought it necessary to discuss the employment of thoracentesis in chronic pleural effusions at the same length as that to which my observations on this means of treatment in the acute effusions into the chest have extended, believing that there is by no means the same difference of opinion in the minds of physicians regarding the former, as unquestionably exists in relation to the latter.

My belief is, that, in many instances of chronic pleural effusions, it will be found an available means of cure; that in others, judiciously employed by itself, or aided by injections, or by the use of the drainage tube, it is capable of greatly alleviating the distress and suffering of not a few cases of this serious chest disease.

[1] See his interesting paper in the ' Dublin Medical Journal ' for 1865.

[2] The drainage tube will further be specially useful in those cases in which the compressed lung is incapable of expansion. By its means the fluid can be completely removed, and so a contracted side—always preferable to an abnormally distended side—will result.

XX.

ON

ANTHRACOSIS; OR, COAL-MINERS' PHTHISIS:

THE

SPURIOUS MELANOSIS OF CARSWELL.

(Reprinted from the 'Glasgow Medical Journal,' 1866.)

A PULMONARY disease, described with sufficient accuracy by J. C. Gregory, William Thomson, Makellar, and others, specially although not exclusively met with in coal miners, now threatens to become very rare in its occurrence; there are indeed indications of its happily altogether disappearing. The increasing rarity of the disease, at all events in its exquisite or well-marked forms, is a subject intimately, and in a most interesting manner, connected with its etiology, and to this particular attention will at one part of the following observations be directed. In the course of hospital experience I have encountered several instances of well-marked carbonaceous infiltration of the lungs; and in particular have met with two examples of the disease differing very remarkably in many important features from each other, both of which terminated fatally. These cases I propose in the commencement of this communication to place on record.

The circumstance of the existence in the pulmonary structure of a varying amount of black pigmentary matter has long been

16

recognised.   Laënnec, in writing of " Mélanoses " of the lungs,[1]
alludes to the discovery of such pigment, more or less abundantly in the lungs of almost all adults, it being found chiefly
in persons advanced in life.   In the lungs of young persons, on
the contrary, he remarks, rarely are any traces to be noticed.
The appearance, as regards colour, presented by the lungs of
young persons, Laënnec likens to that seen in the same organs
in oxen and many other animals ; and he hazards the conjecture
that possibly the pigment, " matière noire," exists only in the
lungs of man and of carnivorous animals; adding, however,
with characteristitic modesty, that his own attention to comparative anatomy had been too limited to admit of his expressing
a confident opinion on that head.   What is of greater interest,
however, and more immediately connected with the subject of
this paper, is the further statement by Laënnec, at the same
place, that he has sometimes surmised that the black matter in
question may in part at least proceed from the smoke of lamps
and combustible bodies used for the purposes of warming and
of lighting ; and again, that in the lungs, as well as in the
bronchial glands, of cottagers unaccustomed to watching or
sitting up late at night, the pigmentary matter is either absent
or present in very small amount.   This experience, Laënnec is
careful to say, is not universal ; for the discovery of pigment in
considerable amount has on the other hand been occasionally
made in the lungs of persons in no peculiar manner exposed to
the causes just alluded to.   The reader familiar with the illustrious work of Laënnec will remember that, although in no
degree detracting from the value of the passage to which reference has now been made, there is in the chapter in which it occurs
not a little confusion, occasioned by the want of a proper distinction, at the time impossible, between the true melanosis of
the lung, an undoubted neoplasm, or new formation of cancerous nature, and the pigmentary substance with which we are at
present more immediately concerned.   To the disease which is
generally known under one or other of the names placed at the
head of this paper, but which has also been described as *Carbonaceous Bronchitis* (Dr. Walshe); *Black Phthisis* (Dr. Makellar); *Black Spit* (J. B. Thomson) ; and *Mélanose du Poumon*

[1] "Traité de L'Auscultation Médiate," deuxième partie, Productions
accidentelles développées dans le Poumon.

(Valleix), the attention of the profession was to a certain extent directed as early as 1813, by Dr. Pearson, writing in the ' Philosophical Transactions ' " On the Colouring Matter of the Black Bronchial Gland, and of the Black Spots of the Lungs ;" but since that date the following important contributions regarding it have appeared :—" Report of a case of peculiar black infiltration of the whole Lungs, resembling Melanosis," by Dr. J. C. Gregory.[1] Article entitled " Spurious Melanosis," in the ' Cyclopædia of Practical Medicine,' by Dr. Carswell. In the same author's well-known work on ' Pathological Anatomy ; Illustrations of the Elementary Forms of Disease,' there is a brief description of the appearances presented by the affected lungs; and likewise, under the head of Melanoma, plate 3, an illustration giving a very correct notion of their universal black discoloration. " On the Existence of Charcoal in the Lungs," by Thomas Graham, F.R.S.[2] " Cases of Spurious Melanosis of the Lungs," by Dr. William Marshall, of Cambuslang.[3] " On Black Expectoration, and the Deposition of Black Matter in the Lungs, particularly as occurring in Coal-Miners, &c.," by Dr. William Thomson.[4] " Melanotic Infiltration of the Lungs, with old and recent Pleuritis," by Dr. Hamilton, of Falkirk.[5] " An Investigation into the Nature of Black Phthisis," by Dr. Makellar.[6] Still more recently a valuable contribution to the pathology of miners' lung has appeared from Professor Virchow, of Berlin ;[7] and Dr. J. B. Thomson, of Perth, has written an interesting paper on the Melanosis of Miners, giving details of his experience as a practitioner in a colliery district for twenty-four years.[8] In several of the best known and most highly esteemed treatises on diseases of the lungs, allusions more or less extended to this peculiar morbid condition exist, as for example in the work of Dr. Walshe.[9]

---

[1] 'Edinburgh Medical and Surgical Journal,' vol. xxxvi, 1831.

[2] 'Eodem Loco,' vol. xlii.

[3] 'Lancet,' 1833-4, vol. ii, p. 271 ; also p. 926.

[4] 'Medico-Chirurgical Transactions,' vol. xx, xxi.

[5] 'Eodem Loco.'

[6] 'Monthly Journal of Medical Science,' 1846.

[7] From notes by Dr. Alexander R. Simpson, 'Edinburgh Medical Journal,' 1858.

[8] 'Edinburgh Medical Journal,' 1858.

[9] 'Diseases of the Lungs,' p. 227.

Of the papers now mentioned, the most important and complete is that by the late Professor William Thomson, of Glasgow ; the references made by that author to the observations and opinions of various writers, ancient and modern, concerning the presence of black matter in the expectoration, obviate the necessity that might otherwise have existed for making a more detailed allusion to the literature of the subject.

The observations which I propose to make on the nature, and more especially on the etiology of carbonaceous infiltration of the lungs, will succeed a brief narrative of the two interesting cases already referred to, as having fallen under my notice in the ordinary course of hospital experience. Several cases of well-marked black expectoration I encountered from time to time ; but, with the exception of another instance of miner's lung complicated with mediastinal cancer, the two to which I presently direct attention were the only fatal cases which I have had the opportunity of observing :—

CASE I.—J. D—, æt. 49, was a patient in the Royal Infirmary for several weeks in the spring and early part of the summer of 1856. He had throughout life worked as an ordinary farm servant, but for some years his occupation had been almost entirely that of attending to a threshing mill, placed in a low-roofed and confined shed. Here, during fully nine months of the year he had worked, in the midst of much dust, from morning till evening ; the remaining three months had been devoted to out-door farm work. This man, of sober habits, had not suffered from any chest affection till commencing, some four or five years before his death, the occupation to which reference has now been made. At that employment he had not worked above a few months when he became short in breathing and subject to cough. After a time he noticed his spit to be dark in colour, and gradually to acquire a black or inky hue. He was able, although with much difficulty, to continue at this work till the beginning of 1856, when from general feebleness, and particularly owing to severe cough and difficulty of breathing, he felt compelled to desist.

When brought under my observation in the hospital, this patient had lost flesh and strength to a great extent, and manifested the appearance of a person who had been for a lengthened period suffering from pulmonary disease. The expectoration was very abundant, and very black. The left front of the chest was universally dull on percussion, and immediately under the clavicle there were the marked signs of extensive excavation. Over the right front the percussion resonance was abnormally clear. The patient had at no time expectorated blood. The course of the disease did not differ in any particular from that of ordinary pulmonary phthisis—hectic fever, night sweats, constant and extremely irritating cough, gradually wore out the poor man's strength. He died on the 2nd day of June.

On examination of the body by Dr. Haldane, the following appearances were presented. There was great emphysema of the upper anterior portion of the right lung. That lung was of a uniform dark colour both externally and internally, while on pressure a fluid of similar colour, and staining the fingers, escaped. In this lung there was no marked condensation. The left lung was firmly adherent, and the corresponding side of the chest contracted, The lung was of a very dark colour, non-crepitant in the lower lobe, yielding, on pressure after section, a very abundant inky fluid. In the upper lobe there were several considerable excavations, and a few small masses of tubercle. Bronchial glands were enlarged, and of extremely black colour. Liver and kidneys congested, but otherwise normal.

The most remarkable feature in this case consists in the circumstance that the subject of it was not a coal-miner, or other operative exposed in any extraordinary manner to the operation of those causes, which, as will be shortly seen, are supposed to engender the disease,—all his life this man had been an agricultural labourer. He was addicted to smoking, but it was ascertained that he did not inhale the fumes as some smokers are known to do. He had not been in any way peculiarly exposed to the inhalation of the smoke of oil-lamps, and had not known other men engaged in precisely the same occupation, suffer as he had done.

So much for the history of the case. It is further of interest to note, that in the left lung a little tubercle was found co-existing with the carbonaceous matter, and that the right lung was greatly emphysematous.

A careful inquiry, instituted at the time of its occurrence, satisfied me, that this case was the only one of its kind which had ever been seen in the district where D— worked for many years, where his pulmonary affection commenced, and from which, when no longer able to follow his employment, he came directly to the Infirmary.

CASE 2.—A. B—, æt. 53, married, a coal miner, native of Gilmerton, in the County of Midlothian, went to work in a coal mine when twelve years of age, and continued at the same employment till he had reached forty-five ; was a healthy man during the earlier portion of his life, but suffered a smart attack of pleurisy in the left side when about thirty. Twenty years ago, that is, eleven years before he gave up his occupation as a miner, he began to suffer from a constant black spit, darkest in colour, and most abundant for a short time after leaving the mine, on the conclusion of each day's work. During the last eleven years of his employment as a miner, he was never free from pains in the chest, cough, and expectoration, while a shortness of breathing, at first trivial in degree, became gradually so serious as to compel him, as he had often noticed others among his fellow-workmen compelled, to abandon the calling of a miner altogether. Having somewhat improved in health, he was able for a time to work in the construction of railways, and for a limited period more particularly in tunnelling, and in the sinking of wells. For nearly two years has been altogether unable to work ; he has during that time been subject to severe irritating cough, with expectoration of black matter, and to greatly increased difficulty of breathing, while his strength and flesh have greatly fallen off. During the same period he has repeatedly spat blood in small quantities. On the 27th of January, 1865, this man came under my care in the Royal Infirmary, he was then much emaciated, and had the appearance of a patient in the advanced stage of phthisis. His sufferings were of a very aggravated description, chiefly from dyspnœa, and urgent cough. The expectoration was copious, and for the most part not difficult. It consisted of black matter, closely resembling ink, with a good deal of frothy mucus, partially stained, and occasionally a little pus. The chest was considerably flattened under both clavicles, more particularly on the right front ; percussion on that side was absolutely dull, and over the upper left front considerably impaired. Loud bronchophony, amounting at one spot over the second rib anteriorly to pectoriloquy, was audible over the right chest. Vocal resonance was increased also over the left sub-clavicular region. Loud and very coarse moist râles, frequently gurgling in character, accompanied a deep tubular sound of breathing over the upper portion of the right front, while, in the lower portions of the right lung, moist râles of finer quality were audible. Posteriorly, the physical signs over the right lung did not differ from these discovered in front, and in the left lung these indicated the existence of pulmonary consolidation with partial softening. Without the previous history of the patient, and still more without aquaintance with the characters presented by the expectoration, there was nothing to distinguish the case of B— from one of ordinary tubercular disease of the lungs advanced to the stage of excavation and disintegration. The sputa, however, did serve thus to distinguish it. I need not particularly dwell on the progress of this case in the hospital. The digestive organs, much affected from the period of his coming under my care, became more seriously disordered : vomiting frequently occurred ; rapid declension of strength, with marked hectic supervened ; and, without the occurrence of any remarkable symptom, death took place at 2 p.m., of the 25th of February. B— had been occasionally delirious at nights for some time ; and the feet had also become œdematous ; the urine was scanty, but never contained albumen.

The body of B— was examined on the 26th February, by Dr. Grainger

Stewart. The chest was much flattened, the body emaciated; heart enlarged, weight 17½ ounces, its right side dilated, substance of heart not materially altered; the blood fluid but thick and very dark. Right lung densely adherent, contained a large amount of black carbonaceous deposit, and had several cavities towards its apex. The bronchial tubes did not exhibit any marked deposit, but were congested and occupied by much black mucus. The left lung was much less adherent, the upper lobe shrunken, and contained a solid mass of carbon, about the size of an apple; there were also cicatrices deeply coloured at different portions of the surface of this lung. The bronchial glands of both lungs were deeply tinged, and those in the right lung were the seat of considerable carbonaceous deposition. The liver was congested and fatty; the spleen exhibited on its surface, and also at several points within its substance, depositions of black pigment; the kidneys were large, weighing 9½ ounces each, but their structure, beyond having a congested appearance, did not seem to be abnormal.

This case is, in all its particulars, an extremely illustrative instance of coal-miners' phthisis, as it has usually presented itself. The man worked as a coal-miner from his youth, became affected with black spit, and in due time, continuing his occupation in pits,—which were generally regarded as the "worst pits for the lungs," to use B—'s own language,—but seeing that they have long since undergone much improvement, or have ceased to be wrought, I need not name — he became the subject of cough, and shortness of breathing. Desisting from his employment as a miner, probably his life, already become burdensome, was thereby somewhat lengthened; but, just as in the cases described by Thomson, Graham, Makellar, and others, the progress of the disease was evidently unarrested, and it is now apparent that deposition and softening, with subsequent excavation of the lung substance, had been slowly going on during the nine years which had elapsed after his leaving the coal-mines. There are a few particulars in this case which are worthy of special notice.

1. Although I have not dwelt upon this circumstance, in the brief record of the case, I wish it to be understood that this man's sufferings were very great—greater than is usual in instances of ordinary pulmonary diseases, and particularly phthisis. Dr. Makellar has more especially depicted the sufferings of such patients, and my observation of B—'s case has convinced me that the portraiture by him has not been overdrawn.

2. The slowness of pulse, coldness of extremities, and blueness or lividity of countenance, described by some authors, were noticed in B—'s case. These features, the two former more especially, have been too readily regarded as the concomitants of a morbid condition of the blood, due to the presence of excess of carbon, at least induced by mal-oxygenation. It is not always so, for in fatal cases of bronchitis, and in instances of long existing cyanosis, and pulmonary emphysema, I have observed a frequency of the heart's action, with unusual maintenance of the animal temperature over the whole body, till dissolution itself has occurred : so was it in the case of B—.

3. The dilated condition of the right ventricle, discovered on dissection, accords with previous observations, and the pigmentary matter found in the substance, as well as on the surface of the spleen, tends to confirm the opinion—to be more prominently set forth in the sequel—that the black matter, whatever its real nature be, is a deposit from the circulating fluid.

The chief or distinguishing character of the pulmonary lesion in this disease is the black appearance assumed by the lungs from the deposition and impaction in their structure of a dark pigmentary matter. Regarding the precise nature of this deposit, as well as its source, a difference of opinion has arisen, and still exists. It is contended, on the one hand, by certain physicians and pathologists—as, for example, by Gregory, William Thomson, Carswell, Makellar, Brockmann, Robin, and others—that the origin of the black matter is *ab extra ;* that it consists, in fact, of carbon inhaled during the occupation which those who chiefly suffer from this affection pursue. It is confessedly among persons who are much exposed to the inhalation of an atmosphere highly charged with carbonaceous particles that anthracosis mainly occurs. The great majority of such sufferers are coal miners ; hence " Miners' Melanosis " and " Miners' Phthisis " have been used as synonyms for the disease. Again, chemical analysis of the black pigment has determined its close resemblance to carbon ; indeed, its being identical with carbon. This was done by Dr. Christison in the instance of one of the earliest recorded cases, that by Dr. J. C. Gregory in 1831, and such experiments have since that time been frequently repeated. Boiled with concentrated nitric acid, the black colour remains unaffected, and, after immersion for some time in a strong solution of chlorine, it is found to be equally black as before. Boiled in a strong solution of caustic potash, and then slowly filtered, the black matter remains on the filter, and this, when washed and carefully dried will burn like charcoal, leaving a grayish ash. Not only so, but a small quantity of the powder left after the action of the nitric acid, may, when properly treated, be caused to yield all the products of the distillation of coal and gas, similar in quality to that so produced, a naphthous fluid and crystalline principle called naphthalline. These circumstances must at once be admitted as establishing the carbonaceous nature of this peculiar lung pigment. Whether the extraneous origin of it admits of as conclusive a proof we have still to inquire. But another and contrary opinion to that now expressed is entertained by certain other physicians and pathologists—among these by Breschet—who, indeed, was the first to broach it—by Trousseau and Leblanc, and more recently, and very decidedly, by the distinguished Professor at Berlin, Virchow. They conceive that the black matter is altered blood pigment, in reality a transformation of hæmatin, that it is deposited from the blood, and has, therefore, an internal and not an extraneous origin. Virchow thus expresses his notion of the pigmentary changes, viz.—" as resulting from extravasations of blood, and subsequent transformations of hæmatin." It is not contended in this view that the pigmentary matter is not closely allied to carbon ; it is not, indeed, sought to be established that it is otherwise than a form of carbon. An opposite conclusion could hardly be arrived at, seeing that, in chemical constitution, so far as is known, this black pigment and carbon are identical. But, then, we are cognisant of no test which is absolutely distinctive of carbon, and the question still remains : Is there any chemical difference between the black pulmonary substance discovered in anthracosis, and the carbon of coal and of smoke? This view may be otherwise expressed by saying, that, although carbonaceous, the black pigmentary matter found in the lungs, and also expectorated in cases of anthracosis, may not after all be the carbon of coal or of smoke. The chemical experiments of Guillot have shown this pigment to be composed of nearly pure carbon ; to be, in fact, much richer in carbon than any form of coal is. It is curious, and likewise instructive, to notice how the different theorists accept and apply these results of a renewed chemical investigation. In the view of Robin, who has always maintained the extraneous origin of the pigmentary matter, the discussion is now to be regarded as closed; the announcement of the results of Guillot's chemical inquiry leaves nothing more to be done.[1] These same results are, however, interpreted by Virchow in a manner totally at variance with the conclusions of the former observers.

Regarding the properties, and more especially the chemical relations of the pigment, both parties may be considered as nearly, although not wholly, agreed; but in respect to its primary origin they seriously differ. *One party* views the inhalation of the carbon, and its impaction in the minute bronchial ramifications and the ultimate air cells, as the ready explanation of its presence in the lungs. *Another view* is entertained by Virchow, that it is deposited from the blood, not as carbon but hæmatin, which undergoes transformation; an anthracosis succeeds the sanguineous extravasation. *A third view*, although it has not been brought prominently forward, may be thus stated; the presence of the black pigmentary matter in the lungs may be, in part, due to the inhalation of minute carbonaceous particles, and in part to the deposition, after some manner or other, of carbon from the blood. It may be contended by those who have formed this last opinion, that the great amount of the deposit in the lungs, its nearly entire limitation to the pulmonary structure, as well as the fact of its steady and often remarkable increase, long after the sufferer has been removed from those circumstances which exposed him to the inhalation of the carbonaceous dust, make this the probable, if not the only tenable, explanation. In regard to this point the inquiry is suggested, whether the carbon—the word is now used as synonymous with black pulmonary pigment —thus deposited from the blood, is a portion of what has been taken into the circulatory system originally at the lungs. That the black matter found in the pulmonary tissue is present in the circulation is at all events deposited from the blood, may be regarded as proved by the fact of the pigmentary substance

---

[1] See Article vii—"Charbon Pulmonaire"—in vol. iii of 'Traité de Chimie anatomique et physiologique normale et pathologique, &c,' par Charles Robin, et F. Verdeil. Paris, 1853.

being found in other situations than the lungs. This statement is, no doubt, opposed to the expressed opinions of Carswell and of others, but it is nevertheless true, for the same black deposit has been discovered many times in the bronchial glands, not unfrequently in the pleura, and, although with much less frequency, nevertheless unequivocally, in the peritoneum, free and intestinal, and in the mesenteric glands. Whether it be the altered hæmatin or the inhaled carbon, and I am disposed to regard the latter as the more likely, which is thus encountered, there can be little doubt that a real deposition from the blood takes place; all of the observed phenomena are not to be explained upon the principle of a simple inhalation and impaction. It is not difficult to understand why, in the latter stages of the lung affection incident to coal miners, when a considerable portion of the pulmonary tissue has suffered destruction, the arrest of the carbon should then take place in an increasing ratio alike as regards rapidity and amount. And for this result we should be prepared, whether the carbon be present in normal or in abnormal degree in the blood.

In the disease known as anthracosis or coal-miners' phthisis, the carbon exists in the circulating fluid in greatly increased amount. At the lungs there is not that free access of oxygen to the blood in the pulmonary capillaries which is necessary for the combustion of the carbon, and, as a necessary consequence, instead of carbonic acid being exhaled, an always increasing amount of carbon is deposited. Dr. Makellar has stated in strong terms, as the result of his long and attentive observation of many exquisite cases of "black phthisis," that when once carbon is lodged in the pulmonary structure by inhalation, there is created by it a disposing affinity for the carbon in the blood, by which there is caused an increase in the amount of the deposit without any more being inhaled." A similar opinion too, has been expressed by Brockmann, who acquired his knowledge of the disease as it exists among the miners of the Hartz mountains.[1]

In the general symptoms presented by the sufferers from anthracosis there exists a close similarity with many cases of tubercular disease of the lungs, and this agreement is also noticeable to a very marked degree, as may have been gathered

[1] See 'Neumeister's Repertorium,' December, 1844.

from the illustrative instances already recorded in this paper, in respect to the physical signs. The distinguishing and highly characteristic feature among the former is the black expectoration. There is often present in the sputa of patients affected by various pulmonary complaints a certain amount of black pigmentary matter; especially will this be noticed in the earlier stage of not a few cases of tubercular disease, and it will generally be found that, in its occurrence and particularly in its amount, the phenomenon in question bears a relation to the nature of the occupation in which such persons have been engaged. This, never otherwise than slight admixture of black pigmentary matter with the sputa, there is really no risk of mistaking for, or confounding with, the pigmentary expectoration of anthracosis. In this disease, besides being thoroughly charged with black matter, the expectoration continues thus altered during the whole course of the malady. No doubt certain changes in its characters are likely to occur, and for the most part do present themselves, for, at first mixed with mucus, this ingredient after a time disappears, and a puriform, to be succeeded by a purulent, sputum takes its place—all this time, however, the expectoration has never lost its very black colour.

It is quite extraordinary how large an amount of black matter will, in cases of anthracosis, be got rid of by expectoration. In one instance which was under my own observation in hospital, for a period of several months, the spit-box was daily filled with a dark, heavy mass. I have had from time to time the opportunity of seeing an old man, formerly a collier, now, at least lately, a toll-man, who, for many years, and to a far greater extent after leaving the coal-pits than while engaged in them, has expectorated very large quantities of black matter. In this case, as in others I have met with, the expectoration is not constant; for the cough, which always exists, will for weeks together become dry, and while dry always very distressing and painful. After the lapse of a few weeks, occasionally of a longer period, the expectoration again returns, being for a time scanty, but gradually becoming more and more copious. When most abundant, the cough and likewise the dyspnœa are most moderate. Dr. Makellar mentions, that in one of his cases the expectoration, as far as consistence went, had the appearance of treacle, being, however, perfectly black; and of this ten to twelve ounces, were expectorated daily. During his attendance on this patient, Dr. Makellar separated the mucus from the black matter by the simple process of diluting the sputa with water, and thereafter separating the precipitated carbon. In this way he was enabled to procure about one and a half drachms of a beautiful black powder, daily, and in the course of a week he had a supply of nearly two ounces. This, Dr. Makellar informs us, he continued for some weeks, and he might have gone on till the period of the patient's death, several months thereafter. The same writer concludes, "It is undoubtedly a striking phenomenon connected with the pathology of the chest, that the human lung can be converted into a manufactory of lamp black!"

Some curious and interesting points suggest inquiry in relation to the expectoration. For example, among coal-miners, the class of operatives chiefly subject to anthracosis, and among them the workers at the stone wall in the pit,—who of all the miners are most frequently affected, and in whom the disease most speedily runs its course—there are very few who are at any time exempt from the black spit. Some there are who have it while at work in the pits, and perhaps for some hours after leaving it, but who find it gone before the stated period of their return to work. Others again, and of this class two interesting examples fell under my observation in the Royal Infirmary during the winter session, 1857-58, and were made the subject of remark at clinical lectures, continue for weeks and months to expectorate black matter : many of them without presenting any of the physical signs or other of the general symptoms of anthracosis. In persons so affected, the inhalation of the carbonaceous particles and their lodgment in the bronchial passages is surely the only satisfactory explanation of the phenomenon. Such patients, for the most part, pay no regard to the black spit ; they treat it as a necessary consequence of their subterranean calling, and do not view it as any indication either of themselves being ill, or of their occupation being unhealthy. Some I have seen have sought relief for other affections, as in the instances occurring in hospital already referred to, both of whom suffered from chronic rheumatism. Still, although in many, as yet, a symptom of no very serious import, it behoves us to bear in remembrance, that in the case of those who have afterwards become the victims of regular carbonaceous infiltration of the lungs, the occurrence of black expectoration has been the very earliest symptom. It will be readily admitted that a free expectoration of inhaled carbonaceous particles is just the most likely circumstance to prevent, at all events, to ward off for a time, its impaction in the air vesicles; and, if this explanation of the pathology of the disease in its earlier stage be essentially the correct one, it is likewise manifest how important an aim it should be to promote in the same stage of anthracosis a free expectoration. In this disease, as in tubercular phthisis, hæmoptysis is not unfrequent; that appears, however, from the cases which have been recorded, seldom to occur in the early progress of the malady, but to be one of the symptoms of the more advanced period when the pulmonary structure has become more or less seriously disorganised. In one of the two cases already recorded hæmoptysis never occurred; in the other case, that of A. B—, it took place for the first time about eleven years after his pulmonary ailment had given by other symptoms unmistakeable evidence of its existence.

The same indications of failing health present themselves in this disease and in phthisis, the same loss of strength and of flesh taking place by degrees, more or less gradually in different cases; for anthracosis is essentially a chronic disease, which tubercular consumption is not always. Great emaciation sometimes occurs in anthracosis. Dropsy, unattended by renal affection, is common in its advanced stages; this, as a peculiarly distressing symptom has been noticed by Makellar and others. Mr. Lawson Tait, who has recently resided in a colliery district, and has had the opportunity of carefully watching a few well-marked instances of the disease, informs me that he was struck by the frequency, as well as by the amount of general dropsical effusion in these cases. Dropsy, with albuminuria, I have also met with, in cases of anthracosis, but rarely. When albumen was present in the urine, it was not abundant, and was unassociated with other and still more significant indications of kidney disease. It was, in all probability, due to renal congestion of a passive kind, primarily to that stasis of blood in the renal capillaries, which, sooner or later, in all diseases characterised by special blood-impurity, results, and is the direct determining cause of serous transudation and albuminuria. Connected with the slight albuminuria thus referred to, I have seen in the urine of anthracosis copious deposition of amorphous urates. I have been much interested in observing, that Dr. Robert Wilson, of Alnwick, who has had large opportunities of studying the diseases of colliers, makes the remark : I have never seen a case of Bright's disease in a pitman. That the disease is not uncommon in the district may be known from the fact that, at the time I write, I have five cases under treatment from albuminuria, and three of them the wives of pitmen."[1]

The cough, and difficulty of breathing are, generally speaking, most severe in this disease. The dyspnœa is, in all probability, intimately connected with the extremely impure condition of the blood, which, as the malady advances, ceases to present the characters of the vitalised fluid, and in appearance resembles a very dark and thick venous blood ; when, as usually happens, the right side of the heart has become dilated, the resulting breathlessness is extreme, and, as in the case of A. B——, most painful to witness. It is at this stage, too, that the general dropsy becomes excessive. The symptoms, moreover, which mark the very advanced stage of tubercular phthisis are often present in anthracosis—the colliquative perspirations, the exhausting diarrhœa, and the wandering mind. The euthanasia, or easy death, not unknown to us in the sufferers from ordinary phthisis, is, I fear, never experienced in the instance of those dying of the disease which is now under consideration. On the contrary, there is, till near the close of life, invariably much suffering, and that of the most distressing nature.

It has already been remarked that the so-called physical signs of disease, in cases of anthracosis, offer a very close resemblance to those which we observe in the different stages of ordinary tubercular disease of the lungs. The varying degrees of dulness on percussion, and of altered resonance of the voice, are not more significant of lung condensed by tubercular deposition, than by carbonaceous infiltration ; while the modifications of bronchial breathing, from a merely comparative harshness, limited in situation to a well-marked tubular

---

[1] "The Coal Miners of Durham and Northumberland, their Habits and Diseases." A paper read before the British Association for the Advancement of Science, at Newcastle, September, 1863. By Robert Wilson, M.D.

sound, and even cavernous râle, are, in some cases quite as
readily recognised in the one condition as in the other. So,
also, when softening and excavation have occurred, the moist
sounds, the crepitant and sub-crepitant râle, and the coarser
gurgling will be audible in anthracosis just as in phthisis. It
is consistent with my own observation, and the two cases which
have been shortly detailed will bear out the remark that a
vomica, the result of softening, and ultimately of destruction of
the pulmonary substance in anthracosis, may have such significant physical signs as cavernous breathing, gurgling râle, and
pectoriloquy to distinguish it, and these quite as well-marked
as when we meet with them in the advanced stages of tubercular
disease. This will not always hold true, for the disease we
have to deal with, an eminently chronic one, is specially apt to
be attended by intercurrent pleural inflammations. Hence,
pleural thickenings and dense adhesions, common enough in
tubercular consumption, are still more so in anthracosis. It is
probably owing to the chronic nature of the disease, but
specially from the frequency of pleural inflammation and
adhesion, that the occurrence of pneumo-thorax has not been
observed in cases of carbonaceous infiltration of the lungs.

The appearance presented by the lungs when affected by
anthracosis is very remarkable. The colour varies from a
well-marked slate colour, to a deep, almost jet, black. The
external surface usually resembling more exactly the former,
while the cut surface presents the darker hue. If the lung is
in the early stage of the disease, no excavations having formed,
it is voluminous, of increased density, evidently condensed
from the occupation of the parenchymatous structure by black
pigmentary matter. If subjected to pressure a considerable
amount of fluid, dark in colour, flows out, staining in a remarkable manner the hands. So deep is the stain thus caused that
it generally requires several applications of soap and water
thoroughly to remove it ; certain parts of the lungs are generally found to be denser, and the tissue in these more completely
occupied by carbonaceous matter than others. A portion of
such will readily sink in water, communicating a deep black
colour to the water as it passes down through it. Unlike the
deposition of tubercular matter which usually commences in
the apex, or towards the summit of the lung, this black matter

is found equally to invade all portions—the base is as subject
to it as the apex. Nor is one lung more likely to be affected
than the other; they suffer equally. This experience in regard
to carbonaceous infiltration, so opposed to what holds true of
tubercular deposition in the lungs, seems again to favour the view
of the former being in the first instance, whenever it occurs, due
to direct inhalation of minute particles. Were it otherwise, is it
not reasonable to suppose that, as is commonly the case with
tubercular deposition, the apices of the lung would chiefly suffer,
and one lung might be found much diseased, while the other was
comparatively unaffected?

It seems to have been at one time imagined that the carbonaceous infiltration and the deposit of tubercular matter in the
lungs were mutually antagonistic. This opinion seems to be
implied in certain of Dr. Makellar's observations, and, were it
correct, undoubtedly we should have arrived at the knowledge
of a very important fact. Such, however, is not the case;
tubercle and this black pigment have been frequently found—
the former in all its stages, recently deposited, crude, and
softening—in the same lung. In the left lung of J. D— it
was so, and I have seen the co-existence of the two, much more
notably illustrated in the lungs removed from the body of a
patient who died of miners' phthisis, by Dr. Maclean, now of
Skye. That, under somewhat different circumstances, tubercle
and carbon co-exist in the lung, the result of numerous *post-
mortem* examinations testify. It is not uncommon to find in
the lungs of elderly or old people the cicatrices of tubercular
cavities, in which more or less of black pigment, not distinguishable from carbon, exists, and such lungs do further not
unfrequently present throughout their entirety an unusually
dark or slaty colour. In the advanced stages of anthracosis
cavities are formed. These, like tubercular vomicæ, vary in
size. Some are very small, others large, capable of holding an
orange; less commonly they are much more extensive. These
excavations are generally found to be partially occupied by a
thick black fluid similar to what has been expectorated during
life. As in tubercular cavities, some of the divisions of the
bronchia, right or left, as the case may be, are seen opening
into them. Blood-vessels also shrivelled and shrunken, as in
the old tubercular excavations of chronic phthisis, are observed

crossing them from wall to wall, and, with these, portions of lung substance in a state of disorganisation, and having the appearance of shreds. The most frequent complication of anthracosis is bronchitis, indeed so frequent is it, and so invariable are the evidences of its previous existence, as discovered on *post-mortem* examination—the congested and thickened mucous membrane, and the dilated bronchial tubes—that bronchial inflammation may be considered an essential part of the malady. It is not uncommon to find more or less of emphysema.

It is now necessary to inquire in what part of the lung tissue the black pigmentary deposit originally occurs? This is undoubtedly various. So much so, indeed, that Virchow holds " the deposit may occur in very different parts of the lung in every case, and no classification can be made of different forms of the disease from the position of the pigment." The opinion generally entertained up to the time Virchow investigated the subject, was that the black matter is found free in the air vesicles, and in the epithelial cells of their walls, while it was limited to this situation. Virchow, however, finds it " free in the alveoli and in the alveolar cells; in the interior of the connective tissue, pleural, subpleural, interlobular, and peribronchial; not unfrequently, also, in the costal and diaphragmatic pleura, and always in the bronchial lymphatic glands." Moreover, he maintains that the black matter is never found in the epithelial cells of the bronchi, and further, that it is invariably noticed in the immediate vicinity of blood-vessels. From the circumstance that the black pigmentary matter is never absent from the bronchial glands, the same observer concludes that there is no evidence of a regular progressive absorption, and moreover, that the limited amount of pigment found in the inter-alveolar septa, and its frequent deposit under the pleura, further militate against this view, and are favorable to the notion of a deposition taking place from the blood. An important particular to attend to is the examination of the black substance itself. Virchow admits that it occurs in " all the forms in which particles of coal dust may present themselves." Sometimes larger, sometimes smaller, these particles may be found of round or angular form; occasionally they are flat and possess an almost crystalline lustre, just as is observed on viewing portions of coal under the microscope. To the circumstance that none of the coal particles which he has ever examined having presented a pure black colour, Virchow attaches great importance. The pigmentary particles removed from the lung in cases of anthracosis are purely black, and the difference in colour between these and coal particles is so remarkable, that he is led to conclude " that the inhalation of particles of carbon cannot be the cause of the pigmentation." Recently a very interesting case of coal-miners' phthisis fell under the notice of Dr. Sanders, and the remarks made by him in regard to it are well worthy of attention. Dr. Sanders observed in the sputum of this patient little hard specks, having all the appearance of coal. One of these specks, nearly of the size of a pin's head, Dr. Sanders sent to Mr. James Bryson, optician, to prepare for the microscope, in order to determine whether it was coal or not. Mr. Bryson had succeeded with some difficulty in grinding the fragment sufficiently thin, and, on comparing the specimen thus prepared with a specimen of Dalkeith coal, it was found that they presented an identical structure consisting of bands of yellow material in a black matrix.[1]

It is quite conclusive, from this interesting observation that in coal-miners' phthisis, fragments of coal, by no means impalpable, do reach the pulmonary structure, and it may reasonably be conjectured that in many other cases, if not in all examples of anthracosis, coal particles in more minute subdivision are inhaled and become firmly impacted.

But in the consideration of the etiology of the subject, it is to be kept in remembrance, that the observation of the disease in the coal pits of Scotland very early gave rise to the notion that the inhalation, not so much of minute coal particles as of an impure atmosphere charged with the products of burnt carbon, by the burning of oil lamps in the confined situation of the pits, was the really efficient cause of anthracosis. This opinion, alluded to by earlier observers, is very strongly expressed in the paper of Mr. J. B. Thomson, of Perth, formerly a practitioner at Tillicoultry, where he had many opportunities of carefully studying the disease. Mr. Thomson has specially grounded the opinion now referred to on the fol-

[1] 'Edinburgh Medical Journal,' September, 1864, p. 274.

lowing considerations :—1st. That in all the low workings in the pit, where oil is used, large masses of black sooty matter, in strings or in flakes, are seen to adhere to and hang from the corners and roof. 2nd. The colliers themselves regard the burning of the oil as the cause of the black spits and the difficult breathing from which they suffer, and they have observed in many pits, in different parts of the country, that those among them who use the oil lamps are the earliest to fall into bad health and the earliest to die. 3rd. The black spit of coal miners is oily or unctuous, corresponding in this respect with the masses which adhere to the walls of the pit and float through the atmosphere. Mr. Thomson asserts "that the use of oil in mines is injurious and probably the exciting cause of black spit." It was noticed by Dr. Makellar, and the observation received confirmation from others, that those men who were frequently engaged in using gunpowder for the purpose of blasting the stone rock, in order to reach the coal seam, suffered more severely from the disease than did others not similarly employed. This was explained by the men engaged in blasting inhaling an atmosphere highly charged with smoke, for after the immediate action of the gunpowder they returned to their work. The opinion as to the injurious effects of blasting I have found to be one commonly entertained by colliers themselves. And I have been able to corroborate the opinion expressed by Mr. Thomson as to the baneful influence of the oil lamp. Where the burning of the oil lamp has been banished the disease has apparently received a most decided check. A further objection is taken by Virchow to the theory of the inhalation of carbonaceous particles being the cause of anthracosis, namely, that these particles are not always met with in the form of granules; at times he remarks the pigment is found "in a diffuse form," "so that cells may be seen grey or black, from the penetration of a matter which the highest microscopic power fails to break up into visible granules;" and he further states, that probably in the case of miners' lung, though much more decidedly in those instances of slighter pulmonary pigmentation which are met with from day to day, a gradual change can be traced by the microscope from a yellowish red, or reddish brown pigment, to a perfect black.

In the careful microscopic examination of recent specimens

of miners' lung I have been unable to verify the statement of Virchow thus alluded to, and I cannot help suspecting that the peculiarities in colour on which he lays so much stress may have been due to the lengthened preservation in spirit of the portions of lung submitted to his scrutiny. The granular form of the pigment is the only form which I have ever seen the particles removed from the sputa, or the lung itself, when examined, to exhibit.

In this paper the attempt has been made to signalise the chief features whether of pathological or etiological interest in cases of anthracosis. It must be admitted that several points in relation to both of these topics require renewed and still more careful investigation. Upon the whole, however, I feel disposed to conclude that—

1. Anthracosis is primarily determined by the inhalation of carbonaceous particles.

2. That in the instance of the coal miner, while capable of being produced in various ways, the chief exciting cause is the inhalation of the very impure atmosphere occasioned by the burning of oil lamps. It would appear that the long-continued inhalation of a very *dusty* atmosphere may, under certain circumstances, engender the same condition. (Case of J. D— detailed in the earlier portion of this paper.)

3. That when once the deposition of carbon in the pulmonary structure has taken place to any extent, and the true function of respiration is thereby interfered with, there occurs a tendency which gradually increases to the arrestment of carbon or carbonaceous pigment in the lungs, and its removal there from the blood.

4. That the presence of black pigmentary deposits in the bronchial glands, the pleura, and less frequently the peritoneum and mesenteric glands, makes it probable that there may in cases of anthracosis be some peculiar process of carbonaceous absorption as well as deposition of carbon.

5. That in this view, the opinion as to the black pulmonary deposit being the result of transformation in hæmatin, although supported by so distinguished an observer as Virchow, cannot be considered as so readily reconcilable with what we know of the natural history, and especially the etiology, of the disease.

It is extremely desirable that the chemical aspects of this

interesting subject should receive renewed investigation, and I would specially invite the chemical inquirer to determine whether the black matter found in the lungs in anthracosis, and that discovered in the bronchial glands, and less frequently in the remoter situations named, be *chemically* identical.

One word in conclusion in reference to the term anthracosis which has been employed in this paper. The expression, not a new one in medical phraseology, because used by some Greek writers to indicate a painful tumour of the eyeball, was first applied to black pigmentary infiltration of the lungs, by Dr. Thomas Stratton, R.N., in an interesting paper, a reference to which will be found below.[1] The word has also been adopted by Virchow, and, on account of its readily understood signification, it is not unlikely that *anthracosis pulmonum* will retain a place in preference to the longer—and of some it must be acknowledged the inaccurate—expressions which different writers have hitherto employed.

---

[1] "Case of Anthracosis or Black Infiltration of the whole Lungs," 'Edinburgh Medical and Surgical Journal,' vol. xlix, 1838, p. 490.

XXI

STRUMA EXOPHTHALMICA [1]

(VASCULAR BRONCHOCELE AND EXOPHTHALMOS).

By PROFESSOR VIRCHOW.

(Translated, with notes and observations, and reprinted from the 'Edinburgh Medical Journal,' April, 1868.)

[IN a recently published part of the important work of Virchow on "Tumours" ('Die Krankhaften Geschwulste'),[2] there occur some statements and reflections in regard to a peculiar form of disease which, both in this country and on the Continent, has of late years attracted very considerable attention. The opinion, as to the nature of so complex a disorder as "Vascular Bronchocele and Exophthalmos," entertained by the eminent professor of Berlin, cannot fail to prove of interest to the members of the profession in general. I have therefore thought it worth while to offer a translation of the author's observations, and to this have added some remarks suggested by their perusal. The latter, for the sake of clearness, and in order to avoid all risk of confusing the reader, are

---

[1] The word "struma," as used by Virchow in the text, and employed by various German writers, means simply bronchocele or goitre—the enlargement of the thyroid gland from whatever cause—and has no relation to that morbid condition or cachexia known as the strumous, or scrofula.—(*Translator.*)

[2] 'Zweiundzwanzigste Vorlesung,' iii Band, i Halfte, S. 73.

thrown entirely by themselves at the close of the translation. The footnotes and references are those of the author unless otherwise distinguished.]

Finally, that is an exceedingly remarkable connection of goitre with affection of the heart (Herzreizung, literally heart-irritation) and large staring eyes (Glotzaugen). So far as is yet known, Flajani[1] was the first to notice the coincidence of goitre with lasting palpitation of the heart. He mentions three cases of this nature, all of which occurred in men, two of the three being youths. In all of these cases, chiefly by means of the external treatment of the bronchocele, a cure was obtained. Of the condition of the eyes he says nothing, but visible enlargement and varicosity of the veins over the thyroid gland were noticed. Parry[2] appears to have been the earliest to observe the third symptom—prominence of the eyes. Next to him, I find two descriptions with post-mortem examinations of accurately investigated cases by Adelmann,[3] in which considerable goitres appeared with enlargement of the heart. During life there existed continued violent palpitation in the region of the heart, great dyspnœa, pain in the abdomen; and in one of the cases it is mentioned that, in addition to these symptoms, "the staring look of the large eyes caused a very remarkable aspect." These facts, notwithstanding, remained nearly unknown till the new experience of Pauli,[4] Von Basedow,[5] and Graves,[6] was published. Although the first communication of Graves appeared in 1835,[7] that of Von Basedow has, notwithstanding, the advantage, the history of the disease having been, in the first place, completely given by him, and, through his knowledge, much information regarding it supplied. By

[1] Guiseppe Flajani, 'Collezione d'osservazioni e riflessioni di Chirurgia,' Roma, 1802, t. iii, p. 270.

[2] Caleb Hillier Parry, "Collections from his unpublished Medical Writings,' London, 1825, vol. ii, p. 3, quoted by Stokes. ' Die Krankheiten des Herzens u. der Aorta.' Uebersetzung von Lindwurm, Würzb., 1855, S. 232.

[3] Adelmann, ' Jahrbücher der philosophisch. medicinischen Gesellschaft zu Wurzburg, 1828, Bd. i, ii, S. 104-8.

[4] Pauli, 'Heidelberger Medic. Annalen,' 1837, S. 218.

[5] Von Basedow, Casper's ' Wochenschrift,' 1840, No. 13, S. 198.

[6] Robert James Graves, ' Klinische Beobachtungen,' Deutsch von Bressler, Leipz., 1843, S. 409.

[7] Stokes, a. a. O., S. 234.

Von Basedow was originated the designation of exophthalmos, of the staring eye (Glotzauges) as the most striking feature, and of the cachexia exophthalmica, large staring eye cachexia (Glotzaugenkachexie), which has more recently become so universally known; and it is from this circumstance that, according to the proposal of G. Hirsch,[1] it has been customary to style the whole assemblage of complex symptoms " Morbus Basedowii." Trousseau,[2] on the other hand, maintains that the disease should be termed " Graves' disease." I hold that this is not correct; for Graves regarded both the palpitation of the heart and the goitre as essentially symptoms of hysteria, while the condition of the eyes is only incidentally mentioned by him; moreover, he is not the first who observed the complex symptoms. By recent writers, prominence has been assigned at one time to one, at another time to another of three principal symptoms; and, according to it, the choice of a designation for the disease has been made. Of late, the name "Struma exophthalmica" (goitre exophthalmique) has become very generally disseminated; but Lebert,[3] having reference to the affection of the heart, suggests for the disease the appellation of " Tachycardia strumosa." [4]

The condition of the thyroid gland is, during life, subject to variety. As a general rule, the swelling is not so great as that of the ordinary goitre, still a very marked enlargement is discovered. The most conspicuous feature of the swelling is an increased development of the vessels, with which, not unfrequently, a diastolic beat and " souffle " (ein diastoliches Klopfen und Rauschen) are perceived, so as to be directly styled "Struma aneurysmatica,"[5] or "Bronchocele vasculosa."[6]

[1] G. Hirsch, ' Klinische Fragmente,' Königsberg, 1858, Heft ii, S. 224.

[2] Trousseau, ' Gazette Hebdomadaire de Médecine,' 1862, No. 30, p. 472.

[3] Lebert, ' Die Krankheiten der Schildrüse,' S. 307.

[4] " Tachycardia " (Ταχύς, quick, Καρδία, the heart), in reference to the rapid and excited action of the organ. The exact term suggested by Lebert is "tachycardia exophthalmica strumosa." See his ' Grundzüge der Artzlichen Praxis,' 1867, S. 230.—(*Translator*).

[5] Henoch, Casper's ' Wochenschrift,' 1848, No. 40, S. 629. Romberg und Henoch, ' Klinische Wahrnehmungen und Beobachtungen,' Berlin, 1851, S. 191. (Of this interesting paper, an abridged rendering by the translator will be found in the ' Edinburgh Medical and Surgical Journal,' April, 1854.) Bullar, ' Medico-Chirurgical Transactions,' 1861, vol. xliv, p. 37.

[6] Laycock, ' Edinburgh Medical Journal,' 1863, p. 1. J. Warburton Begbie, ditto, September, 1863, p. 211.

Sudden appearance of swelling, and its rapid subsidence, have been associated. The results of anatomical inquiries are not agreed upon.[1]

In the only case investigated by me, and of which Traube and Von Recklinghausen have given an account, the gland moderately increased in size, exhibited simply excessive plastic without any gelatinous, nodular, or cystic formation. The lobes of the thyroid reached very distinctly forwards, the interstitial structure was abundant, and the veins only were generally enlarged. Very similar was its condition in the case given by Reith, also in one by Trousseau, which Peter has described, except that, in the last, there is no mention made of the enlargement of the veins. Smith found a very considerable augmentation, especially of the right lobe of the gland, while the arteries were much enlarged and strangely tortuous. Markham observed the gland as being large and firm, at the same time (in a woman of twenty-six years of age) he found an enlarged and persistent thymus gland. In an instance recorded by Hirsch, the thyroid gland was big, hard, and externally covered by enlarged vessels. Heusinger describes the thyroid as double the natural size and uniformly hypertrophied, but without the presence of any abnormal formation. Very similar was its condition, according to the observation of James Begbie. In the case of Schleich, related by Laqueur, Runge found a large gelatinous goitre. Naumann describes the thyroid as very large, its structure uniformly red, and presenting hæmorrhagic spots, the arteries greatly developed. Von Basedow discovered the gland enormously enlarged with hydatid and

[1] Marsh, 'Dublin Journal of Medical Science,' 1842, vol. xx, p. 471. Von Basedow, Casper's 'Wochenschrift,' 1848, No. 49, S. 775. Heusinger (in Braunschweig), Casper's 'Wochenschrift,' 1851, No. 4, S. 53. Naumann, 'Deutsche Klinik,' 1853, No. 25, S. 269. Smith, bei Stokes, a. a. O., S. 239. Banks, 'Dublin Hospital Gazette,' 1855 (quoted by W. Moore, 'Dublin Quarterly Journal,' 1865, November, p. 347). James Begbie, 'Edinburgh Medical and Surgical Journal,' 1855. 'Case-book,' p. 33. F. Praël, sen., 'Archiv f. Ophthalmologie, 1857, Bd. iii, 2, S. 199. Markham, 'Transactions of the Pathological Society of London,' 1858, vol. ix, p. 163. Hirsch, a. a. O., S. 224. L. Laqueur, 'De Morbo Basedowii nonnulla adjecta, singulari observatione,' Dissertatio inauguralis, Berol., 1860, p. 12. Traube und Von Recklinghausen, 'Deutsche Klinik,' 1863, No. 29, S. 286. Trousseau et Peter, 'Gaz. Hebdom.,' 1864, No. 12, p. 181. Archibald Reith, 'Medical Times and Gazette,' November, 1865, p. 521.

varicose degenerations, and Marsh (Sir Henry) saw the thyroid irregularly lobed, containing cysts, which were occupied by a clear fluid, and the jugular veins very greatly distended. Analogous to this was the case recorded by Banks. Lastly, Praël found a ponderous goitre which stretched downwards into the cavity of the chest, its right lobe embracing the trachea, and having passed into a state of cartilaginous degeneration.[1]

It appears from the foregoing comparison of observations, that it is not a determinate variety of goitre, or a fixed enlargement of the same, or definite course, which settles the appearances. Indeed, in many cases the alteration of tissue is so trifling that we may ask, as Graves did, whether it is in reality a bronchocele, or merely a swelling (intumescentia) of the gland which exists. From this consideration, there arises a direct refutation of the opinion entertained by some, that the cause of the exophthalmos is the pressure of the thyroidal tumour on the vessels of the neck.[2] Further, it shows, that at first a simple swelling of the gland exists from which a true bronchocele is formed, and that the goitre runs its usual course from a very moderate, chiefly plastic formation, or advances to a fibrous induration of nodular form. The same series of changes, however, occurs with sufficient frequency in the ordinary goitre, without the appearance of the other symptoms, and accordingly the alteration of the thyroid gland is to be regarded as a secondary phenomenon. That the persistent enlargement of the vessels, and especially of the veins, plays a decided part, may already be conjectured from clinical details. It seems to depend less upon the condition of the arteries; at least in all cases in which these were remarkably changed, there existed also considerable disease in other parts of the vascular system.

In nearly all the cases the heart is greatly enlarged, for the most part dilated, even where the valves are healthy, the left ventricle being chiefly affected. The aorta and great vessels

---

[1] Besides the names already mentioned in the text, that of "cardiagmus strumosus" (καρδιωγμός, a Hippocratic term, synonymous with cardialgia) has been applied to this disease by Hirsch.—(*Translator.*)

[2] Piorry, 'Gazette Hebdomadaire,' 1862, No. 30, p. 477. A. Cros, 'Gazette Hebdom.,' No. 35, p. 548. Nunneley, 'Medico-Chirurgical Transactions,' vol. xlviii, p. 32.

were, in most instances, but by no means in all, atheromatous. Clinical investigation demonstrates that the hypertrophy of the heart belongs to an advanced stage of the disease; accelerated motion (100 beats and upwards in the minute) is the ordinary phenomenon.

The earliest entertained notion in regard to the eyes was that a hydrophthalmos existed: this is now on all sides abandoned. Naumann alone has found a trifling enlargement of the eyeball. The essential change lies in the fatty tissue of the orbit, which is sometimes hypertrophied, but is for the most part expanded by a hyperæmic swelling, capable of being overcome during life by pressure, and readily disappearing after death.[1] Reith alone, besides greatly distended veins, found a small quantity of partially coagulated blood effused over the eyeball.[2] If to this be added a fatty degeneration of the muscles of the eye, as Von Recklinghausen detected, we are enabled to understand how so considerable a prominence of the eyeballs occurs, that in fact the eyelids can no longer be closed,[3] and that in the uncovered portion of the eye inflammation may be induced, which, in turn, may lead to a complete destruction of the cornea and wasting of the eyeball.[4] As a rule, the prominence of the eyes is on both sides and also symmetrical; still it does happen that the protrusion is either earliest seen, or, at all events, is more marked in one eye than the other.[5]

For the present it must be left undecided whether the majority of observers have found enlargement of the spleen to be an essential or merely an accidental result. At all events, we cannot on à priori grounds lightly estimate the disturbance of the digestive function, more particularly the vomiting and

---

[1] Deschambre ('Gazette Hebdomadaire,' 1862, p. 482) quotes an interesting parallel observation by Decès ('Thèse inaugural sur l'Anévrysme cirsoïde,' 1857), where a transitory exophthalmos appeared in a woman who suffered from alternating arterial dilatations in different parts of the body.

[2] A. Reith, l. c., p. 521.

[3] Graves, a. a. O., S. 411. Stokes, a. a. O., S. 231.

[4] Casper's 'Wochenschrift,' 1840, No. 14, S. 221. Von Gräfe, 'Archiv f. Ophthalmologie,' 1857, Bd. iii, 2, S. 282. Teissier, 'Gazette Méd. de Lyon,' 1863, No. 1, 2.

[5] Von Basedow, a. a. O., 1848, No. 49, S. 772. Henoch und Romberg, 'Klinische Wahrnehmungen,' S. 182. Reith, l. c., p. 521. Praül, a. a. O., S. 206, 207.

tendency to diarrhœa, which are often observed. There always remain the three intimate symptoms or triad-affection of the heart, the thyroid gland, and eyes (orbital-polsters, orbit cushions), as the regular, although, in relation to each other, not constant phenomena, and it may be asked what the explanation of this combination is. That the lesion of the thyroid gland is not to be considered as the centre or mainspring of this complex disorder, I have already made apparent. Individual observers indicate that the bronchocele may be altogether absent.[1] Still less can we regard the affection of the fatty tissue in the orbit as of principal importance, particularly as the protrusion of the eyes is sometimes wanting, or else it only becomes apparent at a later stage.[2] Neither can it be held that the hypertrophy of the heart is itself to be looked upon as the point of departure. On the one hand, hypertrophy is not always present; and on the other, considerable hypertrophy of the heart often exists without the staring eyes and without the goitre. The anatomical changes of all these elements cannot then be regarded as diagnostic.

We come, therefore, to the question of the functional disturbances. Here I must specially call attention to the fact, that there exists a peculiar combination of affections of the thyroid gland and heart. This combination, which was formerly mentioned (vol. i, p. 114), is the so-called iodism, or the goitre cachexia (Kropfcachexie). Here we observe, with the disappearance of the goitre as the consequence of a slight iodism, a most remarkable acceleration of the pulse, not unfrequently the production of annoying palpitation. Only the exophthalmos is wanting; instead of it there is another prominent symptom rarely present in the "struma exophthalmica,"[3] to wit, the association of rapid and great emaciation with voracious appetite [mit Bulimie].[4] The point now mentioned, at all times worthy of notice, is so much the more so, from the circumstance that in a case of Oliffe's,[5] the moderate

---

[1] Prael, a. a. O., S. 209.

[2] Henoch und Romberg, 'Klinische Wahrnehmungen,' S. 179, 180.

[3] Trousseau, 'Union Méd.,' 1860, tome 8, p. 437-456.

[4] Emaciation and bulimia do sometimes co-exist in cases of "struma exophthalmica."—(Translator.)

[5] Trousseau, 'Union Méd.,' 1860, tome 8, p. 513.

exhibition of iodine in "struma exophthalmica" produced the worst effects. Trousseau[1] himself has made similar observations, and on this account has not hesitated, in the discussion on iodism in the French Academy of Medicine, to regard as cases of "struma exophthalmica" instances which, by Rilliet, had been described under the name of iodism. Rilliet[2] has, on the contrary, in the most decided manner claimed as examples of iodism recorded cases which had been described under the name of "struma exophthalmica." Extended observations are required in order to clear up this dispute. Neither bronchocele nor iodine produce the phenomena of the "cachexia exophthalmica," or of the "cachexia iodica;" in both cases there must, in addition, be the presence of something peculiar. In reference to this, we must go back to an original predisposition; and I may mention that Bednar[3] has repeatedly found in newly born children the co-existence of an enlargement of the thyroid gland and hypertrophy of the heart. Yet these facts, supposing them to possess a general importance, which is unlikely, do not exclude from the inquiry the existence of a further cause.

In the acceptation of the humoral pathology, it is concluded that there is always a blood derangement when several organs are together affected, without there appearing to be a simple dependence of the disease on one or other of these. Von Basedow[4] has forthwith extended this view to the establishment of an independent dyscrasia, which he has expressed as a hidden scrofula. At a later period, he has pointed out this dyscrasia as being similar to the chlorotic.[5] This opinion has been subsequently embraced by many other observers,[6] and anæmia has become the theoretical foundation of the complex symptoms, while Mackenzie has gone so far as to indicate the condition of the eyes as being neither more nor less than "exophthalmia anæmica." In favour of this view, there is not merely the

---

[1] Trousseau, 'Gazette Hebdom.,' 1860, Avril, p. 219-67.

[2] Rilliet, 'Mémoire sur l'Iodisme constitutionnel, Paris, 1860, p. 83.

[3] Bednar, a. a. O., S. 79.

[4] Von Basedow, a. a. O., 1840, S. 225.

[5] Von Basedow, in the same place, 1848, S. 772.

[6] L. Gros, 'Gaz. Med.,' 1857, p. 232. Hervieux, 'Union Méd.,' 1857, No. 117, p. 477. Beau, 'Gaz. Hebdom.,' 1862, No. 34, p. 539. Fischer, 'Arch. Génér.,' 1859, Dec., p. 671. Begbie, 'Edin. Med. Jour.,' 1863, Sept., p. 201. Praël, a. a. O., S. 210.

frequent occurrence of pulsations, palpitations, and murmurs in the vascular system, as in chlorotic patients, not merely the circumstance that the majority of cases of staring eyes with goitre (Glotzaugen-Kropf) are observed in women,[1] and that on several occasions pregnancy and child-bearing have exerted a remarkably favorable influence on the removal of the malady,[2] but also very specially the experience which we possess in relation to the satisfactory operation of an invigorating treatment.

It is, however, undoubted that the anæmia, granting its existence, cannot directly produce such an effect. At the very least, we must assume that, through the disordered blood, an injurious influence on the nerves takes place. In returning, however, to the nerves, the question arises, whether anæmia is required in order to produce such a condition of the nervous system. Different observers[3] have been content to look upon it as a feeble state of the nervous system (einen Schwächezustand des Nervensystems). Graves and Brück[4] considered it hysterical. Stokes[5] limited himself to pointing out that the essence of the disease consisted in a functional disturbance of the heart, upon which organic change is apt to follow. More recently a further advance has been made, and attention has been directed to the nerves of the heart, and especially to the sympathetic,[6] with perhaps also participation of the spinal cord.[7] Köben, the first to offer this conjecture, supposed that the sympathetic was compressed and irritated by the bronchocele; since then the

---

[1] Trousseau, 'Union Médicale,' 1860, t. viii, S. 437. Charcot, 'Gaz. Med.,' 1856, Sept., p. 584. 'Gaz. Hebdom.,' 1862, Sept., p. 564. Corlieu, 'Gaz. des Hôpitaux,' 1863, p. 125.

[2] Von Basedow (Casper's 'Wochenschrift,' 1848, S. 774) mentions the following remarkable facts: that the mammæ of a man were found greatly enlarged, the left being hard, congested, and painful, yielding colostrum.

[3] Handfield Jones, 'Medical Times and Gazette,' Dec., 1860, p. 541. Fletcher, 'British Med. Journal,' 1863, May. (Hyperneurie.)

[4] Graves, a. a. O., S. 410. A. Th. Brück, Casper's 'Wochenschrift,' 1840, No. 28 (Buphthalmus hystericus), 1848, No. 18, p. 275.

[5] Stokes, a. a. O., S. 244.

[6] Köben, 'De Exophthalmo ac Struma cum Cordis affectione;' Diss. inaug., Berol., 1855. Von Gräfe, a. a. O., S. 280. Trousseau, 'Union Méd.,' 1860, t. viii, p. 487. Arau, 'Gaz. Hebdom.,' No. 49, p. 796. Reith, l. c., p. 522.

[7] Laycock, 'Edin. Med. Jour.,' 1863, Feb., p. 681; July, p. 1.

bronchocele has justly been regarded as pertaining to the
neurosis. In support of this view, some not unimportant facts
in pathological anatomy have been advanced. Peter[1] found
the lowest cervical ganglion enlarged and greatly reddened,
its interstitial tissue increased, the nerve fibres diminished.
Somewhat similar is the account given by Moore[2] of the inquiry
conducted by Cruise and M'Donnel. Reith describes the middle
and lower cervical ganglion on both sides, especially the left,
as enlarged, hard, and firm; and, when viewed under the
microscope, filled with a granular material resembling a lymph
gland in the first stage of tuberculosis. The trunk of the sympathetic itself, as well as its branches proceeding to the "arteria
thyroidea inferior" and "arteria vertebralis," were enlarged.
He held these changes to be tubercular. Directly opposed is
the observation of Von Recklinghausen, in so far as the cord
and ganglia of the sympathetic were small, as if atrophied,
but without histological changes. All now stated was undoubtedly insufficient to explain the real nature of this interesting
affection, especially as the appearances of the "struma exophthalmica"—if we appeal to the familiar physiological experiments of Cl. Bernard—correspond in part to the paralysis, in
part merely to the irritation of the sympathetic; while, again,
there appears to be no true connection, as some of these constant
phenomena in the pupil have not been noticed.[3] Only in isolated
cases has enlargement of the pupil been observed. Stromeyer[4]
compares the "exophthalmia strumosa" with the temporary
incomplete prominence of the globe, which he had noticed in
connection with habitual spasm of the head (Krampfe des
Kopfnickers). When this cramp occurs either from maintaining the erect posture, or from mental emotion, he seeks the
foundation of the staring eyes in spasm of the oblique muscles
of the eye, and the levator muscles of the eyelids. Demme[5]
has also frequently observed with the ordinary goitre partial
changes in the pupils, especially "mydriasis," and a notable

[1] Peter, l. c., p. 182.
[2] Moore, 'Dublin Quar. Jour., 1865, Nov., p. 348.
[3] Henoch und Romberg, 'Klin. Wahrnehmungen,' S. 182. Reith, l. c.,
p. 251.
[4] Stromeyer, 'Handbuch der Chirurgie,' ii, 2, S. 389.
[5] H. Demme, 'Würzb. Med. Zeitschrift,' Bd. iii, S. 269, 273, 297.

elevation of the upper lids. He gives as an anatomical condition at the same time (besides serous swelling and interstitial connective tissue in the recurrent nerve) marked reddening and serous swelling of the sympathetic. These statements, however, suffice just as little as the older descriptions of different changes in the vagus connected with the goitrous condition. Certainly the direction of the inquiry turns, even as in the question of the connection between disease of the supra-renal capsules, bronze-skin,[1] and other cases, more and more to the nerves themselves; while there still exists too little material for enabling us to arrive at a decision.[2] After all, the question resolves itself not so much into an examination of the cases in their later stages, which can be cleared up by autopsies, but into an investigation of the earliest determining cause.

At least, there can no longer be any hesitation in acknowledging the intimate nervous dependence of the complex symptoms as the only probable view. With justice has reference been made to the existence of great derangement of the general nervous system, to the loss of sleep, the often noticed epigastric pulsation, the sensation of heat,[3] and, lastly, to a macular eruption occurring on the head after a slight mechanical irritation.[4] In what particular portion of the nervous system the original seat of the disturbance, and what the disturbance itself

[1] *Bronzing of the skin* occurs in connection with "struma exopthalmica." It exists in a marked degree on the face of a patient (a man) of Dr. Begbie's presently under observation.—(*Translator.*)

[2] Only very recently there died, in my division, a man who had long suffered from very violent palpitation of the heart, with great dyspnœa. His eyes, without being precisely exophthalmic, had an unusual glare (glanz), and gave the impression of being increased in size. A few months previously, Herr Von Gräfe, on account of a commencing glaucoma, had performed iridectomy. Near the close he was affected by dropsy, with very diminished secretion of urine, which was albuminous and rich in uric acid; also with obstinate and violent pain, associated with bloody diarrhœa, great restlessness and fever, with other symptoms. On post-mortem examination I found hypertrophy of the heart, with very extensive myocarditis, a goitre, and very considerable enlargement and interstitial thickening of the sympathetic in the neck, especially of the uppermost and lowest ganglion.

[3] Von Basedow, Casper's 'Wochenschrift,' 1840, No. 13, S. 202; No. 14, S. 220. Teissier, 'Gaz. Méd. de Lyon,' 1862, No. 29; 1863, Nos. 1, 2. Trousseau, 'Gaz. Méd.,' 1864, No. 12, p. 180. Warburton Begbie, 'Edin. Med. Jour.,' 1863, Sept., p. 216.

[4] Trousseau, 'Gaz. Méd.,' 1864, No. 12, p. 180.

is, that must first be more accurately established; and the inquiry must be made also, whence, from what source (whether from the blood) the disturbance has been developed. At all events, it is a step in advance to become acquainted with these complex symptoms, and the jeers of M. Piorry are unable to deter us from acknowledging the entity of the disease.[1] In the history of goitre, it forms an episode as remarkable as it is important; for although this variety of bronchocele seems of itself to have little importance, yet it constitutes a part of a grave malady, and one not unfrequently fatal, although, in other circumstances, readily curable.

As to the ætiology, there remains little more to be said. According to the observations hitherto advanced, it is by no means in goitre-districts of country that this variety has frequently occurred. Still more does the " struma exophthalmica " plainly constitute one of the most important species of sporadic goitre. Females in a greatly preponderating degree suffer,[2] more so in the early period of life, especially about puberty, and in childbed. Uterine derangements act by no means always as exciting causes; and while serious diseases such as typhus, and colds particularly affecting the throat, exert an influence, chlorosis is chiefly to blame. Since the latter disease, according to my understanding, is one of early life—is even a disease of development[3]—we are led to assume the existence of an original predisposition. Romberg and Juncken[4] observed the disease in two sisters.[5] We are still further removed from understanding the cause of the disease in men. Exhausting labour, great and long continued depression of the mind, and

---

[1] Piorry, 'Gaz. Hebdom.,' 1862, p. 477.

[2] It is not without interest that Rorie ('Edin. Med. Jour.,' 1863, Feb., p. 696) frequently found prominence of the eyeballs in persons of weak intellect, and this particularly in women (35 per cent.); inequality of the pupils, also, he noticed not unfrequently. Foderé remarks, concerning cretins:— "Aux uns les yeux sont enfoncés dans la tête, aux autres ils sont très en dehors. En général leur régard est fixe et égaré, et il y a toujours un air d'étonnement."

[3] Virchow, 'Cellular Pathologie (3rd edition), S. 211.

[4] Henoch, Casper's ' Wochenschrift,' 1848, No. 40, S. 627.

[5] Dr. Begbie informs me that, quite recently, he has observed the disease in two sisters, both married. In both, the malady had assumed its unequivocal characters.—(*Translator.*)

weakening diseases, have at times preceded it. According to the comparison instituted by Von Gräfe,[1] the disease appears at a later period, on the average, in men, but, at the same time, is more serious. It is worthy of remark that, not unfrequently, the commencement of the malady has been noticed to be quite sudden, for example, after a fright or hard labour.

Death results with an increase of the appearances, sometimes very quickly, accompanied by great uneasiness and disturbance of the brain, mostly in a gradual manner, with decay of nutrition and strength, which is hastened by urgent diarrhœa, sometimes dysenteric in character, and mucous catarrh of the lungs. At another time, on the other hand, chiefly in recent cases, a complete cure results; the goitre, however, it is true, not always entirely disappearing. Sometimes the preparations of iron have effected this, sometimes digitalis,—it is seldom that iodine is useful. The best consequences have succeeded the employment of cold-water treatment, sea-bathing, and an invigorating diet.[2]

Observations by Translator.—It is necessary, in the first place, to correct an error into which Virchow has fallen when offering the interesting historical summary regarding " Struma Exophthalmica," with which his observations commence. Parry, he remarks, appears to have been the earliest to observe the prominence of the eyes. The fact is, however, that Parry noticed the enlargement of the thyroid gland in connection with disease of the heart, but in the whole course of his statement regarding that connection there is only a single, and that evidently casual, reference to the condition of the eyes. Unquestionably the earliest observer in our own country of the peculiar affection of the eyes, believed by him, at the time, to be a real enlargement, was Dr. Stokes, and next in order to him was the

[1] Von Gräfe, a. a. O., S. 292.

[2] I may take the opportunity of directing attention to a brief but very interesting account of the disease by a physician of Heidelberg, Dr. Theodor Von Dusch, in his recently published volume, entitled 'Lehrbuch der Herzkrankheiten,' Leipzig, 1868.

Dr. Von Dusch's observations on the "Basedow'sche Krankheit" are illustrated by a woodcut representing an example of double exophthalmos, but without goitre, in a man of thirty-two years. The portrait, in the first instance, was photographed from nature.—(*Translator.*)

late Sir Henry Marsh, of Dublin. Antecedent to 1835, the date of his first publication on the subject, Dr. Graves had incidentally had his attention directed to the coincidence of cardiac disease and enlargement of the thyroid gland. In 1839, Dr. Begbie had evidently, in a manner altogether independent, noted the association of the three peculiar symptoms. During the succeeding ten years other instances of the kind occurred to him in practice, and, in 1849, he published an account of them. In doing so, Dr. Begbie was the earliest in this country to assert the entity of the disorder, to advance a theory of its cause, namely, its dependence on anæmia, to indicate its amenability to treatment, and capability of perfect cure, and, lastly, to suggest a plan of treatment, the success of which has, happily in many instances since that time been most satisfactorily proved. Five years subsequently to the incidental observation by Dr. Graves, of enlargement of the thyroid gland with disease of the heart, a German physician, Von Basedow, published a paper, in which terms now sufficiently familiar in connection with the disease, were for the first time employed. For example, "Exophthalmos," "Cachexia exophthalmica," and, in the German, "Glotzaugen" (staring eyes), "Glotzaugenkachexie" (staring-eye or goggle-eye cachexia). In these phrases it will be noticed that no particular reference is made to the condition of the thyroid gland, which in connection with heart-enlargement, had already attracted the attention of Parry and others; but Von Basedow was familiar with the bronchocele as well, and accordingly, in consideration of the correctness of his observation so far, there can be no objection, as has been proposed by Hirsch, and followed by German physicians generally—although scarcely receiving the sanction of Virchow's high authority—to designate the disease "Basedow's disease" ("Basedow'sche Krankheit," "Morbus Basedowii"). The late distinguished and lamented physician of the "Hôtel Dieu," whose unbounded admiration for the character and writings of Dr. Graves is as well known as it is highly appreciated by all readers of the 'Clinical Lectures,' has styled the disease, "Graves' disease" ("Maladie de Graves"), and whether rightly or wrongly so—Virchow, as we have seen, thinks wrongly—there can be no doubt that under this name, as originally employed by Trousseau, it will long be familiarly known and

·described. Were it not that I entirely agree with the late Dr. Todd, of London, in regarding it as no compliment to the great names of our profession " to attach them to any of the numerous ills which flesh is heir to,"[1] I should feel disposed to suggest the appellation of " Stokes' disease." Such, too, is a sufficient reason for not encouraging the use of that name which my filial respect had otherwise most cordially approved, to wit, " Begbie's disease," as already proposed by more than one writer. There is little to be said in favour of the other nomenclature adverted to in the translation, the " Tachycardia strumosa," or "Tachycardia exophthalmica strumosa," of Lebert, and the " Cardiagmus strumosus" of Hirsch and Von Dusch; and it must be confessed that a really good and serviceable title for the disease is still a desideratum.

Like other observers, it is worthy of note, that Virchow indicates no special form of disease as incident to the thyroid gland in this complex disorder. The most marked or characteristic feature is its increased vascularity, and the peculiar pulsation, or pulsatory thrill, which is, at all events, distinguishable over it. Hence the application to this variety of goitre of the terms " vascular bronchocele" and " struma aneurysmatica." While increase of gland structure, and various kinds of degeneration, as, for example, the fibrous and cystic, have been detected in such goitres, there is no doubt whatever that the augmented activity and chronic enlargement of the vessels, particularly the veins in them, is of chief importance.

The central organ of the circulation invariably and, in point of time primarily, suffers. At first, however, and usually for a lengthened period, the heart is only functionally disturbed. Of this disturbance its greatly accelerated action is the prime, as it is the unmistakable indication. After a time, structural change ensues, and that is, for the most part, of the nature of dilatation, or hypertrophy with dilatation. The left ventricle is the chamber chiefly affected. Valvular disease of the heart is certainly rare; when it exists, the imperfection is secondary, never primary. In other words, the increased size of the mitral and tricuspid orifices, discovered on the post-mortem examination of some cases of the disease, bore an intimate relationship

[1] In referring to facial palsy as " Bell's paralysis," in ' Clinical Lectures on Diseases of the Nervous System,' Lecture 4.

to the greatly augmented capacity of both ventricles. This, the earlier result, was evidently the cause on which the insufficiency of the auriculo-ventricular valves depended.[1]

In the great majority of cases, a disturbed action of the heart, generally spoken of as palpitation, is the *first* symptom to attract attention. If, however, a very careful inquiry into the previous history of such patients be made, it will be found that for some time before the distressing action of the heart was noticed—possibly at a considerable period antecedent to the acknowledged existence of any departure from health—there had occurred a diarrhœa or lientery, a menorrhagia or leucorrhœa, an epistaxis, rather a frequently recurring loss of blood from the nose, or a hæmorrhage from piles; and although, in many cases, none of these may have been sufficient to produce the more manifest indications of anæmia, it will, I firmly believe, be further found that impoverishment of blood—readily enough recognisable—exists.

Virchow, like all recent observers of this disease, rejects the notion of the prominence of the eyes being due to "hydrophthalmos." He looks upon a change in the fatty tissue of the orbit —a view originally maintained by Heusinger—as being the essential morbid condition upon which the very strange aspect of the eyes depends. An hypertrophy of the fatty tissue, or its congestion, are the states more particularly indicated. Enlargement of the spleen is referred to by Virchow as having been noticed by some observers, but he truly remarks that the degree of importance to be attached to its occurrence has not been as yet accurately determined.

There are then, it may be stated, *four* essential symptoms in this most interesting malady—namely, 1. Disturbance of the heart's action prone to terminate in structural change; 2. Enlargement—vascular in its nature—of the thyroid gland; 3. Prominence, with peculiar expression, of the eyes; and, 4. Remarkable visible pulsation and vibratory thrill throughout the whole arterial system. Of this "tetrad" of symptoms, the first and fourth are always present; the second and third may each be absent. Without cardiac and vascular derangement, the disease has no existence. An exquisite illustration

---

[1] See, for example, the case of J. K—, as recorded by Dr. Begbie, in Contributions to Practical Medicine,' pp. 143, 148.

of the malady, however, presumes the presence of all the features now mentioned.

In discussing the essential pathology of "struma exophthalmica," Virchow has justly observed that anæmia, granting its existence, cannot directly produce the results which are witnessed. While the "primum mobile" is, however, seated in the blood, it is abundantly evident that an injurious influence is largely exerted on the nerves. A decided advance in our knowledge on this point has recently been made, for Peter, Reith, and Von Recklinghausen have each discovered a distinct lesion of the sympathetic nerve and its ganglia, while Virchow himself so far confirms their interesting and probably important observations as to have found in a case not exactly of the "struma exophthalmica," but bearing a certain resemblance to it, a lesion of the same nervous trunk.

Further observations are, however, required in order to determine, with any amount of accuracy, what value is to be attached to these morbid appearances in relation to the intimate pathology of that strange disease with which they have been found connected.[1]

It cannot be too distinctly stated, nor too carefully borne in remembrance, that, in this disease, *iodine* is an unsuitable remedy—its administration, so valuable in ordinary goitre, is in the "struma exophthalmica" not only useless, but injurious. From *iron*, *digitalis*, and *belladonna*[2] discriminately employed, and from the steady perseverance with an invigorating plan of treatment, the best effects have been found to follow.

[1] I have observed a decided feebleness in the lower extremities, almost amounting to paraplegia, in two or three aggravated cases of the disease. This also points to the implication of the nervous system. In two of these instances the patients walked with considerable difficulty, and had acquired a peculiar rotatory movement in progression.

[2] "On Vascular Bronchocele and Exophthalmos," by the translator; 'Edinburgh Medical Journal,' 1863, p. 217.

XXII.

THE THERAPEUTIC ACTIONS AND USES
OF TURPENTINE.

(Read before the Medico-Chirurgical Society of Edinburgh, 7th June,
1871.)

TURPENTINE, the τερέβινθος or τέρβινθος, and in the earlier
form τέρμινθος, of the Greeks, has an ancient as well as interesting history. Already esteemed as a remedy in Hippocratic
times, and mentioned in three of the treatises which bear the
name of the Father of Medicine,[1] if indeed these were not composed by Hippocrates, there exists little ground for questioning
the identity of the Pistachia Terebinthus,[2] a plant yielding, in
common with certain of the Coniferæ, the liquid turpentine,
with the Terebinthus of the ancient writers. By The ophrastus,
Dioscorides, Galen, and Pliny, many original observations
concerning the use of turpentine are also made, and these are
copied by such subsequent writers as Aetius, Oribasius, Paulus
Ægineta, and Alexander Trallianus. Hippocrates, at least the
Hippocratic author, had ascertained the emmenagogue virtues
of turpentine, and also its action in restraining discharges from
mucous surfaces, particularly those of the genito-urinary pas-

[1] ΗΕΡΙ ΓΥΝΑΙΚΕΙΗΣ ΦΥΣΙΟΣ. ΠΕΡΙ ΓΥΝΑΙΚΕΙΩΝ, τὸ δεύτερον. ΠΕΡΙ
ΣΥΡΙΓΓΩΝ.
[2] "Indeed, this last-mentioned plant is probably the true Terebinthus of
the ancients."—Pereira, 'The Elements of Materia Medica and Therapeutics,'
vol. ii, part i, p. 1183.

sages,[1] and the writers subsequent to him, of whom Dioscorides[2] as a Greek, and Pliny[3] as a Latin author may be particularly cited, indicate their knowledge of its possessing many other important properties.

Coming down to the modern history of turpentine, we meet with a subject naturally complex, from the circumstance that there are *many* officinal substances derived from the coniferous plants. A very clear and instructive narrative of the natural and chemical history of the Terebinthinæ is given by Dr. Christison in his Dispensatory, and the previous labours of M. Guibourt[4] and Dr. Pereira, are by him both acknowledged and rendered further available. The last-mentioned authority, Dr. Pereira, in his able discussion of turpentine, has found it most convenient to treat of the coniferous terebinthinates under four heads :—1. The oleo-resinous juices. 2. The volatile oil obtained by distillation. 3. The resinous

---

[1] After referring to passages in the Hippocratic writings regarding turpentine, Trousseau and Pidoux observe, "Si la première de ces citations est vague et caractérise peu l' action spéciale de la Térébenthine, ce que nous sommes loin de nier, puisque le père de la médecine n'a presque jamais parlé d'un remède excitant sans le déclarer emménagogue, la seconde établit claire-ment que ce grand observateur avait administré la Térébenthine dans les cas où elle est le mieux indiquée, les flux muqueux, et spécialement ceux des voies génito-urinaires."—'Traité de Thérapeutique et de Matière Médicale,' tome seconde, p. 582.

[2] ΠΕΔΑΚΙΟΥ ΔΙΟΣΚΟΡΙΔΟΥ. Περὶ ὕλης ἰατρικῆς, βιβλίον πρῶτον. Περὶ Τέρμινθου. In this passage the learned Anazarbian signalises the possession by turpentine of diuretic and aphrodisiac properties, also its virtues in pulmonary catarrhs and phthisical disorders, in rheumatic affections, in palpebral inflammations, attended by loss of the eyelashes, in scabies, and certain chronic cutaneous eruptions. Moreover, he recommends the employment of turpentine in the form of an electuary, with honey (ἐκλεικτόν, Hippocrates—ἔκλειγμα, Aretaeus: literally, a medicine which melts in the mouth), a method of administration of the remedy, the mention of which (in the words of the French writers already quoted, " remise en honneur de nos jours") gives increased interest to the Hippocratic passage ; finally, turpentine is noticed as affording relief to pain when simply applied to the side, or used as an ointment in pleurisy.

[3] 'C. Plinii Secundi Naturalis Historiæ,' tomus secundus, lib. xiii, cap. vi. "De Terebintho;" also lib. xxiv, cap. vi. In the latter, there occur the following sentences :—" Terebinthi folia et radix collectionibus imponuntur. Decoctum eorum stomachum firmat. Semen in capitis dolore bibitur in vino, et contra difficultatem urinæ. Ventrem leniter emollit. Venerem excitat. Piceæ et laricis folia trita et in aceto decocta dentium dolori prosunt."

[4] 'Histoire Abrégée des Drogues Simples,' tome second, p. 339.

residuum. 4. Tar and pitch. In a closely similar manner
Dr. Christison considers *seriatim* the various substances admitted into the pharmacopœias, and in the following order:—
Frankincense, with its modification, Burgundy pitch, common
turpentine, Venice turpentine, Canada balsam, resin, oil of
turpentine, tar, and pitch. Of these, frankincense (*Thus
Americanum*), Burgundy pitch (*Pix Burgundica*), Canada
balsam (*Terebinthina Canadensis*), resin (*Resina*), oil of turpentine (*Oleum terebinthinæ*), and tar (*Pix liquida*), find their
places in the British Pharmacopœia; the Terebinthina vulgaris
and Terebinthina Veneta are excluded. Among the substances
now named, the oil distilled from the oleo-resin turpentine,
which, again, is obtained from various pines, is a most valuable
therapeutic agent, possessing actions on various organs and
structures of the body which render it available in the treatment of disease. To these, attention will be directed after a
brief consideration of what is known regarding the physiological
action of the drug. The ultimate physiological action of oil of
turpentine may be said to be twofold; it is irritant and stimulant. But these actions embrace others which turpentine very
notably possesses, and we observe that according as its irritant
action is exerted on the intestinal canal, the urinary organs, or
skin, it is a cathartic, a diuretic, or a diaphoretic. As a stimulant, it acts in producing, when a moderate dose has been taken,
a by no means disagreeable sensation of warmth in the stomach,
which is sometimes diffused over the greater part of the abdomen
and chest. It quickens the circulation, and augments the
temperature. Moreover, in limited doses, it unquestionably
produces a stimulating action on the brain, giving rise to
impressions which closely resemble those produced by alcohol,
and with these an ability for sustained mental as well as physical
exertion. Should the quantity taken or administered be more
considerable it may cause remarkable effects on the sensorium.
Such has been known to produce disorder of the intellectual
functions, nearly identical with intoxication. Dr. Copland
in his own person realised this condition. Sir Thomas Watson
also speaks of a patient who was supposed to be dying, but was
found to be only intoxicated by the free dose of turpentine
which he had swallowed.[1] Occasionally the oil has been

---

[1] 'Lectures on the Principles and Practice of Physic,' vol. i, p. 663.

observed to cause sleep. Indeed, a remarkably soothing influence on the nervous system is a by no means uncommon result
of the administration of turpentine. Purkinje noticed this
The same has been experienced by others after taking the oil in
doses of a drachm. Dr. Andrew Duncan observes, "I have
seen large doses produce temporary intoxication, and sometimes
a kind of trance, lasting twenty-four hours, without, however,
any subsequent bad effect."[1] Applied to the skin, turpentine
produces rubefaction, and sometimes a vesicular eruption. A
scarlet eruption over the skin has also been observed to succeed
the internal administration of turpentine. That the external
application may be followed by cutaneous absorption is evident
from the distinct odour of turpentine in the breath of some
persons, over whose chests or other portions of the trunk the
warm terebinthinate epithem has been placed. In the same
way the peculiar, indeed distinctive, odour communicated to
the urine by turpentine, that of violets, may be produced. The
violaceous odour of the urine here referred to, depends on a
portion of the oil having undergone a chemical change in its
passage through the system; but while this is taking place, it
also appears that some portion of the oil leaves the economy by
the urine altogether unchanged. This is illustrated in the
experiments by Moiroud on horses, to whom turpentine had
been given for some days, in the enormous dose of ten or twelve
ounces.[2] It is not by the kidneys alone, however, that the
absorbed turpentine is eliminated. The skin and the bronchial
surfaces act in a similar manner. After the administration of
a few doses, it may be even a single dose, if large, there is a
distinct odour of turpentine recognisable over the cutaneous
surface, and in the breath. It may be further observed, that,
while the violaceous odour of the urine is produced after the
earlier doses of the remedy, in cases in which its continued
administration has been practised, the urine ultimately comes
to have an odour altogether terebinthinate, the by no means
disagreeable aroma, resembling violets, being lost. This effect
may, in all probability, be accounted for by the more pungent
odour of the turpentine concealing the aroma, during the
increased elimination of the remedy by the kidneys, for the

[1] 'The Edinburgh New Dispensatory,' p. 553.
[2] In Pereira's 'Materia Medica,' vol. ii, part i, p. 1188; also Headland on
the 'Action of Medicines in the System,' p. 79.

result of a suspension of the administration of the turpentine is the restoration of the violaceous odour to the urine before the final disappearance from it of all characteristic smell. The persistence of the violaceous odour is a notable feature. That produced by a single small dose of turpentine may be readily detected in the urine for eight-and-forty hours. It is much more persistent than many stronger odours which the urine acquires from the ingesta, as, for example, from asparagus. A further effect of turpentine is irritation of the urinary organs, leading not unfrequently to hæmaturia; and apart from any idiosyncrasy or special susceptibility to the irritant action of turpentine on the kidneys, which is possessed by some few individuals, there appear to be two modes of administration, after either of which the hæmaturia may come. It may succeed the use of the remedy, in a large or considerable dose, given probably with the view of producing catharsis. Here the remedy has either been wholly directed to the urinary organs, the intestinal canal escaping its influence, or, reaching the latter and failing to exert any effect, it has been reabsorbed, and ultimately attracted to the kidneys. This view seems borne out by the circumstance, that, while in one instance the hæmaturia is produced very speedily after the administration of the turpentine, in another, a considerable time has elapsed before the occurrence of the usual irritation. There is one other interesting circumstance in connection with the action of turpentine on the kidneys. It would appear that the production of the violaceous odour may, to a certain extent, be taken as a test of the integrity of these organs.[1] However the drug has been introduced into the system, whether by the mouth or rectum, from the skin, or by inhalation, this seems to hold good; but the most delicate test is that by cutaneous absorption, and it admits of being proved that a shorter time elapses till the odour in question is produced, and when produced, the odour is infinitely more distinct, when no symptom or indication of renal disease is in existence, than when the converse obtains. There may be reason in avoiding the use of turpentine as a counter-irritant in cases where the kidneys are unsound, and the caution regarding its use, which is expressed by some writers, Dr.

[1 *Vide* 'St. Barth. Hosp. Reports,' vol. iii, 1867, p. 216, "On the Passage of certain substances into the Urine in Healthy and Diseased States of the Kidneys," by the Editor.]

George Johnson[1] for example, may prudently be acted upon; nevertheless, it is consistent with my own observation, that, when under such circumstances turpentine is employed as a rubefacient or counter-irritant, the elimination which succeeds its absorption by the skin is effected conspicuously by the bronchial mucous membrane, by the intestines, and probably also by the cutaneous surface.

With these few observations on the physiological action of the drug, I pass to the consideration of its therapeutic actions and uses.

There are certain therapeutic actions of turpentine to which a brief reference is alone required, experience having already incontestably determined its precise value as a remedy. Fore-most among these may be noticed its operations as a *cathartic* and *anthelmintic*. As a simple cathartic, turpentine is rarely employed, and for the good reason that its action, even when administered in large doses, is uncertain. When combined with other purgatives, and more particularly castor-oil, a greater certainty of operation is secured. The combination now referred to is justly esteemed, and, as Dr. Christison remarks, "has often moved the bowels in obstruction from long-continued constipation, after other powerful cathartics had failed." Dr. Kinglake has particularly insisted on the efficient operation of turpentine in cases of obstinate constipation attended by exaggerated tympanites, while Dr. Paris has borne testimony to its value where the obstruction has apparently been dependent on affections of the brain. The anthelmintic virtues of turpentine are chiefly prized in tape-worm, and may be ranked with those of the liquid extract of the male shield-fern and pomegranate-root bark.[2] In the treatment of ascarides the remedy is chiefly

[1] 'Diseases of the Kidney,' p. 133.

[2] "As perhaps the most effectual remedy we possess for the expulsion of tape-worm, oil of turpentine stands deservedly in high repute."—Neligan's 'Medicines, their Uses and Modes of Administration.' Edited by Dr. Macnamara. 6th edition, p. 47. "Oil of turpentine appears to be the best remedy for expelling tape-worms; it is usually given in large doses for this purpose, but I have sometimes found that it fails when thus given, while the continued use of it in small doses succeeds in expelling the parasites. Thus, in the case of the late Mr. Williams, the apothecary in Charlemont Street, ten drops given three times a day, and continued without intermission for six weeks, expelled a long tape-worm, which had resisted the same remedy in large doses."—Graves's 'Clinical Lectures,' Lecture 53. "Oil of turpen-

useful when administered as an enema. It is also efficacious over the lumbrici. Turpentine is a *hæmostatic*—it arrests hæmorrhage. The interest attached to this action of the drug is increased by the consideration that it also causes one variety of hæmorrhage, hæmaturia. The condition which determines the escape of blood from the capillaries is, however, very different in the two cases. The one is an active hæmorrhage, due to the presence of the absorbed turpentine in the blood of the Malpighian capillaries, causing their irritation and rupture ; while the other, that which turpentine cures, is of a passive description, determined in all probability by a neurosis of blood-vessels. Turpentine in the latter instance is an available remedy. I am inclined, from what I have witnessed of its action in cases of purpura hæmorrhagica, with which hæmaturia has been associated, to regard it indeed as the most available remedy. Its action I believe to be through the nervous system, controlling and regulating the current of blood in the minute vessels by stimulation of their contractility. In many, if not in all, of the different forms of hæmorrhage turpentine has been employed, and a strong testimony has been borne by many experienced physicians to its value. Thus, in treating of the means we possess for the arrestment of pulmonary hæmorrhage, Dr. Wood of Philadelphia remarks : " Another hæmostatic medicine, which sometimes acts very promptly and efficiently in hæmoptysis, is oil of turpentine. How it operates is not well understood, though probably by some influence on the capillaries, perhaps through the sympathetic nerve-centres. It is applicable to cases without inflammatory action or febrile excitement ; and if plethora exist, it should be subdued before recourse is had to the oil. Mere frequency of pulse does not contraindicate it. I have found no remedy more efficacious than this under circumstances favorable to its use. In one apparently desperate case I succeeded after failure with all other means. Ten drops of it may be given every hour or two. If the hæmorrhage is very copious, the dose may be much larger."[1]

In hæmatemesis, as well as in hæmoptysis, turpentine was much used by the distinguished John Hunter ; in regard to the tine unquestionably acts as a most virulent poison upon the entozoa, especially upon the tape-worm, which it expels lifeless and livid."—Paris, 'Pharmacologia,' p. 354.

[1] 'A Treatise on the Practice of Medicine,' vol. ii, p. 329.

former, he states that he has seldom found it fail when given in doses of ten drops every two or three hours. In uterine hæmorrhage, the value of the remedy has been tested by many observers. Dr. Copland remarks: " I have had recourse in extreme or prolonged cases to the spirits of turpentine, either in a draught or in an enema, or in the form of epithem or fomentation, applied over the hypogastrium, and always with success. This practice was first adopted by me in 1819, in metro-hæmorrhagia occurring after delivery, and has been pursued by me in other hæmorrhages, whenever it was considered advisable speedily to arrest them. In 1820, I publicly recommended the treatment ; and I know that it has succeeded with those who were thus led to employ it."[1] In the intestinal hæmorrhage of fever, in hæmorrhoidal flux, in epistaxis, and the profuse bleeding which occasionally succeeds the extraction of teeth, in the hæmorrhage from leech-bites and from wounds, internally administered and externally applied, turpentine has often proved eminently useful.[2]

As a *stimulant*, turpentine has been very largely employed in the advanced stages of adynamic fevers. In typhus, more particularly where there exists marked depression of the vital powers, the patient being sunk in the bed, with more or less of stupor or low muttering delirium, and coma evidently threatened, with very probably hiccough, subsultus tendinum, and tympanitic distention of the belly, there is no remedy we possess which is so capable of effectually rousing the vital energy. I appeal with confidence to the experience of physicians who have seen much of fever, when I affirm that, without turpentine, we should, in such circumstances, be, if not powerless, at all events deprived of our most useful and potent auxiliary. In connection with the stimulating effect of turpentine on the nervous system, and through it on the vascular, there is to be taken into account its wonderfully soothing action on the nervous centres, how delirium and restlessness are overcome, and often completely subdued by its use.[3] Not only so, but

---

[1] ' Dictionary of Practical Medicine,' vol. ii, p. 113.

[2] See "Terebinthinæ Oleum," in 'Manual of Practical Therapeutics,' by Edward J. Waring, M.D., p. 724.

[3] Dr. Dewees found the spirit of turpentine, in doses of twenty drops, procure sleep in cases of uterine cancer, when it could not be obtained from opium.—' Diseases of Females,' p. 274.

even maniacal excitement has been similarly overcome. Dr. Graves, in speaking of the administration of turpentine, under just such circumstances, remarks: "Hence the value of this remedy is very great indeed, for it not only opens the bowels (a point of considerable importance in such affections), but also removes tympanites, and exercises a powerful influence in controlling and quieting the nervous system. I have seen persons' lives saved by a few doses of the oil of turpentine, and have watched its tranquilising effect on the nerves with pleasure and surprise."[1] Dr. Copland speaks of the spirits of turpentine exhibited in similar circumstances as " frequently productive of benefit."[2] Dr. Murchison recommends the internal administration of turpentine in the extreme tympanites of typhus; also in the hæmorrhage of enteric fever.[3] The eminent Swedish physician, Dr. Magnus Huss, has emphatically indicated the reliance which may be placed in turpentine, as a remedy in the low forms of chest affection, the catarrh and pneumonia, occurring in fevers. He remarks: "I have a rather long experience of this treatment with turpentine, as I before said in the account of the treatment within the hospital in 1842, with respect to pneumonia typhosa, that the use of the turpentine in certain cases of typhus fever is one among the greatest steps forward the medical art has made of late in the treatment of these forms of disease."[4] Nor is the language employed by Dr. Murchison less assuring. He states: " Its effects in the bronchitis of adynamic fevers are sometimes marvellous. It ought to be given in doses of from ten to twenty minims, with fifteen to thirty minims of chloric ether or sulphuric ether, and half a drachm of spiritus juniperi compositus, in mistura acaciæ, mistura amygdalæ, or yelk of egg. The dose may be repeated every two hours at first, until the desired effect be produced. After a few doses the patient often begins to cough and expectorate large quantities of viscid mucus, with great relief to the

---

[1] Op. cit., p. 101.
[2] 'Dictionary of Practical Medicine,' vol. i, p. 1037.
[3] 'Treatise on Continued Fevers,' pp. 286, 575.
[4] 'Statistics and Treatment of Typhus and Typhoid Fever; from twelve years' experience, gained at the Seraphim Hospital in Stockholm, 1840-1852,' by Magnus Huss, M.D. Translated from the Swedish original, by Ernst Aberg, M.D., p. 139.

respiratory symptoms. The quantity of urine is likewise increased. I have never known strangury produced."[1] Dr. Wood, of Philadelphia, to whose confidence in turpentine as a hæmostatic reference has already been made, uses the remedy largely in the treatment of typhoid fever. He observes: "Should the tongue become very dry, and the abdominal distention remain undiminished, the oil of turpentine will prove an excellent remedy. I cannot too strongly impress upon the profession my convictions of the importance of this medicine. It may be employed in all cases in the advanced stages of this disease when the tongue is dry. But there is a particular condition, and that a not uncommon, and sometimes a very dangerous condition, in which I have often employed it, and hitherto have seldom known it to fail." Dr. Wood here refers to cases in which the tongue, after cleaning, wholly or partially, becomes quite dry, while with this change in the tongue there is generally associated aggravation of other symptoms, but particularly of the tympanites. Turpentine, administered under such circumstances, acts as a stimulant, but also, Dr. Wood believes, as an "alterative to the ulcerated surfaces in the intestinal mucous membrane." The usual dose is ten drops every two hours. It may be given in doses of from five to twenty drops every hour or two. Summing up the evidence which he has collected in regard to the efficiency of the remedy, Dr. Wood, whose enthusiasm in its praise at least merits most attentive consideration, concludes: "I will repeat that the oil of turpentine may be used with great hope of benefit in any case of enteric fever, in the advanced stages, with a dry tongue, but, in the cases above referred to, with great confidence of success, so far as an experience of more than thirty years may be admitted as a ground of confidence."[2]

There is another form of fever in which turpentine has been frequently employed, and by many physicians with success—namely, *puerperal fever*. Dr. Brenan, of Dublin, in 1814, was the first to use it in this disease, in doses of one or two tablespoonfuls every three or four hours, and sweetened; the application of turpentine stupes over the abdomen being also practised. It may be admitted that some of the more distressing symptoms of this disease, more particularly the tympanitic

[1] Op. cit., p. 283.   [2] Op. cit., vol. i, p. 359.

distention of the abdomen, may be effectually relieved by the remedy. The testimony of certain writers subsequent to Brenan, Douglas, and Kinneir, who, like them, upheld the employment of turpentine as almost a specific, has, however, not been confirmed by Dr. Gooch,[1] Dr. Copland, Sir Charles Locock, and Dr. Churchill.[2] Dr. Craigie remarks: " It does not appear, however, either to be alone adequate to the cure of this disease, or to possess any specific powers over the morbid action. It is by no means even always capable of assuaging the violence of the vomiting or the abdominal pains."[3] I am aware that, by some physicians, turpentine is still regarded as the " summum remedium " in this very serious disease, and I feel satisfied that I have witnessed good effects from its use. It is possible that a consideration of some topics which follow may tend to strengthen the reliance which may be placed in its virtues.

There are many forms of *nervous disease* in which turpentine has been administered, and is still justly prized as a remedy. These include both painful and spasmodic affections, and likewise the more formidable convulsive disorders. In epilepsy, turpentine appears to have been earliest prescribed by Dr. John Latham, an allusion to the subject being made in his work on Diabetes, published in 1811. A few years subsequently a strong testimony to the efficiency of the remedy in this disease was borne by the same writer, and by Dr. Edward Percival, of Dublin.[4] They had been accustomed to prescribe turpentine

[1] " Although I have been unsuccessful in the use of turpentine in peritoneal fevers, the testimony of competent witnesses convinces me that there is a class, or perhaps a stage, of these fevers, in which oil of turpentine, given internally, is sometimes highly efficacious, and that cases apparently hopeless have been recovered by it."—' An Account of Some of the Most Important Diseases peculiar to Women,' p. 103.

[2] " Having frequently employed the spirits of turpentine in the more malignant states of fever, and being aware of Dr. Brenan's recommendation of it for the malady, I next prescribed this substance, both by the mouth and in enemata, trusting to it principally, but without obtaining from it all the advantages which I had expected. It should, however, be stated that frequently I was not called to a case until it was far advanced."—(Op. cit., vol. iii, part i, p. 536.) See on the same subject a lengthened and interesting discussion in ' Traité de Thérapeutique et de Matière Médicale,' par A. Trousseau et H. Pidoux, tom. ii, p. 602.

[3] ' Elements of the Practice of Physic,' vol. ii, p. 241.

[4] ' Medical Transactions,' published by the College of Physicians in London, vol. v, p. 65; also ' Edinburgh Medical Review,' 1810.

as an anthelmintic, and had found it effectual in removing the convulsive disorders which are sometimes connected with the presence of tape-worm or lumbrici in the intestines. A more general employment of the remedy, however, had satisfied them that, not when connected with worms alone, but when occurring as an idiopathic disorder, epilepsy may be removed by turpentine. By the physicians now named turpentine was exhibited iu *large* doses. It is in reference to their practice and that of other English physicians that Joseph Frank writes : "Oleum terebinthinæ in epilepsiis non solum a vermibus, sed et in aliis nerveis, et potissimum maniacorum, ad doses incomprehensibiles, recentiores Angli, utinam jure! commendant."[1] Subsequently the remedy came to be employed not in large, but in small doses, and acquired to a considerable extent professional confidence; so much so, that we find Sir Thomas Watson remarking : "If I were called upon to name any single drug from which, in ordinary cases of epilepsy, I should most hope for relief, I should say it was the oil of turpentine. And I find that other physicians have come to the same conclusion."[2] There can be little doubt that the accomplished author, whose words have just been quoted, entertains a different opinion now, and that he, like most physicians, would not be unwilling to subscribe to the statement of Dr. Russell Reynolds—"Bromide of potassium is the one medicine which has, so far as I know, proved of real service in the treatment of epilepsy."[3] In *chorea,* turpentine as a cathartic, and likewise as an external application, has been highly recommended by Dr. Copland[4] and other physicians. Dr. James Jackson, of Boston, U.S., in alluding to the treatment of chorea, says, " But the great remedy is the oil of turpentine. . . . In a severe case,

---

[1] 'Praxeos Medicæ Universæ Præcepta.' Partis secundæ, volumen primum, sectio secunda, p. 407. The following note is appended in illustration of the statement made by Frank in the text : ℞ Olei terebinthinæ, sacchari, āā unciam unam. Misce terendo, affunde aquæ menthæ piperitidis libras duas (!) S. Bis terve in die cochlear majus (!!). Vel, ℞ Olei terebinthinæ drachmas tres. Aquæ fontis libram unam. S. Omni quartâ horâ uncias duas. *Vide* ' The London Medical and Surgical and Pharmaceutical Journal,' 1814, May.

[2] Op. cit., vol. i, p. 662.

[3] ' A System of Medicine,' vol. ii, p. 280.

[4] 'Medical Dictionary,' vol. i, p. 334.

however, or when other remedies fail, this should be used.
. . . In a very young child, you may begin with five
drops three times a day, but the dose should be increased
steadily till relief is obtained, if no objection occurs. . . .
A child of eight or ten years of age will sometimes bear a teaspoonful for a dose. This remedy is successful whether given
early or late in the disease."[1] As an anthelmintic, turpentine
deservedly holds its ground in the treatment of chorea, as well
as other nervous disorders dependent on the reflex irritation
which worms in the intestinal canal produce; but probably the
opinion of Dr. Radcliffe, as expressed in the following statement,
will meet with little contradiction, in so far as the abandonment
of turpentine is concerned : "Turpentine has been given for
various reasons in chorea, as an anthelmintic and purgative
chiefly. At one time I gave it rather as a general stimulant,
and, as it seemed, with benefit to the patient. I then tried
mineral naphtha with the same view, and came to the conclusion
that this medicine was more pleasant than turpentine, less
trying to the system, and not less efficacious. During the last
six or eight years, however, I have rarely given either one or
the other of these medicines, and one chief reason for this
seems to be that I have gradually come to prefer the treatment
of which I have to speak in a few moments."[2] That plan of
treatment, as those familiar with the writings and practice of
the eminent physician now referred to are aware, is "the free
use of alcoholic drinks." For my own part, I am so thoroughly
satisfied with the potency of arsenic in the treatment of chorea,
as to esteem it above all other remedies. In tetanus, infantile
convulsions, puerperal eclampsia, and asthma, turpentine has at
different periods, and by different physicians, been employed as
a remedy; in none of these, however, has it for any time, or
with justness, retained its reputation as a therapeutic agent.
It is necessary now to notice its employment in the treatment
of nerve-pain, or neuralgia, in various of its forms. Of these,
sciatica is the one in which turpentine has been chiefly used.
The remedy is not new; Galen certainly used it; but Dr.
Cheyne, of Dublin, and Dr. Francis Home, were the earliest, in
recent times, to employ it. The latter observes, "I have used

[1] 'Letters to a Young Physician just entering upon Practice, p. 86.
[2] 'Reynolds' System of Medicine,' vol. ii, article "Chorea," p. 138.

it for many years, as an efficacious and valuable medicine."[1]
Seven cases of pure sciatica are detailed, which were treated in
the clinical wards of the Edinburgh Infirmary; of these five
were cured, and the remaining two much relieved. Dr. Home
adds, " I have cured a great number of patients in private
practice, during the many years I have used it." He prescribed
the remedy according to Dr. Cheyne's plan, with a draught of
sack, whey or warm drink after it. The following is the
prescription :

> ℞ Olei terebinthinæ, ʒij ;
> Mellis optimi, ʒj.

M. Fiat linctus. Capiat cochlear parvum mane et vespere, superbibendo
haustum potus communis tepidi.

Dr. Copland[2] speaks very favorably of the use of turpentine
in sciatica, and also in other forms of neuralgia. In France,
turpentine was largely administered, and highly esteemed as a
remedy in neuralgia, by Récamier and Martinet; and although
M. Valleix is not so sanguine in his appreciation of it, he
readily admits its possession of notable therapeutic properties
in this disease.[3] I have frequently employed it in sciatica,
also in crural and brachial neuralgia, and with great benefit, so
much so as to feel satisfied that, in turpentine, we possess a
very valuable remedy for such disorders. I have, on several
occasions, prescribed turpentine in cases of long-standing
sciatica, in which the violence and lengthened continuance of
the pain had greatly reduced the patient's strength, and in one
or two instances had caused great debility. Ordinarily, I have
used it when other remedies had failed; and in one case, which
occurred this last winter, not only had many remedies failed,
but the suffering of the patient was extreme and his prostration
great. His recovery was complete after taking the turpentine
for three weeks. It agrees well with old people, who are so
frequently the sufferers from sciatica and other neuralgias.
The dose varies from ten to thirty minims thrice daily.
Usually I have prescribed twenty minims, to be taken in a little
cold water, thrice daily. The *modus operandi* of turpentine in

---

[1] "Clinical Experiments, Histories, and Dissections," 1783. ' Experiments
upon the Effects of the Oleum Terebinthinæ in the Sciatica,' p. 265.

[2] Op. cit., vol. ii, p. 891.

[3] Valleix, ' Traité des Névralgies,' p. 632.

neuralgia, and particularly in sciatica, is, I am disposed to think, not unfrequently connected with its action on the intestinal mucous surface, with some irritation of which the painful nerve affection is not unfrequently connected. The same remark applies to irritation of the kidney as a cause of sciatica, in which case Sir Thomas Watson has conjectured turpentine does most good.[1] In illustration of this I may refer to an experience by no means uncommon, that after a brisk action of a cathartic, and for this purpose none is more suitable than the combination of turpentine and castor-oil, a severe attack of sciatica has been entirely removed. A better understanding of its action, however, as a remedy will, I hope, be suggested by some considerations which are to follow. Turpentine enemata are likewise useful in sciatica. As an external application in all neuralgic affections, turpentine acts much more efficaciously than the mere counter-irritant and rubefacient effects which it produces will serve to explain; the remedy is absorbed, and in some way or other operates through the blood on the pained nerve. "I have known oil of turpentine," remarks Dr. Pereira, "now and then act most beneficially in sciatica, without giving rise to any remarkable evacuation by the bowels, skin, or kidneys, so that the relief could not be ascribed to a cathartic, a diaphoretic, or a diuretic operation." This statement exactly expresses the experience which I have had of the remedy in the same disease. I venture to believe that the efficiency of the drug, when applied externally, in bronchitis, pleuritis, and pneumonia, also in laryngitis, in which Dr. Copland highly prized it, and in abdominal inflammation, admits of a similar explanation, that there is inherent in turpentine a remarkable power of restraining inflammatory action. In *chronic rheumatism*, and in *lumbago*, the oil of turpentine has been largely employed, more especially as an external application; it has also been administered internally. The stimulating and diaphoretic properties of the drug appear to exert a favourable influence on these disorders, and more particularly when the subjects of them are old and debilitated; but unquestionably the remarkable curative power possessed by turpentine over neuralgias, and chiefly among these sciatica, does not extend to rheumatic disorders properly so called.

[1] Op. cit., vol. i, p. 733.

Bearing some analogy to neuralgia is the severe headache which is apt to occur in nervous and hysterical females. In this painful affection, occurring in young persons of a delicate excitable temperament, without any menstrual or leucorrhœal complication, Dr. Graves placed great reliance on turpentine. He gave it in doses of one or two drachms, to be repeated according to its effects. The best vehicle, he adds, is cold water. Some will bear and derive advantage from two or three doses of this medicine in the day, experiencing from its use a diminution of headache, and removal of flatulency, together with a moderate action of the bowels and kidneys. There is, moreover, another class of sufferers from headache, and this composed of both sexes, who may be relieved by turpentine. I refer to the frontal headache which is most apt to occur after prolonged mental effort, but may likewise be induced by unduly sustained physical exertion, what may be styled the headache of a fatigued brain. A cup of very strong tea often relieves this form of headache, but this remedy, with not a few, is perilous, for, bringing relief to pain, it may produce general restlessness, and, worst of all, banish sleep. Turpentine, in does of twenty or thirty minims, given at intervals of an hour or two, will not only remove the headache, but produce, in a wonderful manner, that soothing influence to which reference has already been made. One dose is not uncommonly sufficient, but it is rarely necessary to repeat the remedy for more than two or three. I willingly subscribe to Dr. Graves's statement, that it is best given in cold water; and have further to urge, that neither the physician nor the patient need be deterred from employing it, from the highly exaggerated notions which have been entertained regarding its disagreeable taste and liability to cause sickness.

In *diseases of the eye,* turpentine has long been a favourite remedy, chiefly in iritis and inflammation of the choroid membrane. In the rheumatic and syphilitic iritis, it was first strongly recommended by Mr. Carmichael, in doses of a drachm thrice daily. Its effects in the treatment of inflammation of the eye may be uncertain, and may have disappointed the expectations of some surgeons; still there can be no doubt that, by oculists generally, turpentine is up to the present time regarded as a valuable antiphlogistic remedy.

Turpentine has been proposed by some writers as a *solvent of biliary concretions or gall-stones;*[1] but although undoubtedly useful as a cathartic and diuretic in jaundice, and as an external application in allaying and even in averting the attacks of gall spasm, there seems no good ground for accepting the action here referred to.[2]

As a local application in burns, in chilblains, and in ulcers of the limbs, turpentine has had its day; but in all of these, as well as in certain other affections, of which it is here unnecessary to make mention, more approved modes of treatment have of late years been adopted.

Reference has already been made to the employment of turpentine by the ancient physicians in affections of the mucous surfaces attended by copious secretion of altered mucus, in a single word, in cases of blennorrhagia, although that term has by some been erroneously restricted to discharges from the vagina or urethra of venereal origin. There can be no doubt that, in the *latter*, when they have become, or have threatened to become, chronic, turpentine is an available remedy. In bronchitis, however, attended by excessive muco-purulent secretion, its remedial virtues are seen most conspicuously. Sir Dominic Corrigan, of Dublin, and Dr. Waters, of Liverpool, have used it, in doses varying from a drachm to an ounce, at intervals of two hours, in cases of severe, or neglected, bronchitis, connected with pulmonary emphysema, and attended by excessive accumulation of secretion in the bronchial tubes. I have seen the remedy signally serviceable in such circumstances. An emetic suggests itself as a likely means of affording relief, but the frequent feeble pulse, and the clammy surface of the body, with features almost collapsed, and livid lips, forbid its employment. Turpentine is then an alternative remedy, and it is a safe one; given internally and diligently applied externally, it will not unfrequently reward the confidence which has been placed in it. In less urgent cases

---

[1] Durande's mixture, which was vaunted for this purpose, consisted of turpentine and ether.

[2] By its diuretic action the oil of turpentine may sometimes usefully influence the kidneys in cases where the epithelium is impregnated with yellow colouring matter, and consequently somewhat impaired in action.—'Thudicum on Gall Stones,' p. 286.

than those now briefly described, but still sufficiently serious, and often little amenable to cure, we have a remedy in turpentine; I mean in chronic pulmonary catarrh attended by fetid secretion. Again, in all cases of bronchial abscess, in pulmonary abscess, and in the formidable gangrene of the lung, turpentine may be hopefully employed, from what has already been observed of its effects. Many years ago, I was strongly impressed by witnessing the remarkable influence produced by small and frequently-repeated doses of turpentine in a case of pulmonary gangrene in the Royal Infirmary; and since then I have always prescribed it in such circumstances. Its action I believe to be stimulating, but also antiseptic, I had almost said specific. Speedily, under its use, the extreme fetor of the breath and expectoration undergo a change; then the latter becomes diminished in amount, while blood disappears from it, and with these changes a corresponding amelioration in the general condition of the patient takes place. Turpentine is borne, in these cases, in a way in which alcoholic stimulants are not. This fact I saw very strikingly illustrated in the case of a man about forty years of age, but of somewhat broken-down constitution, the subject of gangrene of the lower part of the right lung consequent on pneumonia. He was treated by thirty-minim doses of turpentine administered every second or third hour, continued for many days, and the result was most satisfactory. Skoda, the eminent physician of Vienna, has employed the inhalation of turpentine vapour in the treatment of the same disease. The oil of turpentine is poured upon boiling water, and the patient is directed to inhale the vapour every second hour for fifteen minutes at a time.[1] During the early summer of 1870 I saw, with Dr. Somerville, a gentleman who, while convalescent from a severe attack of modified small-pox, had become affected by cough, fetid expectoration, and marked febrile disturbance. Over the upper part of the left mammary region, in this gentleman's chest, there was dulness on percussion, extending below into the region of cardiac dulness, and upwards into the subclavicular region, where it was less pronounced. On auscultation there was audible

---

[1] "Fälle von Lungenbrand behandelt und geheilt durch Einathmen von Terpentinöl-Dämpfen." 'Zietschrift der Kais. Kön. Gesellschaft der Aerzte zu Wien,' 1853, p. 445.

abundant coarse moist rattle, and the resonance of voice was much increased. Over the other portions of the chest the physical signs were normal. The patient complained of the extremely disgusting odour and taste of the expectoration, and was frequently caused to vomit after the effort of coughing had led to its discharge. He was ordered thirty minims of the oil of turpentine in a small wineglassful of cold water every third hour, and this he continued to take for several days. There occurred no disagreeable effects from the remedy, but speedily a notable diminution in the amount of the expectoration, while gradually its fetid character also disappeared. The doses of the turpentine were lessened in amount and frequency after the seventh day, but the remedy was not entirely discontinued till after the twelfth day from its commencement. In this case Dr. Somerville and I noticed the diaphoretic, diuretic, and stimulant action of the turpentine, in addition to its very evident specific operation on the local disease. The patient, whose prostration was very great, while his appetite also was very feeble, had claret wine, but seemed to us to require no other stimulant than the turpentine. His ultimate recovery was complete. I have seen him lately, the picture of good health. I think it unnecessary to furnish the details of other cases similar or nearly so in their nature; but the following remarkable instance of recovery from impaction of a foreign body in the right lung, I need offer no apology for relating.

In April, 1866, I attended, with Dr. Rutherfoord Turnbull, R. F—, residing in Fountainbridge, who, when I first saw him, was expectorating a large quantity of extremely fetid purulent matter, stringy in appearance, and occasionally mixed with blood. This expectoration had been going on for some days previously, and was consequent upon a severe pain towards the lower part of the right side, with which the patient had been seized while at his usual occupation as a groom. There was no difficulty in recognising the existence of pulmonary condensation and evacuation. Its situation was a little below the middle part of the right lung, the physical signs being most distinct posteriorly. I recommended the employment of turpentine, and this, in doses of thirty minims every second hour, was forthwith commenced. It was continued for several days with manifest improvement in the general symptoms, which had previously indicated very considerable prostration. The fetid odour from the sputa, which had been more powerful and penetrating than anything I had before encountered, causing in myself invariably a feeling of nausea, and frequently in his wife, who assiduously nursed the patient, actual sickness, underwent a remarkable modification: not ceasing to be disagreeable, it became much more bearable. Up to the time, however, on which there occurred the interesting circumstance which I have now to record, I was unable to trace any change in the condition of the affected lung. The same dulness on percussion below the lower angle of right scapula, the same absence of all vesicular breathing, and the same somewhat distant but very coarse moist sound, with bronchial breathing and loud bronchophony over a limited space, were present, while the vesicular breathing in the upper portion of the right lung, and over the whole left lung, was greatly exaggerated or puerile. I had requested the patient's wife, his only attendant, to examine carefully the expectoration, and cautioned her not to allow any portion of it to be removed without her having subjected it to a careful scrutiny. This very unpleasant task she had performed with untiring zeal and faithfulness, when one morning, eight days after the commencement of the turpentine administration, she noticed in the sputa, which had been got rid of by an unusually severe fit of coughing, a small dark object, which she immediately removed, and presented to me on my next visit a few hours thereafter. The object thus handed to me possessed the same offensive odour as the expectoration and breath of the patient, was sodden in character, and appeared to be a twig or minute branch of a shrub or tree.

Retained for a short time, it became firm, and ultimately hard, and was then readily enough identified as a small twig of a thorn-bush (Fig. 1). Almost immediate relief succeeded the discharge of this foreign body from the lung, and the patient made

Fig. 1.

a rapid as well as complete recovery. When I examined him some months after the illness now briefly narrated, and some little time after he had resumed his old occupation, I could discover very little wrong with his chest; a degree of dulness on percussion, and feebleness of respiration, alone indicated the site of his very serious lung disease. The narrative would be incomplete without the statement made to me by the patient, after the discovery of the "corpus delicti" in the sputa. He called to remembrance the sudden occurrence of a violent fit of coughing and choking, which was produced by something entering his mouth and passing downwards, when he was riding pretty rapidly through a dense wood in Aberdeenshire, with the wind in his face. This happened nearly six months before the commencement of the illness for which he requested the attendance of Dr. Rutherfoord Turnbull.

It may naturally be asked how the notion of the disease in this case, being dependent on the presence of a foreign body in the lungs, suggested itself to my mind? So interrogated, I have to reply, that there appeared to me something unusual in the whole history of this man's illness. The symptoms did not indicate the original occurrence of pneumonia which had terminated in gangrenous abscess, while the previous healthy condition of the patient, and the entire freedom of the left lung, and no inconsiderable portion of the right, from disease of any kind, made it evident that he laboured under no constitutional dyscrasia, of which the lung disorder was the prominent local manifestation. Further, I was from the first impressed with the very peculiar odour of the breath and expectoration. That differed from the strong and disagreeable smell attaching to both in ordinary pulmonary gangrene, and at the same time irresistibly reminded me of the odour which I had perceived in a case of pulmonary gangrene caused by the presence of a chicken-bone in the lung, under Dr. Bennett's care in the Royal Infirmary, in 1848, and of which a very interesting narrative has been published by Dr. Struthers, of Leith.[1] Small as the foreign body in the case now narrated was, there are instances on record in which bodies equally minute entering the bronchi have given rise to alarming symptoms. Our late lamented friend, Dr. James Duncan, in his interesting probationary essay for the Royal College of Surgeons, on 'Foreign Bodies in the Air-passages,'[2] mentions one which

[1] 'Edinburgh Monthly Journal of Medical Science,' 1852, p. 449.
[2] Op. cit., p. 14.

Note.—The portion of mutton-bone (Fig. 2) which is now exhibited to the Society was expectorated by a lady, a patient of Dr. Struthers, to whose kindness I owe the opportunity of referring to it. In November, 1869, this lady,

occurred to Dr. Donaldson, of Ayr, in which an ear of grass entering gave rise to intense bronchitis, which continued for seven weeks, when the body was expectorated, and the person recovered.

The preceding observations appear to me to warrant the following conclusions :—(1) That turpentine is a powerful stimulant, capable of rousing in a very remarkable manner the vital energies, while it, at the same time, produces a soothing influence on the nervous system. (2) That, in all probability, we possess in turpentine an antiseptic agent, powerful in arresting, it may be in preventing, those morbid changes in the system which are evidently of a septic nature.

while taking mutton-soup at dinner, and being at the same time engaged in speaking to her niece, a little girl, suddenly choked. The disagreeable and painful sensation then excited lasted for fully fifteen minutes, and gradually subsided, leaving her, however, satisfied that a piece of bone had entered the windpipe. On the Tuesday following the Sunday on which the accident took place, the voice became husky, and cough occurred. These symptoms, however, after the lapse of a few days, passed away, but she became subject to attacks of difficulty in breathing, some of which were very severe in character. They occurred at intervals, which rarely exceeded ten days. After some months she became weak, and the cough, which had returned, proved very irritating, and was attended by a scanty expectoration of phlegm. She had consulted medical men in different parts of the country, who regarded her case as one of ordinary bronchial disturbance, and listened incredulously to the tale of the choking fit and passage downwards of the bone. From Dr. Struthers, for reasons of her own, she had purposely concealed all knowledge of the accident. Under his advice, she had, in the summer of 1870,

FIG. 2.

gone to Crieff, and there, being seized with a severe fit of coughing, had brought up the portion of bone. For some days before this took place, she had observed her breath to be very offensive, and likewise the expectoration, which had then greatly increased in quantity. Dr. Gairdner, of Crieff, who had visited this lady when suffering from the severe spasmodic difficulty of breathing which preceded the discharge of the bone, had prescribed some medicine, which she believed to have facilitated its exit. Dr. Struthers has informed me that, on careful examination of the chest, he had detected a roughness of the respiratory murmur, accompanied by wheezing sound, a little below the right sternal clavicular articulation. On the 26th of May, 1871, ten months from the happy event just recorded, I had the opportunity of seeing the patient with Dr. Struthers, and, on examination, failed to discover any evidence whatever of pulmonary affection; her recovery, which was rapid, had evidently also been complete.

The other actions and uses of turpentine—its cathartic, anthelmintic, and hæmostatic virtues, have already been signalised, and I need not again refer to them here.

I am specially anxious to insist on the action turpentine possesses on the nervous system, by which it is rendered a powerful remedy in fevers of the adynamic type, in neuralgia, and not unlikely also in certain cerebral affections, including those of an inflammatory character; also on its antiseptic action, as evidenced by its remarkable influence on pulmonary gangrene and bronchial abscess. It appears to me as not improbable that pyæmia may be favorably influenced by turpentine, and that in this way its action in some cases of puerperal fever may be explained.

I am sanguine enough to believe that, in some cases of diphtheria and of putrid sore throat, we possess an available remedy in turpentine ; and already I have seen it employed in the former, not, however, under circumstances which would justify me in drawing at the present time any decided conclusions from its use.

XXIII.

NOTES ON ALOPECIA AREATA.

(The following observations are taken from a letter addressed to myself, and seem to me worthy of record in this volume.— EDITOR):

Edinburgh, May 4, 1872.

" ALOPECIA AREATA" (Celsus' " Area ") is by no means an uncommon disease here. I meet with it occasionally in hospital practice, but have much more frequently seen it in the better classes.

I have grave doubts of its parasitic nature, and do not believe it to be contagious. I have seen it occur in its most distressing form, affecting the scalp in small detached patches, which generally enlarged, and finally, notwithstanding treatment, local and general, led to baldness—complete, but for a few straggling uncoloured hairs—loss of eyebrows, in the male of all hair from the face, and in both sexes from armpits, pubes, &c. In one gentleman the loss of hair was very rapid and succeeded an injury.[1]

Injuries of the nervous system cause alopecia.—I am strongly disposed to the opinion that alopecia areata depends on a lesion of nutrition, profound in its nature; that in most cases of the kind there is a nervous lesion. This has led me to prescribe in the very earliest stage of the disorder nervine tonics, strychnia,

[1] *Vide* 'Lancet,' 1869, vol. ii, p. 41 ; also 'St. Bartholomew's Hospital Reports,' vol. viii, 1872, p. 159.

&c., and a generous diet, a plan which has, I think, been followed by good results. I do not question the utility of local applications, but these signally fail in some cases.

In the less grave instances of the affection cantharidine lotions and corrosive sublimate washes do good, and I have seen the disease checked in a very short time. This holds good of young girls and boys. I dread its more serious results—a true alopecia, and a general loss of hair over the body—in young adults, females more than males. But both sexes suffer this really very trying deprivation."

XXIV

THE

THERAPEUTIC ACTIONS OF MURIATE OF LIME.

(*Read before the Medico-Chirurgical Society of Edinburgh, May* 15, 1872,
and Reprinted from the ' Edinburgh Medical Journal' for July, 1872.)

AFTER being held in high esteem as a remedy during a considerable period of time, the muriate of lime has of late years passed almost entirely into disuse. The circumstances which have determined this loss of favour are not difficult to discover, and will be exhibited in the brief historical sketch of the remedy to which I shall proceed before endeavouring to show that the muriate of lime possesses therapeutic virtues sufficiently eminent to justify its restoration to a place in professional confidence.

Muriate of lime, calcis murias, hydrated chloride of calcium, hydrochlorate of lime, the chloride of calcium of the British Pharmacopœia, is formed by neutralising hydrochloric acid with carbonate of lime, adding a little solution of chlorinated and slaked lime to the solution, filtering, evaporating until it becomes solid, and finally drying the salt at about 400°.[1] In the British Pharmacopœia, chloride of calcium retains a place ; but while its dose [is mentioned, its importance is only recognised on account of the power it possesses of absorbing water. It is extremely deliquescent in the air, very soluble in water, and

[1] 'British Pharmacopœia,' page 61.

also readily so in rectified spirit. The salt is used in the preparation of chloroform, muriate of morphia, and ether, and likewise in the rectification of spirits. A solution of the chloride of calcium and a saturated solution of the same, are employed as tests, the former for recognising citric acid in citrate of potash, the latter to determine the purity of the spirits of nitrous ether. Formerly, the only officinal preparation of the muriate of lime was its solution in water, the *calcis muriatis solutio* of the Edinburgh, *calcii chloridi liquor* of the London, and *calcis muriatis aqua* of the Dublin Pharmacopœia.

Chloride of calcium is, in large doses, an irritant poison. Dr. Thomas Beddoes administered three drachms and a half of the calx muriata, undiluted, to a dog about six months old. The dog was soon affected with quick breathing and snorting, with convulsive but vain efforts to vomit, and a profuse secretion of saliva, and in about six hours he died. Upon opening this animal the whole of the thoracic viscera were found apparently in a sound state. The villous coat of the stomach, and of the small intestines a great way down, was exceedingly bloodshot. In many parts it was almost black, and converted into a gelatinous slime, which could be taken off by the fingers with great ease.[1] When exhibited in large doses to man, the muriate of lime excites nausea, vomiting, and sometimes purging, causes tenderness of the precordium, quickens the pulse, and occasions faintness, weakness, anxiety and trembling and giddiness. In excessive or poisonous doses, disorder of the nervous system is manifested by failure and trembling of the limbs, giddiness, small contracted pulse, cold sweats, convulsions, paralysis, insensibility, and death. When given in small and repeated doses, it produces increased secretion of mucus, of urine, and perspiration.[2] In adverting to the cathartic properties of chloride of calcium, Sir Robert Christison observes, these have not been particularly examined in its pure state, but it is a convenient remedy of this class when given along with other purgative

[1] 'Observations on the Medical and Domestic Management of the Consumptive; on the Powers of Digitalis Purpurea; and on the Cure of Scrofula,' by Thomas Beddoes, M.D. 'Annals of Medicine' for the year 1801, by Andrew Duncan, sen., M.D., and Andrew Duncan, jun., M.D., vol. i, ustrum ii.

[2] Pereira's 'Elements of Materia Medica and Therapeutics,' vol. i, p. 630.

salts; and it forms almost the only active ingredient of some powerful mineral waters.[1] This holds true of the springs of Airthrie (now better known as Bridge of Allan), Pitcaithley, and Dunblane, all in the County of Perth.

Muriate of lime appears to have been earliest employed as a remedy in disease by the distinguished French physician Fourcroy,[2] who, along with certain Dutch physicians of his day, had much confidence in its power over scrofula. In Germany also it was used about the same time, chiefly, however, on account of the high estimate of its virtues which had been expressed by Fourcroy.[3] At the close of last century and commencement of the present, the remedy seems to have been largely employed and highly prized by many distinguished physicians in our own country. Foremost among these is Dr. Beddoes.[4] The want of success which had attended the use of calomel, sponge, steel, Peruvian bark, tepid salt-water bathing, muriate of barytes, and all the other remedies which were commonly employed, had led Dr. Beddoes to make trial of a remedy which, to use his own words, "was strongly recommended in scrofula by some foreign writer, the muriatic acid saturated with lime, or muriate of lime as it is now styled." Dr. Beddoes gave the remedy to nearly one hundred patients in various conditions of life, the dose being from ten drops of the saturated solution for young children, to two drachms for others, three or four times a day. Dr. Beddoes remarks, that there are few of the common forms of scrofula in which he has not had successful experience of the medicine. In proof of this he gives several cases.

The first case is that of a boy, seven years old, with light hair and eyes, and distinct blue veins winding beneath a fine skin. He had a voracious, nearly insatiable appetite, a protuberant belly, with wasted limbs, and frequent slimy stools. In

---

[1] 'Dispensatory,' page 233.

[2] Antoine François de Fourcroy, born in Paris, 1755; died in 1809.

[3] Thus, Hufeland, in his treatise ' Ueber die Natur Erkentniss-mittel und Heilart der Skrofelkrankheit,' Jena, 1795, bears testimony to its use, chiefly on the authority of Fourcroy. "Fourcroy," he writes, "rühmt es sehr." Calcaria muriatica, or calx salita, was also the basis of a German nostrum, known about the same time as Niemann's. See Phœbus, 'Handbuch der Arzneiverordnungslehre,' p. 95.

[4] Op. cit., page 205.

the evening he had chills, succeeded by heat and night-sweats. The pulse was generally 120 or above. He had taken, without benefit, almost every medicine against worms, or tabes mesenterica, particularly calomel, both in small doses, so as to affect the mouth gently, and in larger, so as to operate smartly on the bowels. A dose of ten drops of muriate of lime, raised gradually to forty, and which the child took with pleasure in small-beer or coffee, began first by stopping the purging, then gradually diminished the hectic flush, and in two months restored the child to health, which has now been permanent for above two years.

The next case, remark the Doctors Duncan, who have quoted both cases in their notice of Dr. Beddoes's work in the 'Annals of Medicine,' 1801, is perhaps no less remarkable. A young lady, aged thirteen, had a very dilated pupil and slender make, in addition to personal appearances nearly the same as those mentioned in the last case. Dr. Beddoes found her with an equally protuberant belly, which became remarkably large, as well as tense in the evenings; she had wasted limbs, frequent loose stools, hectic fever, feet œdematous at night, short cough, and difficult respiration. In three days after beginning to take twenty drops of the muriate of lime, which were gradually raised to sixty drops, the purging ceased. The appetite for animal food soon became strong but natural. In nine days the feet ceased to swell, the hectic symptoms decreased, and the cough disappeared in the course of the third week. In five weeks the forearm, accurately measured round the thickest part, had gained full three quarters of an inch; and at the end of the sixth week no appearance of disease remained.

I have reproduced these cases of Dr. Beddoes because differing in no important particular from instances of a similar kind which have fallen under my care, in which the muriate of lime has apparently been the means of effecting a very salutary change. In the treatment of the chronic diarrhœa of young children, associated with prominence of the belly and hectic symptoms, I am able to bear a strong testimony to the value of the muriate of lime. A few years after the time of Dr. Beddoes's publication, there appeared a paper in the earliest volume of the 'Edinburgh Medical and Surgical Journal,'[1] by Dr. James

[1] Page 147, 1805.

Wood, physician to the Newcastle Infirmary and Dispensary, in which the author observes, " It is not improbable that the muriate of lime is used, and with as much advantage, in every part of the kingdom as it is in this place. With regard to the northern part of it, at least, this probability is much increased by the circumstance of its having obtained a place in the late Edinburgh Pharmacopœia. Still, as I have not met with a single report of the virtues of this invaluable medicine, nor even any allusion to these, in any of the works intended for the quick dissemination of medical facts, I cannot any longer withhold to the more immediate and general practice of the medical world the muriate of lime as a valuable remedy in scrofula and other states of debility." The same writer further states, " I would feel in some degree accountable for the sufferings of all in this complaint (scrofula) if I were not to endeavour to make known, as much as in my power, that these sufferings may be relieved, and frequently entirely prevented, by the remedy I have mentioned." Dr. Wood used the muriate of lime largely in the treatment of incipient phthisis pulmonalis, in all the external forms of scrofula, in rickets, and in all cases of hectic from great discharges. He further mentions that Mr. Ingham, one of the surgeons to the hospital, found the remedy to possess great powers in discussing tumours and obstructions of different kinds. In 1808, the late Dr. James Sauders of this city published his important work on ' Consumption,'[1] and in it we find the following very decided statements :—" I think that I have ascertained that the muriate of lime has a more powerful effect in removing indolent scrofulous tumours than any other substance used as a remedy, but that when they become open sores it is almost useless. This is a very manageable substance ; the dose of it may be gradually increased from five or six grains, three or four times a day, to two drachms ; during its administration no particular change of regimen is necessary; and I have never observed it produce any disagreeable effects, except of the slightest kind, after its use has been long-continued, and the quantity of the dose had become very great. Six years ago, I observed with admiration its effects on a young lady, who was

[1] ' Treatise on Pulmonary Consumption, in which a New View of the Principles of its Treatment is supported by Original Observations on every Period of the Disease,' &c., &c. Edinburgh, 1808.

so disfigured by these swellings that the apex of her head was that of a cone resting on the whole superior or atlantal aspect of the trunk."[1] In the case thus described by Dr. Sanders, the remedy was continued for six months, with the result of the neck resuming its proper shape, and scarcely any enlargement of any gland remaining. He adds, that he has never administered muriate of lime in similar circumstances without producing the most beneficial effects. The chronic enlargement of the lymphatic glands in the neck, associated with a similar condition of the parotid and submaxillary glands, and frequently with fulness of the tonsils, is the form of disease in which I have most frequently had the opportunity of exhibiting the muriate of lime, and my experience of its use in such cases has been so satisfactory as to lead me cordially to join with Dr. Sanders in the remark—" It would give me infinite pleasure if the utility of this remedy in such complaints were completely established." That Dr. Sanders had abundantly satisfied himself of the efficient operation of this remedy may be inferred from the circumstance, that it is in closing his discussion of its use as a deobstruent that the following passage occurs :—" Is there anything more absurd than that life, incomparably the most valuable of all possessions, indeed that without which there is no possession, should be treated with less care and skill than any common article of furniture? We will not allow a footstool to be repaired but by the most expert joiner, while we entrust our lives to the rashness of empiricism."[1]

Through the kindness of Dr. Moir, I have had the opportunity of reading a manuscript lecture of the late eminent Dr. James Hamilton, for the first forty years of this century Professor of Midwifery in the University of Edinburgh, in which, when discussing the treatment of rachitis or rickets, the following occurs :—" The tonic medicines which have been employed are the bark, preparations of iron, and the muriate of lime. According to my experience, preparations of iron and the muriate of lime are the most useful tonic medicines of this disease." In another part of the same lecture, which is devoted to a consideration of the nature and treatment of scrofula, Dr. Hamilton speaks in high terms of the efficacious operation of the muriate of lime in that disease. Dr. Anthony Todd Thompson asserts

<hr>

[1] Page 112.   [2] Op. cit., page 118.

that he has seen more benefit from its continued use than from any other medicine.[1] Dr. de Vering, after bearing a decided testimony to the therapeutic virtues of the muriate of baryta and the muriate of lime in scrofulous affections, indicates his preference for the latter on account of its effects being less violent, and the remedy not requiring the maintenance of the same precautions in its administration.[2]

It would be easy to multiply the references to equally favorable expressions of opinion regarding the therapeutic action of the muriate of lime; I have, however, preferred to cite the testimony of physicians who were distinguished as men of careful observation and matured experience in their own day, and of whom either the personal remembrance or the fame still lives. To be impartial, I have to confess that, at the very time when the muriate had its chief appreciation, and was more commonly employed than either before or since, there were some physicians of undoubted eminence, and one indeed of deserved renown, who had failed to discover its possession of signal therapeutic virtues. Dr. John Thomson, to whom I have just alluded, in his well-known and esteemed treatise on Inflammation, has thus expressed himself:—"Three of the neutral salts have acquired great celebrity for the cure of scrofula, and it is remarkable enough that these should all have been muriates. The first of these was muriate of soda, given as it exists in sea-water. Nothing can be more satisfactory than the evidence which is on record of its efficacy. In reading this, one only wonders how so efficacious a remedy should ever have fallen into neglect. The second, the muriate of barytes, was introduced to the notice of the public under the most favorable auspices, and its antiscrofulous powers extolled by all degrees of men in the medical profession; yet it has had a much shorter-lived reputation than sea-water or its successor the muriate of lime. How long this third muriate will be permitted to enjoy its present fame I shall not venture to say. Not much longer, however, I should imagine, from what I have seen of its use, than till a new remedy shall be found out by those who are still sanguine in their hopes of dis-

---

[1] 'Dispensatory,' 8th edition, p. 748.

[2] 'Manière de Guérir la Maladie Scrofuleuse.' Par le Chevalier Joseph de Vering. 1832. Page 34.

covering a specific for scrofula. To such of you as are but imperfectly acquainted with the past history of the materia medica, and the uncertain nature of medical evidence, in so far as it relates to the operation of remedies for the cure of chronic diseases, the accounts before the public of the virtues of the muriate of lime in curing scrofula must appear satisfactory and complete. It will be well if a little reading or experience does not soon lead you to suspect that the reporters of its efficacy have not, any more than the reporters of the efficacy of the muriates of soda and barytes, learned to distinguish in every instance between a cure and a recovery. Till that distinction, however, is made, and is adhered to more strictly than appears to have been hitherto done in reporting the effects of the remedies employed for the cure of scrofula, a little scepticism, even with regard to the antiscrofulous virtues of muriate of lime, may, I conceive, be safely enough indulged.[1] Few will be prepared to call in question the general appositeness of these remarks, and the interest attached to them is increased owing to the fulfilment of the prophecy made by their distinguished author. In watching the treatment of cases in which muriate of lime has been given, I have been the more careful to abstain from accepting without rigid scrutiny the facts which have seemed to establish the therapeutic action of the remedy, on account of the opinion of Dr. Thomson, just quoted, and of others, to which, with the exception of two, I need not particularly refer.[2] Mr. Benjamin Phillips remarks: "I am not satisfied that it has any very evident action upon scrofulous glands. I cannot say that I have ever seen a case in which, in the absence of other influences, the discutient power of this medicine has been clearly manifested."[3] "Since the publication of the earlier editions of this Dictionary," wrote Mr. Samuel Cooper, "I have seen the muriate of lime given in several cases of scrofula, but without any beneficial effect on the disease."[4]

---

[1] 'Lectures on Inflammation,' by John Thomson, M.D. 1813. See page 196.

[2] See 'A Practical and Historical Treatise on Consumptive Diseases, deduced from original Observations, and collected from Authors of all ages.' By Thomas Young, M.D. London, 1815.

[3] 'Scrofula: its Nature, its Causes, its Prevalence, and the Principles of Treatment.' See page 285.

[4] 'Dictionary of Practical Surgery,' 6th edition, page 1031.

Professional confidence in any remedy might well be unsettled by the expression of opinions so conflicting as those which have now been cited. I do not mean to attempt to reconcile them.

"Non nostrum inter vos tantas componere lites."

Candidly, however, I feel as if the very decided statements, with appeals to extended experience, made by Drs. Beddoes, James Wood, Sanders, Anthony Todd Thompson, and Hamilton, were more than equal to the negative conclusions of Dr. John Thomson, Messrs. Phillips, and Cooper. That the adverse opinion respecting the use of muriate of lime led in some measure at least to its being less employed as a remedy, admits of little doubt; but another and more satisfactory explanation of the circumstance lies in the introduction into practice of iodine and cod-liver oil, the former more especially, as medicinal agents in cases of exactly the same nature as those in which the muriate of lime had been employed. To Dr. Coindet, senior, of Geneva, is due the merit of having discovered, in 1820, the medicinal virtues of iodine, while cod-liver oil, long previously regarded as a panacea, in domestic practice, particularly, however, in strumous disorders, has, since the period of the introduction of iodine, very gradually risen into the well-merited position in professional confidence which it now occupies and bids fair to maintain. To Percival, the elder Bardsley, Scherer, Williams, and chiefly to Dr. Bennett, is this to be ascribed.

The cases in which I have had occasion most frequently to employ the muriate of lime have been instances of struma, the most notable feature of which was the enlargement of the lymphatic glands in the neck. In the earlier cases which fell under my observation, recourse was had to the remedy, either because what appeared to be a fair trial had been already given to iodine, or its preparations, chiefly the iodide of potassium, and syrup of the iodide of iron, or to cod-liver oil. Frequently both iodine and cod-liver oil had been employed without appreciable benefit, or it had happened that these remedies had disagreed—that, owing to the occurrence of sickness and anorexia in the instance of the oil, or of pain in the stomach, coryza, and gravedo in that of iodine, the remedies could not be persistently taken. Under such circumstances, then, muriate of lime was prescribed. For several years, however, with a

growing and latterly extended experience of its virtues, I have
not hesitated to order the remedy when no such proof was
afforded, either of the failure, or of the intolerance on the
patient's part, of the other medicines.   I am not able to affirm
that the remedy has always, that is, in every case, answered my
expectations—of what remedy, even among our "summa re-
media," does an experience of that kind hold true ?—But it is
in my power to assert, that in many instances of very great
enlargement of the cervical glands, and several examples of
other maladies, which will be shortly referred to, have apparently yielded to its use.   The subjects of the former of these
cases have been for the most part young persons of both sexes,
who have presented more or less unequivocally the aspect of a
strumous habit of body.   In a few there has been a more
general enlargement of the lymphatic glands, not confined to
the neck on either side, there has existed glandular swelling in
the axillæ and inguinal regions, while there was also reason for
believing that some at least of the deep-seated lymphatics of the
pelvis were affected.

Muriate of lime requires in such cases to be taken for a
considerable time—for weeks, it may even be months—before
its beneficial effects are visibly produced.   Usually, however,
in the course of a few weeks there occurs a certain degree of
softening in the glandular tumour, and the component glands
in the mass come to be separately distinguishable.   With the
gradual subsidence of the enlargement there is a notable improvement in the appearance of the patient, owing to a favorable change in respect to both appetite and digestion.   Observing
in some instances a tendency to the recurrence of the glandular
swelling, after the discontinuance of the muriate of lime, I have
thought it advisable to counsel its being taken with regularity
for a very considerable period after the entire disappearance of
the cervical fulness.   I have lately seen three patients who
have been taking the medicine with the greatest regularity for
two years, eighteen months, and a year respectively.   Muriate
of lime is best taken in milk, but some patients prefer it in
water.   Generally speaking, I have recommended it to be taken
after meals, twice or thrice daily.   The salt has a mawkish
disagreeable taste, which the milk in part or wholly conceals.
Although far from pleasant, patients rarely complain of the

taste after they have taken the muriate of lime for a short time, and by many, a liking for it is gradually acquired, so that there results in time a much greater disinclination to stopping than to continuing its use. Young children are for the most part readily persuaded to take it. My experience of the value of muriate of lime as a deobstruent in glandular affections has been gathered both from hospital and private practice; and I feel satisfied that in my endeavours thoroughly to test the efficiency of the remedy, it has been in my power, as it has certainly been my desire, to eliminate every conceivable source of fallacy. In hospital and dispensary practice, the muriate of lime has been prescribed for patients whose malady had clearly been intensified by faulty, usually imperfect, diet, as well as by exposure. In private practice, on the other hand, there has been illustrated the influence of hereditary transmission in overcoming the most favorable conditions as regards diet and regimen.

I cannot venture to say in which class of instances, drawn from very different spheres of observation, the powers of the remedy have been most notably produced. One young woman who was sent to the Infirmary from Berwickshire by a medical friend, presented on her admission a deformity of neck which was really frightful, and which nourishing food, and that of the most suitable kind, albuminous and oleaginous, and the diligent use of both internal and external medication for many months, had proved insufficient to overcome. Muriate of lime during this patient's three months' residence in the Infirmary had produced a very decided amelioration, and its continued employment for a much longer period after her return to the country, an altogether satisfactory result. I have frequently had occasion to see two patients, both females of the better classes, whose strumous cervical glands have proved a great cause of annoyance and of mental depression, and in whom the muriate of lime has never failed to produce a marked subsidence of the deformity after its use has been continued for a period of weeks. The remarkable feature in these two cases—and I have seen the same thing, although less notably, in others —is, that after the muriate of lime has been discontinued for a little time, the glandular swelling always returns, but it invariably yields to the influence of the remedy when again employed.

Surely in such an experience as this, there is abundant proof of its therapeutic action. I had lately the satisfaction of recognising, not without some difficulty at first, a young lady, for whom I had prescribed the muriate of lime on account of very extensive enlargement of the glands on both sides of the neck, some of which had suppurated, and by so doing had occasioned increased deformity. This patient had taken the muriate of lime for fully a twelvemonth, having previously consumed large quantities of cod-liver oil, and various of the preparations of iodine and iron, without any benefit whatever. Returning, not for the purpose of receiving further advice, but of exhibiting her changed appearance, I found that cicatrices, with a very trifling hardness of some small glands, alone remained. Several professional friends have, during the past twelve years, informed me of the gratifying results they had witnessed in cases of a similar nature, which had fallen under their observation or more immediate care.

The permanent nature of the cure in many such cases has always appeared to me to offer a further encouragement for the employment of the muriate of lime.

Another form of disease which is apparently benefited by the muriate of lime is met with in childhood, and makes a near approach in its symptoms and general character to the tabes mesenterica. I have observed the exhibition of the remedy in such cases to be followed by the cessation of a protracted diarrhœa and of exhausting perspirations, by a subsidence of fever, hectic in type, by improvement in appetite, the gaining of flesh, and a gradual restoration to the condition of health. In the grave disorders of the alimentary canal occurring in children, the muriate of lime is useful in arresting looseness of the bowels, in promoting digestion and favouring nutrition. I have frequently prescribed the remedy, and been gratified by the results obtained from its use, in cases of children stopping short of any definite disease, but characterised by depraved appetite, loss of flesh, pallor of countenance, protuberant belly, wasted limbs, and more or less of febrile excitement, the latter presenting an intermittent or remittent type, and usually attended by two distinct paroxysms of fever during the twenty-four hours. Dr. Wood, to whose use of the muriate of lime I have already referred, found it most efficacious in the treatment of tabes mesenterica, on account of its checking purging, diminishing the hectic fever, allaying the inordinate appetite which sometimes characterises that disease, and in many cases, he says, ultimately restoring the patient to perfect health. The red appearance of the point and edges of the tongue, associated with diarrhœa and more or less of sickness and failure of appetite—an assemblage of symptoms in children which points to the administration of lime-water, often a most effectual remedy—may be with equal advantage treated with the muriate of lime in repeated doses.

Twenty years ago, when a student in Paris, I was witness to the treatment of lupus by the then eminent physicians of the Saint Louis Hospital, M. Cazenave and M. Devergie. Both insisted strongly on the constitutional treatment of that formidable malady. In the wards of the latter, I saw many instances of lupus exedens materially benefited, and some apparently cured, by the administration of cod-liver oil—in much larger doses, however, than we have been accustomed to give the remedy in this country. It was in the Hospital of St. Louis, in 1850-51, that for the first time I saw patients taking cod-liver oil, not in spoonful doses, but in large glasses or tumblerfuls.[1] Passing from the *clientèle* of M. Devergie into that of M. Cazenave, I found the muriate of lime being prescribed, from a just sense of its remedial powers over a disease so intimately connected as lupus is with the scrofulous constitution. Cazenave gave the muriate in this fashion : a scruple was dissolved in a quart of water, and a teaspoonful of the solution was given every morning, while the dose was increased by a spoonful every four or five days until the patient took twelve spoonfuls a day.[2] In some cases of lupus which have fallen under my own care, I have prescribed a combination of these remedies ; cod-liver oil

[1] 'Traité Pratique des Maladies de la Peau,' par Alph. Devergie. Paris, 1857.—"Mais si l'on réfléchit que c'est le seul moyen qui ait guéri sans le secours d'aucun autre, que pendant dix ans j'ai suivi pas à pas les effets des diverses médications préconisées pour combattre cette maladie, et qu'aujourd'hui j'emploie l'huile de foie de morue d'une manière générale de préférence à tout autre moyen, le médecin insistera sur son usage, et saura donner à des malades tout le courage qu'il leur faut pour avaler le matin et le soir un *très grand verre* d'huile."—(Page 651.)

[2] See ' Manual of Diseases of the Skin,' from the French of M. Cazenave and Schedel, translated by Dr. Burgess (page 258).

in smaller doses than M. Devergie has recommended,·and with
it the muriate of lime. It was in watching the favorable course
of one such case, in which there existed good ground for
believing that the local malady owed its origination not only
to an inherited highly strumous constitution, but to an acquired
syphilitic taint, that I became impressed by the conviction that
the muriate of lime possessed some virtue, as I am satisfied
cod-liver oil does, of an antisyphilitic nature. This much I
am able to affirm, that its alterative powers in certain cases of
cutaneous eruption intimately connected with syphilis, more
especially lupus exedens and non-exedens, and in local psoriasis,
also in some instances of ozœna and chronic tonsillitis, have
appeared to me quite unmistakable.

The recognised dose of the muriate of lime is from 10 to 20
grains; but the solution of the old Edinburgh Pharmacopœia
forms a convenient mode of its administration, and in that form
I have habitually prescribed it. Fifteen drops of this solution,
containing about ten grains of the muriate of lime, may be
considered an average dose for a young adult or adolescent;
and with such a dose given thrice daily in milk, I have usually
commenced; gradually the dose may with advantage be augmented to nearly thirty or forty drops; it is, however, not
advisable, by reason of its occasionally producing such unpleasant effects—as nausea, sickness, pain in stomach, and loss of
appetite—to elevate the dose still further. I have thought that
a little period after food is the better time for its administration,
but this is not of much importance—many patients taking it
with advantage either shortly before or during meals. In the
instance of any young children to whom I have frequently
administered it, the dose must of course be apportioned according to age. I have given it to such in doses of three to ten
drops. Very speedily in some cases, these chiefly of the nature
of diarrhœa and feeble digestion with attenuation in children, I
have witnessed its beneficial effects—quite as speedily, indeed,
as we observe the operation of lime-water as an antacid and
alterative. When given in the more chronic ailments, to which
reference has been made, and more particularly in the strumous
enlargement of glands, a rapid curative action is not to be
looked for. Under such circumstances, indeed, the persistent
use of the remedy is called for. I feel thoroughly satisfied,

however, that in so prescribing and continuing the muriate of
lime, the physician and patient may look forward with confidence to its beneficial operation. Weeks, months, a twelve-
month, are surely not to be considered as very lengthened
periods of time for the removal of a malady which has existed
for many years, and possibly bid defiance to all the other means
of treatment which may have been employed. It has been my
lot within the past three or four years to prescribe the remedy
for patients who have thereafter passed temporarily from my
observation, but at the end of months, twelve months, or even
a longer time, having meantime, conformably to exhortation,
diligently continued the remedy, have again presented themselves, to afford the most gratifying proof of the therapeutic
action in their cases of the muriate of lime.

I have very seldom witnessed the production of any disagreeable effects, and rarely had occasion to interrupt the medicine.
In a few instances I have found that a smaller dose than that
usually prescribed appeared to agree better, and to work out
the therapeutic action of the remedy most satisfactorily.

No notable physiological feature has presented itself to my
notice while watching with care the therapeutical action of the
muriate of lime. Conformably to the experience of experi-
menters, I have observed the acidity of the urine to be lessened
during the administration of the remedy. Dr. Parkes mentions
that the result on the urine of the exhibition of muriate of lime
is a considerable increase in the amount of lime.[1]

Lime, in the form of phosphate or carbonate, is an essential
constituent of the body. As phosphate it is found in all the
solids and fluids. Always united in the solids with organic
substances, as an *element of constitution,* it is scarcely second in
importance to water.[2] It is in the bones that phosphate of lime
chiefly exists, and its absence in due proportion from the bones
is made evident by what we observe in disease. Carbonate of
lime is found in the bones, teeth, and cartilage, and, as a salt
entering into the composition of bone, is only secondary in
consequence to the phosphate. These principles are largely
supplied to the economy by the food which we consume. In

---

[1] 'The Composition of the Urine in Health and Disease,' page 166.

[2] 'The Physiology of Man,' by Austin Flint, jun., M.D., " Introduction,"
page 40.

selecting the chloride of calcium as a therapeutic agent, it is not to be overlooked that, much as chemists have differed regarding the nature of the free acid of the gastric juice, whether hydrochloric or lactic, it is admitted that, besides the acid in question and pepsine, there exists in the solid residue a considerable amount of chlorides and phosphates; and of the former, chloride of calcium is one. We have, then, the satisfaction of knowing that in prescribing the solution of the muriate of lime we are not introducing into the stomach a poison—although I do not undervalue the therapeutic action of poisons—but an agent which, in the healthy state, has its existence in the gastric juice. I am not in a position to affirm, that just as rachitis or rickets is the result of a diminished supply of phosphate of lime to the bones, so the form of that malady in which I have been recommending the employment of muriate of lime may depend on the reduction, or possibly absence, of this substance from the gastric juice. This much we know, that scrofula is essentially a blood disease, transmissible from parent to child, as is the case with rheumatism, gout, and other maladies, the hereditary nature of which is universally admitted, working deterioration in the circulating fluid, and through it, from which their nutrition is derived, injuriously affecting the solid tissues of the body.[1] Of the operation of muriate of lime in scrofula, and more especially in that form of scrofula distinguished by enlargement of the lymphatic glands, I entertain no doubt, having recognised it again and again. To offer a satisfactory explanation of this action I am not prepared, but must rest satisfied by having directed attention to one or two particulars of some importance. I do not wish to be supposed as entertaining a low opinion of iodine as a remedy in scrofula, for the action of which, although we all admit it, it is almost impossible, as Dr. Headland observes, to invent a satisfactory explanation. So far from depreciating iodine, I have very frequently occasion to prescribe it; and in the instance of scrofula associated with anæmia, as we so often find it in the children of the poor resident in towns, have found the syrup of the iodide of iron to be almost as useful as an improved diet and change of air. Let us, however, be, if possible, still further armed against this dreaded and ever formidable foe,

[1] See Headland's 'Action of Medicines on the System,' page 206.

and if, in addition to iodine and bromine, and barium and cod-liver oil, we have muriate of lime, we may, in contending against it, be, I hope, the surer of victory.

I have thus endeavoured to bear a strong testimony, founded on no inconsiderable trial, to the therapeutic virtues of the muriate of lime—virtues which have, in my opinion, been of late years unjustly overlooked.

Permit me, in concluding, to remark that my attention was earliest called to the remedy by one to whom I owe the best lessons I have had in my profession ; to his teaching, therefore, any good which may possibly result from this statement regarding the therapeutic actions of a remedy in which he was wont to place confidence, must be ascribed ;

> " For in my mind
> Is fixed, and now strikes full upon my heart,
> The dear, benign, paternal image, such
> As thine was, when so lately thou didst teach me.
> * * * * * *
> And how I prized the lesson, it behoves
> That long as life endures, my tongue should speak."[1]

---

[1] Dante, ' Dell' Inferno,' Canto xv, Cary's translation.

XXV

THE SWELLED LEG OF FEVERS.

(*Read before the Medico-Chirurgical Society of Edinburgh, 9th June, and reprinted from the 'Edinburgh Medical Journal' for September, 1872.*)

THE occurrence of a peculiar swelling of the lower extremities, usually, although by no means invariably, confined to one limb, in the course of the continued fevers of this country, or, more strictly speaking, as a sequela of such fevers, is familiar to all physicians who have had considerable experience of these diseases. The affection in question is more common in connection with typhus than with typhoid or any other form of fever, but it is not limited in its occurrence to fevers; I have observed a precisely similar condition of the lower limb in pleurisy, and likewise as a sequela of a state of constitutional disturbance lasting for many days, but in none of its leading features resembling any of the recognised forms of continued fever.

The swelled leg, to the pathology of which this communication will be specially addressed, has a history of its own in relation to fevers, and to that history I shall in the first place devote a few remarks.

In the work of Drs. Barker and Cheyne on the 'Epidemic Fever of Ireland' in the years 1817-19, published in 1821, there is the earliest reference which I have been able to find to the occurrence of swelled leg as a sequela of fever. This reference is precise, inasmuch as the enlargement is reported in contradistinction to anasarca, which is also stated to have occurred, and to dropsical swellings, which not unfrequently succeeded recovery from fever. "A swelling of one leg," remark these authors, on the testimony of Dr. Nevin, "was frequently observed at Downpatrick."[1] Again, in reporting the experience of physicians in the Province of Leinster, Drs. Barker and Cheyne observe, " with respect to the sequelæ of the fever, the most remarkable were pulmonary consumption and dropsy; next to these in frequency were chronic rheumatism, mania, or amentia, paralysis, hysteria, and an affection resembling phlegmasia dolens, but not confined to the female sex, which was observed in the fever hospitals both of Dublin and Kilkenny."[2] Some years subsequently to the publication of Drs. Barker and Cheyne's work, there appeared a paper by Dr. Tweedie, of London, in the 'Edinburgh Medical and Surgical Journal,' in which attention was called in a more particular manner than had previously been the case to the swelling of the lower extremity after fever.[3] Dr. Tweedie at that time attributed the swelling to inflammation of the areolar tissue, and made no reference to the state of the veins in the affected limb. The former view of the pathology of the swelling he thought to be rendered probable by the inflammation terminating in two instances in diffuse suppuration. In a more recent publication Dr. Tweedie admits that the swelling may be due to crural phlebitis.[4] Sir Robert Christison, in treating of the sequelæ of continued fever, has remarked as follows :— " During the early stage of convalescence an affection occasionally presents itself, which resembles the phlegmasia dolens of puerperal women, and is sometimes apt to be mistaken for œdema. It is generally preceded by some general fever. Its symptoms are pain, swelling, tension, heat and glistening whiteness of one limb, extending from the groin downwards,

---

[1] 'An Account of the Rise, Progress, and Decline of the Fever lately Epidemical in Ireland, together with Communications from Physicians in the Provinces, and various Official Documents.' By F. Barker, M.D., and J. Cheyne, M.D. London and Dublin, 1821. See page 467.

[2] Op. cit., page 490.

[3] 'Observations on a Peculiar Swelling of the Lower Extremity after Fever. By Alexander Tweedie, M.D., Physician to the London Fever Hospital. Vol. xxx. 1828.

[4] 'Lectures on the Distinctive Characters, Pathology, and Treatment of Continued Fever.' Delivered at the Royal College of Physicians of London. By Alexander Tweedie, M.D., F.R.S. 1862. See page 293.

with inability to move the limb. It generally ends in resolution and recovery; but amendment takes place slowly, and sometimes it terminates in serous effusion and diffuse suppuration of the intermuscular cellular tissue. It is in all probability a variety of subcutaneous cellular inflammation. Of this affection, which was first described by Dr. Tweedie in 1828 as an occasional sequela of fever in the London Fever Hospital, several characteristic examples occurred in the epidemic of Edinburgh in 1817-20.[1] In the fifth volume of the 'Dublin Hospital Reports'[2] will be found a paper by the late Dr. Graves and Dr. Stokes, entitled "Painful Swellings of the Lower Extremities." After recording two interesting cases, one characterised by symptoms of intermittent fever, the other of gastric fever, in both of which painful swelling of the leg occurred, these eminent writers observe : "An accurate observation of numerous cases, both of phlegmasia dolens occurring after delivery and of painful swelling of the extremities appearing during or after fever, has satisfied us of the pathological identity of the two diseases. In both œdema occurs, unattended by redness, but accompanied by increase of heat, with great tenderness and pain, and followed for a considerable time by impaired motion of the limb." Several years subsequent to the publication from which I have now quoted, Dr. Graves drew attention to what he styled a very important form of disease which attacks convalescents from fever, and runs a course of remarkable intensity and rapidity."[3] He alludes in this second communication to the swelled leg, described by himself and Dr. Stokes as occurring during the epidemic of 1826, but adds that the important and fatal form of the disease which he there delineates did not come under his notice till within a more recent period. A careful perusal of the interesting cases recorded in this connection by Dr. Graves leads to the conclusion that they were instances rather of pyæmia than of ordinary phlegmasia dolens. The record in the "Hospital Notes," of the 'Medical Times and Gazette' for 25th April, 1857, of an instructive case of phlegmasia dolens

---

[1] 'The Library of Medicine.' Article, "Continued Fever." Vol. i, page 145. 1840.
[2] 1830. Page 29.
[3] 'Clinical Lectures on the Practice of Medicine.' Edition 1864. See pages 198-201.

after fever, by Dr. Risdon Bennett, in which the affection occurring after fever is stated to be of extreme infrequency in London, called forth an interesting letter in the immediately subsequent number of the same journal by Dr. A. P. Stewart,[1] whose name is so justly connected with the discovery of the non-identity of typhus and typhoid fevers. Dr. Stewart, in this letter, remarks : "During the memorable and destructive epidemic of typhus which prevailed in Glasgow from October, 1836, to May, 1838, phlegmasia dolens and purulent deposits in the joints were by no means rare sequelæ of typhus. Though I cannot at present state the number of these cases witnessed by Dr. A. Anderson and myself, having mislaid my clinical notes, I think I am under the mark when I express my conviction that there could not be fewer than eighteen or twenty." The late Dr. A. Anderson of Glasgow, the colleague of Dr. Stewart, alluded to in the letter which has been quoted, has referred in distinct terms to the latter of these sequelæ. "Sometimes a patient will be recovering very well from fever—say from typhus—when he has the rigor which I have described; and after it he is much worse than you would expect him to be were he only about to take erysipelas. His pulse is exceedingly rapid; he is exhausted, and in particular complains of pains in his joints, in his ankles, wrists, elbows. He becomes very ill. Asthenia is developed, and the most ominous symptom is jaundice; his eyes and skin become yellow. There is swelling and redness about the joints, and he has considerable pain when they are touched or moved. These cases all die, and as far as I have seen they die rapidly, with symptoms of poisoning of the blood, like cases of the worst puerperal fever, or pyæmia after surgical operations. I have seen some dozen of them, and upon inspection found the synovial membrane injected with blood and bathed in pus; pus not the result of ulceration, but the primary secretion from the inflamed membrane, as in purulent ophthalmia."[2] Dr. Magnus Huss, in recording his large experience of typhus and typhoid fevers, as gathered in the Seraphim Hospital of Stockholm, has observed, regarding local œdema as a sequela: "This affection occurs chiefly in the extremities, especially the lower, commonly on one side, seldom

---

[1] 'Medical Times and Gazette,' 2nd May, 1857, page 446.
[2] 'Ten Lectures Introductory to the Study of Fever.' 1861. See page 48.

on both at once. It is caused by coagulation of the blood; that is, the formation of a thrombus in some of the venous trunks leading from the extremity. If the subsequent obstruction be complete, the œdema will be suddenly generated and considerable ; otherwise it is smaller and slower in its formation. Distension of the subcutaneous veins commonly accompanies the œdematous swelling, whether accompanied by pain or not. Except in the cases which will be noticed below, I never saw this state become dangerous in typhus, although it may retard the recovery." . . . . . . " In a few cases (these are the dangerous cases Dr. Huss has referred to) I saw such a thrombus in a venous trunk suppurate, whence all the symptoms which belong to pyæmia resulted, as lobular pneumonia, abscesses, &c."[1] Dr. Murchison, in describing the complications and sequelæ of typhus and typhoid fever, refers to the phlegmasia dolens or white leg. In the experience of Dr. Murchison, this has been a more common sequela of pythogenic or typhoid fever than of typhus. He mentions, that out of nearly seven hundred cases of typhus which came under his care during the epidemic of 1862, the sequela in question did not occur in a single instance.[2] Dr. Maclagan, of Dundee, in exhibiting the statistics of typhus in the Royal Infirmary of that city, makes no reference to the occurrence of swelled leg as a complication or sequela.[3]

So much for the history of this affection. From the preceding statement, it is evident that a swelling of the lower extremity different from ordinary œdema or anasarca has been recognised by various physicians as occurring in the advanced stages of

[1] 'Statistics and Treatment of Typhus and Typhoid Fever.' See page 174.

[2] 'A Treatise on the Continued Fevers of Great Britain.' See pages 186, 504.

[3] 'Edinburgh Medical Journal,' August, 1867. Dr. Maclagan has kindly favoured me with the following :—" On referring to my notes, I find that in 1750 cases of typhus, white leg occurred only twice ; one of the patients was a man, æt. 25, the other a woman, æt. 20. In over 200 cases of enteric fever, it occurred only once, in a man of 32. I have always regarded the malady as of lymphatic rather than venous origin. It is very possible that the circulation through the veins may be secondarily interfered with by the mechanical pressure of the effusion which takes place from the deeper-seated lymphatics. But as I have never watched a case to the close, I can say nothing from personal experience as to the actual state of either system of vessels."

typhus and typhoid fevers. It may be mentioned here that by no authority has the swelled leg been described as a sequela of relapsing fever.

In my own experience, the swelled leg has occurred in typhus as well as in typhoid, but more frequently in the former. To its existence as a chronic affection, but nevertheless arising out of fever, I am specially anxious to direct attention, because it is under such circumstances I have lately and not unfrequently encountered it. Within the last five years I have, on no fewer than nine occasions, had my attention directed to a chronic swelling of the whole leg, from the inguinal region to the front of the foot, which in the majority of instances, while free from pain, has always been attended by very considerable discomfort. In all of these cases the patients have been unable with any exactitude to account for the swelling, but a careful inquiry into the previous history has satisfied me that in nearly all, one or other of the varieties of continued fever, already referred to, has at one time been in existence, and this was distinctly established in some of the number; or pleurisy, or a form of constitutional disturbance, of which mention merely has been made, but to which I shall have more particularly to refer. In these chronic cases, with a single exception, one limb only has been affected, and in the majority it was the left. In the acute cases which I have been able to watch from their commencement there have been three in which both legs were affected; but in each of these the affection, beginning in one limb—in two, the right—and in the third, the left—seemed to pass from the one to the other; in none of the three was there a simultaneous development of the affection in the two legs; it had declined in that first affected before its presence in the other was observed. In one instance, that of a young lady, which I did not see till the whole of the right leg was very greatly enlarged, but with very little suffering, the affection was described to me as commencing near the foot, and gradually rising upwards to the thigh. Thereafter, and under my own observation, the left thigh became affected, and the swelling proceeded downwards to the leg and foot. In the acute cases the swelling has subsided in the course of two or three weeks in some; but in others has lasted for a much longer time. In those remarkable examples to which I have referred as chronic swelled leg, the affection has been in existence for years. One of these, an officer of cavalry, informed me that his right leg had been nearly double the size of his left ever since his convalescence from an acute illness, evidently a continued fever, seven years before I saw him. An elderly gentleman had his left leg enormously swollen since suffering repeated attacks of ague, and one attack of yellow fever fifteen years before his visit to me. A lady upwards of fifty had both legs very greatly swollen since girlhood, and believed that the determining cause of the swelling, which had affected first one limb and then the other, was a low fever, which had seriously as well as permanently impaired her health. In one of the instances of resulting chronic enlargement of the left limb I witnessed the original development of the swelling during the early convalescence from a severe attack of typhus eight years ago, distinguished by the degree of typhomania which had existed during its whole course. The swelling was preceded by uneasiness, followed by great pain in the leg, slight rigors, and renewed feverish disturbance. The enlargement of the calf became very great, and deep-seated suppuration seemed to have occurred in its posterior aspect. The late Dr. Duncan saw this gentleman with me, and his "tactus eruditus" left little doubt in his mind that a large collection of matter already existed. He entered his bistoury, guided by that skill for which he was so eminently distinguished, but no pus escaped then, or at any subsequent period of the case. The swelling continued to be of very considerable dimensions for some weeks, and then gradually diminished. The limb, however, remains to this day enlarged, and after fatiguing exercise is apt to become more than ordinarily swollen. The gentleman has had no pain for a lengthened time, is of very active habits, and, with the exception referred to, is in the enjoyment of complete health.

Several years ago I attended professionally a young gentleman of studious habits, and up to that time healthy, who, after exposure to cold, contracted a severe pleurisy on the right side. While exhibiting the symptoms and physical signs of large pleural effusion, a swelling of the limb on the same side, unattended by pain, occurred. The swelling I at first regarded as an ordinary œdema; but this view of its nature was surrendered, as the limb gradually increased from foot to leg, and from leg to thigh, until it became very greatly enlarged, with notable fulness of the lymphatic glands in the inguinal region. The swelling was white and glistening, did not pit on pressure, and communicated a feeling to the fingers or hand precisely similar to that with which I had already become familiar in the swelled leg of fevers. Meantime the pleural effusion having augmented, and very considerable dyspnœa being occasioned, thoracentesis was had recourse to. The subsequent progress of the case was altogether satisfactory; but the swelled leg, although considerably reduced in size, remained up to the period of this young gentleman's death, which resulted some years afterwards from tubercular disease within the abdomen. I know of other three cases of pleurisy with considerable or large effusion, in which a swelling of the lower limb on the side corresponding to the effusion occurred.[1] Again, I have alluded to the same condition of the lower extremity in connection with a peculiar disturbance of the system, but not resembling fever. It has occurred to me to witness, twice in females, and once in a youth of the other sex, a swelling of the lower extremity identical in its character with the swelled leg of fevers, succeeding no very marked premonitory symptoms, but accompanied by very considerable constitutional disturbance—to wit, failure of appetite, nausea, and feverishness—as well as by pain in the limb. In these instances there existed no other local affection, and they were clearly not examples of idiopathic fever. The swelling continued in each of these for some weeks, and then gradually disappeared. I may mention here that neither in these cases, nor in any of the other and different forms, as I believe them to be, of swelled leg, was there any evidence of renal disorder beyond what is common to every instance of febrile disturbance. There never was albuminuria, and the only change in the urine consisted in its concentration, with more or less increase of lithates.

From the statements already made, and the references to authors which have been adduced, it is evident that there exist different forms of swelled leg as a sequela of fever. The difference in question will be rendered still more apparent by a

---

[1] See paper by writer, "On Paracentesis Thoracis in the Treatment of Pleural Effusions, Acute and Chronic," in 'Edinburgh Medical Journal' for June, 1866.

consideration of the symptomatology of the affection, and to that subject I have now to direct attention.

Before doing so, let me mention that I do not purpose to make any detailed allusion to those instances of swelled leg already signalised, which have been described by the late Drs. Graves and Andrew Anderson, and referred to by Dr. Stewart and Dr. Huss. These were examples of pyæmia, happily not of common occurrence in the progress of either of the ordinary forms of adynamic fever. Dr. Murchison says that he has never known of a case at the London Fever Hospital.[1] The blood-poisoning in such cases has, by some writers, been ascribed to the absorption of irritant matter from the intestinal ulcers in the case of typhoid fever. Were this a true explanation, we should expect pyæmia to be a common accompaniment of this fever, which we have already seen it is not, and, further, to find the blood-poisoning limited in its occurrence to enteric fever. But neither does the latter hold true, for in all of Dr. Stewart's and Dr. Anderson's cases it was typhus, and not typhoid fever. Again, the explanation of the purulent absorption taking place in the former fever from bedsores will not admit of universal application, inasmuch as cases of pyæmia have occurred in typhus which had been entirely free from bedsores, or any cutaneous ulceration. Dr. Murchison has alluded to the possible dependence of such a sequela on the presence of foul air, due to overcrowding and defective ventilation.

On a review, then, of the instances of swelled leg after fever which have fallen under my own observation, together with those recorded by authors, it appears to me that such a division as the following is warranted :—1st. Cases dependent on vascular obstruction; *a*, venous; *b*, lymphatic. 2nd. Cases in which inflammation of the areolar tissue exists. In further illustration of the symptomatology, a brief reference will now be made to these in the order in which they have been named.

Dependent on venous obstruction.—Pain and swelling are admitted to be the characteristic features of interrupted circulation through veins. When, therefore, the convalescent from fever is either suddenly seized with pain in one of the lower extremities, or the limb becomes the seat of gradually augmenting uneasiness, succeeded by swelling, which often attains a

[1] Op. cit., page 190.

very great size, and when the superficial veins are observed to be more or less enlarged, there can be little doubt that obstruction to the return of blood through a large trunk is in existence. In such cases the swelling, besides being confined to one limb, presents an appearance very different from that of ordinary anasarca; it does not pit on pressure, as is the case with dropsical limbs; the swelling, on the other hand, resists pressure, is firm, and has a brawny feeling. The colour of the skin, except where the prominent veins exist, is not much altered; certainly it wants the unusually white appearance which is characteristic of the other forms of swelled leg after fever, and is bluish rather than white. The pain is in some cases very severe, and extends throughout the whole limb, and even into the pelvis. There is always more or less of constitutional disturbance associated with this swelling. Not unfrequently the local affection has been preceded by well-marked rigors; if otherwise, chilliness and discomfort have at least been present for some hours. In just such circumstances other and very alarming symptoms have occurred, indicating the implication of the heart itself, and exhibiting, I cannot help concluding, very decidedly that a part of the vascular system intimately connected with its central organ has been primarily involved. Let me illustrate this by the few details with which I have become acquainted in the case of a gentleman suffering from swelled leg whom I have frequently seen. When in India this gentleman had an attack of low fever, subsequent to which his right leg became greatly swollen. While so suffering, he became suddenly affected by pain and a feeling of very great uneasiness in the region of the heart, accompanied by breathlessness, and shortly afterwards fainted. He was seen by medical men, who regarded his condition at the moment, and for some time thereafter, as perilous, owing to the existence of some profound embarrassment of the circulation. Happily, however, he gradually recovered, but, at the distance of fully four years from the original attack, continues to have a swelled leg, not painful, although at times uncomfortable, and giving rise to inconvenience. I do not know how to account for the sudden and alarming seizure from which this gentleman suffered, except by supposing that a portion of clot originally obstructing the femoral or iliac vein on the affected side, had found its way to the right chambers of the heart, whei it may have been detained, or, passing thence through the pulmonary artery, may, in part, have reached the lungs. That further mischief in the latter view, of the nature of metastatic inflammation, did not result in this case, may lead to the conviction of its rarity, but cannot, I think, be regarded as disproving the pathological inference which I have now suggested. Virchow has strongly insisted on the fact that thrombi from the remote venous system of the body produce pulmonary obstructions and metastatic depositions in the lungs. He has argued that secondary disturbances, as, for example, in the lungs, are frequently caused, not by the introduction of softened masses, which rapidly become liquid, into the blood, but by the separation of larger or smaller portions from the end of a softening thrombus, which is carried on in the current of blood, and becomes ultimately impacted in remote vessels.[1] Such fragments becoming detached in the venous system, and ultimately producing pulmonary embolism, must needs reach the heart, and in so doing may give rise to such symptoms as distinguished the interesting case to which reference has now been made.

When regard is had to the authoritative statement of Virchow in connection with the observations which have been made by Graves, Stokes, Anderson, and Stewart, it may, I think, be affirmed that one variety of the swelled leg of fevers depends on venous obstruction.

That the peculiar condition of the lower limb which we are considering may arise from other causes is, however, abundantly evident, and I have now to direct attention to its probable dependence in some cases on *an obstructed state of the lymphatics*. Dr. Murchison records an instance of typhus fever followed by phlegmasia dolens of left leg, jaundice, and death, in which, upon examination after death, the heart was found to be fatty, and the liver in a state of acute atrophy, while no clot existed in the femoral vein, but, on the contrary, both left femoral and iliac veins were in a healthy state. Clearly, in this as well as in other instances, a cause different from venous obstruction must have determined the swelling of the limb. In certain of the cases which have fallen under my own observation I have observed a distinct enlargement of the lymphatic glands in the

[1] 'Die Cellular Pathologie,' p. 183.

groin of the affected limb, while in one instance there existed a distinct fulness of the same glands within the pelvis. Further, in some cases, and these distinguished by the glandular increase referred to, the limb, besides being swollen and firm, as in the phlegmasia dependent on venous obstruction, has presented a peculiar appearance on the surface. Wanting entirely the bluish hue, with notable prominence of the superficial veins, it has had marks which may, I think, be justly ascribed to dilated cutaneous lymphatic vessels. Hyaline lines in various parts of the thigh and leg, not unlike the marks over the abdomen which we observe in women who have borne children. I have seen the same appearance, and a remarkable one it is, under other circumstances. Through the kindness of Mr. Lister, I saw it in a lady, sent by a medical man at a distance to consult him, whose nates and breasts presented these hyaline lines, and I think I am correct in saying that Mr. Lister adopted the view of their being due to dilatation of the superficial lymphatic vessels. The plate which is here produced represents the lower limbs of a young man who was for several months under my care in the Royal Infirmary, suffering from renal disease. When in the hospital his legs became œdematous, but we were struck by the appearance of peculiar markings over the thighs first of all, but subsequently over the whole limbs. These markings were precisely similar to the lines which I have been describing as occurring in other cases. In the space of a few weeks, the œdema meantime increasing, the limbs assumed the very remarkable appearance represented in the plate, which, considering the changes we were able to observe in them from day to day, led me to conclude that we had to deal with dropsical limbs modified by lymphatic dilatation. Ascites supervening in this case, and proving little amenable to medicinal treatment, I tapped the abdomen on three occasions, and thereafter, as we observe from time to time in instances of chronic renal disease, the dropsy in the limbs rapidly subsided, the strange appearance, resembling the cerebral convolutions, greatly vanished, and there remained, when the patient left the hospital, limbs but slightly enlarged, bearing, however, the hyaline lines which I have endeavoured to describe. The inguinal lymphatic glands were decidedly enlarged in this case also.

The view as to the chronic enlargement of the leg consequent on fevers being due in some cases to lymphatic obstruction, has been strongly impressed on my mind by observing the right leg and thigh of an elderly gentleman who sought my advice about a twelvemonth ago. In this case the whole limb presented the same appearance as that already described in the instances of supposed lymphatic obstruction—much swollen, firm, not pitting on pressure, brawny. In addition to these characters, there were on the surface linear elevations not unlike the rugæ so strikingly delineated in the plate, and the lymphatic glands in the groin, and certain of the pelvic lymphatics were very much enlarged. The right thigh of this gentleman at its largest part was twenty-six inches in circumference, while the left thigh was nineteen. Again, the circumference of the right knee was nineteen inches, of the left fourteen, of the right foot at instep ten inches. The swelling was wholly free from pain, and the limb had never been painful. In the evening, and to a still greater extent after any fatiguing exercise, the whole leg became increasingly distended. There existed a mass of enlarged lymphatics in the left side of the neck. The swelling of the leg had made its appearance earliest in the groin, and had gradually extended downwards. A precisely similar condition to that affecting this gentleman's leg I met with in the right arm and shoulder of a lady about forty-five years of age. I cite these cases here, not as examples of swelling of the limbs due to obstructed lymphatics resulting from fever—although I believe that in both some form of fever had previously existed, and that out of it the swelling was developed—but refer to them on account of their presenting, in an exquisite degree, the very same characters which I have observed in certain of the swelled legs of fever; and this circumstance strengthens the conviction I have long entertained, that the swelled leg of fever is sometimes due to obstructed lymphatic vessels, as distinguished from obstructed venous trunks. That such a condition as the former of these should result during the advanced stages, or shortly after the termination of adynamic fever, need not surprise us, when we consider what the true office or function of the lymphatic system is, and how actively engaged it becomes in all febrile disorders. We know that the ingredients of the lymph, which these vessels contain, are derived from the meta-

morphosis of the tissues in which they exist, and that, returning
as the lymph does to the circulation through the receptaculum
chyli, it cannot be regarded, as John Hunter did, solely as an
excrementitious fluid.   The probability is that, in part, materials
of waste are carried by the lymphatics to the blood for the
purposes of excretion; and that a portion of the fluid, on the
other hand, undergoes some renovating process by which it is
made available for further nutrition.   Now, in fevers, there is
often a rapid waste of tissues, and chiefly of those tissues in
which lymphatic vessels abound.   I allude particularly to the
muscles.   We can therefore understand that the absorbing
function which the lymphatics have to perform is in the
advanced stages of fever, when the process of tissue disintegration is active, very considerably heightened.   At that stage the
removal these vessels perform is of material for elimination,
ultimately through the busy agency of the kidneys chiefly.
But when convalescence is established, and the repair of the
system is in progress, it may be presumed that they are still
actively engaged in absorbing material, which, after mixing
with the chyle and circulating in the blood, is to be again fitted
for the purposes of nutrition.   If the question is put, why, in
the case of the swelled leg of fever is it, that the lymphatics of
the lower extremity are affected, and not those in other parts
of the body, the upper extremity for example, which is fully
supplied with similar vessels? we may observe, first of all,
that two instances have been referred to, in one of which the
upper extremity and shoulder were affected, and in the other
the pelvic and cervical lymphatics; and although the complete
history of these cases could not be obtained, I think it very
probable that in both, the primary disturbance of the lymphatic
system occurred during or shortly after fever.   Again, a reason
for the lower extremity suffering when the upper parts of the
body escape, may be that valves, which materially assist in
carrying on the circulation of the lymph, are very frequent in
the upper, while they are only sparsely distributed in the lymphatics of the lower extremity.   We must further keep in
remembrance, that nearly all the accidents, so to speak, which
are apt to occur in the vascular system, including arteries,
veins, and lymphatics, in the progress of fever, affect the lower
extremity by preference.

Allusion has been made to the painless haracter of the swelled leg of fever, when due to lymphatic obstruction, and this strikingly contrasts with the suffering of the patient when the venous system, on the other hand, is evidently involved. Into the lymphatics, no nerves have been traced. The uneasiness and discomfort which arise when the swelling has attained considerable dimensions may readily be accounted for, the former by the pressure exerted on contiguous tissues, and the latter from the great weight of the limb. In cases of swelled leg of fever, due to lymphatic obstruction, I have never known the serious results of blood-poisoning, nor embolism, nor purulent deposits in remote parts, to occur; and if satisfied as to the exact pathological character of the swelling, whether in its recent, acute, or more chronic form, the physician may offer a favorable prognosis in so far as the risk to life is concerned. Care here, however, is requisite, inasmuch as instances occur in which both venous and lymphatic systems are involved, and in such the prognosis, even when the latter condition is predominant, must be guarded. It is interesting, in connection with the observations now made, to find Virchow, when alluding to the occurrence of an epidemic of puerperal fever, remarking, in respect to the fatal cases, that in all of those which were accompanied by pulmonary metastasis, there existed thrombosis in the pelvis or lower extremity, while in the inflammation of lymphatic vessels there never occurred this alarming sequela.[1]

There remains for a brief consideration the third form of swelled leg of fever, namely, *cases in which inflammation of the areolar tissue exists*. The instances of swelled leg occurring in the course of fevers which have fallen under my own observation, and have been specially characterised by the affection of both legs, first one and then the other becoming swollen, have appeared to be in some particulars essentially different from the cases already described, in which venous or lymphatic obstruction has been the determining pathological condition. Reference has already been made to the circumstance of the swelling commencing in the foot or lower part of one leg, and

[1] Op. cit. In reference to such facts, the author justly observes, "Solche statistische Resultate haben eine gewisse zwingende Nothwendigkeit, selbst woder strenge Anatomische Nachweis fehlt."

then gradually rising upwards to the thigh, and ultimately affecting the thigh of the other limb, and descending from that to the leg and foot. An inflammatory affection of the areolar tissue would best account for this peculiar progress. I think it very likely that in such cases the lymphatic system of the limb does not always escape implication. This remark being grounded on the fact, that the cases have at times appeared to present a mixed character, having the general pain of the limb or limbs, which distinguish the inflammation of the cellular tissue, while more or less of the lymphatic fulness and superficial markings, with glandular enlargement, have been visible. Superficial abscess in such cases is not of unfrequent occurrence, but the dangers which must always be regarded as present in such instances of swelled leg, due to venous obstruction, and specially so when suppuration has taken place, are happily absent in the cases we are now considering. Embolism and metastatic inflammation would appear to be the very unfavorable, or hazardous results of swelled leg, due to venous obstruction, the mischief, as truly in the latter case as in the former, being primarily intravascular.

These are dangers which do not present themselves in the cases of swelled leg due to inflammation of the cellular tissue of the limb. While by no means denying that purulent absorption may not in such circumstances be induced, I am satisfied that its occurrence need not be dreaded as a likely event.

I must bring these observations to a close, by offering a very few remarks in regard to treatment.

When occurring in its acute form, whatever may be the cause of its development, swelling of the lower limb in fever will require rest. I am inclined to believe that some of the instances of long-continued swelling have resulted from too little attention being given to this point during the acute stage.

When pain and tenderness are prominent symptoms, fomentations, which may be made with opium or other anodynes, ought to be constantly applied. I have known the employment of leeches, more especially when distinct hardness and tenderness over a venous trunk in the limb were discoverable, to be followed by very considerable relief.

The further treatment of the acute stages will consist in the use of febrifuge and calmative remedies, attending to the state of the "primæ viæ," and carefully watching in the instance of the venous obstruction for those complications to which reference has been made. Till all febrile disturbance has passed, and the swelling of the limb has greatly, if not entirely, subsided, the patient so affected should be strictly confined to the recumbent posture. In the event of abscesses forming in the limb, and proving the cause of irritation and inconvenience, they will require to be cautiously opened.

A very careful regulation of diet, the avoidance of articles of food calculated to produce excitement of the vascular system, and of stimulants, unless when demanded by weakness or notable sudden failure of strength, should be practised. The only remedial means which I have found available in the treat-ment of the chronic swelled leg of fever, is very careful bandag-ing of the limb from the foot upwards to the thigh. In some cases this has been a great source of increased comfort, where formerly it had been had recourse to in a less perfect manner. Fatigue and want of due rest in the recumbent posture are potent causes of the aggravation both of swelling and discom-fort, and as much as possible both should be avoided. From local stimulation, and the employment of deobstruent remedies internally, I have seen no advantage to follow.

XXVI.

THE BROMIDE QUESTION.

A LETTER.

Reprinted from the 'Practitioner,' Feb., 1874.

EDINBURGH, *Jan.* 15, 1874.

DEAR DR. ANSTIE,—I have read with much interest in the 'Practitioner' for this month, your translation of the paper by Professor Binz, of Bonn, on "the therapeutic employment of bromide of potassium," and your own account of "the English stand-point respecting the value of bromide of potassium."

Were it not that you have inadvertently fallen into error in ascribing to me the authorship of the article on bromide of potassium which appeared in the 'Edinburgh Medical Journal' for December, 1866, I should not have troubled you with this letter. My appreciation of the value of bromide of potassium as a remedy in various diseases is, however, so high, that I am jealous of any testimony which has been borne to its therapeutic actions failing to exert the influence which such testimony justly possesses. Permit me therefore to state that the article in question was written by my father, the late Dr. Begbie, whose patient investigation of the virtues possessed by bromide of potassium, and strong recommendation of its use, did much to secure for it the confidence of the profession in this part of the country, and largely contributed to its general popularity.

Having made this correction, I am encouraged by the perusal of what you have written to add my testimony to the value of bromide of potassium in the treatment of various diseases. This I shall do in a categorical manner, in something of the same way as you have recently done.

1. *Epilepsy.*—In this disease my experience of bromide of potassium entirely confirms the statements of Dr. Russell Reynolds. I have repeatedly seen cures, in the strictest sense of the word, result from its employment, after the failure moreover, in many cases, of other remedies. Not only have severe fits ceased to return under its use, but the general health of patients, and more especially their mental condition, which had seriously suffered, have been completely restored.

Years have elapsed in certain instances since the occurrence of a fit, and individuals who had, owing to the frequency and severity of their attacks, been rendered incapacitated for their employment, have been enabled to resume their occupations and continue them without interruption.

Some patients have been benefited but not cured. The fits in such have been rendered less frequent in their occurrence, and less severe, but have not been entirely removed. Still, in these cases the bromide of potassium has been truly the *summum remedium*. No regulation of diet, no peculiar stringency of regimen, no other remedy than bromide of potassium—and many remedies have been tried—has exerted the like beneficial influence. Accordingly, it has in such cases been continued for the purpose, as you and Dr. Hughlings Jackson have observed, of reducing the frequency and severity of the fits. Some cases of epilepsy have in my hands been in no respect benefited by the bromide of potassium. A few have apparently been aggravated. I have not been able to satisfy myself of the reason for this varied but exceptional experience. It is, however, a common experience in the use of other admirable remedies. *Nullum medicamentum est idem omnibus.*

Looking back upon my experience of epilepsy, I feel inclined to remark that, were I deprived of the bromide of potassium, I should conclude that my best hope of being useful to the sufferers from this last disease had been taken away. I cordially embrace the aphoristic deliverance of the authority whom you quote in the concluding sentence of your paper : "It has changed the whole prognostic significance of epileptic attacks."

2. *Insomnia.*—In the procuring of sleep, bromide of potassium may be said to fall far short of opium, chloral, henbane, and other narcotics; and yet in many cases of insomnia it is superior as a remedy to the whole of these. Its innocency is in the first place to be set against their potency, not unmixed as that potency is with injury or even danger.

In the sleeplessness which precedes mental shock, as is occasioned by long-continued mental strain or by worry, the bromide of potassium in full dose is oftentimes singularly efficacious, not only procuring much-needed sleep, but tranquillising the whole nervous system, and rendering the individual, otherwise quite unfit, capable of mental exertion.

I have repeatedly prescribed the remedy with the happiest results in cases of insomnia accompanied by general restlessness and incapacity for exertion, consequent upon long-sustained mental effort with anxiety in professional men, and on prolonged devotion to business in persons following different kinds of mercantile pursuits, in whom rest, change of air and scene, the most careful attention to diet and regimen, including treatment in hydropathic establishments, and the use of other drugs, had entirely failed to produce any good result. I do not affirm that the bromide of potassium always succeeds, or that it has always succeeded in such cases. I entirely concur in your observation that the insomnia of aged persons is apt to be aggravated by the bromide of potassium, although I have not found it to be always so, as your experience appears to have been. In one case of an old lady the remedy certainly did harm. She, however, had notable calcareous degeneration of the arterial tissues; and from my observations in her case and in other old persons, I have been led to surmise that the condition in question interferes with the physiological action of the salt, and with its therapeutic action likewise. Bromide of potassium is believed to contract the minute vessels, and if degeneration of their walls exists to a marked degree, in failing to produce this effect it is possible that the presence of the salt in the blood may excite cerebral disturbance in place of quelling it. Whether this theory be correct or not, I have for a considerable time avoided the use of bromide of potassium in old people whose vessels were evidently the seat of general atheromatous degeneration, but have prescribed it in the insomnia of the aged when this morbid condition of the vascular system was not conspicuous.

A further and most important use of bromide of potassium is as an adjunct to chloral. I have found twenty grains of the former greatly increase the efficiency of a like dose of the latter.

The insomnia of delirium tremens is often overcome by large and frequently repeated doses of bromide of potassium, and so also is the sleepless excitement of puerperal mania. In these maladies the combination of bromide of potassium and chloral is chiefly to be recommended.

I have had occasion to verify the important observation of Dr. Begbie, that the craving for alcoholic stimulants which is so distressing a feature of dipsomania, is to a certain extent, even in some bad cases, and to a much greater degree in the milder, restrained by bromide of potassium.

3. *Spasmodic diseases.*—In controlling habitual cramps of the lower extremities, I have found no remedy so useful as bromide of potassium; and undoubtedly the very distressing cramps of the formidable Asiatic cholera were found during the last prevalence of that disease to be subject to its influence.

In spasmodic asthma I have had a considerable experience of bromide of potassium, and have here but to rank its virtues very highly. In a review of the late lamented Dr. Hyde Salter's excellent work on asthma, undertaken at the request of my friend Dr. Sanders, then editor (1869) of the 'Edinburgh Medical Journal,' I took occasion to express a favorable opinion of this salt as a remedy in asthma, and, at the same time, surprise that it had not even been named by Dr. Salter.

Perhaps in the treatment of asthma no remedy has appeared to me so useful as the iodide of potassium, but in my experience bromide of potassium has effected a cure when the iodide has failed. The union of these two salts, and their combination with arsenic, has been still more efficacious.

4. *In the incontinence of urine of young children,* bromide of potassium has answered when even belladonna had not succeeded, and these two remedies are probably the most available in this often troublesome disorder.

A less experience of its use in the following diseases has led me to the conclusion that in each of them the bromide of potassium is a remedy well deserving trial :—Hysteria, more especially its convulsive forms (in these Sir Charles Locock had reliable proof of its value), gonorrhœa, and certain non-malignant enlargements of the liver and spleen, the former more especially when connected with the too free use of alcoholic drinks.

I forbear from mentioning the diseases in which the use of bromide of potassium has been followed by results either negative or wholly unsatisfactory. Let me, however, state that I have grave doubts of its being, in the strict sense of the term, a febrifuge. In relieving the restlessness and insomnia of the febrile state, it unquestionably does good : but such therapeutic action does not entitle bromide of potassium to rank as an antipyretic.

I agree to the fullest extent in your judgment of the value of such articles as that of Professor Binz, in forcing us to scrutinise our grounds of belief in the action of remedies with additional rigour. Although I regard Professor Binz as essentially wrong, it will be my duty, after reading his paper, to reconsider the position I have been led to assume.

Believe me, dear Dr. Anstie, yours sincerely,

J. W. BEGBIE.

XXVII.

ALBUMINURIA

IN CASES OF

VASCULAR BRONCHOCELE AND EXOPHTHALMOS.

(*Read before the Medico-Chirurgical Society of Edinburgh, 4th March,
and reprinted from the ' Edinburgh Medical Journal' for April*, 1874.)

THAT albuminuria may exist independently of Bright's disease, and be therefore unconnected with any structural change
in the kidneys, is a proposition which few physicians, if any,
will be prepared to call in question.

No doubt, the presence of albumen in the urine is the most
significant feature in the symptomatology of Bright's disease,
otherwise there could have existed no warrant whatever for the
employment of the term as a synonym for that disease. The
use of the expression in this way is, however, faulty, and will
become more and more unsuitable as the discovery of albumen
in the urine, under other circumstances than those which
indicate the existence of a grave renal disease in one or other
of its different forms, is made. The presence of albumen in
the urine as a notable feature in some cases of vascular bronchocele and exophthalmos has been familiar to me for some
time ; while a very special interest is attached to the circumstances under which the albuminuria has in a few instances
been met with.

I have been unable to find any reference to the association
of an albuminous condition of the urine with those remarkable
symptoms, the union of which characterises the disease now
well-known through the writings of Graves, Stokes, Basedow,
Begbie, Trousseau, and other writers. This is, I believe, only
to be accounted for by the circumstance that the condition of
the urine has hitherto in this disease not been made the subject
of any careful examination. It will of course be understood
that I exclude from this reference the albuminuria of passive
renal congestion, which is so often witnessed in cases of heart
disease, and likewise when the primary vascular impediment is
seated in the lungs, and sometimes also in the liver. From
this reference I also exclude those instances of vascular bronchocele and exophthalmos in their advanced stages, in which
the heart, and in their turn, not unfrequently the kidneys, have
become involved in organic changes. In the latter, dropsy and
albuminuria are constantly present, but under these circumstances they are to be properly regarded as symptoms, not of
the disease itself, but of those complications which are prone to
occur in its course.

The albuminuria incident to cases of vascular bronchocele
and exophthalmos in their earlier stages is essentially a temporary albuminuria, and is evidently unconnected with any form
of renal degeneration. But although temporary, disappearing
as the other symptoms of the disease are either relieved or
removed, the albuminuria has generally been considerable in
degree, and sometimes even excessive.

In this respect the coagulability of the urine in cases of vascular bronchocele and exophthalmos has presented a remarkable
contrast to the temporary albuminuria which is found in certain
other diseases. I have indeed never seen so large an amount
of albumen in the urine in any other disease, when the cause of
the albuminuria was not inflammatory or organic.

My attention having been called to the association of an
albuminous condition of the urine with vascular bronchocele
and exophthalmos, in the first instance, owing to the existence,
in certain cases, of œdema of the feet and ankles, I became
satisfied that the association is by no means of infrequent
occurrence. I have found albuminuria in a considerable
number of the cases which have lately fallen under observation,

and it is more than likely that it may have existed in other instances, although unrecognised from causes to which reference will be made. Albuminuria has existed in persons of both sexes suffering from this disease, and has been more common in cases of female than male patients; but when the much greater frequency of vascular bronchocele and exophthalmos among women than men is kept in view, the symptom has been present in a larger proportion of males than females. In some it has been an evanescent symptom, lasting only for a short time, and when so, only present in limited degree. In others, the albuminuria has been very considerable—it has even been excessive, and it has lasted for weeks, indeed for months—while the other notable symptoms of the complex malady continued, and only disappeared as the latter became relieved or removed. Œdema of the lower limbs, although in the first instance calling attention to the condition of the urine, has not been observed to bear any constant relation to the albuminuria; on the contrary, œdema, and sometimes considerable anasarca of the legs, have been present without any appearance of albumen in the urine; and albumen, when present, has generally existed without any form of dropsical swelling. In the most notable cases of albuminuria in connection with vascular bronchocele and exophthalmos, dropsy has not been present.

In prosecuting my inquiry on this subject, a very interesting circumstance became manifest, namely, that the albuminuria was in certain cases limited to the period of digestion— present immediately after a meal, and absent when the person fasted. I had in one case been not a little puzzled by noticing the strange variety presented by the urine within very short periods—the albumen present in considerable quantity one day, and absent the next—present in the urine of the forenoon, and not to be detected in that passed before dinner. By obtaining repeatedly specimens of the urine in this case, and in one or two others, I was able to satisfy myself that in this disease the albuminuria is apt to possess the remarkable character of only occurring during or immediately after the digestion of the food.

This appears to me to be a most interesting feature, and it is also in various ways a very important one. The existence of albumen might readily escape detection if the physician relied on the results of one examination, as he is not unapt to do; and even when taking more than usual care, it is quite possible that in several specimens of urine furnished by the same patient for examination it might be found that no albumen existed. Conceive a patient so affected consulting a medical man before breakfast or luncheon; his urine, carefully examined, found to be non-albuminous; but, from some cause or other—and we know how fickle some patients are—calling for another physician shortly after a meal, when a large precipitate of albumen occurred on applying heat as well as on the addition of a little nitric acid. Remarkable as this character of the albuminuria which occurs in cases of vascular bronchocele and exophthalmos is, there is another feature pertaining to it which is even more striking. The albumen is present in much larger quantity after breakfast than either after luncheon or dinner. In one case of this kind, which I was able to observe at intervals for a considerable time, the urine presented the following characters :—It was passed in average amount, was of healthy colour, reaction, and density. On no occasion was the density observed to fall below 1015, and it never rose above 1025; the average density was that of health, 1020. Very occasionally this urine deposited lithates, and from time to time contained a slight excess of earthy phosphates. Sugar was never present. Albumen existed in this urine daily for upwards of a twelve-month, but only at certain times of the day, and these times were readily found to be shortly after meals. After breakfast, however, the amount of the albumen was invariably greater than after luncheon, dinner, or an evening meal. Being greatly interested in these peculiar phenomena presented by the urine in the case of a gentleman whom I had recommended to spend the spring months in the south of England, I requested him to take an opportunity of consulting Dr. George Johnson, of London, whose opinion in all departments of urinary pathology is so deservedly held in high esteem. In connection with this case, Dr. Johnson wrote to me as follows:—" I saw two days ago a patient of yours, who asked me to write to you. As he told me that the explanation which I gave him of his symptoms is essentially the same as that which you gave him, I need not enter into minute detail in writing to you. I found that the urine passed after his breakfast contained a large amount of albumen; that passed at 3 p.m. contained none; that in the evening, three hours after dinner, contained a small quantity. He has been overworked, and is evidently a nervous, excitable man. I conclude that there is no structural change in the kidney, but that his kidney is irritated and congested at intervals during the process of excreting the products of faulty digestion. I confess that I am at a loss to account for the fact of the urine being more constantly and copiously albuminous after breakfast than after dinner. I repeated to him the usual directions as to avoiding cold and wet and fatigue, and long fasting. I also advised him to make trial of an exclusively milk diet. He told me that you had made the same suggestions to him. I prescribed a mixture of tincture of quinine and tincture of nux vomica, acid hydrochloric diluted, and syrup of ginger, to be taken after food, and advised him to take an occasional dose of chloral hydrate when he is restless or disturbed by dreams.

" It occurs to me to ask whether the breakfast taken after a long interval from the previous meal, and when, consequently, the absorption of materials is likely to be more rapid, gets into his vessels quickly, and in a crude and half-digested state? If this be so, food taken at shorter intervals would seem to be indicated. The urine passed in my room an hour and a half after breakfast, became nearly solid with heat and nitric acid. I have often met with cases in which the urine has been albuminous only after food and exercise, but I have not before met with one in which the *breakfast* appeared to be so especially noxious to the kidney."

A brief account of the case to which Dr: Johnson alludes in his interesting communication just quoted, will now be given, before offering certain considerations which its observation has suggested.

A gentleman, of about thirty years of age, had long been in a somewhat delicate state of health, although no particular attention had been called to his symptoms till the summer of 1871. He was then suffering from debility, great nervousness, and palpitation of the heart. These had succeeded a condition of looseness of the bowels, which had existed for a considerable time. The prominence and peculiar expression of the eyes in this gentleman were, at the time now referred to, quite characteristic, and suggested the very probable discovery of a goitre. This, although the patient had been quite unaware of its existence, was readily detected in the form of a soft pulsating tumour on both sides of the neck. The visible pulsation of arteries in the neck and limbs was present in a notable degree. On examining the urine of this gentleman, it was found to contain a considerable amount of albumen; but speedily the discovery was made that the albuminuria was not persistent, but, on the contrary, variable in its occurrence. The urine passed after meals was found to be more constantly and highly coagulable than that passed while fasting, and at times the urine was found to be free from albumen. Dr. Henderson, of Helensburgh, under whose care this gentleman had been, had noted the variable character of the albuminuria, and had distinctly traced its occurrence to the periods of digestion. Both before and after this gentleman's visit to the south of England and residence on its coast, rest from professional duties—which in his case were arduous—had been enjoined, and various experiments in diet and regimen had been practised. He had also several remedies in addition to those prescribed by Dr. Johnson. From bromide of potassium and belladonna he undoubtedly received benefit, but more especially from digitalis. To the latter, indeed—which, in the form of its tincture, he took persistently for months, in doses of from ten to twenty drops thrice daily, frequently combined with iron, and sometimes alone—he has himself ascribed the chief benefit. Under its use the prominent eyes have retired, the goitre has nearly if not entirely disappeared, the cardiac pulsations have fallen from 140 per minute to the normal standard, and the distressing palpitation from which he suffered has been succeeded by calmness in the heart's action. The nervousness and apprehension so characteristic of his malady, and which in his case were often most distressing, have given place to mental calmness and tranquility. He has become greatly changed for the better in appearance ; having been formerly very notably thin, he has now become very fairly nourished. He has returned to his professional duties, and during the past winter has discharged them regularly and comfortably. For months there has been no appearance of albumen in his urine. The last time I had an opportunity of examining the urine, which was passed shortly after breakfast, it contained no trace of albumen.   The recovery in this gentleman has been complete.

It is surely a satisfactory consideration that a condition of excessive albuminuria—the urine becoming nearly solid on the application of heat and addition of nitric acid—may, after all, not indicate the existence of any structural change in the kidney.   Of course, in connection with the albuminuria, the presence or absence of certain other important features must, under such circumstances, be taken into account.   Apart from the intermittent character of the coagulability, the facts that the quantity and density and colour of the secretion did not deviate from the healthy standard, and still more, that diligent and repeated examination by the microscope failed to detect the vestige of a cast of any kind, were to be regarded as the proofs of the renal derangement being functional and not organic.   Still, there is occasion for reiterating the assurance that albuminuria is not Bright's disease, and for pointing out that, when unconnected with the presence of blood or pus in it, there may be even a highly coagulable condition of the urine, due to causes which are wholly independent of any structural change in the renal substance.   Such, I am persuaded, may confidently be affirmed of the albuminuria which is apt to occur in cases of vascular bronchocele and exophthalmos.

Some little time after my attention had been called to the peculiar features of the albuminuria which is incident to cases of vascular bronchocele and exophthalmos, and to which reference has now been briefly made, a very instructive instance of the malady fell under my notice in the person of a medical man, who had been for some years engaged in active practice in the south of England.   Calling one day for advice, the gentleman in question told me that he was the subject of Bright's disease, and feared that little or nothing could be done for his relief.   He certainly looked ill, was thin and sallow in appearance, and evidently deeply depressed in spirits.   Having, however, noticed, as he entered my room for the first time, that he possessed the prominent eyes, with peculiar staring expression, so characteristic of vascular bronchocele and exophthalmos, I ventured—in reliance on my previous observations —to offer the comforting suggestion, that possibly, if not probably, the presence of albumen in his urine might be due to causes which were capable of being removed, and did not indicate the existence of any serious disease. This remark he received with politeness, but with very evident incredulity, mentioning that his condition had already been condemned by medical authority, that he did not expect to be cured, but only felt justified in expecting a little prolongation of life with greatly impaired health. On carefully examining this gentleman, a bronchocele of considerable size, soft, and pulsating, of whose existence he had been unaware, was discovered. His pulse was small, and as frequent as 140 per minute. The urine, on its earliest examination, while the patient was fasting, and between 1 and 2 p.m., was to his own surprise, found to be free from albumen, its density 1020, and of acid reaction. Subsequent examinations of the urine determined its decided coagulability after meals, and its freedom from albumen while abstinence from food was practised. This gentleman was exceedingly nervous, and very desponding. Under treatment a considerable improvement took place. As he had occasion to pass through London, I begged him to see Dr. Johnson, and it is to him Dr. Johnson alludes in a letter of date 27th October, 1872, from which I now quote :—" There is a striking resemblance between his case and that of the Scotch clergyman, whom you were so good as to send to me. Dr. —— is extremely feeble and nervous, and I fear that the prognosis is bad. I quite agree with you, that a long sea voyage would be the best course for him, but he seemed unwilling to do anything that would separate him from his family." I have not seen this gentleman for some time, but his progress can be traced in the correspondence I have had with him. On the 28th of March, 1873, he wrote :—" I have gone very comfortably through the winter, considering all things. I am much stouter than when you saw me, and much stronger. I do a good deal of walking in the course of the day. My heart still beats very rapidly, but its action is not so irregular as formerly. Whether albuminuria exists, I cannot say, as I never test for it, and try to banish the thought of it altogether from my mind. The goitre is decidedly less in size, but is still visible."

I obtained two specimens of urine passed on the 10th of April, 1873. That voided before food was taken, contained deposit of lithates, and was absolutely free from albumen. That passed an hour after breakfast had a density of 1016, and contained a very faint trace of albumen. The letter which accompanied the specimens of urine will exhibit the peculiar nervousness under which my friend still laboured. " I send you," he wrote, " two little bottles with urine which I passed to-day. Please do not send me a bad report, as it will only frighten me. I dread the thought of renal disease so much, that I try to banish the very existence of kidneys from my thoughts. That I shall look with anxiety for your next letter, and yet dread its arrival, your knowledge of my nervous condition will assure you." Happily, I had no occasion to send " a bad report," while, in consideration of his highly sensitive and nervous state, I wrote over the seal of my communication, " good news."

Since the summer of 1873, this gentleman's condition has steadily improved. On the 28th October he wrote :—" I am glad to be able to tell you that my wife was confined on the 27th ultimo, and has done very well indeed. For myself, the only trouble I now have is occasional palpitation." Again, on the 8th December :—" My general health is now very good. I am as fat as ever I was, and my eyes have lost that unnatural stare. There is still a slight enlargement of the thyroid gland, and sometimes—though rarely—my kidneys act very little. Digitalis and iron remedy this. My heart still beats fast." My last communication, of date 17th Jan., 1874, gave a most satisfactory account of his progress, and was written a few days before he embarked as surgeon of a ship sailing with the royal mails for Madeira, Ascension, and the Cape of Good Hope. Before obtaining this appointment, my friend was obliged to go before the medical officer of the General Post-Office for examination as to personal and professional fitness. In this communication, he says :—" I find no remedy relieve me so much as bromide of potassium, in 20-grain doses, thrice daily. Aconite and digitalis do not relieve me much."

This case is certainly a very gratifying and encouraging one. Not only has there been an almost entire disappearance of albumen from the urine, but the other symptoms from which the patient suffered in very notable degree—the palpitation of the heart and throbbing of the arteries, the bronchocele and exophthalmos—have all become very greatly lessened, and

will, I fully expect, soon entirely disappear. This hope is
justified by the results of experience in other cases. It has
occurred to me to witness, within the past two years, three
cases of vascular bronchocele and exophthalmos, all in females,
in two of which albuminuria existed, gradually improve under
the same treatment as that which has been pursued in the
instances more fully detailed, and ultimately in these a complete
cure has been obtained. In the second patient, whose case has
been narrated at some length, renal casts were said to have
been seen. This may very possibly have been so, but repeated
careful examinations of the urine, made while he remained
under my care, failed to detect their presence. I have, indeed,
in no instance of the albuminuria occurring in cases of vascular
bronchocele and exophthalmos, found renal casts. This remark
applies equally to the examples of excessive albuminuria, and
the more numerous instances of the disease in which the coagulability of the urine has neither been great nor long-continued.
Albuminuria is not a constant symptom of vascular bronchocele
and exophthalmos, but it is a frequent one. I am inclined to
think that it may hereafter be found a more frequent symptom
than my own observations presently entitle me to call it. From
the circumstance that I have had no opportunity of carefully
watching some instances of vascular bronchocele and exophthalmos which have recently fallen under my notice, having in
such been able to make an examination of the urine only on a
solitary occasion, it is very probable that albuminuria may
have escaped detection. It existed in a patient of Dr. Rosa,
whom I saw lately, a married woman, æt. 36, the mother of
seven children, in whom the malady succeeded the occurrence
of lienteric diarrhœa and prolonged lactation. Dr. Affleck
informs me that he has found albuminuria of the nature I have
been describing, to exist in a sufferer from vascular bronchocele
and exophthalmos recently under his care.

Having indicated the nature of the albuminuria which is
found in certain cases of vascular bronchocele and exophthalmos,
it now becomes necessary to inquire a little more fully into its
pathology. Albumen is, in all probability, not a constituent of
healthy urine. It has, indeed, been stated by Dr. Gigon of
Angoulême, that albumen exists in normal urine, and can be
thrown down by chloroform. Becquerel, Aran, and Parkes

have satisfied themselves that the precipitate which is produced by the addition of chloroform to the urine is not albumen, but a mixture of chloroform, mucus, and organic substances. Albumen, however, is so frequently present in the urine, and occurs under so vast a variety of circumstances, that it becomes a matter of very great importance to determine its clinical significance. The existence of blood, pus, or spermatic fluid in the urine renders it coagulable; but it is scarcely necessary to state that in the cases of vascular bronchocele and exophthalmos to which I have referred, there were none of these conditions. Again, the excessive use of a diet composed chiefly or entirely of albuminous matter, such as eggs, has been found by various observers—among others, Barreswil, Hammond, and Brown-Séquard—to produce albumen in the urine. Barreswil, after taking ten eggs, passed albuminous urine for twenty-four hours. There can be little doubt that, in some persons peculiarly constituted, the partaking of certain articles of food difficult of digestion by them, produces albuminuria for a time. Of this nature was the case of the student mentioned by Sir Robert Christison, in whom a large amount of cheese or pastry produced albumen in the urine. Apart, however, from errors of diet, as Dr. Parkes has stated, temporary albuminuria will occur in persons with very slight disease. Beneke, when suffering from dyspepsia, noticed albumen in his own urine four times in four weeks. Clemens, Rayer, Martin Solon, and many other physicians, have made similar observations. It may be admitted, then, that albumen, although not an ingredient of healthy urine, may occur in the urine of healthy persons, or of persons whose disorder of health is, at the time of its presence, very slight. Attention has recently been called by Dr. George Johnson to the occurrence of albuminuria in healthy persons after bathing in cold water. Again, albuminuria is apt to occur in relation to a great many disorders which are not essentially connected with structural change in the kidneys. Not to dwell upon pregnancy, as a condition of the system with which albuminuria is associated, there is the puerperal state. Again, there is a large number of febrile and inflammatory diseases in the urine of which albumen very often occurs. Among these may be mentioned scarlet fever, measles, erysipelas, smallpox, diphtheria, typhus and typhoid fever, cholera, &c., and, of inflammatory diseases, pneumonia. Over and above these relationships, there are various forms of visceral disease—of disease affecting the heart, liver, and lungs—in the urine of which albumen appears; and the physician, in his observation of such cases, is on the outlook for its occurrence, and ascribes it, when it does come, to the general impediment to the circulation which the following diseases—(I name them as illustrative examples only) dilatation of the heart, cirrhosis of the liver, emphysema of the lungs—produce; for, owing to these, the renal circulation necessarily suffers. In such diseases, the albuminuria is almost invariably associated with a diminished secretion of urine. It is not necessarily so in the albuminuria of vascular bronchocele and exophthalmos,—the quantity is generally unaffected, and so are the other characters of the urine.

Dr. Roberts, of Manchester, has very clearly pointed out, that, in endeavouring to determine whether the presence of albumen in the urine be dependent upon the existence of organic disease of the kidneys or not, the question in each individual case must be considered in connection with the three following points :—1. The temporary or persistent duration of the albuminuria; 2. The quantity of the albumen present, and the occurrence and character of a deposit of renal derivatives; 3. The presence or absence of any disease outside the kidneys which will account for the albuminuria.[1]

Now, viewing the albuminuria of vascular bronchocele and exophthalmos under these aspects, the following observations may be made :—1. The albuminuria is temporary; for, according to Dr. Parke's definition of that condition, it has totally disappeared while the patient is under observation ; but, instead of lasting a few days or weeks, as holds true of most instances of temporary albuminuria, properly so called, it has lasted for many months, indeed for a year. Intermittent or remittent albuminuria would be a better signification than temporary, for the albuminuria of vascular bronchocele and exophthalmos, but, better still, because more definite, albuminuria occurring during or after digestion. 2. The amount of albumen which is present in the urine when the cause of its manifestation is independent of organic or inflammatory disease is usually

[1] 'On Urinary and Renal Diseases.' Second edition, p. 172.

small; very often it is not more than a mere trace. The amount of albumen in the urine when passive congestion of the kidneys results from cardiac or other visceral disease may indeed be considerable, but I do not remember ever to have seen the urine under such circumstances very highly co-agulable; very highly or excessively albuminous has, however, been the character of the urine in at least one example of vascular bronchocele and exophthalmos, the recovery in which has been complete. Again, in the temporary albuminuria of other maladies, there is generally some deviation, often notable, from the normal condition of the urine in other respects; the quantity, density, and reaction of the urine are often affected; and there is the presence of lithates in excess, or an undue amount of earthy phosphates. Not so, generally at least, in the cases of vascular bronchocele and exophthalmos which I have seen. With the exception of its containing albumen in consid-erable or large amount, the urine has been healthy. Neither has there been in the latter any deposit derived from the kidneys. In this respect, indeed, there is the interesting fact of a copious presence of albumen in the urine, without any trace of casts of one kind or another, and without any renal epithelium or blood. Further, the form of albuminuria which we are now considering, differs from any other form hitherto described, in being limited to the period of digestion of the food. 3. The presence of disease apart from the kidneys is of course conspicuous in vascular bronchocele and exophthalmos, while the peculiar morbid condition of the nervous sytem and of the blood-vessels in that disease, as well as the spanæmia which exists, must, I think, be taken into consideration in our endeavour to determine the pathology of the albuminuria, which we now know to be in some way or other associated with it.

In vascular bronchocele and exophthalmos, there is always present much disturbance of the nervous system—the sufferers from this disease are invariably highly nervous—they are often hysterical. The primary disorder of the circulation, both cardiac and vascular, is of the nature which we associate with derangement of the nervous system. The organs and parts of the body in which the local manifestations of disturbance are seated, are organs and parts freely supplied with blood-vessels.

and blood,—the thyroid gland, the spleen, which, although not invariably, is often affected, and the deep ocular tissues. To these must be added the kidney. From the failure of due nervous influence, the small vessels, and, it may be presumed, the capillaries, in the thyroid gland, and the deep-seated orbital vessels, become dilated, and the circulation through them in consequence interfered with. We can infer from the consideration of the essential nature of the renal circulation that if an obstruction to the return of blood through the inter-tubular capillaries and veins exists, either from an obstruction in the heart or lungs, or from a disordered state of the vessels themselves—a condition which I believe to exist in vascular bronchocele and exophthalmos—favoured by the more or less watery state of the blood itself, there will occur a transudation of serum, carrying with it albumen, through the walls of the Malpighian capillaries into the tubes, and thus the urine will be rendered coagulable.

But in order to explain the limitation of the albuminuria to the period during and after digestion of the food, it is necessary to regard the increased afflux of blood which then takes place, as leading to an altered physical relation between the blood and the walls of the vessels, and likewise determining an engorgement of the Malpighian capillaries, while the loss of tonicity in the efferent vessels is thus rendered temporarily more injurious. In other words, the renal circulation, in its comparatively tranquil condition, is unaffected by the disordered state of the capillaries and small vessels; but when excited, by the stimulus of a recent meal, it is unequal to the task, and the resulting interference determines the albuminuria.

But, further, there is something in the character of this albuminuria to ally it with the albuminuria of indigestion, to the occurrence of which a brief reference has been made. Sufferers from vascular bronchocele and exophthalmos have frequently an inordinate appetite and craving for food. They have bulimia; and, in the cases I have shortly recorded, this symptom was notably present. A large meal taken hurriedly is not unlikely to influence, as a remote cause, the production of the albuminuria. I think Dr. Johnson's explanation of the greater amount of albumen in the urine after breakfast than dinner, may be correct—the same explanation had occurred to my own mind—that the earlier meal taken after a long fast gets into the blood-vessels quickly, and in consequence leads to a greater disturbance of the renal circulation. Besides, hot tea and coffee, with eggs, consumed at breakfast, may be presumed to be articles more likely than others to furnish to the blood the offending material.

I have not attempted to exhaust this interesting subject, but have for the present limited myself to pointing out the occurrence of a form of albuminuria which, so far as I am aware, has not in its details been previously described by any observer, namely, albuminuria occurring during and after digestion in cases of vascular bronchocele and exophthalmos.

XXVIII.

HÆMATINURIA.

(Read before the Medico-Chirurgical Society of Edinburgh, 7th April, 1875, and reprinted from the 'Edinburgh Medical Journal' for May, 1875.)

THIS disease, in which the passage of the colouring matter of the blood, hæmatin, with the urine takes place, has of late years been described by Dr. George Harley,[1] Dr. Dickinson,[2] Dr. Greenhow,[3] and Sir William Gull,[4] while Dr. Roberts, of Manchester, in his work on Urinary and Renal diseases, besides detailing interesting examples of the disorder which have fallen under his own observation, has given an excellent summary of the whole subject of hæmatinuria.[5]

Antecedent to the publication by Dr. George Harley, in the 'Transactions of the Royal Medical and Chirurgical Society,' of two cases of this remarkable malady, the circumstance of hæmatin or hæmato-globuline existing in the urine without the association of blood-discs had been noticed by different pathologists.

[1] "On Intermittent Hæmaturia; with Remarks upon its Pathology and Treatment." 'Medico-Chirurgical Transactions.' Second series, vol. xxx, p. 161.

[2] "Notes on Four Cases of Intermittent Hæmaturia." 'Medico-Chirurgical Transactions.' Second series, vol. xxx, p. 175.

[3] "Case of Intermittent or Paroxysmal Hæmaturia." 'Transactions of the Clinical Society of London.' Vol. i, p. 40.

[4] "A case of Intermittent Hæmaturia, with Remarks," 'Guy's Hospital Reports.' Third series, vol. xii, p. 381.

[5] Second edition, p. 139.

Thus, Neubauer and Vogel remark—"The urine sometimes presents a bloody or reddish-brown, or brownish-black, or even an inky coloration, and yet, under the most careful microscopic observation, blood-corpuscles cannot be detected in it." Urine of this kind, these authors go on to observe, " is occasionally met with in diseases, which are associated with, what is called, a dissolved state of the blood—in scurvy, in putrid and typhus fevers, in malignant remittent fever, after the inhalation of arseniuretted hydrogen."[1]

Dr. Parkes observes—"Hæmatine appears in the urine in two states, either in the blood-corpuscles or separate from these; . . . in the second, the pigment is completely dissolved in the urine, to which it gives a more or less brown or black colour. Dissolved hæmatine," Dr. Parkes adds, "appears to indicate not local disease and rupture of the vessels, but a special affection of the blood, either general or local, produced by some septic or profound cachectic diseases. In bad typhus, malignant variola, pernicious remittents, &c., in scurvy, and sometimes in morbus Brightii, the urine may be very dark from hæmatine; and the very dark urines, if bile and vegetable pigments be absent, almost always indicate its presence."[2]

Dr. Thudichum describes hæmatin or hæmato-globuline as dissolved blood-corpuscles, "for," he observes, "it is in fact a mixture of the albuminous fluid filling the corpuscles—globuline, and of the colouring matter, which may be obtained in crystals under certain conditions—hæmato-crystalline." The distinction drawn by Dr. Thudichum between dissolved blood and dissolved blood-corpuscles, hæmato-globuline, is without doubt of importance. He was the earliest to direct attention to this particular, and to point out that "urine may contain albumen and hæmato-globuline at the same time, yet they must be present in the same proportions as in the blood, before we can say that they are due to hæmorrhage and consequent solution of the blood."[3]

[1] 'A Guide to the Qualitative and Quantitative Analysis of the Urine.' New Sydenham Society's translation, p. 310.

[2] 'The Composition of the Urine in Health and Disease, and under the Action of Remedies,' p. 183.

[3] 'A Treatise on the Pathology of the Urine,' p. 235.

The clinical history of the hæmatinuria may be said to date from an earlier period than that of the publications referred to, inasmuch as cases of a very similar nature had already been described or alluded to by Dr. Prout,[1] Dr. Elliotson,[2] and Sir Thomas Watson,[3] also by Mons. Rayer, and Mons. Gergères, of Bordeaux.[4] More recently Dr Pavy,[5] Dr. Alfred Wiltshire,[6] and Dr. Murchison,[7] have contributed to the illustration of this disorder.

In the accounts of hæmatinuria which have been given by the different authors to whom I have referred, there exists a very close resemblance. The disorder is essentially intermittent in character, or, as it has been styled, paroxysmal. The attack is preceded by a shivering, or at least a notable feeling of cold, and after the passage of the dark-coloured urine, any general disturbance of the system, and lumbar uneasiness or pain, if such have existed, decline. There is unquestionably such movement of the nervous system in many of the cases as to suggest the relationship of hæmatinuria and ague. Of twenty cases collected by Dr. Roberts, "four had at one time or another suffered from undoubted ague, but in the remainder no evidence or suspicion of ague or malarial poison existed."[8] Sir Thomas Watson, in his Lectures, makes special reference to a connection subsisting between urinary hæmorrhage and ague. Dr. Elliotson, in the clinical lecture already mentioned, gives the following very interesting case :—"It was that of a man with a diseased heart and symptoms of ague ; he was admitted into hospital on the 24th November. He was one of those unfortunate persons who were sent by a very wise Government to Walcheren, where so many thousands of our countrymen lost

---

[1] 'The Nature and Treatment of Stomach and Renal Diseases.' Fifth edition, p. 414.

[2] Clinical Lectures. "Diseases of the Heart united with Ague." 'Lancet,' vol. i, 1831-32, p. 500.

[3] 'Lectures on the Principles and Practice of Physic.' Fourth edition, vol. ii, p. 726.

[4] 'Traité des Maladies des Reins.' Tome troisième, p. 370.

[5] 'Transactions of the Pathological Society of London.' Vol. xviii, p. 157.

[6] *Eodem loco.* Vol. xvi, p. 183.

[7] *Eodem loco.* Vol. xviii, p. 180.

[8] Op. cit., p. 141.

their lives for no purpose whatever. He had this violent fever
of the place, and from that time was never perfectly well. He
is forty years of age; he looked sallow and of a dirty pale hue,
and on that account I asked him if he had had ague; to which
he replied that he had had the fever at Flushing. Now this
man was labouring under frequent chills, but had not regular
paroxysms of ague. You will find it a common circumstance
for ague not to be perfect in all its stages, but for various
degrees of shaking to take place from time to time. That was
the case with this man. The singular circumstance, however,
in this man's disease was, that, when his paroxysms came on
he discharged bloody urine. . . . Now, in this man, the
kidneys discharged blood, at least there was blood in the urine;
at first pure blood, and afterwards less and less, and this he
said was invariably the case—hæmaturia every time the cold
fit came on. This circumstance, however, made no difference
in the treatment, and I gave him sulphate of quinine. I
mentioned, however, that he had had a disease of the heart.
There was a great impulse of the left ventricle; but this was
only a recent occurrence, and the cause of it I do not know.
There was also a strong, full, sharp pulse, and on that account
I bled him to a pint, put him on low diet, and kept his bowels
open every day. He was bled on the 25th to another pint, on
account of the violent action. The aguish symptoms were now
quite certain, for I had observed them myself, and I therefore
gave him 5 grains of sulphate of quinine three times a day.
He was bled again on the 6th of December to 16 ounces. He
bore it well, and, in fact, was all the better for it. He then
took 10 grains of sulphate of quinine three times a day till he
became perfectly well, so far as his aguish symptoms were
concerned. He lost the rigors, he lost the cold fit, and lost
the bloody urine. The bloody urine was intermittent like the
rigors; that is an interesting circumstance. I never met with
an instance of a similar description. There can be no doubt of
its truth, because the man showed his urine, and the blood was
abundant in it. He was presently quite well, so far as this was
concerned, and the symptoms arising from hypertrophy of the
heart were much diminished. Having had aguish fever, however, in the severe form which he suffered, whenever the east
wind blows, or he is exposed to cold and wet, or commits any

errors in diet, or is guilty of any debauchery, he will be liable
to a return of the disease."

I think it worth while to give Dr. Elliotson's concluding
remarks on the case, which have a special reference to its
treatment. " You have seen several times, in the course of the
winter, that when blood-letting is indicated, the indication; to
give sulphate of quinine does not interfere with the depletion.
This man was bled on account of the great impulse of the heart,
three times to a pint, and the symptoms for which the bleeding
was instituted were not aggravated by the quinine, nor, on the
other hand, was the cure of the aguish symptoms by the quinine
at all impeded by the bleeding. The diseased heart and
bloody urine appeared to have no connection with the other,
but the bloody urine depended on the ague. Although the
man considered himself quite well, his ague and hæmaturia
having been cured, and the impulse of the heart having been
considerably diminished, yet he will, of course, through the
Walcheren expedition, be a shattered man as long as he
lives."

M. Rayer, in treating of renal hæmorrhages, notices, under
his third group—" Hémorrhagies Rénales Essentielles "—the
case of Dr. Elliotson just quoted, and likewise a very interesting one recorded by M. Gergères, in which the relation of
aguish symptoms and hæmaturia is very clearly exhibited.[1]
Rayer also refers to a similar instance previously published
by a Dr. Stewart.[2] It is, of course conjectural that these

---

[1] " Un cas analogue est rapporté par le Docteur Gergères :—Un jeune
homme, capitaine de navire, jouissant habituellement d'une bonne santé, fut
pris pendant deux heures de frissons très vifs, après lesquels se développa
une forte chaleur : pendant cette période, le malade eut besoin d'uriner;
mais, au lieu d'urine, il rendit par l'urèthre une grande quantité de sang.
Quelques heures après, une sueur s'établit, et le malade se crut guéri. Le
lendemain, à la même heure, retour des mêmes accidens fébriles, et de
l'évacuation du sang. M. Gergères prescrit un traitement émollient tant
interne qu'externe. Les symptômes cédèrent encore à la même heure que
dans le premier accès. Le troisième jour, les mêmes phénomènes se repro-
duisirent encore avec plus de violence. Dès-lors on s'empressa, vers la fin
de l'acces, d'administrer le sulfate de quinine à la dose de vingt cinq grains ;
ce moyen mit fin à tous les accidens, et en empêcha le retour."

[2] " Antérieurement Stewart avait publié l'observation d'une hematurie
periodique, traitée sans succés, depuis huit mois, par la diète et le régime

were instances of hæmatinuria. I agree, however, with Dr. Harley in thinking it[1] highly probable that the case recorded by Dr. Elliotson is the exact counterpart of those he has described.

Paroxysmal hæmatinuria appears to be almost limited to the male sex; only one of the twenty cases collected by Dr. Roberts occurred in a female. In the same series of cases, the age of the patients at the commencement of the disease ranged from two to forty-eight years. Two cases were under twenty, seven between twenty and thirty, six between thirty and forty, two between forty and fifty, while in three the date of invasion is not specified.

Whether connected with malaria or not, there can be no doubt as to the important influence of cold, more especially when associated with damp, in exciting the paroxysm of hæmatinuria. To this circumstance all observers of the disease have borne testimony. It is well illustrated in the two cases which have fallen under my notice, and to which I shall now call attention, leaving a few remarks on the pathology and treatment of this obscure disease for the close of my communication.

A. H—, æt 25, a clerk; in height 5 feet 4½ inches; of weight 8 stone 7 lbs.; an orphan. Has two brothers both of whom are healthy. First seen on the 11th December, 1874, and again on the 18th of the same month, when he informed me that, for fully three months, he has not ceased to pass dark urine daily after midday. He had good health till September, 1873, when he for the first time noticed the dark colour of the urine. The dark appearance of the urine was not at that time persistent; it occurred on an average about once a week for some weeks. After a few weeks, the urine resumed its normal appearance, and this continued till the autumn of 1874. He had overtaxed his strength by walking to Queensferry, a distance of nine miles, to visit the Channel Fleet, and had also been exposed to cold and damp. After this the dark urine reappeared. He has never received any blow or injury over the loins, nor has he at any time experienced pain in the lumbar region.[2]

---

antiphlogistique, et qui guérit dans l'espace de trois mois par le quinquina et les toniques. Le sixième mois de ce traitement, le malade était complete-ment rétabli."

[1] Op. cit., p. 173.

[2] I make this observation more particularly in connection with the fol-lowing interesting statement of Sir William Gull:—"There is reason for thinking that a blow or injury to the loins may give rise to this complaint

The urine has on no occasion been dark before 11 a.m. His usual breakfast has consisted of a cup of tea with sugar and cream or milk, or of porridge with milk, with a small piece of ham, and a little bread or toast. On Sundays, when keeping in the house, during the whole day, the dark urine does not appear. Before the dark urine is passed, he invariably feels general discomfort, and a sensation of coldness over the whole frame, but this has never amounted to a shivering or rigor. He is very pale, with a distinct icteric tint of the conjunctivæ. A well-marked anæmic murmur is audible over the base of the heart, accompanying the systolic sound, and a loud *bruit de diable* exists in the neck. There are no scorbutic marks on the surface of the body, no petechial spots, and no other form of hæmorrhage has at any time occurred. The patient's blood, when viewed under the microscope, shows no excess of colourless corpuscles; there is, however, manifest diminution of the red globules. The urine, after reposing for a brief time in a conical glass vessel, presents the following characters:—is of dark colour resembling port wine, possessing a fleshy odour, of acid reaction, having a density of 1022, highly coagulable on the application of heat and addition of nitric acid, a dirty-brown precipitate being thrown down by the former, and by the latter a deep chocolate-coloured mass.

A very considerable brownish sediment falls to the bottom of the glass, and this, when viewed under the microscope, is found to consist of reddish or brownish-red granular matter, with numerous granular casts of the tubuli uriniferi.

Dr. Affleck, who kindly undertook a careful chemical examination of the urine of this patient, both when abnormally coloured and when free from blood pigment, has favoured me with the following report:—" The investigation bore reference more especially to the amount of urea, and to the presence of the bile acids. 1. As to the urea. I found, after repeated experiments, in which a marked uniformity of result was obtained, that the urine, without hæmato-globuline, contained nearly one fourth more urea than that with it, viz. 92 and 93 grains in the former, and 71 and 81 grains in the latter, per 12 ounces of urine respectively. 2. As to the bile acids. After a long and careful search, I failed to find any distinct evidence of their presence in either specimen of urine. The plan pursued was that laid down by Neubauer and Vogel in their

—intermittent hæmatinuria. Thus, a young lady, in getting into a railway carriage, fell and hurt her back. Soon afterwards she passed dark bloody-looking water. I carefully examined the secretion by the aid of the microscope, but found in it no blood-corpuscles, and only the granular pigment-matter of disintegrated blood-corpuscles."—Op. cit., p. 390.

work. Ample time was given, and full justice done to all parts of the process, and I believe, had bile acids been present in any appreciable quantity, they would have been detected." Dr. Affleck adds, "I ought to mention, that in both investigations I enjoyed the able assistance of Mr. A. D. Murray. Although the result is largely negative, yet even this may not be without its use."

Respecting the elimination of urea, Dr. George Harley had observed, that during the attack of intermittent hæmaturia in the cases recorded by him, the passage of urea was excessive, and that copious deposition of urates also took place.[1] Dr. Dickinson and Dr. Gee found the urea above the average, but quite within the limit of normal variation.[2] The former physician, however, in an earlier account of the disease, has remarked, "The urine during these attacks always contained a great excess of urea."[3] The difference between the urine of ordinary hæmaturia and that of intermittent or paroxysmal hæmatinuria is well expressed by Dr. Harley:—"In ordinary hæmaturia, the urine is not only coagulable by heat and nitric acid, but contains blood-corpuscles, which are gradually deposited on standing; while in this form of intermittent hæmaturia, as in some cases of the non-intermittent variety, the urine, although coagulable by heat and nitric acid, contains no blood-corpuscles, and the colouring matter is not deposited on standing. Besides this, the urine contains numerous granular tube-casts, an increased percentage of urea, and a deposit of amorphous urates."[4]

As to the presence or absence of bile acids, I had suggested to Dr. Affleck the importance of determining this point in the urine of hæmatinuria, keeping in view the observation of Kühne, that the bile acids have a powerful dissolving effect on the blood-cells, and the suggestion of Dr. Parkes, that some cases of hæmaturia in the urine, might be owing to an action of this kind in febrile icterus.

On the 11th of December, the patient, whose case I have been relating, began to take quinine in five-grain doses, thrice

---

[1] Loc. cit., p. 170.
[2] Ditto, p. 177.
[3] 'Transactions of the Pathological Society of London,' vol. xvi, p. 175.
[4] Ditto, vol. xvi, p. 168.

daily. He had formerly, while under the care of Dr. Menzies, been treated with gallic acid, in doses of 15 grains, thrice daily; but this astringent, so useful in many cases of ordinary hæmaturia, had in no measure influenced the discharge of blood pigment.

A few days thereafter, no appreciable change having taken place, the dose of quinine was elevated to 7 grains, thrice daily, before meals, and in addition, the patient was ordered 10 grains of the citrate of iron and ammonia an hour after meals. The effect of this treatment was apparently to lessen the amount of blood-colouring matter in the urine, and for two days together, on one or two occasions, the dark colour entirely disappeared. While continuing the medicines, the hæmatinuria returned during the very cold weather which immediately preceded last Christmas; still its occurrence was limited to the afternoons; and when the patient confined himself entirely to the house, it did not appear. Rather unpleasant symptoms of cinchonism having presented themselves, while it was evident the remedies had failed to check the discharge of hæmatin, I ordered, on the 28th of December, 20 grains of the chloride of ammonium, sal ammoniac, to be taken, simply dissolved in water, thrice daily· On the 20th of January 1875, I found that from the day on which this medicine was commenced, no dark urine had been passed. In connection with this observation, however, it must be kept in view that the atmospheric temperature, which had, previous to the 1st of January, been very low, then rose, and milder weather continued to prevail. After this date, the patient has on two occasions omitted the remedy, with the effect of the hæmatinuria returning. I had prescribed the tincture of the perchloride of iron in 15-drop doses, thrice daily, and while taking this medicine, the dark urine reappeared. It should be mentioned, that when the hæmatin was absent from the urine, the characters presented by the secretion were, as nearly as possible, those of health; and in particular, there existed no coagulability with heat or nitric acid.

On no occasion did I observe the hæmato-crystalline, although very diligently looked for, on account of Sir William Gull's observation. "The granules," remarks Sir William, "when carefully examined, are found to consist chiefly of very small prismatic crystals of hæmatin; and even such granules as are not so distinctly crystalline are, on changing the focus, seen to have a somewhat crystalline appearance." The minute granules in the case I have described were at no time crystalline in appearance.[1]

The case now briefly narrated is the second instance of hæmatinuria with which I have met. An earlier one came under my notice in February, 1873, having been sent to me by Dr. Macleod of Hawick. From Dr. Macleod I have received the letter written to him after examining this patient, a gentleman of upwards of fifty years of age. I now take the liberty of transcribing certain portions of that communication :

"Mr. H—'s case is one of great interest. No urines could be more different than the two specimens he brought with him to-day, voided within a few hours of each other; the one normal in its character, containing no trace of albumen or blood; the other of a deep porter colour, due to the presence of blood colouring-matter. The blood no doubt comes from the kidney. Under the microscope there are visible granular casts of the tubuli uriniferi, a few crystals of oxalate of lime, and some of uric acid; also much amorphous and granular matter, but no blood-discs. The latter circumstance is of much significancy, and allies the case with the so-called hæmatinuria—that is, the passage in the urine of hæmatin as distinguished from hæmaturia. I do not think there exists any evidence of renal calculus (of the existence of which malady the patient himself was suspicious), and I believe that the affection in Mr. H— is connected with the ague, or feverish disorder resembling ague, from which he suffers. The presence of blood in the urine, Mr. H— tells me, is generally to be traced to exposure to cold, while warmth wards off the attack. I think Mr. H—'s case less serious on account of its being hæmatinuria. He must be very careful in avoiding exposure to cold and fatigue; he ought to clothe warmly, wearing flannel next the skin, and particularly across the loins; live generously, but on simple food, not eating much animal food, and drinking only light wine. Will you order for him thirty drops of the liquor ferri per-nitratis, to be taken thrice daily after meals, with four minims of the liquor arsenicalis? After a little time, full doses of quinine may be tried; and in the event of any severe or protracted attack occurring, I should wish Mr. H— to take the oil of turpentine, in doses of twenty or thirty drops, repeatedly. I think you may speak encouragingly to Mr. H—."

[1] This seems a disease in which the employment of Mr. Mahomed's interesting test of the presence of blood in the urine in minute quantity, or rather of the crystalloids of the blood, might with some advantage be made. By a careful use of the guaiacum and ozonic ether test, infinitesimal traces of blood can be detected in the urine. See "The Etiology of Bright's

Dr. Macleod subsequently informed me that this gentleman had his first attack of hæmatinuria about eight years before his visit to me, and that it occurred after a severe chill or rigor when seal-shooting in the Hebrides. Subsequent attacks took place under circumstances somewhat similar; one in particular, in autumn weather, when exposed to cold in the coursing field. Mr. H— now resides in the north of England, and has from time to time consulted Dr. William Murray, of Newcastle. From the patient himself I had recently the following interesting letter :—"I cannot say I am any better. The attacks now are brought on by a much slighter exposure to cold, and consequently are more frequent; but I do not suffer the same amount of pain, nor have I the shivering fits as formerly, but I am altogether weaker. I seldom go out since the cold weather set in, and only in a covered conveyance ; still, even with this precaution, I am sure to suffer from an attack of more or less severity, my urine at the time varying in colour from pale coffee to blood. During last summer, for about two months, when the temperature ranged about 60°, I was free from attacks, as I am now when I keep in the house at 60°. I have said that the extreme pain and shivering have not accompanied late attacks, and sometimes I am not sure in slight ones whether it is an attack or not until I attempt to make water; then I can tell at once, by the penis being drawn back almost entirely into the body, if the water is to be ever so little discoloured. I think I did not mention this when I saw you, nor am I sure that I had then noticed it. I had an attack of jaundice last May."

The last statement is one of importance. There is some connection, I believe, between liver disorder and the passage of hæmatin in the urine. Dr. Roberts remarks—"In most cases the patient has presented a somewhat sallow and icteric aspect, or has looked pale and sickly." Dr. Harley's first patient was slightly jaundiced, "as a result," Dr. Harley adds, "most probably, of the malarial poison, from the effects of which he had not as yet entirely recovered. The varying condition of the three urines," the same writer observes, "clearly pointed to intense congestion of the chylopoietic

Disease and the Prealbuminuric Stage," by Fred. A. Mahomed, M.R.C.S., 'Medico-Chirurgical Transactions,' vol. lvii.

viscera of a transient and periodic character. Fitting the practice to the theory, mercurials, and afterwards quinine, were taken by this gentleman, in order to remove the congestion of the chylopoietic viscera, and check the periodicity of the disease. The results were most favorable; for although four years have passed away, he has never had a recurrence of these urinary symptoms." In Dr. Harley's second case, the sallowness which the patient exhibited appeared to be due to some disturbance of the hepatic functions. The man admitted that he was a very bilious subject. Similar treatment resulted in the patient's complete recovery. The notable connection of liver disorder with hæmatinuria, just like that of ague, while seen in certain instances, has not been observed in any considerable number of the recorded cases. The influence of cold is, however, universal; and this remarkable circumstance has in some individuals been observed, that " the hæmorrhage," to use Dr. Dickinson's words, " has always ceased on the removal of the cold which produced it, and has recurred with undiminished readiness on the next exposure."[1]

Dr. George Johnson, it is well known, has called particular attention to the circumstance of temporary albuminuria following cold bathing.[2] Recently the subject of albuminuria, hæmaturia, and hæmatinuria, in their relation to thermic neuroses, and to taking cold, has received a most interesting illustration by Dr. Laycock.[3]

In the paper to which I refer, Dr. Laycock has given some instructive examples of transient neurotic albuminuria, and he has pointed out that there is much in common, in certain cases, between albuminuria and hæmaturia, and, it may be added, hæmatinuria. Dr. Laycock believes, and he appeals to facts in support of this belief, that " in the process known as taking cold, there is always a change induced in the trophic nervous system [this does not, in his view, mean the vaso-motor system only, but that larger system which, including the vaso-motor as a higher and special evolution of it, presides over the primary or vegetative organic processes of nutrition, so as to modify

---

[1] Op. cit., p. 179.
[2] ' British Medical Journal,' vol. ii, for 1873.
[3] " On Neurotic Albuminuria and Hæmaturia." 'Dublin Journal of Medical Science,' July, 1874.

the chemical conditions of the blood-corpuscles, lymph, and tissues in general, as well as the contraction of the blood-vessels and the distribution of the blood], both locally and generally, such that one or other of a numerous group of trophic changes result in organs and tissues, and that this morbid and morbific change is one of the primary and most essential conditions of the process."

There can be little doubt that, in the curious disease which we are considering—a person apparently in his usual health, on being exposed to cold, even to a modified degree of cold, passing bloody urine, which phenomenon ceases for the time when the individual is placed in a higher temperature—an injurious impression is made on the nervous system by the cold, and it is when the surface of the body is chilled, that the kidney disturbance is effected. That the renal function should be so seriously, although only temporarily, influenced, as to determine the passage of either albumen, blood, or blood-colouring matter, it may, I think, be presumed, and more particularly in the latter case, which we are considering, that some morbid change in the blood itself, although it has as yet eluded detection, has existed ; some product, probably, of faulty hepatic function being the "fons et origo mali." According to our present knowledge, unquestionably defective, I think it very probable, that in paroxysmal hæmatinuria the primary morbid change takes place in the blood. The kidney, however, speedily suffers. Sir William Gull, in the course of some interesting and suggestive observations on the pathology of this disease, specifies "pains in the loins," as showing, along with the remarkable urinary changes, that the kidneys are affected. But lumbar pain is by no means a necessary, I doubt if it be more than an occasional, concomitant of the disordered secretion; while the appearance the urine presents, and its features, when carefully examined, are quite sufficient to establish the implication of the kidney. The kidney forms the hæmatin, the colouring matter of the urine ; and in order to accomplish this important function, the organ must be in a tolerably healthy condition. Sir William Gull illustrates this by a reference to what occurs in certain cases of post-scarlatinal nephritis. "We frequently," he says, "see hæmatinuria as a sequela of scarlet fever. The usual history is as follows :—After an attack of scarlet fever the child passes albumen and blood in its urine. The microscope shows that blood-corpuscles are present. The affection is a simple hæmorrhage from the kidneys. But when the child advances towards recovery, and the kidneys begin to resume their functions, although albumen may be present in the urine, we no longer find blood-corpuscles, these being replaced by hæmatin. The urine is dusky, but contains no blood-corpuscles. The kidneys have regained their functions so far that they can now break up the blood-corpuscles. In the next stage the urine, still containing albumen in small quantities, presents uric acid and urates, and we then know that the kidneys are beginning to recover themselves. In the fourth stage the urine contains no albumen, but urates, urea, and its natural colouring matter. The kidneys have then totally regained their functions, and we have seen, step by step, the dynamical power of these organs return."

The analogy between the urine thus affected and hæmatinuria as it occurs in cases such as those I have described, is a tenable one. It is not of course perfect, for in the cases we have been considering, the uric acid excreting function of the kidney is preserved, and, as we have seen, the power of discharging urea may even be increased. Still, the function of converting hæmatin into normal urinary pigment is interrupted; or, as Sir William Gull expresses it, the kidneys " ought to eliminate the hæmatin in the condition of urine pigment; instead of that they eliminate the hæmatin itself."

As to treatment, warmth is evidently the remedial agent of the highest efficiency in this disease. It is alike preventive and curative. In many cases the attack is warded off so long as the surface of the body is kept warm; and in all instances on record, the restoration of heat, when that has been removed, has led to the cessation of the attack.

The astringent remedies which are so useful in the treatment of ordinary hæmaturia signally fail to exert any therapeutic action in paroxysmal hæmatinuria. This, at all events, may be affirmed of acetate of lead, gallic acid, and the preparations of iron, although the latter are indispensable in combating the resulting anæmia.

Quinine, in full doses, is unquestionably a valuable remedy. Next to heat, it may for the present be considered as the remedy of most value in paroxysmal hæmatinuria. It has, however, failed in other hands; and in the case, the details of which I have now given, it also failed, while another remedy apparently succeeded. That remedy was the chloride of ammonium—the sal ammoniac. It would be very absurd to extol the virtues of the muriate of ammonia in paroxysmal hæmatinuria on the strength of one case only; but I am anxious to bring its employment to the notice of the profession, being very hopeful of its being found serviceable in this as well as in other diseases of neurotic origin.

I was led to employ it in the case now narrated from reflecting on the very remarkable deobstruent and alterative properties which that salt possesses, more especially in relation to hepatic disorders, and, further, from its frequently great power in relieving neuralgic suffering.

Acting directly on the nervous system and on the blood, it appeared to me a medicine, likely to exert a beneficial influence in a disease, in which disturbance of nervous system and of blood unquestionably coexisted. In this expectation I have not been disappointed in the only case in which I have as yet had the opportunity of employing it.

XXIX.

ANCIENT AND MODERN PRACTICE OF MEDICINE.

(*An Address in Medicine, delivered at the Forty-third Annual Meeting of the British Medical Association, held in Edinburgh, August, 1875, and reprinted from the 'British Medical Journal,' August 7th, 1875.*)

When the late distinguished Professor of Logic and Metaphysics in the University of Edinburgh inquired, " Has the *practice* of medicine made a single step since Hippocrates ?" and in vindication of his own belief in the negative conclusion, referred to the recorded opinions of several eminent authorities of modern times in the profession, he put a question which no thoughtful mind within the pale of medicine will be inclined to evade, and the consideration of which, after some sort, may suitably engage our attention in such a meeting as the present.

Sir William Hamilton, in penning the question referred to, had under review 'An Account of the Life, Lectures, and Writings of William Cullen, M.D.,' the famous Professor of the Practice of Medicine in the University of Edinburgh from 1769 to 1790, by Dr. John Thomson ; and having noticed, in terms of well-deserved commendation, the masterly execution of his task by the eminent author of the 'Lectures on Inflammation,' and accompanied him in a brief survey of the doctrines promulgated by the renowned triumvirate of the early part of the eighteenth century, to wit, Hoffmann, Stahl, and Boerhaave, he

was tempted by a mild reflection of Cullen on the practice of
Stahl, which censure, indeed, was judged too indiscriminating
by Dr. Thomson, to indulge in a philippic against the modern
practitioners of the healing art, quoting what for his purpose
appeared to be the apposite'phrase of Hoffmann, " Fuge medicos
et medicamenta si vis esse salvus," and that of Celsus, " Optima
medicina est non uti medicinâ." The vehemence of Sir William
Hamilton's denunciation is more fully explained by a note
published in 1853, to the original article, which had appeared
in the 'Edinburgh Review' for July, 1832, where it is shown
that the dangers which are to be apprehended in the practice
of medicine arise, in Sir William Hamilton's opinion, from the
illiterate rashness of its practitioners, for he transfers to his
pages, with very evident satisfaction, the statement of Dr.
Gregory : "I think it more than possible that in fifty or a
hundred years the business of physician will not be regarded
even in England, as either a learned or a liberal profession."
If the medical faculty of the University of Edinburgh had in
any measure justly laid itself open to the charge of hastening
the decadence of learning in the profession, it will be admitted
by every dispassionate inquirer that the statutes and regulations
of that University relative to degrees in medicine entitle it, at
the present time, to be regarded as in the van of those bodies,
which are striving for the honour and advance of the medical
profession. It is, indeed, impossible to read the animadversions
of Sir William Hamilton without coming to the conclusion
that learning in the practitioners of medicine, by which he
evidently understood general culture and, in particular, classical
attainments, was, in his opinion, the great desideratum.
Between learning of the nature referred to, and usefulness in
medicine, as dependent upon ample professional qualifications,
there is really nothing antagonistic. Not a few of the most
distinguished men in the profession in quite recent times have
been accomplished scholars. But, while this holds true, let it
be distinctly understood that learning of the kind in question
is not supreme ; it is secondary in importance to ability in the
healing art. I make bold to say that not a few physicians,
with no pretension whatever to learning, have served their
generation well, and have done much to recommend the profession they zealously cultivated, if they cannot be said to have

adorned it. If, therefore, it were necessary to decide between the claims of medicine as a learned or so-called liberal profession and as an useful art, the preference must be awarded to the latter. Let us be thankful, however, that no such issue is before us. Medicine *is* a liberal profession, and will, doubtless, continue to be so, although the diffusion throughout its ranks of polite learning may have become diminished, a result which is to be in no small measure attributed to the very great enlargement which has taken place in all that is proper to medicine itself. Think of the rapid advances which have been made during the last thirty years in such departments of medicine as animal chemistry, physiology, pathology, and psychology; and then consider how limited is the time at the disposal of him who is expected to acquire at least a competent knowledge of these sciences, for the cultivation of other subjects, however elevating and attractive. That there exists nothing hostile in the study of medicine, as now pursued, to distinction in other walks, is evident from the circumstance that members of our profession, in no way favorably placed for the study, have achieved distinction in scholarship. Look at the career of the late Francis Adams, toiling as a country surgeon in Aberdeenshire, and yet distinguished as the translator of Hippocrates, Aretæus, and Paulus Ægineta. Who can fail to sympathise with the feelings of that accomplished man when, in drawing his *magnum opus* to a close, he thus expressed himself: " I shall conclude this argument and my present task, by quoting the memorable words in which Cicero apologises for his having spent a certain portion of his time in the cultivation of elegant literature and of philosophy, leaving the reader to apply the same in the case of Hippocrates, and, I may be permitted to add, in that of the humble editor of the present volume, who trusts he shall not be set down as an idle and unprofitable practitioner of the art because he has found leisure, amidst the turmoil and distraction of a professional life, to communicate to his countrymen the important opinions contained in the genuine remains of the Coan sage."

It has been my happy lot to meet with others who, although less distinguished, some indeed wholly unknown to fame, have cultivated, in circumstances quite as trying, their natural taste for classical and other learning.

> " Along the cool sequester'd vale of life
> They kept the noiseless tenor of their way."

In remote districts of the country, undergoing a daily round of fatigue and anxiety, which must needs try the strength both of body and mind to the very utmost, mine, moreover, has been the privilege to meet and have friendly intercourse with men, who were ably discharging the duties of their calling, and were at the same time being leant upon by the whole community in which their lot was cast, not only as the advisers in sickness, but as persons on whose counsel and judgment all reliance was to be placed.

Having formed the acquaintance of such men, I have with pride reflected on the circumstance that the individuals who were the recipients of so much confidence, and whose friendship was so highly prized, were members of the profession to which we have the happiness to belong. It is not the least of the advantages possessed by membership of this great Association, that in our annual meeting the bands of fellowship among us are apt to be greatly strengthened.

The question of Sir William Hamilton, to which reference has been made, leads us, in the first place, to a brief consideration of the practice of medicine at the period of Hippocrates.

Intimately acquainted, as Sir William Hamilton was, with the whole history of philosophy, he knew the close alliance which existed between philosophy and medicine in ancient times. The most renowned philosophers, antecedent to and contemporaneous with Hippocrates, applied themselves to the study of medicine. Numerous are the references to medicine in the writings of these philosophers. Take, for example, the following passage from the *Phædrus* of Plato, in which not only is the relation referred to, but the name of Hippocrates is introduced.

Socrates remarks : Rhetoric is like medicine.

Phædrus. How is that?

Socrates. Why, because medicine has to define the nature of the body, and rhetoric of the soul, if you would proceed not empirically but scientifically ; in the one case, to impart health and strength by giving medicine and food ; in the other, to implant the conviction which you require by the right use of the words and principles.

Phædrus. You are probably right in that.

Socrates. And do you think that you can know the nature of the soul intelligently without knowing the nature of the whole?

Phædrus. Hippocrates the Asclepiad says that this is the only method of procedure by which the nature of the body can be understood.

Socrates. Yes, friend, and he says truly. Still, we ought not to be content with the name of Hippocrates, but to examine and see whether he has reason on his side.

Phædrus. True.

Socrates. Then, consider what this is which Hippocrates says, and which right reason says about this or any other nature.[1]

(' The Dialogues of Plato,' by B. Jowett, M.A., vol. i, page 605.) in speculations as to the phenomena of disease, it is in the highest degree improbable that these philosophers ever practised the healing art. It is, indeed, worthy of remark that in subsequent, although still ancient times, the intimate connection which had subsisted between philosophy and medicine was not regarded as favorable to the growth of the latter, and the share he had in effecting their divorcement is held by Celsus as a reason for eulogising Hippocrates. " Hujus autem, ut quidam crediderunt, discipulus Hippocrates Cous, primus quidem ex omnibus memoriâ dignis, ab studio sapientiæ disciplinam hanc separavit, vir et arte et facundiâ insignis " (*De Medicinâ,* liber primus). Medicine, however, had been cultivated after a fashion long antecedent to the birth-time of philosophy. The doctor-priests of the Grecian temples, or Asclepiadæ, had acknowledged Æsculapius as its origin. The Asclepia, or temples, were erected in many parts of Greece, were ruled by the Asclepiadæ, and used in a manner not very unlike that in which hospitals are employed in modern times. To them the sick resorted for advice and cure. In one of the most distinguished of these temples, namely, that of Cos, built on the island of the same name, one of the Sporades, a group of scattered islands, as their appellation denotes, in the Ægean Sea, off the island of Crete and west coast of Asia Minor, Hippocrates, inheriting a recognised position, acted as an

[1] ' The Dialogues of Plato,' by B. Jowett, M.A., vol. i, page 605.

Æsculapian priest. He had been born, in all probability, in the four hundred and sixtieth year before the birth of Christ. But Hippocrates had not only the advantage of the most favorable study in the Asclepion of Cos; we know, on excellent authority, that, under the direction of Herodicus of Selymbria in Thrace, he became intimately acquainted with the practice then pursued in the gymnasia, while, through the instructions of Gorgias and Democritus, the former of Leontini in Sicily, the latter of Abdera in Thrace, and himself illustrious as the originator of the doctrine of atoms, he became thoroughly versed in the literature and philosophy of the age.

The foundation of the practice of Hippocrates, with which we are now more immediately concerned, was experience; but this experience of Hippocrates was rational in character, not a mere blind or misguided empiricism. No one could be more convinced of the fallaciousness of a blind empiricism than he was, and his condemnation of it may be recognised in the earliest, the best known, and, perhaps, the grandest of all the Hippocratic aphorisms, "ἡ πεῖρα σφαλερὴ ἡ κρίσις χαλεπή," "experimentum periculosum, judicium difficile." Hippocrates believed in the existence of a principle, a spiritual essence, the preserver of all things in nature, the restorer of whatever had become disordered. The regulation and superintendence of all the actions of the system were due to this principle, to which he gave the name of Φύσις, Nature. Thus, he was led to consider that the chief duty of the physician consisted in watching the operations of Nature, endeavouring, as might be the case, to promote or restrain these, possibly in some, but these very rare instances, to counteract them. "Our natures," he remarks, or if not he, one of his immediate descendants, who may reasonably be supposed to be expressing the views of the master, "our natures are the physicians of our diseases." "Νουσῶν φύσιες ἰητροί." It is in reference to this exposition of the function at once of Nature and the physician in relation to disease, that Sydenham, "the chief of English practical physicians," who in many particulars resembled the Father of Medicine, observes: "He it is whom we can never duly praise. He it is who then laid the solid and immovable foundation for the whole superstructure of medicine, when he taught that 'our natures are the physicians of our diseases.'" And, again,

" The great sagacity of this man had discovered that Nature by herself determines diseases and is of herself sufficient in all things against all of them." The belief which Hippocrates had in this " vis conservatrix," " vis naturæ medicatrix," would, in the first place, make him, as we know from his writings he really was, a very close observer of the operations of nature. It would further render him cautious in regard to interference with these, and resolute in his determination, as it has been said, "to have two special objects in view, with regard to diseases, namely, to do good, and to do no harm." There is, however, no ground for concluding that Hippocrates was an inert or purely expectant practitioner. On the contrary, there is abundant proof in the works which bear his name that, in limiting, as Sydenham has expressed it, " the province of medical art to the support of Nature when she was enfeebled, and to the coercion of her when she was outrageous," Hippocrates found occasion to be bold and decided in his method of treatment. His employment of powerful remedies is best exhibited in the instances of diseases which, according to the humoral doctrine promulgated by him, were to be relieved by the discharge of some peccant humour. Evacuants of various kinds were used with this intention, purgatives more especially, but likewise emetics, diuretics, and sudorifics. He drew blood by means of the lancet, the scarificator, and the cupping instrument, but with what careful consideration and thoughtfulness is well shown in the treatise Περὶ Διαίτης 'Οξέων, ' On the Regimen in Acute Diseases,' in which he remarks concerning the treatment of pleuritis : " But if the pain be not removed by the fomentations, we ought not to foment for a long time, for this dries the lungs and promotes suppuration ; but if the pain point to the clavicle, or if there be heaviness in the arm or about the breast, or above the diaphragm, one should open the inner vein at the elbow and not hesitate to abstract a large quantity of blood, until it becomes much redder, or, instead of being pure red, it becomes livid ; for both these states occur." What forcibly strikes the reader of the passage now quoted, and of those passages which immediately precede and follow it, is, as indeed Galen among the ancient and many of the modern commentators of Hippocrates have carefully noted, the manner in which the Father of Medicine commences with the milder means of affording relief from the pain of pleuritis, such as the employment of fomentations, the rules for the preparation and application of which, as laid down by him, are simply admirable; and only in the event of these failing to accomplish the object in view he counsels that recourse should be had to bloodletting and the use of other powerful remedies, including cathartics. In another part of the same treatise, the following rule is laid down for the employment of bloodletting : "Bleed in the acute affections, if the disease appear strong and the patients be in the vigour of life, and if they have strength." Surely, this is a most cautious limitation of the circumstances in which the remedy is, in the mind of the writer, to be advantageously employed. In one passage, however, if not in more than one of the Hippocratic writings, there is reference made to the production of "deliquium animi," "leipothymia," or "leipopsychia," as the Greeks termed it, by bloodletting in the treatment of acute diseases. This rule, which was opposed by the ancient authorities generally, cannot be said to have been invariably acted upon by Hippocrates.

A study of the method of treatment pursued by the Father of Medicine and his immediate descendants exhibits the fact that their rules of procedure were all based on experience. He had the merit of discovering the great truth that accurate observation in medicine is the real foundation of all knowledge, and he proceeded in the true spirit of the inductive philosophy to generalise solely from the phenomena thus observed. It can never cease to afford material for wonder that through the genius of one man so much was accomplished, when we reflect on the circumstance that in the time of Hippocrates human anatomy had scarcely, if at all, been practised, that physiology was virtually unknown, and the use of remedial agents was almost entirely limited to articles of the vegetable kingdom, and these the indigenous plants of Greece and the neighbouring countries. To the subject of diet and regimen, however, Hippocrates paid the greatest attention. In the Hippocratic writings there occur terms which exactly correspond with those we so frequently employ : full, ordinary, and low diet. In the treatise Περὶ Ἀγμῶν the following passage occurs :—"A diet slightly restricted will be sufficient in those cases in which there was no external wound at first, or when the bone does-not protrude; but one should live rather sparingly until the tenth day, as being now deprived of exercise; and tender articles of food should be used, such as moderately loosen the bowels; but one should abstain altogether from flesh and wine, and then by degrees resume a more nourishing diet." And so, not to multiply quotations, in the treatise already referred to, and in 'Αφορισμοί, there are many interesting and instructive suggestions to be found regarding the administration of food and wine. It is sufficient, in passing, to make a brief reference to the paramount importance Hippocrates attached to the doctrine of crisis, and to the bearing which this had on the treatment of diseases. The doctrine of crisis, indeed, was an essential part of his system of humoralism, and had in consequence an intimate connection with the method of treatment he pursued. Critical events were evacuations of different kinds, occurring chiefly by the skin, bowels, and kidneys.

With the views he entertained as to crisis, there is further intimately blended the so-called Hippocratic doctrine of critical days. Galen expressly affirms that Hippocrates was the first author who treated of these; but, whether this be true or not, we know that he attached very considerable importance to the doctrine. "Fevers," he remarks, "come to a crisis on the same days as to number on which men recover and die." It was the particular attention given by Hippocrates to the tendencies manifested by diseases to recovery, or, on the other hand, to an unfavorable termination, also to the occurrence of evacuations or of crises in their course, that led to the remarkable care with which he studied the whole subject of prognosis. There is no more interesting or valuable work in the whole Hippocratic collection than the one entitled Προγνωστικόν, ' Prænotiones,' ' Prognostics' ; and happily concerning its authenticity, as the undoubtedly genuine work of the Father of Medicine himself, there has never been any question.

Again, we should be doing serious injustice to the Father of Medicine were we not to notice, and that in terms of the very highest commendation, the profound sagacity exhibited by him in the observation of the influence of external agents on men in health and on disease. This is fully exhibited in the treatise Περὶ 'Αερῶν, 'Υδατῶν, Τοπῶν, in which the operation of the atmosphere, of particular seasons, situation and dwellings of

the people, in the production of health and diseases of different
kinds is discussed. Dr. Adams says of it that "it relates to a
subject of commanding interest, and deserves to be carefully
studied, as containing the oldest exposition which we possess
of the opinions entertained by an original and enlightened
mind on many important questions connected with public
hygiene and political economy, two sciences which of late
years have commanded a large amount of professional attention." Since this passage was written by Dr. Adams, greatly
increased interest has been awakened in these subjects. I
venture to affirm that the most enlightened inquirer concerning
public health, be he legislator or physician, will find much to
instruct him in the pages of Hippocrates.

The narration of individual cases of disease commenced with
Hippocrates; he may, indeed, be said to have been the
originator of the clinical study of medicine. By way of comparison between ancient and modern medicine, some clinical
observations of Hippocrates may be quoted in the first place,
and thereafter certain passages cited from a modern clinical
lecture not unworthy of being placed alongside of the former.
In the first book of the 'Epidemics,' 'Επιδημίων, a, it is thus
written:—"Philiscus, who dwelt near the wall, was laid up.
On the first day, fever acute; he perspired; night very disturbed. Second day, aggravation of symptoms; in the evening,
an injection procured a good stool; night quiet. On the morning of the third day, and up to noon, appeared free from pain;
but in the evening, acute fever, with perspiration; thirst, tongue
dry; passed black urine; night disturbed; he did not sleep at
all; his mind wandered on all subjects. On the fourth day,
general paroxysms; urine black; night more endurable; urine
of improved colour. On the fifth day, about noon, a little
blood escaped from the nostrils; urine varied in appearance
with thready clouds resembling semen irregularly suspended in
it. The urine did not deposit. A suppository caused passage
of some feculent matter with wind. Night distressing; little
sleep; talkativeness; delirium; extremities very cold, and could
not be warmed; the patient voided black urine; he rested a
little towards daybreak; lost speech; had a cold sweat; extremities livid. About the middle of the sixth day, he died.
The respiration was throughout large and rare, like that of a

person who required to be reminded to breathe. The spleen was swollen, and formed a roundish tumour. The perspiration continued to be cold to the end; the paroxysms were on even days." It is to the description here given of the patient's breathing that I wish particularly to call attention. The words employed by Hippocrates are " Τούτῳ πνεῦμα διὰ τέλεος ἀραιὸν μέγα." Galen's commentary on the passage justifies the rendering which has been adopted. Further, we know that the word ἀραιός when used by Hippocrates, whether in reference to the respiration or the pulse, invariably signifies "infrequent," "few in number," "with intervals." Before offering a few observations on this clinical history, I shall give an extract, or rather extracts, from a case recently recorded by Dr. Laycock (' Dublin Journal of Medical Science,' 1873). "J. O'H—, æt. 56, labourer, admitted to hospital November 18th, 1863. No family history obtainable. Previously to admission was employed in sinking a well, which kept him constantly wet; he has not been a temperate man, but enjoyed good health up to four days before his admission. On that day he complained of pain in the chest and some shortness of breath. He attributed this to overwork, but it was so severe as to oblige him to leave off work, and he consequently went to bed. Next day felt better; but the day after he felt very giddy, and was forced to return to bed. On the 17th, about 7 a.m., his wife found him lying half out of bed, and passing urine on the floor; when spoken to, said his left arm felt very heavy, and he could not move it, and that the left leg was the same; he also complained of headache, frontal and temporal, but not severe." There follows a detailed and interesting statement regarding the patient's condition on admission to the Royal Infirmary. I quote the account of his breathing :—" Breathing appears calm for the most part, with frequent intervals of accelerated and laborious breathing. When the act of respiration is suspended, the fact of coughing once or twice does not seem to bring it back ; but if the patient is roused and made to speak, respiration is resumed. The cessation appears to be quite regular in point of time, occupying generally about thirty seconds, and respiration then continues for about twenty-five respirations. The heart's action at such times was accelerated and tumultuous." The progress of the case is recorded as follows :—" On

December 1st complained of pain in the right side; friction sounds detected; coughs slightly; no expectoration; delirium occurred during the succeeding night; the following morning said he was better, and the ascending and descending respiration was not observed; friction heard in the right infra-axillary region; the right side moved but slightly in respiration, which was chiefly diaphragmatic; dulness was perceived over the right base posteriorly, where also friction and fine crepitation were heard. On the 3rd December the respiratory phenomena were less marked; but on the 4th, weeping was observed in the afternoon, although the patient was cheerful about himself, and the peculiar breathing was again manifested. On the 5th, heart's action was calmer; œdema of the left hand commenced. On the 9th, œdema of the lower part of the left thigh; foot and lower part of the leg very cold. On the 12th, a fresh pulmonary attack commenced, the left pleura now being the seat. During the three following days there was considerable delirium; he was very troublesome at night, crying out and groaning. On the evening of the 16th, he had more frequent paroxysms of apnœa; the cardiac action was hurried, about 130 per minute, but regular. On the 18th the symptoms were found to have subsided somewhat; but on the evening of that day dyspnœa came on, with greatly increased feebleness; pulse about 60, and irregular; respirations hurried and forcible, from 45 to 50 per minute. The pulmonary symptoms had become greatly aggravated, and the patient died about one o'clock on the morning of the 20th. Post mortem was not permitted."

The case of Philiscus, as recorded by Hippocrates, is one of great interest. The occurrence of accession of fever towards the evening of the third day, freedom from fever having been noted in the morning, with supervention of several unfavorable symptoms, in particular great thirst, dry condition of the tongue, black urine, delirium, and coldness of the extremities, led Galen, in his commentary, to remark that the fatal issue of the disease might have been anticipated. It is, however, in respect to the peculiar character of the breathing that the case of Philiscus acquires its chief interest, and it is in this particular that a resemblance is to be found between the ancient and the modern clinical examples now quoted. The attention of Hippocrates had been arrested by the peculiar character of the breathing which existed throughout the fatal illness of Philiscus. Surely, it is matter of interest and for reflection that the respiration described by Hippocrates as ἀραιὸν μέγα, " rare and large," and to which Galen has attached the meaning " like a person who forgot for a time the need of breathing, and then suddenly remembered," or " the respiration throughout, like that of a person recollecting himself, was rare and large," has attracted great attention in quite recent times. The expression used by French writers, " besoin de respirer," corresponds in some measure to the meaning which is sought to be conveyed by the Greek words. In Latin, 'the rendering is, " Spiratio huic perpetuo rara et magna fuit." Daremberg, the learned French editor of Hippocrates, thus translates the passage : " La respiration fût constamment grande, rare comme chez quelqu'un qui ne respire que par souvenir." The relation of this peculiar character of the breathing with which, under the name of " ascending and descending inspiration " of the eminent Dublin physician, Dr. Stokes, the profession is now familiar, to lesion of the nervous system, was, of course, unknown to Hippocrates, and for many subsequent ages could not be known to those who were ignorant alike of anatomy and physiology. In recent times, it has been described by the late Dr. Cheyne, of Dublin. " For several days," wrote Dr. Cheyne, in 1816, in his account of a patient, aged sixty, who had fatty degeneration of the heart, with irregular and intermittent pulse, and whose death was due to apoplexy, " his breathing was irregular; it would cease for a quarter of a minute, then it would become perceptible, though very low, then by degrees it became heaving and quick, and then it would gradually cease again. This revolution in the state of his breathing occupied about a minute, during which there were about thirty acts of respiration." Subsequently, Dr. Stokes connected the peculiar respiration with a weakened state of the heart, " a phenomenon to be looked for in many cases of fatty degeneration." I have never seen it, remarks the same authority, except in examples of that disease. In his description of it, Dr. Stokes observes : " It consists in the occurrence of a series of inspirations, increasing to a maximum, and then declining in force and length, until a state of apparent apnœa is established. In this condition, the patient may remain for such a length of time as to make his attendants

believe that he is dead, when a low inspiration, followed by
one more decided, marks the commencement of a new ascending
and then descending series of inspirations. This symptom, as
occurring in its highest degree, I have only seen during a few
weeks previous to the death of a patient. I do not know any
more remarkable or characteristic phenomena than those
presented in this condition, whether we view the long-continued
cessation of the breathing, yet without any suffering on the
part of the patient, or the maximum point of the series of
inspirations, when the head is thrown back, the shoulders
raised, and every muscle of inspiration thrown into the most
violent action; yet all this without any *râle* or sign of mechanical obstruction." Dr. Stokes refers to the fact of the
sighing respiration, which is closely allied to the more formidable ascending and descending respiration, being observed in
persons who are labouring under certain forms of gastric and
hepatic derangement, and in connection with undeveloped gout,
and likewise to the significant fact of Laennec having described
a form of asthma with puerile respiration, while the illustrious
French physician attributed the malady to some special modification of nervous influence.[1]

Dr. Little, of Dublin, in an able paper published in 1868,
while allying the peculiar breathing, as Dr. Stokes had done,
with organic disease of the heart, does not admit its special
connection with fatty degeneration, but believes it to accompany
atheroma of the aorta, valvular lesions, and hypertrophy, as
well as dilatation of the left ventricle. Dr. Little has suggested
as a theory of its causation, that, in consequence of the existence
of one or other of the lesions mentioned, there is an unequal
action of the two ventricles. Consequently, the left ventricle
is unable to propel the aërated blood, and stops now and then.
This blood, therefore, remains in the lungs, pulmonary veins,
and left auricle; and, as it has already been fully oxygenated,

---

[1] "Cependant le malade étouffe; et, comme nous venons de le dire, il
aurait besoin d'une respiration plus étendue que celle que permit son orga-
nisation : ou, en d'autres termes, l'expiration est très parfaite, le besoin seul
de respirer est augmenté. Ce n'est pas dans le poumon qu'il faut chercher
la cause de la maladie; et lors même qu'adoptant en entier la théorie
chimique de la respiration, on voudrait supposer qu'un besoin extraordinaire
d'oxygénation du sang est la cause de la dyspnée, il faudrait encore remonter
plus haut et reconnaître que le mal est dans l'innervation même."

it no longer stimulates the respiratory centre through the vagus. Thus, the venous blood which is requisite to excite the vagus branches is not supplied, consequently respiration ceases, and the breathing takes on this irregular action. By degrees, the contractions of the ventricle partially free the auricle and pulmonary veins; venous blood is again sent to the lungs, which stimulates the filaments of the pneumogastric and causes respiration to begin. Dr. Laycock, in his valuable contribution to the pathology of the ascending and descending respiration, or, as he terms it, " recurrent brief apnœa," from which I have already quoted, while offering objections to the completeness of the explanation according to Dr. Little's ingenious theory, does not hesitate to concur in the opinion that the vagus system is involved.

It is worthy of remark that, in the case of Philiscus detailed by Hippocrates, sleeplessness was a notable feature; and, although the febrile condition under which the patient laboured may be the explanation of this symptom, it is at least as reasonable to suppose that the neurosis of the vagus on which the peculiarity of his breathing depended was its cause.

Laennec, the illustrious French physician, the modern discoverer of auscultation, he to whom we are indebted for the introduction of auscultation, and for the great light which his discovery shed on the diagnosis and treatment of diseases of the chest, has rendered due credit to Hippocrates. To the Father of Medicine indeed, and to Aretæus, among the ancients, Laennec confesses that he was alone indebted for any information on the subject which he has so signally made his own. He expressly states that Hippocrates practised immediate auscultation. " Hippocrate avait tenté l'auscultation immédiate ; " and, in proof of his having made trial of this means of diagnosis, he refers to the well-known passage in the treatise Περὶ Νουσῶν, τὸ Δεύτερον, ' De Morbis,' Liber secundus, a work which there is good reason for believing, although not composed by Hippocrates himself, was written either by one or more of his contemporaries or by some among his immediate descendants in the school of Cos, in which it is made clear that Hippocrates fell into error in supposing his ability to distinguish between the presence of water and of pus in the chest, by the peculiar sound heard on applying the ear. It is in the same chapter,

and in close relation to the same subject, that Laennec makes
the remarkable statement—a statement which cannot be read
without feelings of admiration for the candour and modesty
of that distinguished man—that he had read the passage in
Hippocrates many years before the commencement of certain
experiments in physics, which suggested to him the idea
of mediate auscultation, but he never entertained the idea
of repeating the experiment of Hippocrates; it passed
entirely into forgetfulness; he simply regarded it as one
of the errors into which that great man had fallen. But
the passage reverted to his mind when he commenced his
researches; and he felt surprise that its consideration had not
proved suggestive to some readers. The error made by Hippocrates, Laennec further remarks, might have led him to the
discovery of many valuable truths. He concludes a remarkable
passage in the following words: "But Hippocrates stopped
with an incorrect observation, and his successors overlooked its
import. This, at first sight, may appear surprising; nevertheless, nothing is more common. No man is permitted to
embrace all the relations and consequences of the most simple
fact; and the secrets of Nature are more frequently disclosed
by accidental circumstances than they are wrested by scientific
efforts" ('*De l'Auscultation Médiate*,' Première Partie, chapitre
iii). Under the designation of Hippocratic succussion, we
possess, as is well known, a means of physical exploration of
the chest, which was practised by the Father of Medicine. In
the same treatise as that already referred to, the method of
procedure in the use of this means is laid down. It is directed
that, after the patient has been carefully washed with warm
water, he is to be placed in a firm seat, and his hands held by
an assistant; the physician meantime, taking him by the
shoulders, shakes him, and attentively listens in order to
determine on which side of the chest a sound is occasioned.
Further, the rules for the treatment of empyema by operation
are given with precision; it is directed that recourse is not to
be had to paracentesis before the fifteenth day from the
commencement of the effusion: where pain is chiefly felt and
swelling is most conspicuous, the opening is to be made, while
a preliminary incision through the integuments precedes the
penetration of the pleura effected by a sharper and more pointed

instrument, protected by a piece of cloth. In some instances, it is mentioned, the perforation of the thoracic parietes was made, not through an intercostal space but through a rib, a plan revived in recent times by M. Reybard. When a sufficient quantity of pus has been permitted to flow, the wound is to be closed by means of a portion of linen cloth attached to a thread. Daily a similar quantity of pus is to be evacuated. On the tenth day, when the whole of the collection has been allowed to escape, a mixture of tepid oil and wine is to be injected through the opening, for the purpose of cleansing the lung. This part of the operation is to be practised twice daily ; the injection of the morning being withdrawn and replaced by a fresh quantity in the evening, and so on. At length, when the purulent fluid has become clear and thin, a metallic sound is to be introduced, the size of which is to be gradually lessened as the fluid itself diminishes ; thus, the wound is permitted to cicatrise.

The interest attached to the description now quoted is heightened by a consideration of certain shrewd observations bearing on the same subject, and which occur, not in the same treatise alone, but in other of the Hippocratic works, notably in the book of ' *Aphorisms.*' An empyema on the left side, the author remarks, is less dangerous than on the right. When the pus was clear, and studded more or less with sanguinolent threads, that appearance indicated the probability of a satisfactory recovery ; but, on the other hand, if, on the first day of its removal, the fluid possessed a colour like the yolk of egg, while on the succeeding day it was thick, having a pale green hue, and emitting a fœtid odour, it was likely that the sufferer would not recover, but shortly die. Again, the sufferers from empyema and dropsies treated by incision or by the cautery, certainly perish if the pus or water be suddenly evacuated. Every one acquainted with the history of paracentesis thoracis knows that it dates from the period of the Father of Medicine. The dogmatic statements which are to be found in the Hippocratic writings may not all be accepted without question in the present day, but it is remarkable how much truth there is in several of these. One of the highest living authorities on diseases of the chest, Dr. Walshe, commends the precept of Hippocrates that paracentesis should not be performed before the fifteenth day of effusion, unless the accumulation of fluid be so great as *per se* to threaten life; while he questions the accuracy of the observation made in the ancient time, and adhered to pretty closely in subsequent ages, that success is less likely to follow operations when the fluid has been from the first purulent in character than when sero-albuminous (' *Diseases of the Lungs*,' 4th edition, p. 281).

The modern history of thoracentesis is very interesting. Since the writings of Trousseau in its recommendation, and the still more powerful example of our transatlantic brethren, chiefly Dr. Bowditch, the remedy has become one commonly resorted to. In the article "Pleurisy," contributed to the third volume of Dr. Reynolds' ' *System of Medicine* ' by a physician, whose premature death the profession had recently to deplore, will be found an interesting account of what Dr. Anstie called a new era in the treatment of pleurisy. The new era is, however, signalised rather by the discovery and introduction of such new instruments as the suction-instrument of Dr. Wyman, so efficient in the hands of Dr. Bowditch, and the aspirator of M. Dieulafoy, than by any novel suggestion regarding the treatment of the disease. If, as is not unlikely, we have recently attained to something like perfection in the diagnosis and treatment of pleurisy, a dispassionate review of the history of the disease in ancient and modern times will justify the application of the dictum of Seneca, "Multum egerunt qui ante nos fuerunt sed non peregerunt."

It would be very easy to multiply references to important and suggestive passages in the Hippocratic writings tending to establish yet more fully the truth of the statement that the Father of Medicine was enabled, by the exercise chiefly of his most remarkable powers of observation, to acquire a really wonderful amount of accurate information regarding the causes and progress of diseases as well as the influence exerted by various remedies over them. Enough has, however, been stated to justify Sir William Hamilton in exalting the reputation and praise of Hippocrates. Was Sir William entitled to depreciate the medical practitioners of his own time, which he surely did when exclaiming, "Has the practice of medicine made a single step since Hippocrates?" For centuries after the Hippocratic epoch it may truly be said that little or no advance in medicine was effected. Many learned and ingenious men no doubt did appear in the ranks of the profession, and by them the position which had been achieved for medicine by Hippocrates was, at all events, maintained. In ancient times by far the most renowned of these was Galen, who, embracing warmly the views of Hippocrates, was the first formally to expound and then systematically to formulate the doctrine of humoralism or humorism. It might be a sufficient answer to the query of Sir William Hamilton to signalise the discovery in modern days of vaccination and the introduction of sulphuric ether and chloroform as anæsthetics; the last mentioned, as the author of ' *Rab and His Friends*,[1] says, " one of God's best gifts to his suffering children." These were unknown to Hippocrates, and surely our possession of them indicates at least one step in advance. But we are able to point to the abandonment of many remedies altogether worthless which were used in ancient times, and to the introduction, as well as much more satisfactory employment of others; while, owing to the remarkable and altogether indisputable progress which has been made in the prosecution, first of all, of the study of anatomy, then of physiology, and subsequently of pathology, we are justly entitled to conclude that the more advanced our knowledge of the minute structure of the body becomes, the more extensive our acquaintance with the function and uses of its several parts, and the more refined our understanding of the various morbid processes by which these are altered and destroyed, so much the more thorough and reliable will be our application and adaptation of the means of cure to the treatment of diseases. Any scientific practice of medicine before the physician had been able to acquaint himself with human anatomy was not to be expected; and it is truly marvellous that Hippocrates, Aretæus, Galen, and the Arabian physicians, notably Rhazes, were able to achieve so much, and to hand down to posterity a body of well-observed facts and careful deductions from these facts, wearing so much the aspect of science.

Medicine can, however, be said to have started on a scientific basis when Mundinus, early in the fourteenth century, applied himself with diligence to the dissection of the human body, and published a treatise on anatomy, ' *Anatomi Omnium*

[1] John Brown, M.D., L.L.D., (died May, 1882) ED.

Humani Corporis Interiorum Membrorum,' which, till the middle of the sixteenth century, was the recognised text-book of the schools. The statutes of the University of Padua prescribed that all anatomical lectures were to adhere to the literal text of the Bologna professor. Mundinus died in 1326,[1] universally respected; and no advances in anatomical knowledge were made after his time till Bereuger, of Carpi, published, in 1521, a commentary upon Mundinus. There succeeded Berenger, Vido Vidius, Jacob Sylvius, and the renowned Flemish anatomist Andreas Vesalius. Of the last named Hallam remarks that "if he was not quite to anatomy what Copernicus was to astronomy, he has yet been said, a little hyperbolically, to have discovered a new world" (*'Literary History,'* vol. i, p. 467). He was the first anatomist who ventured to emancipate himself, and that thoroughly, from the trammels of Galen, who up to that time had been regarded with an altogether blind veneration. Fallopius and Eustachius, two well-known names, names not to be forgotten by any one at all acquainted with anatomy, were the contemporaries, although younger, of Vesalius; and of the same period, or shortly subsequent, were Realdus Columbus, Arantius, and Fabricius ab Aquapendente, the discoverer of the valves in the veins, and the instructor of our own immortal Harvey. The splendid discovery of the circulation of the blood was followed by that of the absorbent system, in which Asellius, a professor at Pavia, Rudbeck, a professor at Upsala, and Bartholin, a Dane, were chiefly concerned; while to Pecquet, a professor at Montpellier, belongs the credit of describing the thoracic duct and its uses. Other important anatomical discoveries, and discoveries also in physiology, were being made simultaneously, or shortly thereafter, in connection with which the names of Malpighi, Glisson, Wharton, Highmore, Richard Lower, Leeuwenhoeck, Ruysch, Valsalva, and many others start up. The most eminent of the pupils of Valsalva was the distinguished Morgagni, who, following the plan pursued by Bonnet in his 'Sepulchretum Anatomicum,' first published at Geneva, the place of his birth, in 1679, described by Haller as "immor-

---

[1] Mundinus, sagt John Adelphus in der von ihm besorgten Strassburger Ausgabe vom Jahre 1513, "quem omnis studentium universitas colit ac venerat ut deum."—Haeser, *'Lehrbuch der Gerschichte der Medicin.'*

tale opus," became himself professor in the University of Padua, and was the founder of pathological anatomy (' *Der Begründer der Neüeren Pathologischen Anatomie*,' Haeser, *Seite* 654). His works ' *Adversaria Anatomica*,' and still more his celebrated treatise ' *De Sedibus et Causis Morborum per Anatomiam Indagatis*,' immensely advanced his favourite science.

While chemistry, about the same time, was advancing towards the dignity of a science, chiefly through the genius of our distinguished countryman, the Honourable Robert Boyle, there arose the sect of the so-called chemical physicians. Of this sect, the earliest was François Deleboe Sylvius (' *Der berühmteste Vertreter der Iatrochemischen Schule*,' Haeser, *Seite* 571), who was born at Hanau in Flanders, in 1614, and, after a time, became professor of the practice of medicine at Leyden. The chemical theory of medicine had, however, passed from Paracelsus, who was born towards the close of the fifteenth century, through Van Helmont, by more than eighty years his junior, to Sylvius. The leading principles of the chemiatric physicians was that diseases owed their origin to derangement in a process of fermentation, which was constantly at work in the human body. While most of the maladies which were produced in this way arose from excess of acid, some were regarded as of alkaline origin. One eminent English physician embraced the doctrine of Sylvius. Thomas Willis was born in 1621, and in 1659 published his celebrated treatise entitled ' *Diatribæ duæ Medico-Philosophicæ; quarum prior agit de Fermentatione, altera de Febribus*.' The object of this work was to prove that, in every organ of the body, there existed its own special fermentation, and that disease of every kind resulted from the disturbance of these fermentative processes. Willis was one of the earliest members of the Royal Society, and left behind him the character of an orthodox, pious, and charitable physician.[1] It is recorded of Dr. Willis that, being consulted regarding the delicate condition of the children of the Duke of York, afterwards James II, he spoke his mind freely, and thereby gave great offence. Bishop Burnet has related that "Willis, the great physician, being called to consult for one of his, the Duke of York's, sons, gave his opinion in the words, ' mala stamina

---

[1] ' The Roll of the Royal College of Physicians of London,' by William Monk, M.D., vol. i, p. 524.

26

vitæ,' which gave such offence that he was never called for afterwards." The reputation of Willis, unquestionably a very able man, has been obscured by that of another English physician, his junior by only three years. The physician in question was Thomas Sydenham, " whose character," as Dr. John Brown felicitously remarks in that delightful essay of his, ' *Locke and Sydenham*,' " is as beautiful and as genuinely English as his name." He was born in Winford Eagle in Dorsetshire, in 1624. A parallel has been drawn between Hippocrates and Sydenham by more than one modern writer. ' *Wiederherstellung des Hippokratesmus durch Thomas Syden-ham*,' is the title of a chapter by Haeser, the erudite German historian of medicine, and a very instructive one it is, on the life and writings of the English physician. He has frequently been called the English Hippocrates, and, in truth, the appellation is deserved; for, like the illustrious Greek physician,. the great aim he set before him was the cure of disease, and, although possessing a mind which delighted in speculative inquiry, he never permitted the theories he formed and ably defended to interfere with his treatment. That was based on a rational empiricism, such as we have seen in the instance of Hippocrates; he carefully watched the operation of the remedies he employed, and from these he drew the indications for further guidance. Sydenham was humoral in his pathology, and he further agreed with Hippocrates in the doctrine of crisis, and the subsidiary views as to coction and crasis. We find him frequently referring to the Father of Medicine, as, for example, when he inquires what is gout. It is a provision of Nature to purify the blood of old men, and to purge the deep parts of the body ; such at least is the language of Hippocrates. The same may be said of all other diseases, fully formed, and "That practice, and that alone, will do good which elicits the indications of cure out of the phenomena of the disease itself. This made Hippocrates divine." It was from Sydenham that the school of empirical physicians in England sprung—a term to be used, as Hallam has expressed it, "in a good sense," as denoting the regard its disciples had to observation and experience or to the Baconian principles of philosophy.

Another school of medicine had arisen in Italy through the instrumentality of Giovanni Alfonso Borelli, a profound mathematician, who endeavoured to explain the operation of the various functions of the body on mechanical principles. His views and principles were, through the excessive zeal of his pupils, carried beyond their legitimate length. Of these, Lorenzo Bellini, of Florence and Pisa, was the chief. There were other eminent adherents the iatro-mathematical school in Italy; while Pitcairne, Freind, and Mead, in their time, were in this country attached to it; and it secured the sympathies of the illustrious nosologist François Boissier de Sauvages in France, in the eighteenth century.

To the chemiatric and iatro-mathematical schools there succeeded a third, of which Van Helmont was the founder. Embracing the views of the former to a certain extent, he made this important addition, that all the changes occurring in the body, whether arising spontaneously or produced by remedies, are determined by a specific agent inherent in the living system, to which he gave the name of Archeus. This archeus explained, in Van Helmont's opinion, all physiological actions, and accounted for the maintenance of health as well as the occurrence of disease. Founding on the views promulgated by Van Helmont, although widely differing from him, came the earliest of the three distinguished men to whom a brief reference was made at the commencement of this address. Rejecting the doctrines of the chemical and mathematical physicians, Stahl concentrated attention on what he denominated vital actions. He, too, referred these actions to a dominating principle; and the Anima of Stahl—so he named it—resembles, in some measure at least, the Archeus of Van Helmont. To Stahl belongs the great merit of having pointed out that, contrary to the prevalent opinions of the schools, the operations of the animal economy cannot be explained by either chemical or mechanical laws; that there exists something over and above these; and that something is of the nature of vital action. The anima of Stahl, however, was a hypothetical principle, and he signally failed to gain for his theory any general support. Hoffmann, his distinguished colleague in the University of Halle, and his rival, conferred a lasting benefit on science by pointing out that the actions which were ascribed by Stahl to the government of his "anima" were in reality determined by nervous influence. "It was reserved for Hoffmann," says

Dr. John Thomson, " to take a comprehensive view of the nervous system, not only as the organ of sense and motion, but also as the common centre by which all the different parts of the animal economy are connected together, and through which they mutually influence each other." Facts, and many of these most important in their nature, regarding the nervous system, had been recorded before the time of Hoffmann. The renowned professors in the early Alexandrian school, Herophilus, and Erasistratus, and Galen, with others among the ancients, Willis, Vieussens, Mayow, Baglivi, and Pacchioni, much nearer his own day, had laid the foundation for the reasoning of Hoffmann; but, as Cullen has observed, " he was the first who gave any tolerably simple and clear system on the subject, or pointed out any extensive application of it to the explanation of diseases." There is little need for reminding you of the triumphant discoveries in the nervous system which have been made since the time of Hoffmann—such discoveries as have rendered the names of Charles Bell and Marshall Hall in particular, but many others in lesser degree, famous. In no department of pathological inquiry is there at the present time exhibited a greater amount of zeal, or are important facts being more frequently brought to light, than in that pertaining to the nervous system. How signal our advance in treatment also, as determined by that which can alone with any certainty determine treatment—a sound diagnosis! We can distinguish between functional and organic diseases of the brain, spinal cord, and nerves; and use our remedies in a way of which not only the ancient physicians, but many among the moderns, could not have dreamt.

The names of Stahl and Hoffmann, the German professors in Halle, of whom a few words have been said, are inseparably linked with that of the illustrious Dutch professor in the University of Leyden, Hermann Boerhaave. The aim of Boerhaave was essentially eclectic; he culled from the writings of his predecessors all that was valuable, and with these and the results of his own extended observation endeavoured to erect a system of medicine. His system was faulty in ascribing too little importance to the influence exerted by the brain and nervous system generally over the animal functions. The pathology of Boerhaave was as defective as his physiology; his explanations of morbid phenomena were more applicable to the body considered as an inert hydraulic machine, than as an organised living and sentient system. Intellectually and morally distinguished, few greater men than Boerhaave have adorned our profession in any age or country. After his decease, his reputation, which as a living teacher had been of the most exalted description, rather increased than declined. This result was due in great measure to the publication of commentaries on his works by two of his most distinguished pupils, Haller and Van Swieten. The former of these is justly considered as the father of modern physiology. The magnificent researches of Haller regarding development, growth of bone, and the circulation, deserve the praise and gratitude of posterity not more than the impulse of his ardent spirit and example in laborious inquiry, by which the zeal of his associates and successors was kindled. Of Haller's powerful opponent in the controversy regarding irritability and sensibility—Dr. Whytt— I can only make mention. Contemporaneously with Haller, and conferring benefits on the practice of medicine resembling those which Haller rendered to physiology, was William Cullen. A very erroneous impression of this great Scottish teacher has been entertained by many; more particularly, however, by foreigners. By such, Cullen has been called a purely speculative physician. The condemnation of this opinion is readily supplied by his own words. "There is nothing," he observes, I desire so much as that every disease we treat here should be a matter of experience to you ; so that you must not be surprised that I use only one remedy when I might employ two or three; for in using a multiplicity of remedies, when a cure does succeed, it is not easy to perceive which is the most effectual. But I wish that you may always have some opportunity of judging with regard to their proper effects." Again, he says: "Every wise physician is a dogmatist; but a dogmatical physician is one of the most absurd animals that lives. We say he is a dogmatist in physic who employs his reason, and, from some acquaintance with the nature of the human body, thinks he can throw some light upon diseases, and ascertain the proper methods of cure ; and I have known none who were not dogmatists, except those who seemed to be incapable of reasoning, or who were too lazy for it. On the

other hand, I call him a dogmatical physician who is very
ready to assume opinions, to be prejudiced in favour of them,
and to retain and assert very tenaciously, and with too much
confidence, the opinions or prejudices which he has already
taken up in common life, or in the study of the sciences. Now,
I profess to be a dogmatist, but I should be sorry if any person
thought me dogmatical; for there are but few theoretical
opinions which I have received or offered to communicate with
regard to disease, concerning which I am not ready to doubt,
and to admit grounds for doubting, as soon as they are offered
to me. I know there are no universal rules in the practice of
physic; but there are general rules, which all admit of, with
more or fewer exceptions, in theory and practice." The
foundation of the practice of physic was expressly stated by
Cullen to lie in fact and experience. "All our knowledge of
Nature consists," he says, "in experience."

To Cullen we are largely indebted for the introduction into
general use by medical men in this country of such remedies
as the acid tartrate of potash, tartar emetic, hyoscyamus, and
James's powder, or the pulvis antimonialis. Tartar emetic
Cullen largely employed as an antiphlogistic, sometimes after
bloodletting, and sometimes in place of that remedy. He had
noticed something of the contra-stimulant action of antimony
in the form of tartar emetic, described by Dr. Marryatt, of
Bristol, in 1790, and afterwards so strongly insisted upon by
Rasori, a professor in Pavia, and by others. A successor of
Cullen, one of the most distinguished physicians in recent times,
as he certainly was also one of the most benevolent of men, the
reverend Dr. Alison, who occupied the chair, which you,[1] sir,
now so worthily fill, when this Association held its former
meeting in Edinburgh, he, whom Dr. Stokes has recently
described as "the best man I ever knew," and in so alluding
to Dr. Alison may be said to have turned many hearts towards
himself—for what student who knew Dr. Alison did not venerate
him? and who can ever cease to cherish his memory?—when
indicating the way by which, in his opinion, the further
improvement in the art of medicine was likely to be effected,
signalised the two following lines of inquiry; first, in the
discovery of specifics which may counteract the different

[1] Professor Gairdner, of Glasgow.—ED.]

diseased actions of which the body is susceptible, as effectually as the cinchona counteracts the intermittent fever, citric acid the scurvy, or vaccination the small-pox; and, second, in the investigation of causes of disease, whether external or internal— *i.e.* of the conditions under which either the vital action of the solids or the vital properties of the fluids of the body may become liable to deviation from their natural state. It will be readily admitted by all candid inquirers that, under the latter head, very signal advances have been made during the last half century. Look, for example at the etiological investigations regarding continued fevers, and the bearing of these upon treatment, with which the names of Jenner, Stewart, Bartlett, Murchison, and Buchanan, are so intimately connected. Again, consider the great advances in knowledge of parasitic diseases— the entozoa more particularly—and their appropriate treatment, for which we are largely indebted to Küchenmeister, Von Siebold, Davaine, and Cobbold. Nothing more interesting or more remarkable in the line of therapeutics has recently appeared than the wonderfully successful treatment of hydatids of the lung by the internal administration of turpentine in the hands of Dr. Bird, of Melbourne, Australia.[1] This is a medicine in estimation of which, were time at my disposal, I could say much, having had occasion to watch its influence very closely when administered in cases of pulmonary gangrene and bronchial affections attended by copious expectoration of fetid pus. In these diseases, I regard turpentine as an invaluable remedy.

Of specifics, we still possess but few; while the desire to increase their number is not only legitimate, but is likely sooner or later to be gratified. Of the class of specifics, no remedy better deserves the name than quinine. The potent action of quinine in intermittent fevers thoroughly justifies the application to it of the term specific ; and it is to be noted that the curative action in question is to be seen not only in febrile disorders of the intermittent type, but in neuralgias which

---

[1] Dr. Bird had formerly used bromide of potassium, twenty grains, with one fluid drachm of tincture of kamala in infusion of serpentary, three times a day regularly. ('On Hydatids of the Lung.' Melbourne: 1874.) I am, however, assured by a recovered patient that, in the treatment of pulmonary hydatids, Dr. Bird now places great reliance on turpentine administered internally.

manifest a similar character. Many ingenious theories regarding the *modus operandi* of cinchona or quinine in these diseases
have been advanced; but up to the present time, we are
entirely ignorant respecting the method of action of a medicine
in whose power we justly place the very highest confidence.
The remarkable effects of quinine in reducing the temperature
in pyrexiæ, and the still more remarkable influence of cold in
the same way in hyperpyrexiæ, of which Dr. Wilson Fox has
given some happy illustrations, are noteworthy facts in the
recent history of therapeutics.

A remedy of marvellous power and usefulness, the virtues of
which we are still only learning, is the iodide of potassium.
This medicine was prepared soon after the discovery of iodine
by Courtois in 1812, and has been chiefly employed as a
deobstruent, alterative, and diuretic. I am satisfied that the
diuretic properties of iodide of potassium deserve to be more
widely recognised than is generally the case. Its specific action
is seen in syphilitic periostitis; for truly the rapidity and completeness with which pain and swelling decline and disappear
in instances of enlargements over the tibiæ and other bones in
cases of secondary syphilis, are not less remarkable than the
readiness with which an attack of intermittent fever or neuralgia
yields to quinine. The late Dr. Todd, of London, remarked: " If
there is anything in addition to quinine which deserves the
name of a specific, it is the iodide of potassium in syphilitic
periostitis." Another remarkable action of this medicine is in
aortic aneurysm. Iodide of potassium, administered for the
most part in tolerably large doses, in this terrible disease exerts
a wonderful influence, not only in relieving the neuralgic pains,
which are frequently so harassing, but in subduing the local
pressure occasioned by encroachments of the aneurysm and in
leading, apparently, to firm coagulation within the sac.

It is in the treatment of thoracic aneurysm by iodide of
potassium that physicians have learned the very remarkable
tolerance of the drug manifested by sufferers from that disease.
No reasonable suggestion has hitherto been offered regarding
the *modus operandi* of iodide of potassium in aneurysm. The
influence it exerts on the progress of aneurysm appears to have
been discovered not only empirically, but by the merest hazard,
writes Dr. Walshe, " in this point of view, the story of all our

really valuable medicines is simply repeated." (*'Diseases of the Heart,'* 4th edition, page 512). The names of Bouillaud, Nélaton, and Chuckerbutty are specially connected with the early employment of the iodide of potassium in the treatment of aneurysm ; while the profession is largely indebted to Dr. G. W. Balfour of Edinburgh for his patient investigation into the subject. (*' Edinburgh Medical Journal,'* 1868.)

Twenty years ago, little was known regarding the virtues of bromide of potassium. If any standard work on the materia medica of that date be consulted, it will merely be found recorded of this salt that it is diuretic and cathartic, and, like the preparations of iodine, a powerful deobstruent and alterative. Its dose, moreover, is stated in such works at from three to twelve grains thrice daily. Since then, and more particularly within the last few years, bromide of potassium has rapidly advanced in professional estimation ; and, at the present time, it may with confidence be affirmed that there are very few medicines which are more largely employed, and the use of which is attended by more signal benefits. As a calmative and hypnotic, bromide of potassium is largely confided in ; but its specific operation in epilepsy is of the most striking description. "It is to be demonstrated, in my opinion," writes Dr. Russell Reynolds, "that there is something specific in the action of bromide of potassium in epilepsy." And the same author observes : " Bromide of potassium is the one medicine which has, so far as I know, proved of real service in the treatment of epilepsy." My own experience of the use of bromide of potassium in epilepsy has been of the most encouraging description. I have repeatedly witnessed cures in the strictest sense result from its employment. Let me briefly refer to one such.

S. A—, a bookbinder, aged 50, had for twenty years been subject to severe fits, occurring irregularly by night and by day, often attended by biting of the tongue. The usual interval between the fits had been a fortnight, and on no occasion had a longer period than six weeks elapsed. In January, 1870, this patient, whose mental capacity had at that time become considerably enfeebled, so much so as to make it necessary for him to give up his business, began the bromide of potassium, and continued it for eighteen months without any pause. The dose never exceeded twenty grains thrice daily. The result of this treatment was an entire cessation of the epilepsy ; there has been no recurrence of the disease. His mental vigour has returned. He long ago resumed his occupation, and has since been busily engaged in it without any interruption.

I could multiply instances of this kind; and so, I believe, could many practitioners who, in the treatment of epilepsy with bromide of potassium, have been mindful to adhere to the rule upon which Dr. Reynolds insists, that the remedy " should not be discontinued in the treatment of a case of epilepsy because of its apparent failure, but that the dose should be gradually increased, and the exhibition of the drug most patiently carried on for a period of many months, or even years." Epilepsy is a disease which specially attracted the attention of the ancient physicians. It was termed νόσος ἱερὰ, the sacred disease, by the Greeks; and Aretæus expressly mentions why the appellation sacred was given to epilepsy " for more reasons than one," he remarks, " from the greatness of the evil, for the word ἱερός also means great, or because the cure of it is not human, but divine; or from the notion that the disease occurred from the entrance of a demon into the man." Plato, in the ' Timæus,' ascribes the use of the term sacred to the circumstance of the head or brain being the part of the body affected in epilepsy. "When the phlegm is mingled," he says, "with black bile, and dispersed about the courses of the head, which are the divinest parts of us, and disturbs them in sleep, the attack is not so severe; but when assailing those who are awake, it is hard to be got rid of; and being an affection of a sacred part, is most justly called sacred." Hippocrates combated the notion entertained by his countrymen that epilepsy was peculiarly a sacred disease, one specially inflicted by the gods. In the treatise Περὶ Ἱερῆς Νούσου, he emphatically points out that the incomprehensible nature of the malady is no reason for concluding it to be divine; inasmuch as many other diseases, and notably the paroxysms of intermittent fevers, are just as much above the reach of the human understanding. He believes that epilepsy, like other diseases, results from natural causes. The reader of the remarks on epilepsy in the pages of Hippocrates and Aretæus cannot fail to have his opinion of these great men enhanced; but he also cannot fail to reach the conclusion that the moderns, understanding the nature of convulsive diseases, their connection with altered conditions of the blood, with, for example, anæmia and uræmia, their dependence at one time on central, at another on peripheral, irritation of the nervous system, are infinitely better prepared for their treatment than they were; and this unquestionably holds true of epilepsy.

The use of the remedies we have been briefly reviewing has, in the first instance, been adopted either by mere accident or empirically; nor have we, on this account, any cause for feeling regret. We do not know in what the preservative power of vaccination consists; and yet millions of lives have already been saved by this precaution (Œsterlen). A recent and very interesting example of the way in which therapeutical knowledge may be advanced is afforded by what has occurred in the Andaman islands. Dr. Dougall, a distinguished graduate of the University of Edinburgh, has apparently discovered that leprosy sores and other ailments attendant upon that disease can be cured by the aid of oil from the Gurjun tree, which is very common in these islands. Take another disease known to the ancients, although its pathology, still to a considerable extent obscure, has been carefully investigated only in recent times. I mean diabetes; and regarding it, we may compare the treatment pursued by Aretæus, for example, and that which we now employ, with the result of feeling thoroughly assured that many steps have been taken in the right direction, and with signal advantage to suffering humanity, since the writings of the distinguished Cappadocian physician. I do not think the opinion unfounded that, owing to the recent advances in the knowledge of tubercular diseases, etiologically and pathologically, we may look forward with confidence to a decided gain in their efficient treatment; but even now may we not be said to possess in cod-liver oil a very potent means of modifying the progress of pulmonary tuberculosis? In the treatment of this disease and of other allied constitutional disorders, cod-liver oil was first employed in the Manchester Infirmary, chiefly by the elder Bardsley, after the commencement of the present century. Previously to that time, however, an oil obtained by ebullition with water from the fresh livers of several fishes, the ling and skate as well as the cod, had long been a domestic panacea in strumous affections and chronic rheumatism.

Subsequently to its use in the Manchester Hospital, cod-liver oil was largely used in Germany; but, falling into disuse in this country, its restoration to professional and public favour has followed the publication of Dr. Hughes Bennett's recommendation of its virtues, in his excellent treatise on that subject. Sir Thomas Watson has very happily expressed the characteristic effect of the remedy in phthisis, when he says: "It is antagonistic to a much greater extent than any other drug of the consuming power of the disease." There are probably few medical men who have seen much of this sad malady who would hesitate to concur in the opinion of a very high authority—Dr. Williams—that cod-liver oil is more beneficial in the treatment of pulmonary consumption than any other agent, medicinal, dietetic, or regiminal, that has yet been employed. We may justly congratulate ourselves on the possession of cod-liver oil; but it becomes us to remember that the ancient physicians used oil inunction in phthisis. This is expressly stated by Aretæus; and he, as well as Hippocrates, lauds the use of milk in the same disease, preferring it to all other kinds of food. "For," says the former, "milk is pleasant to take, is easy to drink, gives solid nourishment, and is more familiar than any other food from childhood. In colour it is pleasant to see; as a medicine, it seems to lubricate the windpipe, to clean as with a feather the bronchi, and to bring off phlegm, improve the breathing, and facilitate the discharges downwards. To ulcers, it is a sweet medicine, and milder than anything else. If one will, then, only drink plenty of milk, he will not require anything else. For it is a great thing that, in a disease, milk should serve both for medicine and nourishment." In fevers Hippocrates did not allow milk, more particularly in such fevers as were attended by bilious discharges from the bowels. The modern practice is not, in this very important particular, in agreement with the ancient; the highest authorities, as, for example, Gairdner, Murchison, and Parkes, the last mentioned, on weighty theoretical grounds, considering milk the best food in fevers.

We have been alluding to the manner in which the practice of medicine has been advanced, and may doubtless be still further advanced, by the simple method of observation and experience. It is true that we cannot entirely depend upon empirical laws. We cannot, for example, feel assured that quinine will certainly cure an attack of intermittent fever, mercury syphilis; or, for that matter, that a dose or doses of any given medicine will exert their thoroughly ascertained physiological or therapeutic action; still, such laws are of the highest value, and we cannot help employing them.

The recent progress of chemistry, physiology, and pathology, has naturally led to the establishment of an advanced school of therapeutics, from whose labours signal benefits may not only be anticipated for medicine, but have already been conferred upon it. To Dr. Lauder Brunton, for example, belongs the great merit of conceiving accurately the therapeutic action of the nitrite of amyl from its physiological properties, and thereby of adding a useful remedy to our armamentarium. And so, also, to Dr. Fraser we are indebted for the elaborate investigations regarding the Calabar bean, which have resulted in a demonstration of its therapeutic value. Care must, however, be taken that the results of scientific inquiry and those of patient, oftentimes laborious, observation in the field of practical medicine running counter, do not interfere with the ultimate grand object of our profession—the healing of the sick.

We are not entitled to withhold remedies because we do not understand their exact nature, nor the minute changes they produce in the animal economy. Œsterlen has well expressed the attitude which, as practitioners of medicine, we are called upon to assume. "The patient requires our aid, and we must decide for or against the employment of a particular medicine, and upon the manner in which to employ it. If we possess sufficient experience, knowledge of the subject, and practical tact, we shall no doubt be able to do all for that patient which circumstances permit."

Let each one of us be fully persuaded in his own mind. While deeply interested in, and much instructed by, the experiments performed by a Committee of this Association, regarding the use of mercury, for example, I remain as thoroughly convinced as ever that the much abused drug in question exerts a powerful action on the function of the liver, and is to be trusted as a most efficient remedy in controlling not a few of its disorders.

I regard cold as a powerful antiphlogistic, and its external application, already briefly referred to, as a remedy of unquestiouable value in the treatment of hyperpyrexia; but my own observation, and the fullest attention I have been able to give to the recorded observations of others, have convinced me that the real reason for the present abandonment of a remedy of superior power—to wit, bloodletting—does not lie alone in the advance of scientific pathology. "The thinking man," writes one of the most philosophical of living physicians, Dr. Stokes, " finds it hard to believe that the fathers of British Medicine were always in error, or that they were bad observers and mistaken practitioners. They, indeed, have rested from their labours, but their works remain; and he who reads the writings of Sydenham, of Haygarth, and of Fothergill; of Heberden and Fordyce; of Gregory, Cullen, Alison, Cheyne, or Graves; must have a very inapprehensive mind if he fail to discover that there were giants in those days; and that the advocacy of such ideas only indicates a state of mind not consonant with the modesty of science."

INDEX.

A.

ABDOMINAL TYPHUS (typhoid fever), albuminuria in, 17
ACCENTUATED CARDIAC SECOND SOUND, 163
— diagnostic value of, 161
— in dilatation of the aorta, 167
— mechanism of, 167
ACUTE PLEURISY, bleeding in, 222
— paracentesis in, 205
ACUTE RHEUMATISM succeeded by chorea, 21
ADDRESS to the British Medical Association on Ancient and Modern Practice of Medicine, delivered at Edinburgh 1875, 381
ADULT, croup fatal in, 113
AFFLECK, Dr., on analysis of urine in hæmatinuria, 372
ALBUMINURIA a frequent symptom in exophthalmic goitre, 358
— arsenic in, *vide* Editor's preface
— critical, 3, 14
— desquamative, 44
— in abdominal typhus (typhoid fever), 17
— in Asiatic cholera, 9
— in cases of vascular bronchocele and exophthalmos, 349
— — independent of organic renal disease, 355
— in certain forms of dyspepsia, 359
— in erysipelas, 11
— in organic visceral diseases, characters of, 360
— in pneumonia, 14
— in pyretic conditions, characters of, 360
— in scarlatina, 4, 9
— in typhus fever, 17
— in vascular bronchocele and exophthalmos, its relation to digestion, 351
— — explanation of its occurrence, 361

ALBUMINURIA, inflammatory, 13
— most marked after breakfast in cases of vascular bronchocele and exophthalmos, 352
— not Bright's disease, 355
— remitting in vascular bronchocele and exophthalmos, 360
— temporary, 1
ALISON, Dr., urged search for specifics, and necessity of study of etiology, 406
ALOPECIA AREATA, 305
— a neurosis, 305
— elements of prognosis in, 306
— non-parasitic, 305
— treatment of, 305
AMAUROSIS in diabetes, 136
ANCIENT AND MODERN PRACTICE OF MEDICINE, address on the, 381
ANÆMIA and chorea, 24
— cause of vascular bronchocele, 180
ANÆMIC THEORY of vascular bronchocele, 173
ANEURYSM of aorta with laryngeal spasm, tracheotomy in, 103
" ANIMA " of Stahl, 403
ANTHELMINTIC ACTION of turpentine, sometimes best secured by repeated small doses, 286
ANTHRACOSIS and tubercle, 257
— dropsy in, 254
— or coal-miners' phthisis, 241
— pulmonum, symptoms of, 248
— theories as to etiology, 249
AORTA, aneurysm of, with spasm of larynx for which tracheotomy was performed, 103
AORTIC ANEURYSM, second sound of heart accentuated in, 163
— dilatation, second sound of heart accentuated in, 163
APNŒA, recurrent brief, of Laycock, 395
" ARCHEUS " of Van Helmont, 403
AREA of Celsus, 305

PRINTED BY J. E. ADLARD, BARTHOLOMEW CLOSE, E.C.